"The present collection brings together
seven of the finest examples of the
novelette . . . Here we have stories of
innocence, of self-deception and
discovery, of sin and violence, of
guilt and fear, of social death and
a break into freedom and fulfillment,
of death and transfiguration.

"In tone these stories range from the
satirical to the lyrical, from the comic
to the tragic; in method, from objective
to subjective; in mode, from chronicle
to anecdotal reminiscence, from narrative
to drama. Each is different from every
other in nearly all ways."

—*from the Introduction*
BY MARK SCHORER

LEO HAMALIAN and EDMOND L. VOLPE are professors of English at The City College of New York. They are co-editors of five first-rate anthologies, including *Great Stories by Nobel Prize Winners* and *Essays of Our Time.*

MARK SCHORER is a professor of English and chairman of the department at The University of California at Berkeley. He is the author of three novels, including *The Wars of Love;* of a short story collection, *The State of Mind;* of a critical study of William Blake; and of many critical essays that have appeared in the quarterly magazines and elsewhere. He has just completed a biography, *Sinclair Lewis: An American Story.* Mr. Schorer has held three Guggenheim Fellowships, a Fulbright to Italy, has taught in the American Studies Seminar in the University of Tokyo and is at present a Bollingen Fellow.

Seven Short Novel Masterpieces

EDITED BY

LEO HAMALIAN AND EDMOND L. VOLPE

WITH AN INTRODUCTION BY

MARK SCHORER

The Popular Living Classics Library · New York

NED L. PINES, President

FRANK P. LUALDI, Publisher

POPULAR LIBRARY EDITION
Published in February, 1964

ACKNOWLEDGMENTS

The editors wish to express their gratitude to the following publishers and agents for permission to reprint the following works:

First Love by Ivan Turgenev. Translated by Isabel F. Hapgood and published by Charles Scribner's Sons. Reprinted by courtesy of the publisher.

Master and Man by Leo Tolstoy. Published in *The Complete Works of Leo Tolstoy* by Thomas Y. Crowell Company. Reprinted by courtesy of the publisher.

The Lesson of the Master by Henry James. Copyright 1891 by The Macmillan Company. Reprinted by permission of Paul R. Reynolds & Son, 599 Fifth Avenue, New York 17, N. Y.

Daughters of the Vicar by D. H. Lawrence. Reprinted from *The Prussian Officer and Other Stories*. The story is also included in *The Complete Short Stories of D. H. Lawrence* published by William Heinemann Ltd. Reprinted by permission of The Viking Press, Inc. and The Estate of the late Mrs. Frieda Lawrence. All rights reserved.

Table of Contents

Introduction

The essential fact about the *novella* or novelette is also the obvious fact: it is longer than the short story and shorter than the novel. This quantitative distinction points to the qualitative character of the novelette: it aims at something like the concentration of the short story at the same time that it employs the complexities of the novel. One does not wish to suggest that these are literary compromises; rather, they are the positive qualities of a form that, in the words of Ludwig Lewisohn, brings together "isolation of material and depth of tone, restraint upon over-elaboration, and yet the final effect of brimming fullness."

If we can define the difference between the short story as opposed to the novelette and novel at all, it would seem to be in this distinction: that the short story is an art of moral revelation, the novel an art of moral evolution. In the first we expect in at least one of the characters an alteration in awareness, a growth in perception, some act of discovery whether of self or of the world or of both; in the second we usually get, and often in a number of characters, an alteration in being, a growth in character, some act of discovery that changes the self or the world or both.

The structural difference between the two forms is of special significance. Growth in character involves a whole different order of social and moral complexity from growth in psychological perception, no matter how acute the latter may be. The two are not separate, of course, and the lesser is not to be scorned, but psychological perception is nevertheless only a part of that larger quality that we call the moral imagination. The short story can ordinarily reveal to us only a facet of the author's view of life, and even though that facet is bright and sharp, even though it is symbolic of the author's whole view, that whole can come to us as impression only from implied details that are not really there; but the novelette shares with the novel those more complex and extensive materials and relationships that can evoke those larger overtones that represent the whole of an author's attitude, that make us feel the whole of his brooding presence behind the story rather than let us see only his infinitely graceful but still severed hand. It is hardly surprising that a form that can take advantage of the best qualities of two other forms should have become a favorite with many of the greatest writers in the literary tradition of the West. The present collection brings together seven of the finest examples.

These examples remind us at once that, whatever large generalizations we can make about the novelette as a literary form, these neglect to take into account the most important fact about it, the extraordinary range and variety of which it is capable in every regard—in theme, subject, style, tone, method. Here we have stories of innocence, of self-deception and discovery, of sin and violence, of guilt and fear, of social death and a break into freedom and fulfillment, of death and transfiguration. In tone these stories range from the satirical to the lyrical, from the comic to the tragic; in method, from objective to subjective; in mode, from chronicle to anecdotal reminiscence, from narration to drama. Each is different from every other in nearly all ways.

The oldest and best-known of these stories is *Candide,* Voltaire's eighteenth century satire on philosophical innocence. Raised in the absurd but popular doctrine of universal benevolence, a sentimental optimism that decreed the harmonious causation of all events, Candide and his friends live through an extravagant series of assaults horrendous and violent beyond the expectations of even the most confirmed cynic, all to demonstrate the existential fact of the arbitrary nature of evil. Sometimes shaken in his simple faith, Candide can still at the end of the story, after all the horrors through which he has passed, accept the word of the "philosophical" tutor, Pangloss, that all this was necessary to their now eating candied fruit and pistachio nuts, albeit in the midst of sordid suffering still.

Another kind of innocence is the subject of a very different treatment in Turgenev's *First Love.* It is the story of an inexperienced boy of sixteen who falls in love with a charming and coquettish young princess of twenty-one. He is the youngest of a whole troupe of suitors whom she keeps at arm's length until he discovers that it is to his own father that she has yielded her favors. Told as a reminiscence of lost youth, it ends with the decrescendo of old age, when the protagonist, after all the intervening years, is suddenly moved to pray for his long-dead father and his long-lost princess. Few love stories evoke so richly the emotions of youth, the blindness, the painful ecstasies, the heartbreak.

The Lesson of the Master is one of several stories by Henry James that deal with the problem of the integrity, indeed, the "perfection," of the artist, and the Master's lesson is that to these ends, the artist must sacrifice precisely the ecstasies and the heart-break of personal entanglements, together with all material comforts, must remain outside life, as it were, to represent life itself most perfectly in art. Whereas most stories present, in one way or another, a protagonist who becomes more intimately involved with life than he had formerly been, the James story forces the choice of withdrawal upon its hero.

Benito Cereno, perhaps the best known of Melville's *Piazza Tales,* is based on a true adventure and the account of it left by a Captain Delano in his *A Narrative of Voyages and Travels,* published in 1817. Melville does not depart far from his source in this story about mutiny on a slave ship in which the masters of the ship are forced into slavery, but he brings to that original an atmosphere of nightmare and mystery and horror, all heightened by the naive good will of Captain Delano, that makes of it one of the masterpieces of the macabre.

Macabre in a very different way is Franz Kafka's *The Metamorphosis.* It opens with an outrageous, impossible event:

> "As Gregor Samsa awoke one morning from a troubled dream, he found himself changed in his bed to some monstrous kind of vermin."

A travelling salesman of the lower middle class, a perfectly ordinary young man, he had indeed been transformed overnight into a giant cockroach. The story proceeds in the same matter-of-fact tone with which it opened, but now every detail and event is completely realistic as we follow Gregor's fate through his family's horror, their rejection of the creature, his suffering and demise, the disposal of his corpse by a charwoman, and the renewed happiness of his parents and his sister. Long before we come to that end, we are aware that we are not reading a fantasy but a moral fable, and a fable that can be understood in a number of ways. The story can be read as Gregor's primarily, as a study of guilt and self-destruction; or it can be read as primarily his family's, as a study of the fear of change, which is the process of living toward death, and of the fear of death itself and the mind's rejection of it.

Death and life, or rather life and death-in-life, is likewise the theme of D. H. Lawrence in *Daughters of the Vicar*, but his treatment is explicitly psychological whereas Kafka, concerned as his story is with the most profound psychological truths, nevertheless permits himself no explicit psychologizing. Lawrence differs, too, in his concern with a specific social scene and time, whereas Kafka's story exists abstractly, outside time and space. Lawrence writes of two respectable young women, one of whom remains safely within the conventions of her class when she marries, and thereby dooms herself to a life of dry suffocation and the stultification of self, while her sister, yielding to impulse, defies the conventions of her class, marries beneath her, and seizes upon the chance for self-fulfillment and heightened life.

Finally, and more literally, Tolstoy in *Master and Man* is concerned with death, with the triumph of unselfishness over death and the transfiguration of the self in that triumph. A selfish merchant and his servant lose their way in a snowstorm, and the master, who is warmly dressed and well-fed, determines in what is perhaps the only generous impulse of his life to save his servant if he can, and he lies on his nearly frozen body to keep it warm. When they are dug out of the snow, the servant is alive and the master is dead. Dying, his last thought had filled him "with joyful emotion. He felt himself free and that nothing could hold him back any longer."

In all these stories we are always observing human change. Candide's circumstances change, but the conditions of comedy prevent him from changing his views very much. The young hero of *First Love* matures through the shock of his discovery and finds that he can forgive his father. Paul Overt in *Lesson of the Master* finds himself unwillingly but not without submissiveness changing the course of his life for a monk-like dedication to "the real thing." Benito Cereno feels upon himself the enduring doom of his slave, and like the punished slave, himself soon goes to his death. Change and fear of change are the very themes of *Metamorphosis*. A double and contrasting choice of change is the basis of Lawrence's plot.

Inexplicably, perhaps, Tolstoy seems to tell us, men can choose to convert their shabby humanity into heroism.

All living is the process of always changing, and the essence of fiction, as these short novels show us so successfully, is to capture and thereby to make permanent, in its endless variety of kind and mood, that process of life that is in itself necessarily transient.

MARK SCHORER
Berkeley, California

October 31, 1960

Candide

BY VOLTAIRE
(FRANÇOIS MARIE AROUET) 1694-1778

On November 1, 1755, an earthquake shook Lisbon, causing widespread destruction and death. To Voltaire, the tragedy demonstrated the absurdity of the prevailing optimism of the period, expressed philosophically by Leibnitz, to the effect that everything happened for the best in the best of all possible worlds. The witty, satiric Candide, published in 1759, was Voltaire's devastating attack on this philosophy. During the two centuries since its publication, the story has been respected and loved by millions of delighted readers. Indeed, it would be difficult to name a single short novel which is more universally admired.

The author was born in Paris, received his education under the Jesuits, and began writing at an early age. His expert satire kept him in trouble for much of his career. In May, 1717, he was sent to the Bastille and held until April, 1718. In 1726, the Chevalier de Rohan, a powerful nobleman, angered by Voltaire's stinging wit, had the writer beaten by hoodlums and then thrown into the Bastille. He was released only when he promised to leave the country. A man of tremendous energy, Voltaire also waged a vigorous battle against religious intolerance.

13

Candide

CHAPTER I

HOW CANDIDE WAS BROUGHT UP IN A NOBLE CASTLE AND HOW HE WAS EXPELLED FROM THE SAME

In the castle of Baron Thunder-ten-tronckh in Westphalia there lived a youth, endowed by Nature with the most gentle character. His face was the expression of his soul. His judgment was quite honest and he was extremely simple-minded; and this was the reason, I think, that he was named Candide. Old servants in the house suspected that he was the son of the Baron's sister and a decent honest gentleman of the neighborhood, whom this young lady would never marry because he could only prove seventy-one quarterings, and the rest of his genealogical tree was lost, owing to the injuries of time.

The Baron was one of the most powerful lords in Westphalia, for his castle possessed a door and windows. His Great Hall was even decorated with a piece of tapestry. The dogs in his stable-yards formed a pack of hounds when necessary; his grooms were his huntsmen; the village curate was his Grand Almoner. They all called him "My Lord," and laughed heartily at his stories.

The Baroness weighed about three hundred and fifty pounds, was therefore greatly respected, and did the honors of the house with a dignity which rendered her still more respectable. Her daughter Cunegonde, aged seventeen, was rosy-cheeked, fresh, plump and tempting. The Baron's son appeared in every respect worthy of his father. The tutor

Pangloss was the oracle of the house, and little Candide followed his lessons with all the candor of his age and character.

Pangloss taught metaphysico-theologo-cosmolonigology. He proved admirably that there is no effect without a cause and that in this best of all possible worlds, My Lord the Baron's castle was the best of castles and his wife the best of all possible Baronesses.

"'Tis demonstrated," said he, "that things cannot be otherwise; for, since everything is made for an end, everything is necessarily for the best end. Observe that noses were made to wear spectacles; and so we have spectacles. Legs were visibly instituted to be breeched, and we have breeches. Stones were formed to be quarried and to build castles; and My Lord has a very noble castle; the greatest Baron in the province should have the best house; and as pigs were made to be eaten, we eat pork all the year round; consequently, those who have asserted that all is well talk nonsense; they ought to have said that all is for the best."

Candide listened attentively and believed innocently; for he thought Mademoiselle Cunegonde extremely beautiful, although he was never bold enough to tell her so. He decided that after the happiness of being born Baron of Thunder-ten-tronckh, the second degree of happiness was to be Mademoiselle Cunegonde; the third, to see her every day; and the fourth to listen to Doctor Pangloss, the greatest philosopher of the province and therefore of the whole world.

One day when Cunegonde was walking near the castle, in a little wood which was called The Park, she observed Doctor Pangloss in the bushes, giving a lesson in experimental physics to her mother's waiting maid, a very pretty and docile brunette. Mademoiselle Cunegonde had a great inclination for science and watched breathlessly the reiterated experiments she witnessed; she observed clearly the Doctor's sufficient reason, the effects and the causes, and returned home very much excited, pensive, filled with the desire of learning, reflecting that she might be the sufficient reason of young Candide and that he might be hers.

On her way back to the castle she met Candide and blushed; Candide also blushed. She bade him good-morning in a hesitating voice; Candide replied without knowing what he was saying. Next day, when they left the table after dinner, Cunegonde and Candide found themselves behind a screen; Cunegonde dropped her handkerchief, Candide picked it up; she innocently held his hand; the young man innocently kissed the young lady's hand with remarkable vivacity, tenderness and grace; their lips met, their eyes sparkled, their knees trembled, their hands wandered. Baron Thunder-ten-tronckh passed near the screen, and, observing this cause and effect, expelled Candide from the castle by kicking him in the backside frequently and hard. Cunegonde swooned; when she recovered her senses, the Baroness slapped her in the face; and all was in consternation in the noblest and most agreeable of all possible castles.

CHAPTER II

WHAT HAPPENED TO CANDIDE AMONG THE BULGARIANS

Candide, expelled from the earthly paradise, wandered for a long time without knowing where he was going, weeping, turning up his eyes to Heaven, gazing back frequently at the noblest of castles which held the most beautiful of young Baronesses; he lay down to sleep supperless between two furrows in the open fields; it snowed heavily in large flakes. The next morning the shivering Candide, penniless, dying of cold and exhaustion, dragged himself towards the neighboring town, which was called Waldberghoff-trarbkdikdorff. He halted sadly at the door of an inn. Two men dressed in blue noticed him.

"Comrade," said one, "there's a well-built young man of the right height." They went up to Candide and very civilly invited him to dinner.

"Gentlemen," said Candide with charming modesty, "you do me a great honor, but I have no money to pay my share."

"Ah, sir," said one of the men in blue, "persons of your figure and merit never pay anything; are you not five feet five tall?"

"Yes, gentlemen," said he, bowing, "that is my height."

"Ah, sir, come to table; we will not only pay your expenses, we will never allow a man like you to be short of money; men were only made to help each other."

"You are in the right," said Candide, "that is what Doctor

Pangloss was always telling me, and I see that everything is for the best."

They begged him to accept a few crowns, he took them and wished to give them an I O U; they refused to take it and all sat down to table. "Do you not love tenderly . . ."

"Oh, yes," said he. "I love Mademoiselle Cunegonde tenderly."

"No," said one of the gentlemen. "We were asking if you do not tenderly love the King of the Bulgarians."

"Not a bit," said he, "for I have never seen him."

"What! He is the most charming of Kings, and you must drink his health."

"Oh, gladly, gentlemen." And he drank.

"That is sufficient," he was told. "You are now the support, the aid, the defender, the hero of the Bulgarians; your fortune is made and your glory assured."

They immediately put irons on his legs and took him to a regiment. He was made to turn to the right and left, to raise the ramrod and return the ramrod, to take aim, to fire, to double up, and he was given thirty strokes with a stick; the next day he drilled not quite so badly, and received only twenty strokes; the day after, he only had ten, and was looked on as a prodigy by his comrades.

Candide was completely mystified and could not make out how he was a hero. One fine spring day he thought he would take a walk, going straight ahead, in the belief that to use his legs as he pleased was a privilege of the human species as well as of animals. He had not gone two leagues when four other heroes, each six feet tall, fell upon him, bound him and dragged him back to a cell. He was asked by his judges whether he would rather be thrashed thirty-six times by the whole regiment or receive a dozen lead bullets at once in his brain. Although he protested that men's wills are free and that he wanted neither one nor the other, he had to make a choice; by virtue of that gift of God which is called *liberty*, he determined to run the gauntlet thirty-six times and actually did so twice. There were two thousand men in the regiment. That made four thousand strokes which laid bare the muscles and nerves from his neck to his backside. As they were about to proceed to a third turn, Candide, utterly exhausted, begged as a favor that they would be so kind as to smash his head; he obtained this favor; they bound his eyes and he was made to kneel down. At that moment the King of the Bulgarians came by and inquired the victim's crime;

and as this King was possessed of a vast genius, he perceived from what he learned about Candide that he was a young metaphysician very ignorant in worldly matters, and therefore pardoned him with a clemency which will be praised in all newspapers and all ages. An honest surgeon healed Candide in three weeks with the ointments recommended by Dioscorides.* He had already regained a little skin and could walk when the King of the Bulgarians went to war with the King of the Abares.

CHAPTER III

HOW CANDIDE ESCAPED FROM THE BULGARIANS AND WHAT BECAME OF HIM

Nothing could be smarter, more splendid, more brilliant, better drawn up than the two armies. Trumpets, fifes, hautboys, drums, cannons, formed a harmony such as has never been heard even in hell. The cannons first of all laid flat about six thousand men on each side; then the musketry removed from the best of worlds some nine or ten thousand blackguards who infested its surface. The bayonet also was the sufficient reason for the death of some thousands of men. The whole might amount to thirty thousand souls. Candide, who trembled like a philosopher, hid himself as well as he could during this heroic butchery.

At last, while the two Kings each commanded a *Te Deum* in his camp, Candide decided to go elsewhere to reason about effects and causes. He clambered over heaps of dead and dying men and reached a neighboring village, which was in ashes; it was an Abare village which the Bulgarians had burned in accordance with international law. Here, old men dazed with blows watched the dying agonies of their murdered wives who clutched their children to their bleeding breasts; there, disembowelled girls who had been made to satisfy the natural appetites of heroes gasped their last sighs; others, half-burned, begged to be put to death. Brains were

* A Greek doctor.

scattered on the ground among dismembered arms and legs.

Candide fled to another village as fast as he could; it belonged to the Bulgarians, and Abarian heroes had treated it in the same way. Candide, stumbling over quivering limbs or across ruins, at last escaped from the theatre of war, carrying a little food in his knapsack, and never forgetting Mademoiselle Cunegonde. His provisions were all gone when he reached Holland; but, having heard that everyone in that country was rich and a Christian, he had no doubt at all but that he would be as well treated as he had been in the Baron's castle before he had been expelled on account of Mademoiselle Cunegonde's pretty eyes.

He asked an alms of several grave persons, who all replied that if he continued in that way he would be shut up in a house of correction to teach him how to live. He then addressed himself to a man who had been discoursing on charity in a large assembly for an hour on end. This orator, glancing at him askance, said: "What are you doing here? Are you for the good cause?"

"There is no effect without a cause," said Candide modestly. "Everything is necessarily linked up and arranged for the best. It was necessary that I should be expelled from the company of Mademoiselle Cunegonde, that I ran the gauntlet, and that I beg my bread until I can earn it; all this could not have happened differently."

"My friend," said the orator, "do you believe that the Pope is Anti-Christ?"

"I had never heard so before," said Candide, "but whether he is or isn't, I am starving."

"You don't deserve to eat," said the other. "Hence, rascal; hence, you wretch; and never come near me again."

The orator's wife thrust her head out of the window and seeing a man who did not believe that the Pope was Anti-Christ, she poured on his head a full . . . O Heavens! To what excess religious zeal is carried by ladies!

A man who had not been baptized, an honest Anabaptist named Jacques, saw the cruel and ignominious treatment of one of his brothers, a featherless two-legged creature with a soul; he took him home, cleaned him up, gave him bread and beer, presented him with two florins, and even offered to teach him to work at the manufacture of Persian stuffs which are made in Holland. Candide threw himself at the man's feet, exclaiming: "Doctor Pangloss was right in telling me that all is for the best in this world, for I am vastly more touched by your extreme generosity than by the harshness of the gentleman in the black cloak and his good lady."

The next day when he walked out he met a beggar covered with sores, dull-eyed, with the end of his nose fallen away, his mouth awry, his teeth black, who talked huskily, was tormented with a violent cough and spat out a tooth at every cough.

CHAPTER IV

HOW CANDIDE MET HIS OLD MASTER IN PHILOSOPHY, DOCTOR PANGLOSS, AND WHAT HAPPENED

Candide, moved even more by compassion than by horror, gave this horrible beggar the two florins he had received from the honest Anabaptist, Jacques. The phantom gazed fixedly at him, shed tears and threw its arms round his neck. Candide recoiled in terror.

"Alas!" said the wretch to the other wretch, "don't you recognise your dear Pangloss?"

"What do I hear? You, my dear master! You, in this horrible state! What misfortune has happened to you? Why are you no longer in the noblest of castles? What has become of Mademoiselle Cunegonde, the pearl of young ladies, the masterpiece of Nature?"

"I am exhausted," said Pangloss. Candide immediately took him to the Anabaptist's stable where he gave him a little bread to eat; and when Pangloss had recovered: "Well!" said he, "Cunegonde?"

"Dead," replied the other.

At this word Candide swooned; his friend restored him to his senses with a little bad vinegar which happened to be in the stable. Candide opened his eyes. "Cunegonde dead! Ah! best of worlds, where are you? But what illness did she die of? Was it because she saw me kicked out of her father's noble castle?"

"No," said Pangloss. "She was disembowelled by Bulgarian soldiers, after having been raped to the limit of possibility; they broke the Baron's head when he tried to defend her; the

Baroness was cut to pieces; my poor pupil was treated exactly like his sister; and as to the castle, there is not one stone standing on another, not a barn, not a sheep, not a duck, not a tree; but we were well avenged, for the Abares did exactly the same to a neighboring barony which belonged to a Bulgarian Lord." At this, Candide swooned again; but, having recovered and having said all that he ought to say, he inquired the cause and effect, the sufficient reason which had reduced Pangloss to so piteous a state.

"Alas!" said Pangloss, " 'tis love; love, the consoler of the human race, the preserver of the universe, the soul of all tender creatures, gentle love."

"Alas!" said Candide, "I am acquainted with this love, this sovereign of hearts, this soul of our soul; it has never brought me anything but one kiss and twenty kicks in the backside. How could this beautiful cause produce in you so abominable an effect?"

Pangloss replied as follows: "My dear Candide! You remember Paquette, the maidservant of our august Baroness; in her arms I enjoyed the delights of Paradise which have produced the tortures of Hell by which you see I am devoured; she was infected and perhaps is dead. Paquette received this present from a most learned monk, who had it from the source; for he received it from an old countess, who had it from a cavalry captain, who owed it to a marchioness, who derived it from a page, who had received it from a Jesuit, who, when a novice, had it in a direct line from one of the companions of Christopher Columbus. For my part, I shall not give it to anyone, for I am dying."

"O Pangloss!" exclaimed Candide, "this is a strange genealogy! Wasn't the devil at the root of it?"

"Not at all," replied that great man. "It was something indispensable in this best of worlds, a necessary ingredient; for, if Columbus in an island of America had not caught this disease, which poisons the source of generation, and often indeed prevents generation, we should not have chocolate and cochineal; it must also be noticed that hitherto in our continent this disease is peculiar to us, like theological disputes. The Turks, the Indians, the Persians, the Chinese, the Siamese and the Japanese are not yet familiar with it; but there is a sufficient reason why they in their turn should become familiar with it in a few centuries. Meanwhile, it has made marvellous progress among us, and especially in those large armies composed of honest, well-bred stipendiaries who decide the destiny of States; it may be asserted that when thirty thousand men fight a pitched battle against an equal number of troops, there are about twenty thousand with the pox on either side."

"Admirable!" said Candide. "But you must get cured."

"How can I?" said Pangloss. "I haven't a sou, my friend, and in the whole extent of this globe, you cannot be bled or receive an enema without paying or without someone paying for you."

This last speech determined Candide; he went and threw himself at the feet of his charitable Anabaptist, Jacques, and drew so touching a picture of the state to which his friend was reduced that the good easy man did not hesitate to succor Pangloss; he had him cured at his own expense. In this cure Pangloss only lost one eye and one ear. He could write well and knew arithmetic perfectly. The Anabaptist made him his bookkeeper. At the end of two months he was compelled to go to Lisbon on business and took his two philosophers on the boat with him. Pangloss explained to him how everything was for the best. Jacques was not of this opinion.

"Men," said he, "must have corrupted nature a little, for they were not born wolves, and they have become wolves. God did not give them twenty-four-pounder cannons or bayonets, and they have made bayonets and cannons to destroy each other. I might bring bankruptcies into the account and Justice which seizes the goods of bankrupts in order to deprive the creditors of them."

"It was all indispensable," replied the one-eyed doctor, "and private misfortunes make the public good, so that the more private misfortunes there are, the more everything is well."

While he was reasoning, the air grew dark, the winds blew from the four quarters of the globe and the ship was attacked by the most horrible tempest in sight of the port of Lisbon.

CHAPTER V

STORM, SHIPWRECK, EARTHQUAKE, AND WHAT HAPPENED TO DR. PANGLOSS, TO CANDIDE AND THE ANABAPTIST JACQUES

Half the enfeebled passengers, suffering from that inconceivable anguish which the rolling of a ship causes in the nerves and in all the humors of bodies shaken in contrary directions, did not retain strength enough even to trouble about the danger. The other half screamed and prayed; the sails were torn, the masts broken, the vessel leaking. Those worked who could, no one cooperated, no one commanded. The Anabaptist tried to help the crew a little; he was on the main deck; a furious sailor struck him violently and stretched him on the deck; but the blow he delivered gave him so violent a shock that he fell head-first out of the ship. He remained hanging and clinging to part of the broken mast. The good Jacques ran to his aid, helped him to climb back, and from the effort he made was flung into the sea in full view of the sailor, who allowed him to drown without condescending even to look at him. Candide came up, saw his benefactor reappear for a moment and then be engulfed for ever. He tried to throw himself after him into the sea; he was prevented by the philosopher Pangloss, who proved to him that the Lisbon roads had been expressly created for the Anabaptist to be drowned in them. While he was proving this *a priori,** the vessel sank, and every one perished except Pangloss, Candide and the brutal sailor who had drowned the virtuous Anabaptist; the blackguard swam successfully to the shore and Pangloss and Candide were carried there on a plank.

When they had recovered a little, they walked toward Lisbon; they had a little money by the help of which they hoped to be saved from hunger after having escaped the storm. Weeping the death of their benefactor, they had scarcely set foot in the town when they felt the earth trem-

* Deductive method of argument.

ble under their feet; the sea rose in foaming masses in the port and smashed the ships which rode at anchor. Whirlwinds of flame and ashes covered the streets and squares; the houses collapsed, the roofs were thrown upon the foundations, and the foundations were scattered; thirty thousand inhabitants of every age and both sexes were crushed under the ruins. Whistling and swearing, the sailor said: "There'll be something to pick up here."

"What can be the sufficient reason for this phenomenon?" said Pangloss.

"It is the last day!" cried Candide.

The sailor immediately ran among the debris, dared death to find money, found it, seized it, got drunk, and having slept off his wine, purchased the favors of the first woman of good will he met on the ruins of the houses and among the dead and dying. Pangloss, however, pulled him by the sleeve. "My friend," said he, "this is not well, you are disregarding universal reason, you choose the wrong time."

"Blood and 'ounds!" he retorted, "I am a sailor and I was born in Batavia; four times have I stamped on the crucifix during four voyages to Japan; you have found the right man for your universal reason!"

Candide had been hurt by some falling stones; he lay in the street covered with debris. He said to Pangloss: "Alas! Get me a little wine and oil; I am dying."

"This earthquake is not a new thing," replied Pangloss. "The town of Lima felt the same shocks in America last year; similar causes produce similar effects; there must certainly be a train of sulphur underground from Lima to Lisbon."

"Nothing is more probable," replied Candide; "but, for God's sake, a little oil and wine."

"What do you mean, probable?" replied the philosopher; "I maintain that it is proved."

Candide lost consciousness, and Pangloss brought him a little water from a neighboring fountain.

Next day they found a little food as they wandered among the ruins and regained a little strength. Afterwards they worked like others to help the inhabitants who had escaped death. Some citizens they had assisted gave them as good a dinner as could be expected in such a disaster; true, it was a dreary meal; the hosts watered their bread with their tears, but Pangloss consoled them by assuring them that things could not be otherwise. "For," said he, "all this is for the best; for, if there is a volcano at Lisbon, it cannot be anywhere else; for it is impossible that things should not be where they are; for all is well."

A little, dark man, a familiar of the Inquisition, who sat beside him, politely took up the conversation, and said: "Apparently, you do not believe in original sin; for, if everything is for the best, there was neither fall nor punishment."

"I most humbly beg your excellency's pardon," replied Pangloss still more politely, "for the fall of man and the curse necessarily entered into the best of all possible worlds."

"Then you do not believe in free will?" said the familiar.

"Your excellency will pardon me," said Pangloss; "free will can exist with absolute necessity; for it was necessary that we should be free; for in short, limited will . . ."

Pangloss was in the middle of his phrase when the familiar nodded to his armed attendant who was pouring out port or Oporto wine for him.

CHAPTER VI

HOW A SPLENDID AUTO-DA-FE WAS HELD TO PREVENT EARTHQUAKES, AND HOW CANDIDE WAS FLOGGED

After the earthquake which destroyed three-quarters of Lisbon, the wise men of that country could discover no more efficacious way of preventing a total ruin than by giving the people a splendid *auto-da-fé*.* It was decided by the university of Coimbre that the sight of several persons being slowly burned in great ceremony is an infallible secret for preventing earthquakes. Consequently they had arrested a Biscayan convicted of having married his fellow-godmother, and two Portuguese who, when eating a chicken, had thrown away the bacon; after dinner they came and bound Dr. Pangloss and his disciple Candide, one because he had spoken and the other because he had listened with an air of approbation; they were both carried separately to extremely cool apartments, where there was never any discomfort from the sun; a week afterwards each was dressed in a sanbenito and their

* "Act of faith"—the burning of heretics.

heads were ornamented with paper mitres; Candide's mitre and sanbenito were painted with flames upside down and with devils who had neither tails nor claws; but Pangloss's devils had claws and tails, and his flames were upright.

Dressed in this manner they marched in procession and listened to a most pathetic sermon, followed by lovely plain song music. Candide was flogged in time to the music, while the singing went on; the Biscayan and the two men who had not wanted to eat the bacon were burned, and Pangloss was hanged, although this is not the custom. The very same day, the earth shook again with a terrible clamor.

Candide, terrified, dumbfounded, bewildered, covered with blood, quivering from head to foot, said to himself: "If this is the best of all possible worlds, what are the others? Let it pass that I was flogged, for I was flogged by the Bulgarians, but, O my dear Pangloss! The greatest of philosophers! Must I see you hanged without knowing why! O my dear Anabaptist! The best of men! Was it necessary that you should be drowned in port! O Mademoiselle Cunegonde! The pearl of women! Was it necessary that your belly should be slit!"

He was returning, scarcely able to support himself, preached at, flogged, absolved and blessed, when an old woman accosted him and said: "Courage, my son, follow me."

CHAPTER VII

HOW AN OLD WOMAN TOOK CARE OF CANDIDE AND HOW HE REGAINED THAT WHICH HE LOVED

Candide did not take courage, but he followed the old woman to a hovel; she gave him a pot of ointment to rub on, and left him food and drink; she pointed out a fairly clean bed; near the bed there was a suit of clothes. "Eat, drink, sleep," said she, "and may our Lady of Atocha, my Lord Saint Anthony of Padua and my Lord Saint James of Compostella take care of you; I shall come back tomorrow."

Candide, still amazed by all he had seen, by all he had suffered and still more by the old woman's charity, tried to kiss her hand. " 'Tis not my hand you should kiss," said the old woman, "I shall come back tomorrow. Rub on the ointment, eat and sleep."

In spite of all his misfortune, Candide ate and went to sleep. Next day the old woman brought him breakfast, examined his back and smeared him with another ointment; later she brought him dinner, and returned in the evening with supper. The next day she went through the same ceremony.

"Who are you?" Candide kept asking her. "Who has inspired you with so much kindness? How can I thank you?"

The good woman never made any reply; she returned in the evening without any supper. "Come with me," said she, "and do not speak a word."

She took him by the arm and walked into the country with him for about a quarter of a mile; they came to an isolated house, surrounded with gardens and canals. The old woman knocked at a little door. It was opened; she led Candide up a back stairway into a gilded apartment, left him on a brocaded sofa, shut the door and went away. Candide thought he was dreaming, and felt that his whole life was a bad dream and the present moment an agreeable dream. The old woman soon reappeared; she was supporting with some difficulty a trembling woman of majestic stature, glittering with precious stones and covered with a veil.

"Remove the veil," said the old woman to Candide. The young man advanced and lifted the veil with a timid hand. What a moment! What a surprise! He thought he saw Mademoiselle Cunegonde, in fact he was looking at her, it was she herself. His strength failed him, he could not utter a word and fell at her feet. Cunegonde fell on the sofa. The old woman dosed them with distilled waters; they recovered their senses and began to speak: at first they uttered only broken words, questions and answers at cross purposes, sighs, tears, exclamations. The old woman advised them to make less noise and left them alone.

"What! Is it you?" said Candide. "You are alive, and I find you here in Portugal! Then you were not raped? Your belly was not slit, as the philosopher Pangloss assured me?"

"Yes, indeed," said the fair Cunegonde; "but those two accidents are not always fatal."

"But your father and mother were killed?"

" 'Tis only too true," said Cunegonde, weeping.

"And your brother?"

"My brother was killed too."

"And why are you in Portugal? And how did you know I was here? And by what strange adventure have you brought me to this house?"

"I will tell you everything," replied the lady, "but first of all you must tell me everything that has happened to you since the innocent kiss you gave me and the kicks you received."

Candide obeyed with profound respect; and, although he was bewildered, although his voice was weak and trembling, although his back was still a little painful, he related in the most natural manner all he had endured since the moment of their separation. Cunegonde raised her eyes to heaven; she shed tears at the death of the good Anabaptist and Pangloss, after which she spoke as follows to Candide, who did not miss a word and devoured her with his eyes.

CHAPTER VIII

CUNEGONDE'S STORY

"I was fast asleep in bed when it pleased Heaven to send the Bulgarians to our noble castle of Thunder-ten-tronckh; they murdered my father and brother and cut my mother to pieces. A large Bulgarian six feet tall, seeing that I had swooned at the spectacle, began to rape me; this brought me to, I recovered my senses, I screamed, I struggled, I bit, I scratched, I tried to tear out the big Bulgarian's eyes, not knowing that what was happening in my father's castle was a matter of custom; the brute stabbed me with a knife in the left side where I still have the scar."

"Alas! I hope I shall see it," said the naïf Candide.

"You shall see it," said Cunegonde, "but let me go on."

"Go on," said Candide.

She took up the thread of her story as follows: "A Bulgarian captain came in, saw me covered with blood, and the soldier did not disturb himself. The captain was angry at the brute's lack of respect to him, and killed him on my body. Afterwards, he had me bandaged and took me to his billet as a prisoner of war. I washed the few shirts he had and did the cooking; I must admit he thought me very pretty;

and I will not deny that he was very well built and that his skin was white and soft; otherwise he had little wit and little philosophy; it was plain that he had not been brought up by Dr. Pangloss. At the end of three months he lost all his money and got tired of me; he sold me to a Jew named Don Issachar, who traded in Holland and Portugal and had a passion for women. This Jew devoted himself to my person but he could not triumph over it; I resisted him better than the Bulgarian soldier; a lady of honor may be raped once, but it strengthens her virtue. In order to subdue me, the Jew brought me to this country house. Up till then I believed that there was nothing on earth so splendid as the castle of Thunder-ten-tronckh; I was undeceived.

"One day the Grand Inquisitor noticed me at Mass; he ogled me continually and sent a message that he wished to speak to me on secret affairs. I was taken to his palace; I informed him of my birth; he pointed out how much it was beneath my rank to belong to an Israelite. A proposition was made on his behalf to Don Issachar to give me up to His Lordship. Don Issachar, who is the court banker and a man of influence, would not agree. The Inquisitor threatened him with an *auto-da-fé*. At last the Jew was frightened and made a bargain whereby the house and I belong to both in common. The Jew has Mondays, Wednesdays and the Sabbath day, and the Inquisitor has the other days of the week. This arrangement has lasted for six months. It has not been without quarrels; for it has often been debated whether the night between Saturday and Sunday belonged to the old law or the new. For my part, I have hitherto resisted them both; and I think that is the reason why they still love me.

"At last My Lord the Inquisitor was pleased to arrange an *auto-da-fé* to remove the scourge of earthquakes and to intimidate Don Issachar. He honored me with an invitation. I had an excellent seat; and refreshments were served to the ladies between the Mass and the execution. I was indeed horror stricken when I saw the burning of the two Jews and the honest Biscayan who had married his fellow-godmother; but what was my surprise, my terror, my anguish, when I saw in a sanbenito and under a mitre a face which resembled Pangloss's! I rubbed my eyes, I looked carefully, I saw him hanged; and I fainted. I had scarcely recovered my senses when I saw you stripped naked; that was the height of horror, of consternation, of grief and despair. I will frankly tell you that your skin is even whiter and of a more perfect tint than that of my Bulgarian captain. This spectacle redoubled all the feelings which crushed and devoured me. I exclaimed, I tried to say: 'Stop, Barbarians!' but my voice failed and my cries would have been useless. When you had been well flogged, I said to myself: 'How does it happen that the charming Candide and the wise Pangloss are in Lisbon, the one to receive a hundred lashes, and the other to be hanged, by order of My Lord the Inquisitor, whose darling I am? Pangloss deceived me cruelly when he said that all is for the best in the world.'

"I was agitated, distracted, sometimes beside myself and sometimes ready to die of faintness, and my head was filled with the massacre of my father, of my mother, of my brother, the insolence of my horrid Bulgarian soldier, the gash he gave me, my slavery, my life as a kitchen wench, my Bulgarian captain, my horrid Don Issachar, my abominable Inquisitor, the hanging of Dr. Pangloss, that long plain song *miserere** during which you were flogged, and above all the kiss I gave you behind the screen that day when I saw you for the last time. I praised God for bringing you back to me through so many trials, I ordered my old woman to take care of you and to bring you here as soon as she could. She has carried out my commission very well; I have enjoyed the inexpressible pleasure of seeing you again, of listening to you, and of speaking to you. You must be very hungry; I have a good appetite; let us begin by having supper."

Both sat down to supper; and after supper they returned to the handsome sofa we have already mentioned; they were still there when Signor Don Issachar, one of the masters of the house, arrived. It was the day of the Sabbath. He came to enjoy his rights and to express his tender love.

* A Latin chant: "Have mercy, O God."

CHAPTER IX

WHAT HAPPENED TO CUNEGONDE, TO CANDIDE, TO THE GRAND INQUISITOR AND TO A JEW

This Issachar was the most choleric Hebrew who had been seen in Israel since the Babylonian captivity. "What!" said he. "Bitch of a Galilean, isn't it enough to have the Inquisitor? Must this scoundrel share with me too?"

So saying, he drew a long dagger which he always carried and, thinking that his adversary was unarmed, threw himself upon Candide; but our good Westphalian had received an excellent sword from the old woman along with his suit of clothes. He drew his sword, and although he had a most gentle character, laid the Israelite stone-dead on the floor at the feet of the fair Cunegonde.

"Holy Virgin!" she exclaimed, "what will become of us? A man killed in my house! If the police come we are lost."

"If Pangloss had not been hanged," said Candide, "he would have given us good advice in this extremity, for he was a great philosopher. In default of him, let us consult the old woman."

She was extremely prudent and was beginning to give her advice when another little door opened. It was an hour after midnight, and Sunday was beginning. This day belonged to My Lord the Inquisitor. He came in and saw the flogged Candide sword in hand, a corpse lying on the ground, Cunegonde in terror, and the old woman giving advice. At this moment, here is what happened in Candide's soul and the manner of his reasoning: "If this holy man calls for help, he will infallibly have me burned; he might do as much to Cunegonde; he had me pitilessly lashed; he is my rival; I am in the mood to kill, there is no room for hesitation."

His reasoning was clear and swift; and, without giving the Inquisitor time to recover from his surprise, he pierced him through and through and cast him beside the Jew.

"Here's another," said Cunegonde, "there is no chance of

31

mercy; we are excommunicated, our last hour has come. How does it happen that you, who were born so mild, should kill a Jew and a prelate in two minutes?"

"My dear young lady," replied Candide, "when a man is in love, jealous, and has been flogged by the Inquisition, he is beside himself."

The old woman then spoke up and said: "In the stable are three Andalusian horses, with their saddles and bridles; let the brave Candide prepare them; mademoiselle has moidores* and diamonds; let us mount quickly, although I can only sit on one buttock, and go to Cadiz; the weather is beautifully fine, and it is most pleasant to travel in the coolness of the night."

Candide immediately saddled the three horses. Cunegonde, the old woman and he rode thirty miles without stopping. While they were riding away, the Holy Hermandad † arrived at the house; My Lord was buried in a splendid church and Issachar was thrown into a sewer.

Candide, Cunegonde and the old woman had already reached the little town of Avacena in the midst of the mountains of the Sierra Morena; and they talked in their inn as follows.

CHAPTER X

HOW CANDIDE, CUNEGONDE AND THE OLD WOMAN ARRIVED AT CADIZ IN GREAT DISTRESS, AND HOW THEY EMBARKED

"Who can have stolen my money and my diamonds?" said Cunegonde, weeping. "How shall we live? What shall we do? Where shall we find Inquisitors and Jews to give me others?"

"Alas!" said the old woman, "I strongly suspect a reverend Franciscan father who slept in the same inn at Badajoz with

* Portuguese coin.
† An association that tracked down criminals.

us; Heaven forbid that I should judge rashly! But he twice came into our room and left long before we did."

"Alas!" said Candide, "the good Pangloss often proved to me that this world's goods are common to all men and that every one has an equal right to them. According to these principles the monk should have left us enough to continue our journey. Have you nothing left then, my fair Cunegonde?"

"Not a maravedi,"* said she. "What are we to do?" said Candide.

"Sell one of the horses," said the old woman. "I will ride postillion behind Mademoiselle Cunegonde, although I can only sit on one buttock, and we will get to Cadiz."

In the same hotel there was a Benedictine prior. He bought the horse very cheap. Candide, Cunegonde and the old woman passed through Lucena, Chillas, Lebrixa, and at last reached Cadiz. A fleet was there being equipped and troops were being raised to bring to reason the reverend Jesuit fathers of Paraguay, who were accused of causing the revolt of one of their tribes against the kings of Spain and Portugal near the town of Sacramento. Candide, having served with the Bulgarians, went through the Bulgarian drill before the general of the little army with so much grace, celerity, skill, pride and agility, that he was given the command of an infantry company. He was now a captain; he embarked with Mademoiselle Cunegonde, the old woman, two servants, and the two Andalusian horses which had belonged to the Grand Inquisitor of Portugal.

During the voyage they had many discussions about the philosophy of poor Pangloss. "We are going to a new world," said Candide, "and no doubt it is there that everything is for the best; for it must be admitted that one might lament a little over the physical and moral happenings in our own world."

"I love you with all my heart," said Cunegonde, "but my soul is still shocked by what I have seen and undergone."

"All will be well," replied Candide; "the sea in this new world already is better than the seas of our Europe; it is calmer and the winds are more constant. It is certainly the new world which is the best of all possible worlds."

"God grant it!" said Cunegonde, "but I have been so horribly unhappy in mine that my heart is nearly closed to hope."

"You complain," said the old woman to them. "Alas! you have not endured such misfortunes as mine."

* A small coin.

Cunegonde almost laughed and thought it most amusing of the old woman to assert that she was more unfortunate. "Alas! my dear," said she, "unless you have been raped by two Bulgarians, stabbed twice in the belly, have had two castles destroyed, two fathers and mothers murdered before your eyes, and have seen two of your lovers flogged in an *auto-da-fé*, I do not see how you can surpass me; moreover, I was born a Baroness with seventy-two quarterings and I have been a kitchen wench."

"You do not know my birth," said the old woman, "and if I showed you my backside you would not talk as you do and you would suspend your judgment."

This speech aroused intense curiosity in the minds of Cunegonde and Candide. And the old woman spoke as follows.

CHAPTER XI

THE OLD WOMAN'S STORY

"My eyes were not always bloodshot and red-rimmed; my nose did not always touch my chin and I was not always a servant. I am the daughter of Pope Urban X * and the Princess of Palestrina. Until I was fourteen I was brought up in a palace to which all the castles of your German Barons would not have served as stables; and one of my dresses cost more than all the magnificence of Westphalia. I increased in beauty, in grace, in talents, among pleasures, respect and hopes; already I inspired love, my breasts were forming; and what breasts! White, firm, carved like those of the Venus de' Medici. And what eyes! What eyelids! What black eyebrows! What fire shone from my two eyeballs, and dimmed the glitter of the stars, as the local poets pointed out to me. The women who dressed and undressed me fell into ecstasy when they beheld me in front and behind; and all the men would have liked to be in their place.

"I was betrothed to a ruling prince of Massa-Carrara. What a prince! As beautiful as I was, formed of gentleness and charms, brilliantly witty and burning with love; I loved him with a first love, idolatrously and extravagantly. The marriage

* An imaginary Pope.

ceremonies were arranged with unheard of pomp and magnificence; there were continual fêtes, revels and comic operas; all Italy wrote sonnets for me and not a good one among them.

"I touched the moment of my happiness when an old marchioness who had been my prince's mistress invited him to take chocolate with her; less than two hours afterwards he died in horrible convulsions; but that is only a trifle. My mother was in despair, though less distressed than I, and wished to absent herself for a time from a place so disastrous. She had a most beautiful estate near Gaeta, we embarked on a galley, gilded like the altar of St. Peter's at Rome. A Salle pirate swooped down and boarded us; our soldiers defended us like soldiers of the Pope; they threw down their arms, fell on their knees and asked the pirates for absolution *in articulo mortis.**

"They were immediately stripped as naked as monkeys and my mother, our ladies of honor and myself as well. The diligence with which these gentlemen strip people is truly admirable; but I was still more surprised by their inserting a finger in a place belonging to all of us where we women usually only allow the end of a syringe. This appeared to me a very strange ceremony; but that is how we judge everything when we leave our own country. I soon learned that it was to find out if we had hidden any diamonds there; 'tis a custom established from time immemorial among the civilised nations who roam the seas. I have learned that the religious Knights of Malta never fail in it when they capture Turks and Turkish women; this is an international law which has never been broken.

"I will not tell you how hard it is for a young princess to be taken with her mother as a slave to Morocco; you will also guess all we had to endure in the pirates' ship. My mother was still very beautiful; our ladies of honor, even our waiting maids possessed more charms than could be found in all Africa; and I was ravishing, I was beauty, grace itself, and I was a virgin; I did not remain so long; the flower which had been reserved for the handsome prince of Massa-Carrara was ravished from me by a pirate captain; he was an abominable negro who thought he was doing me a great honor. The Princess of Palestrina and I must indeed have been strong to bear up against all we endured before our arrival in Morocco!

* At the point of death.

But let that pass; these things are so common that they are not worth mentioning.

"Morocco was swimming in blood when we arrived. The fifty sons of the Emperor Muley Ismael had each a faction; and this produced fifty civil wars, of blacks against blacks, browns against browns, mulattoes against mulattoes. There was continual carnage throughout the whole extent of the empire.

"Scarcely had we landed when blacks of a party hostile to that of my pirate arrived with the purpose of depriving him of his booty. After the diamonds and the gold, we were the most valuable possessions. I witnessed a fight such as is never seen in your European climates. The blood of the northern peoples is not sufficiently ardent; their madness for women does not reach the point which is common in Africa. The Europeans seem to have milk in their veins; but vitriol and fire flow in the veins of the inhabitants of Mount Atlas and the neighboring countries. They fought with the fury of the lions, tigers and serpents of the country to determine who should have us. A Moor grasped my mother by the right arm, my captain's lieutenant held her by the left arm; a Moorish soldier held one leg and one of our pirates seized the other. In a moment nearly all our women were seized in the same way by four soldiers. My captain kept me hidden behind him; he had a scimitar in his hand and killed everybody who opposed his fury. I saw my mother and all our Italian women torn in pieces, gashed, massacred by the monsters who disputed them. The prisoners, my companions, those who had captured them, soldiers, sailors, blacks, browns, whites, mulattoes and finally my captain were all killed and I remained expiring on a heap of corpses. As every one knows, such scenes go on in an area of more than three hundred square leagues and yet no one ever fails to recite the five daily prayers ordered by Mahomet.

"With great difficulty I extricated myself from the bloody heaps of corpses and dragged myself to the foot of a large orange tree on the bank of a stream; there I fell down with terror, weariness, horror, despair and hunger. Soon afterwards, my exhausted senses fell into a sleep which was more like a swoon than repose. I was in this state of weakness and insensibility between life and death when I felt myself oppressed by something which moved on my body. I opened my eyes and saw a white man of good appearance who was sighing and muttering between his teeth: *O che sciagura d'essere senza coglioni!"*

CHAPTER XII

CONTINUATION OF THE OLD WOMAN'S MISFORTUNES

"Amazed and delighted to hear my native language, and not less surprised at the words spoken by this man, I replied that there were greater misfortunes than that of which he complained. In a few words I informed him of the horrors I had undergone and then swooned again. He carried me to a neighboring house, had me put to bed, gave me food, waited on me, consoled me, flattered me, told me he had never seen anyone so beautiful as I, and that he had never so much regretted that which no one could give back to him.

" 'I was born at Naples,' he said, 'and every year they make two or three thousand children there into capons; some die of it, others acquire voices more beautiful than women's, and others become the governors of States. This operation was performed upon me with very great success and I was a musician in the chapel of the Princess of Palestrina.'

" 'Of my mother,' I exclaimed.

" 'Of your mother!' cried he, weeping. 'What! Are you that young princess I brought up to the age of six and who even then gave promise of being as beautiful as you are?'

" 'I am! my mother is four hundred yards from here, cut into quarters under a heap of corpses . . .'

"I related all that had happened to me; he also told me his adventures and informed me how he had been sent to the King of Morocco by a Christian power to make a treaty with that monarch whereby he was supplied with powder, cannons and ships to help to exterminate the commerce of other Christians. 'My mission is accomplished,' said this honest eunuch, 'I am about to embark at Ceuta and I will take you back to Italy. *Ma che sciagura d'essere senza coglioni!'*

"I thanked him with tears of gratitude; and instead of taking me back to Italy he conducted me to Algiers and sold me to the Dey. I had scarcely been sold when the plague which had gone through Africa, Asia and Europe, broke out furiously in Algiers. You have seen earthquakes; but have you ever seen the plague?"

"Never," replied the Baroness.

"If you had," replied the old woman, "you would admit that it is much worse than an earthquake. It is very common in Africa; I caught it. Imagine the situation of a Pope's daughter aged fifteen, who in three months had undergone poverty and slavery, had been raped nearly every day, had seen her mother cut into four pieces, had undergone hunger and war, and was now dying of the plague in Algiers. However, I did not die; but my eunuch and the Dey and almost all the seraglio of Algiers perished.

"When the first ravages of this frightful plague were over, the Dey's slaves were sold. A merchant bought me and carried me to Tunis; he sold me to another merchant who resold me at Tripoli; from Tripoli I was re-sold to Alexandria, from Alexandria re-sold to Smyrna, from Smyrna to Constantinople. I was finally bought by an Aga of the Janizaries, who was soon ordered to defend Azov against the Russians who were besieging it.

"The Aga, who was a man of great gallantry, took his whole seraglio with him, and lodged us in a little fort on the Islands of Palus-Maeotis, guarded by two black eunuchs and twenty soldiers. He killed a prodigious number of Russians but they returned the compliment as well. Azov was given up to fire and blood, neither sex nor age was pardoned; only our little fort remained; and the enemy tried to reduce it by starving us. The twenty Janizaries had sworn never to surrender us. The extremities of hunger to which they were reduced forced them to eat our two eunuchs for fear of breaking their oath. Some days later they resolved to eat the women. We had with us a most pious and compassionate Imam who delivered a fine sermon to them by which he persuaded them not to kill us altogether. 'Cut,' said he, 'only one buttock from each of these ladies and you will make very good cheer; if you have to return, there will still be as much left in a few days; Heaven will be pleased at so charitable an action and you will be saved.'

"He was very eloquent and persuaded them. This horrible operation was performed upon us; the Imam anointed us with the same balm that is used for children who have just been circumcised; we were all at the point of death.

"Scarcely had the Janizaries finished the meal we had supplied when the Russians arrived in flat-bottomed boats; not a Janizary escaped. The Russians paid no attention to the state we were in. There are French doctors everywhere; one of them who was very skilful, took care of us; he healed us and I shall remember all my life that, when my wounds were cured, he made propositions to me. For the rest, he told us all to cheer up; he told us that the same thing had happened in several sieges and that it was a law of war.

"As soon as my companions could walk they were sent to Moscow. I fell to the lot of a Boyar who made me his gardener and gave me twenty lashes a day. But at the end of two years this lord was broken on the wheel with thirty other Boyars owing to some court disturbance, and I profited by this adventure; I fled; I crossed all Russia; for a long time I was servant in an inn at Riga, then at Rostock, at Wismar, at Leipzig, at Cassel, at Utrecht, at Leyden, at the Hague, at Rotterdam; I have grown old in misery and in shame, with only half a backside, always remembering that I was the daughter of a Pope; a hundred times I wanted to kill myself but I still loved life. This ridiculous weakness is perhaps the most disastrous of our inclinations; for is there anything sillier than to desire to bear continually a burden one always wishes to throw on the ground; to look upon oneself with horror and yet to cling to oneself; in short, to caress the serpent which devours us until he has eaten our heart?

"In the countries it has been my fate to traverse and in the inns where I have served I have seen a prodigious number of people who hated their lives; but I have only seen twelve who voluntarily put an end to their misery: three negroes, four Englishmen, four Genevans and a German professor named Robeck. I ended up as servant to the Jew, Don Issachar; he placed me in your service, my fair young lady; I attached myself to your fate and have been more occupied with your adventures than with my own. I should never even have spoken of my misfortunes, if you had not piqued me a little and if it had not been the custom on board ship to tell stories to pass the time. In short, Mademoiselle, I have had experience, I know the world; provide yourself with an entertainment, make each passenger tell you his story; and if there is one who has not often cursed his life, who has not often said to himself that he was the most unfortunate of men, throw me headfirst into the sea."

CHAPTER XIII

HOW CANDIDE WAS OBLIGED TO
SEPARATE FROM THE FAIR
CUNEGONDE AND THE
OLD WOMAN

The fair Cunegonde, having heard the old woman's story, treated her with all the politeness due to a person of her rank and merit. She accepted the proposition and persuaded all the passengers one after the other to tell her their adventures. She and Candide admitted that the old woman was right.

"It was most unfortunate," said Candide, "that the wise Pangloss was hanged contrary to custom at an *auto-da-fé;* he would have said admirable things about the physical and moral evils which cover the earth and the sea, and I should feel myself strong enough to urge a few objections with all due respect."

While each of the passengers was telling his story the ship proceeded on its way. They arrived at Buenos Ayres. Cunegonde, Captain Candide and the old woman went to call on the governor, Don Fernando d'Ibaraa y Figueora y Mascarenes y Lampourdos y Souza. This gentleman had the pride befitting a man who owned so many names. He talked to men with a most noble disdain, turning his nose up so far, raising his voice so pitilessly, assuming so imposing a tone, affecting so lofty a carriage, that all who addressed him were tempted to give him a thrashing. He had a furious passion for women. Cunegonde seemed to him the most beautiful woman he had ever seen. The first thing he did was to ask if she were the Captain's wife. The air with which he asked this question alarmed Candide; he did not dare say that she was his wife, because as a matter of fact she was not; he dared not say she was his sister, because she was not that either; and though this official lie was formerly extremely fashionable among the ancients, and might be useful to the moderns, his soul was too pure to depart from truth.

"Mademoiselle Cunegonde," said he, "is about to do me the honor of marrying me, and we beg your excellency to be present at the wedding."

Don Fernando d'Ibaraa y Figueora y Mascarenes y Lampourdos y Souza twisted his moustache, smiled bitterly and ordered Captain Candide to go and inspect his company. Candide obeyed; the governor remained with Mademoiselle Cunegonde. He declared his passion, vowed that the next day he would marry her publicly, or otherwise, as it might please her charms. Cunegonde asked for a quarter of an hour to collect herself, to consult the old woman and to make up her mind.

The old woman said to Cunegonde: "You have seventy-two quarterings and you haven't a shilling; it is in your power to be the wife of the greatest Lord in South America, who has an exceedingly fine moustache; is it for you to pride yourself on a rigid fidelity? You have been raped by Bulgarians, a Jew and an Inquisitor have enjoyed your good graces; misfortunes confer certain rights. If I were in your place, I confess I should not have the least scruple in marrying the governor and making Captain Candide's fortune."

While the old woman was speaking with all that prudence which comes from age and experience, they saw a small ship come into the harbor; an Alcayde and some Alguazils were on board, and this is what had happened. The old woman had guessed correctly that it was a long-sleeved monk who stole Cunegonde's money and jewels at Badajoz, when she was flying in all haste with Candide. The monk tried to sell some of the gems to a jeweller. The merchant recognised them as the property of the Grand Inquisitor. Before the monk was hanged he confessed that he had stolen them; he described the persons and the direction they were taking. The flight of Cunegonde and Candide was already known. They were followed to Cadiz; without any waste of time a vessel was sent in pursuit of them. The vessel was already in the harbor at Buenos Ayres. The rumor spread that an Alcayde was about to land and that he was in pursuit of the murderers of His Lordship the Grand Inquisitor. The prudent old woman saw in a moment what was to be done.

"You cannot escape," she said to Cunegonde, "and you have nothing to fear; you did not kill His Lordship; moreover, the governor is in love with you and will not allow you to be maltreated; stay here."

She ran to Candide at once. "Fly," said she, "or in an hour's time you will be burned." There was not a moment to lose;

but how could he leave Cunegonde and where would he take refuge?

CHAPTER XIV

HOW CANDIDE AND CACAMBO WERE RECEIVED BY THE JESUITS IN PARAGUAY

Candide had brought from Cadiz a valet of a sort which is very common on the coasts of Spain and in the colonies. He was one-quarter Spanish, the child of a half-breed in Tucuman; he had been a choirboy, a sacristan, a sailor, a monk, a postman, a soldier and a lackey. His name was Cacambo and he loved his master because his master was a very good man. He saddled the two Andalusian horses with all speed. "Come, master, we must follow the old woman's advice; let us be off and ride without looking behind us."

Candide shed tears. "O my dear Cunegonde! Must I abandon you just when the governor was about to marry us! Cunegonde, brought here from such a distant land, what will become of you?"

"She will become what she can," said Cacambo. "Women never trouble about themselves; God will see to her. Let us be off."

"Where are you taking me? Where are we going? What shall we do without Cunegonde?" said Candide.

"By St. James of Compostella," said Cacambo, "you were going to fight the Jesuits; let us go and fight for them; I know the roads, I will take you to their kingdom, they will be charmed to have a captain who can drill in the Bulgarian fashion; you will make a prodigious fortune; when a man fails in one world, he succeeds in another. 'Tis a very great pleasure to see and do new things."

"Then you have been in Paraguay?" said Candide.

"Yes, indeed," said Cacambo. "I was servitor in the College of the Assumption, and I know the government of *Los Padres** as well as I know the streets of Cadiz. Their govern-

* The Priests.

ment is a most admirable thing. The kingdom is already more than three hundred leagues in diameter and is divided into thirty provinces. *Los Padres* have everything and the people have nothing; 'tis the masterpiece of reason and justice. For my part, I know nothing so divine as *Los Padres* who here make war on the Kings of Spain and Portugal and in Europe act as their confessors; who here kill Spaniards and at Madrid send them to Heaven; all this delights me; come on, you will be the happiest of men. What a pleasure it will be to *Los Padres* when they know there is coming to them a captain who can drill in the Bulgarian manner!"

As soon as they reached the first barrier, Cacambo told the picket that a captain wished to speak to the Commandant. This information was carried to the main guard. A Paraguayan officer ran to the feet of the Commandant to tell him the news. Candide and Cacambo were disarmed and their two Andalusian horses were taken from them. The two strangers were brought in between two ranks of soldiers; the Commandant was at the end, with a three-cornered hat on his head, his gown tucked up, a sword at his side and a spontoon in his hand. He made a sign and immediately the two newcomers were surrounded by twenty-four soldiers. A sergeant told them that they must wait, that the Commandant could not speak to them, that the reverend provincial father did not allow any Spaniard to open his mouth in his presence or to remain more than three hours in the country.

"And where is the reverend provincial father?" said Cacambo.

"He is on parade after having said Mass, and you will have to wait three hours before you will be allowed to kiss his spurs."

"But," said Cacambo, "the captain, who is dying of hunger just as I am, is not a Spaniard but a German; can we not break our fast while we are waiting for his reverence?"

The sergeant went at once to inform the Commandant of this.

"Blessed be God!" said that lord. "Since he is a German I can speak to him; bring him to my arbor."

Candide was immediately taken to a leafy summerhouse decorated with a very pretty colonnade of green marble and gold, and lattices enclosing parrots, hummingbirds, guinea hens and many other rare birds. An excellent breakfast stood ready in gold dishes; and while the Paraguayans were eating maize from wooden bowls, out of doors and in the heat of the sun, the reverend father Commandant entered the arbor.

He was a very handsome young man, with a full face, a fairly white skin, red cheeks, arched eyebrows, keen eyes, red ears, vermilion lips, a haughty air, but a haughtiness which was neither that of a Spaniard nor of a Jesuit. Candide and Cacambo were given back the arms which had been taken from them and their two Andalusian horses; Cacambo fed them with oats near the arbor, and kept his eye on them for fear of a surprise. Candide first kissed the hem of the Commandant's gown and then they sat down to table. "So you are a German?" said the Jesuit in that language.

"Yes, reverend father," said Candide.

As they spoke these words they gazed at each other with extreme surprise and an emotion they could not control.

"And what part of Germany do you come from?" said the Jesuit.

"From the filthy province of Westphalia," said Candide; "I was born in the castle of Thunder-ten-tronckh."

"Heavens! Is it possible!" cried the Commandant.

"What a miracle!" cried Candide.

"Can it be you?" said the Commandant.

"'Tis impossible!" said Candide. They both fell over backwards, embraced and shed rivers of tears.

"What! Can it be you, reverend father? You, the fair Cunegonde's brother! You, who were killed by the Bulgarians! You, the son of My Lord the Baron! You, a Jesuit in Paraguay! The world is indeed a strange place! O Pangloss! Pangloss! How happy you would have been if you had not been hanged!"

The Commandant sent away the negro slaves and the Paraguayans who were serving wine in goblets of rock crystal. A thousand times did he thank God and St. Ignatius; he clasped Candide in his arms; their faces were wet with tears.

"You would be still more surprised, more touched, more beside yourself," said Candide, "if I were to tell you that Mademoiselle Cunegonde, your sister, whom you thought disembowelled, is in the best of health."

"Where?"

"In your neighborhood, with the governor of Buenos Ayres; and I came to make war on you."

Every word they spoke in this long conversation piled marvel on marvel. Their whole souls flew from their tongues, listened in their ears and sparkled in their eyes. As they were Germans, they sat at table for a long time, waiting for the reverend father provincial; and the Commandant spoke as follows to his dear Candide.

CHAPTER XV

HOW CANDIDE KILLED HIS DEAR CUNEGONDE'S BROTHER

"I shall remember all my life the horrible day when I saw my father and mother killed and my sister raped. When the Bulgarians had gone, my adorable sister could not be found, and my mother, my father and I, two maidservants and three little murdered boys were placed in a cart to be buried in a Jesuit chapel two leagues from the castle of my fathers. A Jesuit sprinkled us with holy water; it was horribly salt; a few drops fell in my eyes; the father noticed that my eyelids trembled, he put his hand on my heart and felt that it was still beating; I was attended to and at the end of three weeks was as well as if nothing had happened. You know, my dear Candide, that I was a very pretty youth, and I became still prettier; and so the Reverend Father Croust, the Superior of the house, was inspired with a most tender friendship for me; he gave me the dress of a novice and some time afterwards I was sent to Rome. The Father General wished to recruit some young German Jesuits. The sovereigns of Paraguay take as few Spanish Jesuits as they can; they prefer foreigners, whom they think they can control better. The Reverend Father General thought me apt to labor in his vineyard. I set off with a Pole and a Tyrolese. When I arrived I was honored with a subdeaconship and a lieutenancy; I am now colonel and priest. We shall give the King of Spain's troops a warm reception; I guarantee they will be excommunicated and beaten. Providence has sent you to help us. But is it really true that my dear sister Cunegonde is in the neighborhood with the governor of Buenos Ayres?"

Candide assured him on oath that nothing could be truer. Their tears began to flow once more. The Baron seemed never to grow tired of embracing Candide; he called him his brother, his savior.

"Ah! My dear Candide," said he, "perhaps we shall enter the town together as conquerors and regain my sister Cunegonde."

"I desire it above all things," said Candide, "for I meant to marry her and I still hope to do so."

"You, insolent wretch!" replied the Baron: "Would you have the impudence to marry my sister who has seventy-two quarterings! I consider you extremely impudent to dare to speak to me of such a foolhardy intention!"

Candide, petrified at this speech, replied: "Reverend Father, all the quarterings in the world are of no importance; I rescued your sister from the arms of a Jew and an Inquisitor; she is under considerable obligation to me and wishes to marry me. Dr. Pangloss always said that men are equal and I shall certainly marry her."

"We shall see about that, scoundrel!" said the Jesuit Baron of Thunder-ten-tronckh, at the same time hitting him violently in the face with the flat of his sword. Candide promptly drew his own and stuck it up to the hilt in the Jesuit Baron's belly; but, as he drew it forth smoking, he began to weep. "Alas! My God," said he, "I have killed my old master, my friend, my brother-in-law; I am the mildest man in the world and I have already killed three men, two of them priests."

Cacambo, who was acting as sentry at the door of the arbor, ran in.

"There is nothing left for us but to sell our lives dearly," said his master. "Somebody will certainly come into the arbor and we must die weapon in hand."

Cacambo, who had seen this sort of thing before, did not lose his head; he took off the Baron's Jesuit gown, put it on Candide, gave him the dead man's square bonnet, and made him mount a horse. All this was done in the twinkling of an eye. "Let us gallop, master; every one will take you for a Jesuit carrying orders and we shall have passed the frontiers before they can pursue us."

As he spoke these words he started off at full speed and shouted in Spanish: "Way, way for the Reverend Father Colonel . . ."

CHAPTER XVI

WHAT HAPPENED TO THE TWO TRAVELLERS WITH TWO GIRLS, TWO MONKEYS, AND THE SAVAGES CALLED OREILLONS

Candide and his valet were past the barriers before anybody in the camp knew of the death of the German Jesuit. The vigilant Cacambo had taken care to fill his saddlebag with bread, chocolate, ham, fruit, and several bottles of wine. On their Andalusian horses they plunged into an unknown country where they found no road. At last a beautiful plain traversed by streams met their eyes. Our two travellers put their horses to grass. Cacambo suggested to his master that they should eat and set the example.

"How can you expect me to eat ham," said Candide, "when I have killed the son of My Lord the Baron and find myself condemned never to see the fair Cunegonde again in my life? What is the use of prolonging my miserable days since I must drag them out far from her in remorse and despair? And what will the Journal de Trévoux say?"

Speaking thus, he began to eat. The sun was setting. The two wanderers heard faint cries which seemed to be uttered by women. They could not tell whether these were cries of pain or of joy; but they rose hastily with that alarm and un-easiness caused by everything in an unknown country. These cries came from two completely naked girls who were run-ning gently along the edge of the plain, while two monkeys pursued them and bit their buttocks. Candide was moved to pity; he had learned to shoot among the Bulgarians and could have brought down a nut from a tree without touch-ing the leaves. He raised his double-barrelled Spanish gun, fired, and killed the two monkeys.

"God be praised, my dear Cacambo, I have delivered these two poor creatures from a great danger; if I committed a sin by killing an Inquisitor and a Jesuit, I have atoned for it by saving the lives of these two girls. Perhaps they are young ladies of quality and this adventure may be of great advantage to us in this country."

He was going on, but his tongue clove to the roof of his mouth when he saw the two girls tenderly kissing the two monkeys, shedding tears on their bodies and filling the air with the most piteous cries.

"I did not expect so much human kindliness," he said at last to Cacambo, who replied: "You have performed a wonderful masterpiece; you have killed the two lovers of these young ladies."

"Their lovers! Can it be possible? You are jesting at me, Cacambo; how can I believe you?"

"My dear master," replied Cacambo, "you are always surprised by everything; why should you think it so strange that in some countries there should be monkeys who obtain ladies' favors? They are quarter men, as I am a quarter Spaniard."

"Alas!" replied Candide, "I remember to have heard Dr. Pangloss say that similar accidents occurred in the past and that these mixtures produce Aigypans, fauns and satyrs; that several eminent persons of antiquity have seen them; but I thought they were fables."

"You ought now to be convinced that it is true," said Cacambo, "and you see how people behave when they have not received a proper education; the only thing I fear is that these ladies may get us into difficulty."

These wise reflections persuaded Candide to leave the plain and to plunge into the woods. He ate supper there with Cacambo and, after having cursed the Inquisitor of Portugal, the governor of Buenos Ayres and the Baron, they went to sleep on the moss. When they woke up they found they could not move; the reason was that during the night the Oreillons, the inhabitants of the country, to whom they had been denounced by the two ladies, had bound them with ropes made of bark. They were surrounded by fifty naked Oreillons, armed with arrows, clubs and stone hatchets. Some were boiling a large cauldron, others were preparing spits and they were all shouting: "Here's a Jesuit, here's a Jesuit! We shall be revenged and have a good dinner; let us eat the Jesuit, let us eat the Jesuit!"

"I told you so, my dear master," said Cacambo sadly. "I knew those two girls would play us a dirty trick."

Candide perceived the cauldron and the spits and exclaimed: "We are certainly going to be roasted or boiled. Ah! What would Dr. Pangloss say if he saw what the pure state of nature is? All is well, granted; but I confess it is very cruel to have lost Mademoiselle Cunegonde and to be spitted by the Oreillons."

Cacambo never lost his head. "Do not despair," he said to the wretched Candide. "I understand a little of their dialect and I will speak to them."

"Do not fail," said Candide, "to point out to them the dreadful inhumanity of cooking men and how very unchristian it is."

"Gentlemen," said Cacambo, "you mean to eat a Jesuit today? 'Tis a good deed; nothing could be more just than to treat one's enemies in this fashion. Indeed the law of nature teaches us to kill our neighbor and this is how people behave all over the world. If we do not exert the right of eating our neighbor, it is because we have other means of making good cheer; but you have not the same resources as we, and it is certainly better to eat our enemies than to abandon the fruits of victory to ravens and crows. But, gentlemen, you would not wish to eat your friends. You believe you are about to place a Jesuit on the spit, and 'tis your defender, the enemy of your enemies you are about to roast. I was born in your country; the gentleman you see here is my master and, far from being a Jesuit, he has just killed a Jesuit and is wearing his clothes; which is the cause of your mistake. To verify what I say, take his gown, carry it to the first barrier of the kingdom of *Los Padres* and inquire whether my master has not killed a Jesuit officer. It will not take you long and you will have plenty of time to eat us if you find I have lied. But if I have told the truth, you are too well acquainted with the principles of public law, good morals and discipline, not to pardon us."

The Oreillons thought this a very reasonable speech; they deputed two of their notables to go with all diligence and find out the truth. The two deputies acquitted themselves of their task like intelligent men and soon returned with the good news. The Oreillons unbound their two prisoners, overwhelmed them with civilities, offered them girls, gave them refreshment, and accompanied them to the frontiers of their dominions, shouting joyfully: "He is not a Jesuit, he is not a Jesuit!"

Candide could not cease from wondering at the cause of his deliverance. "What a nation," said he. "What men! What

manners! If I had not been so lucky as to stick my
sword through the body of Mademoiselle Cunegonde's brother
I should infallibly have been eaten. But, after all, there is
something good in the pure state of nature, since these people, instead of eating me, offered me a thousand civilities as
soon as they knew I was not a Jesuit."

CHAPTER XVII

ARRIVAL OF CANDIDE AND HIS VALET
IN THE COUNTRY OF ELDORADO
AND WHAT THEY SAW THERE

When they reached the frontiers of the Oreillons, Cacambo
said to Candide: "You see this hemisphere is no better than
the other; take my advice, let us go back to Europe by the
shortest road."

"How can we go back," said Candide, "and where can we
go? If I go to my own country, the Bulgarians and the
Abares are murdering everybody; if I return to Portugal I
shall be burned; if we stay here, we run the risk of being
spitted at any moment. But how can I make up my mind to
leave that part of the world where Mademoiselle Cunegonde
is living?"

"Let us go to Cayenne," said Cacambo, "we shall find
Frenchmen there, for they go all over the world; they
might help us. Perhaps God will have pity on us."

It was not easy to go to Cayenne. They knew roughly the
direction to take, but mountains, rivers, precipices, brigands
and savages were everywhere terrible obstacles. Their horses
died of fatigue; their provisions were exhausted; for a whole
month they lived on wild fruits and at last found themselves
near a little river fringed with cocoanut-trees which supported their lives and their hopes.

Cacambo, who always gave advice as prudent as the old
woman's, said to Candide: "We can go no farther, we have
walked far enough; I can see an empty canoe in the bank,
let us fill it with cocoanuts, get into the little boat and drift
with the current; a river always leads to some inhabited place.

If we do not find anything pleasant, we shall at least find something new."

"Come on then," said Candide, "and let us trust to Providence."

They drifted for some leagues between banks which were sometimes flowery, sometimes bare, sometimes flat, sometimes steep. The river continually became wider; finally it disappeared under an arch of frightful rocks which towered up to the very sky. The two travellers were bold enough to trust themselves to the current under this arch. The stream, narrowed between walls, carried them with horrible rapidity and noise. After twenty-four hours they saw daylight again; but their canoe was wrecked on reefs; they had to crawl from rock to rock for a whole league and at last they discovered an immense horizon, bordered by inaccessible mountains. The country was cultivated for pleasure as well as for necessity; everywhere the useful was agreeable. The roads were covered or rather ornamented with carriages of brilliant material and shape, carrying men and women of singular beauty, who were rapidly drawn along by large red sheep whose swiftness surpassed that of the finest horses of Andalusia, Tetuan, and Mequinez.

"This country," said Candide, "is better than Westphalia."

He landed with Cacambo near the first village he came to. Several children of the village, dressed in torn gold brocade, were playing quoits outside the village. Our two men from the other world amused themselves by looking on; their quoits were large round pieces, yellow, red and green which shone with peculiar lustre. The travellers were curious enough to pick up some of them; they were of gold, emeralds and rubies, the least of which would have been the greatest ornament in the Mogul's throne.

"No doubt," said Cacambo, "these children are the sons of the King of this country playing at quoits."

At that moment the village schoolmaster appeared to call them into school.

"This," said Candide, "is the tutor of the Royal Family."

The little beggars immediately left their game, abandoning their quoits and everything with which they had been playing. Candide picked them up, ran to the tutor, and presented them to him humbly, giving him to understand by signs that their Royal Highnesses had forgotten their gold and their precious stones. The village schoolmaster smiled, threw them on the ground, gazed for a moment at Candide's face with much surprise and continued on his way. The travellers did not fail to pick up the gold, the rubies and the emeralds.

"Where are we?" cried Candide. "The children of the King must be well brought up, since they are taught to despise gold and precious stones."

Cacambo was as much surprised as Candide. At last they reached the first house in the village, which was built like a European palace. There were crowds of people round the door and still more inside; very pleasant music could be heard and there was a delicious smell of cooking. Cacambo went up to the door and heard them speaking Peruvian; it was his maternal tongue, for everyone knows that Cacambo was born in a village of Tucuman where nothing else is spoken.

"I will act as your interpreter," he said to Candide, "this is an inn, let us enter."

Immediately two boys and two girls of the inn, dressed in cloth of gold, whose hair was bound up with ribbons, invited them to sit down to the table d'hôte. They served four soups each garnished with two parrots, a boiled condor which weighed two hundred pounds, two roast monkeys of excellent flavor, three hundred colibris in one dish and six hundred hummingbirds in another, exquisite ragouts and delicious pastries, all in dishes of a sort of rock crystal. The boys and girls brought several sorts of drinks made of sugarcane. Most of the guests were merchants and coachmen, all extremely polite, who asked Cacambo a few questions with the most delicate discretion and answered his in a satisfactory manner.

When the meal was over, Cacambo, like Candide, thought he could pay the reckoning by throwing on the table two of the large pieces of gold he had picked up; the host and hostess laughed until they had to hold their sides. At last they recovered themselves.

"Gentlemen," said the host, "we perceive you are strangers; we are not accustomed to seeing them. Forgive us if we began to laugh when you offered us in payment the stones from our highways. No doubt you have none of the money of this country, but you do not need any to dine here. All the hotels established for the utility of commerce are paid for by the government. You have been ill entertained here because this is a poor village; but everywhere else you will be received as you deserve to be."

Cacambo explained to Candide all that the host had said, and Candide listened in the same admiration and disorder with which his friend Cacambo interpreted. "What can this country be," they said to each other, "which is unknown to the rest of the world and where all nature is so different from ours? Probably it is the country where everything is for the best; for there must be one country of that sort. And, in spite of what Dr. Pangloss said, I often noticed that everything went very ill in Westphalia."

CHAPTER XVIII

WHAT THEY SAW IN THE LAND OF ELDORADO

Cacambo informed the host of his curiosity, and the host said: "I am a very ignorant man and am all the better for it; but we have here an old man who has retired from the court and who is the most learned and most communicative man in the kingdom." And he at once took Cacambo to the old man. Candide now played only the second part and accompanied his valet. They entered a very simple house, for the door was only of silver and the panelling of the apartments in gold, but so tastefully carved that the richest decorations did not surpass it. The antechamber indeed was only encrusted with rubies and emeralds; but the order with which everything was arranged atoned for this extreme simplicity.

The old man received the two strangers on a sofa padded with colibri feathers, and presented them with drinks in diamond cups; after which he satisfied their curiosity in these words: "I am a hundred and seventy-two years old and I heard from my late father, the King's equerry, the astonishing revolutions of Peru of which he had been an eyewitness. The kingdom where we now are is the ancient country of the Incas, who most imprudently left it to conquer part of the world and were at last destroyed by the Spaniards. The princes of their family who remained in their native country had more wisdom; with the consent of the nation, they ordered that no inhabitants should ever leave our little kingdom, and this it is that has preserved our innocence and our felicity. The Spaniards had some vague knowledge of this country, which they called Eldorado, and about a hundred years ago an Englishman named Raleigh came very near to it; but, since we are surrounded by inaccessible rocks and precipices, we have hitherto been exempt from the rapacity of the nations of Europe who have an inconceivable lust for the pebbles and mud of our land and would kill us to the last man to get possession of them."

The conversation was long; it touched upon the form of the government, manners, women, public spectacles and the arts. Finally Candide, who was always interested in metaphysics, asked through Cacambo whether the country had a religion.

The old man blushed a little. "How can you doubt it?" said he. "Do you think we are ingrates?"

Cacambo humbly asked what was the religion of Eldorado.

The old man blushed again. "Can there be two religions?" said he. "We have, I think, the religion of every one else; we adore God from evening until morning."

"Do you adore only one God?" said Cacambo, who continued to act as the interpreter of Candide's doubts.

"Manifestly," said the old man, "there are not two or three or four. I must confess that the people of your world ask very extraordinary questions."

Candide continued to press the old man with questions; he wished to know how they prayed to God in Eldorado.

"We do not pray," said the good and respectable sage, "we have nothing to ask from him; he has given us everything necessary and we continually give him thanks."

Candide was curious to see the priests; and asked where they were.

The good old man smiled. "My friends," said he, "we are all priests; the King and all the heads of families solemnly sing praises every morning, accompanied by five or six thousand musicians."

"What! Have you no monks to teach, to dispute, to govern, to intrigue and to burn people who do not agree with them?"

"For that, we should have to become fools," said the old man; "here we are all of the same opinion and do not understand what you mean with your monks."

At all this Candide was in an ecstasy and said to himself: "This is very different from Westphalia and the castle of His Lordship the Baron; if our friend Pangloss had seen Eldorado, he would not have said that the castle of Thunder-ten-tronckh was the best of all that exists on the earth; certainly, a man should travel."

After this long conversation the good old man ordered a carriage to be harnessed with six sheep and gave the two travellers twelve of his servants to take them to court. "You will excuse me," he said, "if my age deprives me of the honor of accompanying you. The King will receive you in a manner which will not displease you and doubtless you will pardon the customs of the country if any of them disconcert you."

Candide and Cacambo entered the carriage; the six sheep galloped off and in less than four hours they reached the King's palace, which was situated at one end of the capital. The portal was two hundred and twenty feet high and a hundred feet wide; it is impossible to describe its material. Anyone can see the prodigious superiority it must have over the pebbles and sand we call *gold* and *gems*.

Twenty beautiful maidens of the guard received Candide and Cacambo as they alighted from the carriage, conducted them to the baths and dressed them in robes woven from the down of colibris; after which the principal male and female officers of the Crown led them to his Majesty's apartment through two files of a thousand musicians each, according to the usual custom. As they approached the throne-room, Cacambo asked one of the chief officers how they should behave in his Majesty's presence; whether they should fall on their knees or flat on their faces, whether they should put their hands on their heads or on their backsides; whether they should lick the dust of the throneroom; in a word, what was the ceremony?

"The custom," said the chief officer, "is to embrace the King and to kiss him on either cheek."

Candide and Cacambo threw their arms round his Majesty's neck; he received them with all imaginable favor and politely asked them to supper. Meanwhile they were carried to see the town, the public buildings rising to the very skies, the market-places ornamented with thousands of columns, the fountains of rose-water and of liquors distilled from sugarcane, which played continually in the public squares paved with precious stones which emitted a perfume like that of cloves and cinnamon.

Candide asked to see the law courts; he was told there were none, and that nobody ever went to law. He asked if there were prisons and was told there were none. He was still more surprised and pleased by the palace of sciences, where he saw a gallery two thousand feet long, filled with instruments of mathematics and physics.

After they had explored all the afternoon about a thousandth part of the town, they were taken back to the King. Candide sat down to table with his Majesty, his valet Cacambo and several ladies. Never was better cheer, and never was anyone wittier at supper than his Majesty. Cacambo explained the King's witty remarks to Candide and even when translated they still appeared witty. Among all the things which amazed Candide, this did not amaze him the least.

They enjoyed this hospitality for a month. Candide repeatedly said to Cacambo: "Once again, my friend, it is quite true that the castle where I was born cannot be compared with this country; but then Mademoiselle Cunegonde is not here and you probably have a mistress in Europe. If we remain here, we shall only be like everyone else; but if we return to our own world with only twelve sheep laden with Eldorado pebbles, we shall be richer than all the kings put together; we shall have no more Inquisitors to fear and we can easily regain Mademoiselle Cunegonde."

Cacambo agreed with this; it is so pleasant to be on the move, to show off before friends, to make a parade of the things seen on one's travels, that these two happy men resolved to be so no longer and to ask his Majesty's permission to depart.

"You are doing a very silly thing," said the King. "I know my country is small; but when we are comfortable anywhere we should stay there; I certainly have not the right to detain foreigners, that is a tyranny which does not exist either in our manners or our laws; all men are free, leave when you please, but the way out is very difficult. It is impossible to ascend the rapid river by which you miraculously came here and which flows under arches of rock. The mountains which surround the whole of my kingdom are ten thousand feet high and are perpendicular like walls; they are more than ten leagues broad, and you can only get down from them by way of precipices. However, since you must go, I will give orders to the directors of machinery to make a machine which will carry you comfortably. When you have been taken to the other side of the mountains, nobody can proceed any farther with you; for my subjects have sworn never to pass this boundary and they are too wise to break their oath. Ask anything else of me you wish."

"We ask nothing of your Majesty," said Cacambo, "except a

few sheep laden with provisions, pebbles and the mud of this country."

The King laughed. "I cannot understand," said he, "the taste you people of Europe have for our yellow mud; but take as much as you wish, and much good may it do you."

He immediately ordered his engineers to make a machine to hoist these two extraordinary men out of his kingdom. Three thousand learned scientists worked at it; it was ready in a fortnight and only cost about twenty million pounds sterling in the money of that country. Candide and Cacambo were placed on the machine; there were two large red sheep saddled and bridled for them to ride on when they had passed the mountains, twenty sumpter sheep laden with provisions, thirty carrying presents of the most curious productions of the country and fifty laden with gold, precious stones and diamonds. The King embraced the two vagabonds tenderly. Their departure was a splendid sight and so was the ingenious manner in which they and their sheep were hoisted on to the top of the mountains. The scientists took leave of them after having landed them safely, and Candide's only desire and object was to go and present Mademoiselle Cunegonde with his sheep.

"We have sufficient to pay the governor of Buenos Ayres," said he, "if Mademoiselle Cunegonde can be bought. Let us go to Cayenne, and take ship, and then we will see what kingdom we will buy."

CHAPTER XIX

WHAT HAPPNED TO THEM AT SURINAM AND HOW CANDIDE MADE THE ACQUAINTANCE OF MARTIN

Our two travellers' first day was quite pleasant. They were encouraged by the idea of possessing more treasures than all Asia, Europe and Africa could collect. Candide in transport carved the name of Cunegonde on the trees. On the second day two of the sheep stuck in a marsh and were swallowed up with their loads; two other sheep died of fatigue a few days later; then seven or eight died of hunger in a desert; several days afterwards others fell off precipices. Finally, after they had travelled for a hundred days, they had only two sheep left.

Candide said to Cacambo: "My friend, you see how perishable are the riches of this world; nothing is steadfast but virtue and the happiness of seeing Mademoiselle Cunegonde again."

"I admit it," said Cacambo, "but we still have two sheep with more treasures than ever the King of Spain will have, and in the distance I see a town I suspect is Surinam, which belongs to the Dutch. We are at the end of our troubles and the beginning of our happiness."

As they drew near the town they came upon a negro lying on the ground wearing only half his clothes, that is to say, a pair of blue cotton drawers; this poor man had no left leg and no right hand. "Good heavens!" said Candide to him in Dutch, "what are you doing there, my friend, in that horrible state?"

"I am waiting for my master, the famous merchant Monsieur Vanderdendur."

"Was it Monsieur Vanderdendur," said Candide, "who treated you in that way?"

"Yes, sir," said the negro, "it is the custom. We are given a pair of cotton drawers twice a year as clothing. When we work in the sugar mills and the grindstone catches our fingers, they cut off the hand; when we try to run away, they cut off a leg. Both these things happened to me. This is the price paid for the sugar you eat in Europe. But when my mother sold me for ten patagons on the coast of Guinea, she said to me: 'My dear child, give thanks to our fetishes, always worship them, and they will make you happy; you have the honor to be a slave of our lords the white men and thereby you have made the fortune of your father and mother.' Alas! I do not know whether I made their fortune, but they certainly did not make mine. Dogs, monkeys, and parrots are a thousand times less miserable than we are; the Dutch fetishes who converted me tell me that we are all of us, whites and blacks, the children of Adam. I am not a genealogist, but if these preachers tell the truth, we are all second cousins. Now, you will admit that no one could treat his relatives in a more horrible way."

"O Pangloss!" cried Candide. "This is an abomination

you had not guessed; this is too much, in the end I shall have to renounce optimism."

"What is optimism?" said Cacambo.

"Alas!" said Candide, "it is the mania of maintaining that everything is well when we are wretched." And he shed tears as he looked at his negro; and he entered Surinam weeping.

The first thing they inquired was whether there was any ship in the port which could be sent to Buenos Ayres. The person they addressed happened to be a Spanish captain, who offered to strike an honest bargain with them. He arranged to meet them at an inn. Candide and the faithful Cacambo went and waited for him with their two sheep. Candide, who blurted everything out, told the Spaniard all his adventures and confessed that he wanted to elope with Mademoiselle Cunegonde.

"I shall certainly not take you to Buenos Ayres," said the captain. "I should be hanged and you would, too. The fair Cunegonde is his Lordship's favorite mistress."

Candide was thunderstruck; he sobbed for a long time; then he took Cacambo aside. "My dear friend," said he, "this is what you must do. We have each of us in our pockets five or six millions worth of diamonds; you are more skilful than I am; go to Buenos Ayres and get Mademoiselle Cunegonde. If the governor makes any difficulties give him a million; if he is still obstinate give him two; you have not killed an Inquisitor so they will not suspect you. I will fit out another ship, I will go and wait for you at Venice; it is a free country where there is nothing to fear from Bulgarians, Abares, Jews or Inquisitors."

Cacambo applauded this wise resolution; he was in despair at leaving a good master who had become his intimate friend; but the pleasure of being useful to him overcame the grief of leaving him. They embraced with tears. Candide urged him not to forget the good old woman. Cacambo set off that very same day; he was a very good man, this Cacambo.

Candide remained some time longer at Surinam waiting for another captain to take him to Italy with the two sheep he had left. He engaged servants and bought everything necessary for a long voyage. At last Monsieur Vanderdendur, the owner of a large ship, came to see him.

"How much do you want," he asked this man, "to take me straight to Venice with my servants, my baggage and these two sheep?"

The captain asked for ten thousand piastres. Candide did not hesitate. "Oh! Ho!" said the prudent Vanderdendur to himself, "this foreigner gives ten thousand piastres immediately! He must be very rich." He returned a moment afterwards and said he could not sail for less than twenty thousand.

"Very well, you shall have them," said Candide.

"Whew!" said the merchant to himself, "this man gives twenty thousand piastres as easily as ten thousand." He came back again, and said he could not take him to Venice for less than thirty thousand piastres.

"Then you shall have thirty thousand," replied Candide.

"Oho!" said the Dutch merchant to himself again, "thirty thousand piastres is nothing to this man; obviously the two sheep are laden with immense treasures; I will not insist any further; first let me make him pay the thirty thousand piastres, and then we will see."

Candide sold two little diamonds, the smaller of which was worth more than all the money the captain asked. He paid him in advance. The two sheep were taken on board. Candide followed in a little boat to join the ship which rode at anchor; the captain watched his time, set his sails and weighed anchor; the wind was favorable. Candide, bewildered and stupefied, soon lost sight of him. "Alas!" he cried, "this is a trick worthy of the old world."

He returned to shore, in grief; for he had lost enough to make the fortunes of twenty kings. He went to the Dutch judge; and, as he was rather disturbed, he knocked loudly at the door; he went in, related what had happened and talked a little louder than he ought to have done. The judge began by fining him ten thousand piastres for the noise he had made; he then listened patiently to him, promised to look into his affair as soon as the merchant returned, and charged him another ten thousand piastres for the expenses of the audience.

This behavior reduced Candide to despair; he had indeed endured misfortunes a thousand times more painful; but the calmness of the judge and of the captain who had robbed him, stirred up his bile and plunged him into a black melancholy. The malevolence of men revealed itself to his mind in all its ugliness; he entertained only gloomy ideas.

At last a French ship was about to leave for Bordeaux and, since he no longer had any sheep laden with diamonds to put on board, he hired a cabin at a reasonable price and announced throughout the town that he would give the passage, food and two thousand piastres to an honest man who would make the journey with him, on condition that this man was the most unfortunate and the most disgusted with his condition in the whole province. Such a crowd of applicants arrived that a fleet would not have contained them. Candide, wishing to choose among the most likely, picked out twenty persons who seemed reasonably sociable and who all claimed to deserve his preference. He collected them in a tavern and gave them supper, on condition that each took an oath to relate truthfully the story of his life, promising that he would choose the man who seemed to him the most deserving of pity and to have the most cause for being discontented with his condition, and that he would give the others a little money. The sitting lasted until four o'clock in the morning. As Candide listened to their adventures he remembered what the old woman had said on the voyage to Buenos Ayres and how she had wagered that there was nobody on the boat who had not experienced very great misfortunes. At each story which was told him, he thought of Pangloss.

"This Pangloss," said he, "would have some difficulty in supporting his system. I wish he were here. Certainly, if everything is well, it is only in Eldorado and not in the rest of the world."

He finally determined in favor of a poor man of letters who had worked ten years for the booksellers at Amsterdam. He judged that there was no occupation in the world which could more disgust a man. This man of letters, who was also a good man, had been robbed by his wife, beaten by his son, and abandoned by his daughter, who had eloped with a Portuguese. He had just been deprived of a small post on which he depended and the preachers of Surinam were persecuting him because they thought he was a Socinian. It must be admitted that the others were at least as unfortunate as he was; but Candide hoped that this learned man would help to pass the time during the voyage. All his other rivals considered that Candide was doing them a great injustice; but he soothed them down by giving each of them a hundred piastres.

CHAPTER XX

WHAT HAPPENED TO CANDIDE AND
MARTIN AT SEA

So the old man, who was called Martin, embarked with Candide for Bordeaux. Both had seen and suffered much; and if the ship had been sailing from Surinam to Japan by way of the Cape of Good Hope they would have been able to discuss moral and physical evil during the whole voyage. However, Candide had one great advantage over Martin, because he still hoped to see Mademoiselle Cunegonde again, and Martin had nothing to hope for; moreover, he possessed gold and diamonds; and, although he had lost a hundred large red sheep laden with the greatest treasures on earth, although he was still enraged at being robbed by the Dutch captain, yet when he thought of what he still had left in his pockets and when he talked of Cunegonde, especially at the end of a meal, he still inclined towards the system of Pangloss.

"But what do you think of all this, Martin?" said he to the man of letters. "What is your view of moral and physical evil?"

"Sir," replied Martin, "my priests accused me of being a Socinian; but the truth is I am a Manichean."

"You are poking fun at me," said Candide, "there are no Manicheans left in the world."

"I am one," said Martin. "I don't know what to do about it, but I am unable to think in any other fashion."

"You must be possessed by the devil," said Candide.

"He takes so great a share in the affairs of this world," said Martin, "that he might well be in me, as he is everywhere else; but I confess that when I consider this globe, or rather this globule, I think that God had abandoned it to some evil creature—always excepting Eldorado. I have never seen a town which did not desire the ruin of the next town, never a family which did not wish to exterminate some other family. Everywhere the weak loathe the powerful before whom they cower and the powerful treat them like flocks of sheep whose wool and flesh are to be sold. A million drilled assassins go from one end of Europe to the other murdering and robbing with discipline in order to earn their bread, because there is no honester occupation; and in the towns which seem to enjoy peace and where the arts flourish, men are devoured by more envy, troubles and worries than the afflictions of a besieged town. Secret griefs are even more cruel than public miseries. In a word, I have seen so much and endured so much that I have become a Manichean."

"Yet there is some good," replied Candide.

"There may be," said Martin, "but I do not know it."

In the midst of this dispute they heard the sound of cannon. The noise increased every moment. Every one took his telescope. About three miles away they saw two ships engaged in battle; and the wind brought them so near the French ship that they had the pleasure of seeing the fight at their ease. At last one of the two ships fired a broadside so accurately and so low down that the other ship began to sink. Candide and Martin distinctly saw a hundred men on the main deck of the sinking ship; they raised their hands to Heaven and uttered frightful shrieks; in a moment all were engulfed.

"Well!" said Martin, "that is how men treat each other."

"It is certainly true," said Candide, "that there is something diabolical in this affair."

As he was speaking, he saw something of a brilliant red swimming near the ship. They launched a boat to see what it could be; it was one of his sheep. Candide felt more joy at recovering this sheep than grief at losing a hundred all laden with large diamonds from Eldorado.

The French captain soon perceived that the captain of the remaining ship was a Spaniard and that the sunken ship was a Dutch pirate; the captain was the very same who had robbed Candide. The immense wealth this scoundrel had stolen was swallowed up with him in the sea and only a sheep was saved.

"You see," said Candide to Martin, "that crime is sometimes punished; this scoundrel of a Dutch captain has met the fate he deserved."

"Yes," said Martin, "but was it necessary that the other passengers on his ship should perish too? God punished the thief, and the devil punished the others."

Meanwhile the French and Spanish ships continued on their

way and Candide continued his conversation with Martin. They argued for a fortnight and at the end of the fortnight they had got no further than at the beginning. But after all, they talked, they exchanged ideas, they consoled each other. Candide stroked his sheep. "Since I have found you again," said he, "I may very likely find Cunegonde."

CHAPTER XXI

CANDIDE AND MARTIN APPROACH THE COAST OF FRANCE AND ARGUE

At last they sighted the coast of France.

"Have you ever been to France, Monsieur Martin?" said Candide.

"Yes," said Martin, "I have traversed several provinces. In some half the inhabitants are crazy, in others they are too artful, in some they are usually quite gentle and stupid, and in others they think they are clever; in all of them the chief occupation is making love, the second scandal-mongering and the third talking nonsense."

"But, Monsieur Martin, have you seen Paris?"

"Yes, I have seen Paris; it is a mixture of all the species; it is a chaos, a throng where everybody hunts for pleasure and hardly anybody finds it, at least so far as I could see. I did not stay there long; when I arrived there I was robbed of everything I had by pickpockets at Saint-Germain's fair; they thought I was a thief and I spent a week in prison; after which I became a printer's reader to earn enough to return to Holland on foot. I met the scribbling rabble, the intriguing rabble and the fanatical rabble. We hear that there are very polite people in the town; I am glad to think so."

"For my part, I have not the least curiosity to see France," said Candide. "You can easily guess that when a man has spent a month in Eldorado he cares to see nothing else in the world but Mademoiselle Cunegonde. I shall go and wait for her at Venice; we will go to Italy by way of France; will you come with me?"

"Willingly," said Martin. "They say that Venice is only for the Venetian nobles but that foreigners are nevertheless well received when they have plenty of money; I have none, you have plenty, I will follow you anywhere."

"Apropos," said Candide, "do you think the earth was originally a sea, as we are assured by that large book belonging to the captain?"

"I don't believe it in the least," said Martin, "any more than all the other whimsies we have been pestered with recently!"

"But to what end was this world formed?" said Candide.

"To infuriate us," replied Martin.

"Are you not very much surprised," continued Candide, "by the love those two girls of the country of the Oreillons had for those two monkeys, whose adventure I told you?"

"Not in the least," said Martin. "I see nothing strange in their passion; I have seen so many extraordinary things that nothing seems extraordinary to me."

"Do you think," said Candide, "that men have always massacred each other, as they do today? Have they always been liars, cheats, traitors, brigands, weak, flighty, cowardly, envious, gluttonous, drunken, grasping, and vicious, bloody, backbiting, debauched, fanatical, hypocritical and silly?"

"Do you think," said Martin, "that sparrow hawks have always eaten the pigeons they came across?"

"Yes, of course," said Candide.

"Well," said Martin, "if sparrow hawks have always possessed the same nature, why should you expect men to change theirs?"

"Oh!" said Candide, "there is a great difference; *free will* . . ." Arguing thus, they arrived at Bordeaux.

CHAPTER XXII

WHAT HAPPENED TO CANDIDE AND MARTIN IN FRANCE

Candide remained in Bordeaux only long enough to sell a few Eldorado pebbles and to provide himself with a two-seated post chaise, for he could no longer get on without his philosopher Martin; but he was very much grieved at having to part with his sheep, which he left with the Academy of

Sciences at Bordeaux. The Academy offered as the subject for a prize that year the cause of the redness of the sheep's fleece; and the prize was awarded to a learned man in the North, who proved by A plus B minus C divided by Z that the sheep must be red and die of the sheep-pox.

However, all the travellers Candide met in taverns on the way said to him: "We are going to Paris." This general eagerness at length made him wish to see that capital; it was not far out of the road to Venice.

He entered by the Faubourg Saint-Marceau and thought he was in the ugliest village of Westphalia. Candide had scarcely reached his inn when he was attacked by a slight illness caused by fatigue. As he wore an enormous diamond on his finger, and a prodigiously heavy strongbox had been observed in his train, he immediately had with him two doctors he had not asked for, several intimate friends who would not leave him and two devotees who kept making him broth.

Said Martin: "I remember that I was ill too when I first came to Paris; I was very poor; so I had no friends, no devotees, no doctors, and I got well."

However, with the aid of medicine and bloodletting, Candide's illness became serious. An inhabitant of the district came and gently asked him for a note payable to bearer in the next world; Candide would have nothing to do with it. The devotees assured him that it was a new fashion; Candide replied that he was not a fashionable man. Martin wanted to throw the inhabitant out the window; the clerk swore that Candide should not be buried; Martin swore that he would bury the clerk if he continued to annoy them. The quarrel became heated; Martin took him by the shoulders and turned him out roughly; this caused a great scandal, and they made an official report on it.

Candide got better; and during his convalescence he had very good company to supper with him. They gambled for high stakes. Candide was vastly surprised that he never drew an ace; and Martin was not surprised at all.

Among those who did the honors of the town was a little abbé from Périgord, one of those assiduous people who are always alert, always obliging, impudent, fawning, accommodating, always on the lookout for the arrival of foreigners, ready to tell them all the scandals of the town and to procure them pleasures at any price. This abbé took Candide and Martin to the theatre. A new tragedy was being played. Candide was seated near several wits. This did not prevent his weeping at perfectly played scenes. One of the argumentative bores near him said during an interval: "You have no business to weep, this is a very bad actress, the actor playing with her is still worse, the play is still worse than the actors; the author does not know a word of Arabic and yet the scene is in Arabia; moreover, he is a man who does not believe in innate ideas; tomorrow I will bring you twenty articles written against him."

"Sir," said Candide to the abbé, "how many plays have you in France?"

"Five or six thousand," he replied.

"That's a lot," said Candide, "and how many good ones are there?"

"Fifteen or sixteen," replied the other.

"That's a lot," said Martin.

Candide was greatly pleased with an actress who took the part of Queen Elizabeth in a rather dull tragedy which is sometimes played. "This actress," said he to Martin, "pleases me very much; she looks rather like Mademoiselle Cunegonde; I should be very glad to pay her my respects."

The abbé offered to introduce him to her. Candide, brought up in Germany, asked what was the etiquette, and how queens of England were treated in France.

"There is a distinction," said the abbé. "In the provinces we take them to a tavern; in Paris we respect them when they are beautiful and throw them in the public sewer when they are dead."

"Queens in the public sewer!" said Candide.

"Yes, indeed," said Martin, "the abbé is right; I was in Paris when Mademoiselle Monime* departed, as they say, this life; she was refused what people here call the *honors of burial*—that is to say, the honor of rotting with all the beggars of the district in a horrible cemetery; she was buried by herself at the corner of the Rue de Bourgogne; which must have given her extreme pain, for her mind was very lofty."

"That was very impolite," said Candide.

"What do you expect?" said Martin. "These people are like that. Imagine all possible contradictions and incompatibilities; you will see them in the government, in the law courts, in the churches and the entertainments of this absurd nation."

---

* A contemporary actress.

"Is it true that people are always laughing in Paris?" said Candide.

"Yes," said the abbé, "but it is with rage in their hearts, for they complain of everything with roars of laughter and they even commit with laughter the most detestable actions."

"Who is that fat pig," said Candide, "who said so much ill of the play I cried at so much and of the actors who gave me so much pleasure?"

"He is a living evil," replied the abbé, "who earns his living by abusing all plays and all books; he hates anyone who succeeds, as eunuchs hate those who enjoy; he is one of the serpents of literature who feed on filth and venom; he is a scribbler."

"What do you mean by a scribbler?" said Candide.

"A scribbler of periodical sheets," said the abbé. "A Fréron." *

Candide, Martin and the abbé from Périgord talked in this manner on the stairway as they watched everybody going out after the play.

"Although I am most anxious to see Mademoiselle Cunegonde again," said Candide, "I should like to sup with Mademoiselle Clairon,† for I thought her admirable."

The abbé was not the sort of man to know Mademoiselle Clairon, for she saw only good company. "She is engaged this evening," he said, "but I shall have the honor to take you to the house of a lady of quality, and there you will learn as much of Paris as if you had been here for four years."

Candide, who was naturally curious, allowed himself to be taken to the lady's house at the far end of the Faubourg Saint-Honoré; they were playing faro; twelve gloomy punters each held a small hand of cards, the foolish register of their misfortunes. The silence was profound, the punters were pale, the banker was uneasy, and the lady of the house, seated beside this pitiless banker, watched with lynx's eyes every double stake, every seven-and-the-go, with which each player marked his cards; she had them unmarked with severe but polite attention, for fear of losing her customers; the lady called herself Marquise de Parolignac. Her fifteen-year-old daughter was among the punters and winked to her to let her know the tricks of the poor people who attempted to repair the cruelties of fate. The abbé from Périgord, Candide

* A journalist who had attacked Voltaire.
† A noted actress.

and Martin entered; nobody rose, nobody greeted them, nobody looked at them; every one was profoundly occupied with the cards.

"Her Ladyship the Baroness of Thunder-ten-tronckh was more civil," said Candide.

However the abbé whispered in the ear of the Marquise, who half rose, honored Candide with a gracious smile and Martin with a most noble nod. Candide was given a seat and a hand of cards, and lost fifty thousand francs in two hands; after which they supped very merrily and everyone was surprised that Candide was not more disturbed by his loss. The lackeys said to each other, in the language of lackeys: "He must be an English Milord."

The supper was like most suppers in Paris; first there was a silence and then a noise of indistinguishable words, then jokes, most of which were insipid, false news, false arguments, some politics and a great deal of scandal; there was even some talk of new books.

"Have you seen," said the abbé from Périgord, "the novel by Gauchat, the doctor of theology?"

"Yes," replied one of the guests, "but I could not finish it. We have a crowd of silly writings, but all of them together do not approach the silliness of Gauchat, doctor of theology. I am so weary of this immensity of detestable books which inundates us that I have taken to faro."

"And what do you say about the *Mélanges* by Archdeacon Trublet?" said the abbé. "Ah!" said Madame de Parolignac, "the tiresome creature! How carefully he tells you what everybody knows! How heavily he discusses what is not worth the trouble of being lightly mentioned! How witlessly he appropriates other people's wit! How he spoils what he steals! How he disgusts me! But he will not disgust me any more; it is enough to have read a few pages by the Archdeacon."

There was a man of learning and taste at table who confirmed what the marchioness had said. They then talked of tragedies; the lady asked why there were tragedies which were sometimes played and yet were unreadable. The man of taste explained very clearly how a play might have some interest and hardly any merit; in a few words he proved that it was not sufficient to bring in one or two of the situations which are found in all novels and which always attract the spectators; but that a writer of tragedies must be original without being bizarre, often sublime and always natural, must know the human heart and be able to give it speech,

must be a great poet but not let any character in his play
appear to be a poet, must know his language perfectly, speak
it with purity, with continual harmony and never allow the
sense to be spoilt for the sake of the rhyme.

"Anyone," he added, "who does not observe all these rules
may produce one or two tragedies applauded in the theatre,
but he will never be ranked among good writers; there are
very few good tragedies; some are idylls in well-written and
well-rhymed dialogue; some are political arguments which
send one to sleep, or repulsive amplifications; others are the
dreams of an enthusiast, in a barbarous style, with broken
dialogue, long apostrophes to the gods (because he does not
know how to speak to men), false maxims and turgid com-
monplaces."

Candide listened attentively to these remarks and con-
ceived a great idea of the speaker; and, as the marchioness
had been careful to place him beside her, he leaned over to
her ear and took the liberty of asking her who was the man
who talked so well.

"He is a man of letters," said the lady, "who does not play
cards and is sometimes brought here to supper by the abbé;
he has a perfect knowledge of tragedies and books and he
has written a tragedy which was hissed and a book of which
only one copy has ever been seen outside his bookseller's
shop and that was one he gave me."

"The great man!" said Candide. "He is another Pangloss."

Then, turning to him, Candide said: "Sir, no doubt you
think that all is for the best in the physical world and in the
moral, and that nothing could be otherwise than as it is?"

"Sir," replied the man of letters, "I do not think anything
of the sort. I think everything goes awry with us, that nobody knows his rank or his office, nor what he is doing, nor
what he ought to do, and that except at supper, which is
quite gay and where there appears to be a certain amount of
sociability, all the rest of their time is passed in senseless
quarrels: Jansenists with Molinists,* lawyers with churchmen,
men of letters with men of letters, courtiers with courtiers,
financiers with the people, wives with husbands, relatives with
relatives—'tis an eternal war."

Candide replied: "I have seen worse things; but a wise
man, who has since had the misfortune to be hanged, taught
me that it is all for the best; these are only the shadows in a
fair picture."

* Jesuits.

"Your wise man who was hanged was poking fun at the world," said Martin; "and your shadows are horrible stains."

"The stains are made by men," said Candide, "and they cannot avoid them."

"Then it is not their fault," said Martin.

Most of the gamblers, who had not the slightest understanding of this kind of talk, were drinking; Martin argued with the man of letters and Candide told the hostess some of his adventures.

After supper the marchioness took Candide into a side room and made him sit down on a sofa.

"Well!" said she, "so you are still madly in love with Mademoiselle Cunegonde of Thunder-ten-tronckh?"

"Yes, madame," replied Candide.

The marchioness replied with a tender smile: "You answer like a young man from Westphalia. A Frenchman would have said: 'It is true that I was in love with Mademoiselle Cunegonde, but when I see you, madame, I fear lest I should cease to love her.' "

"Alas! madame," said Candide, "I will answer as you wish."

"Your passion for her," said the marchioness, "began by picking up her handkerchief; I want you to pick up my garter."

"With all my heart," said Candide; and he picked it up.

"But I want you to put it on again," said the lady; and Candide put it on again.

"You see," said the lady, "you are a foreigner; I sometimes make my lovers in Paris languish for a fortnight, but I give myself to you the very first night, because one must do the honors of one's country to a young man from Westphalia."

The fair lady, having perceived two enormous diamonds on the young foreigner's hands, praised them so sincerely that they passed from Candide's fingers to the fingers of the marchioness. As Candide went home with his abbé from Périgord, he felt some remorse at having been unfaithful to Mademoiselle Cunegonde. The abbé sympathised with his distress; he had only had a small share in the fifty thousand francs Candide had lost at cards and in the value of the two half-given, half-extorted, diamonds. His plan was to profit as much as he could from the advantages which his acquaintance with Candide might procure for him. He talked a lot about Cunegonde and Candide told him that he should ask that fair one's forgiveness for his infidelity when he saw her at Venice. The abbé from Périgord redoubled his politeness and civilities and took a tender interest in all Candide said, in all he did, and in all he wished to do.

"Then, sir," said he, "you are to meet her at Venice?"

"Yes, sir," said Candide, "without fail I must go and meet Mademoiselle Cunegonde there."

Then, carried away by the pleasure of talking about the person he loved, he related, as he was accustomed to do, some of his adventures with that illustrious Westphalian lady.

"I suppose," said the abbé, "that Mademoiselle Cunegonde has a great deal of wit and that she writes charming letters."

"I have never received any from her," said Candide, "for you must know that when I was expelled from the castle because of my love for her, I could not write to her; soon afterwards I heard she was dead, then I found her again and then I lost her, and now I have sent an express messenger to her two thousand five hundred leagues from here and am expecting her reply."

The abbé listened attentively and seemed rather meditative. He soon took leave of the two foreigners, after having embraced them tenderly.

The next morning when Candide woke up he received a letter composed as follows: "Sir, my dearest lover, I have been ill for a week in this town; I have just heard that you are here. I should fly to your arms if I could stir. I heard that you had passed through Bordeaux; I left the faithful Cacambo and the old woman there and they will soon follow me. The governor of Buenos Ayres took everything, but I still have your heart. Come, your presence will restore me to life or will make me die of pleasure."

This charming, this unhoped-for letter, transported Candide with inexpressible joy; and the illness of his dear Cunegonde overwhelmed him with grief. Torn between these two sentiments, he took his gold and his diamonds and drove with Martin to the hotel where Mademoiselle Cunegonde was staying. He entered trembling with emotion, his heart beat, his voice was broken; he wanted to open the bed curtains and to have a light brought.

"Do nothing of the sort," said the waitingmaid. "Light would be the death of her." And she quickly drew the curtains.

"My dear Cunegonde," said Candide, weeping, "how do you feel? If you cannot see me, at least speak to me."

"She cannot speak," said the maidservant.

The lady then extended a plump hand, which Candide watered with his tears and then filled with diamonds, leaving a bag full of gold in the armchair. In the midst of these transports a police officer arrived, followed by the abbé from Périgord and a squad of policemen.

"So these are the two suspicious foreigners?" he said.

He had them arrested immediately and ordered his bravoes to hale them off to prison.

"This is not the way they treat travellers in Eldorado," said Candide.

"I am more of a Manichean than ever," said Martin.

"But, sir, where are you taking us?" said Candide.

"To the deepest dungeon," said the police officer.

Martin, having recovered his coolness, decided that the lady who pretended to be Cunegonde was a cheat, that the abbé from Périgord was a cheat who had abused Candide's innocence with all possible speed, and that the police officer was another cheat of whom they could easily be rid. Rather than expose himself to judicial proceedings, Candide, enlightened by this advice and impatient to see the real Cunegonde again, offered the police officer three little diamonds worth about three thousand pounds each.

"Ah! sir," said the man with the ivory stick, "if you had committed all imaginable crimes you would be the most honest man in the world. Three diamonds! Each worth three thousand pounds each! Sir! I would be killed for your sake, instead of taking you to prison. All strangers are arrested here, but trust to me. I have a brother at Dieppe in Normandy, I will take you there; and if you have any diamonds to give him he will take as much care of you as myself."

"And why are all strangers arrested?" said Candide.

The abbé from Périgord then spoke and said: "It is because a scoundrel from Atrebatum listened to imbecilities; this alone made him commit a parricide, not like that of May 1610, but like that of December 1594, and like several others committed in other years and in other months by other scoundrels who had listened to imbecilities."

The police officer then explained what it was all about.

"Ah! the monsters!" cried Candide. "What! Can such horrors be in a nation which dances and sings! Can I not leave at once this country where monkeys torment tigers? I have seen bears in my own country; Eldorado is the only place where I have seen men. In God's name, sir, take me to Venice, where I am to wait for Mademoiselle Cunegonde."

"I can only take you to Lower Normandy," said the officer.

Immediately he took off their irons, said there had been a mistake, sent his men away, took Candide and Martin to Dieppe, and left them with his brother. There was a small Dutch vessel in the port. With the help of three other diamonds the Norman became the most obliging of men and embarked Candide and his servants in the ship which was about to sail for Portsmouth in England. It was not the road to Venice; but Candide felt as if he had escaped from Hell, and he had every intention of taking the road to Venice at the first opportunity.

CHAPTER XXIII

CANDIDE AND MARTIN REACH THE COAST OF ENGLAND; AND WHAT THEY SAW THERE

"Ah! Pangloss, Pangloss! Ah! Martin, Martin! Ah! my dear Cunegonde! What sort of a world is this?" said Candide on the Dutch ship.

"Something very mad and very abominable," replied Martin.

"You know England; are the people there as mad as they are in France?"

"'Tis another sort of madness," said Martin. "You know these two nations are at war for a few acres of snow in Canada, and that they are spending more on this fine war than all Canada is worth. It is beyond my poor capacity to tell you whether there are more madmen in one country than in the other; all I know is that in general the people we are going to visit are extremely melancholic."

Talking thus, they arrived at Portsmouth. There were multitudes of people on the shore, looking attentively at a rather fat man who was kneeling down with his eyes bandaged on the deck of one of the ships in the fleet; four soldiers placed opposite this man each shot three bullets into his brain in the calmest manner imaginable; and the whole assembly returned home with great satisfaction.

"What is all this?" said Candide. "And what Demon exercises his power everywhere?" He asked who was the fat man who had just been killed so ceremoniously.

"An admiral," was the reply.

"And why kill the admiral?"

"Because," he was told, "he did not kill enough people. He fought a battle with a French admiral and it was held that the English admiral was not close enough to him."

"But," said Candide, "the French admiral was just as far from the English admiral!"

"That is indisputable," was the answer, "but in this country it is a good thing to kill an admiral from time to time to encourage the others."

Candide was so bewildered and so shocked by what he saw and heard that he would not even set foot on shore, but bargained with the Dutch captain (even if he had to pay him as much as the Surinam robber) to take him at once to Venice. The captain was ready in two days. They sailed down the coast of France; and passed in sight of Lisbon, at which Candide shuddered. They entered the Straits and the Mediterranean and at last reached Venice. "Praised be God!" said Candide, embracing Martin, "here I shall see the fair Cunegonde again. I trust Cacambo as I would myself. All is well, all goes well, all goes as well as it possibly could."

CHAPTER XXIV

PAQUETTE AND FRIAR GIROFLÉE

As soon as he reached Venice, he inquired for Cacambo in all the taverns, in all the cafés, and of all the ladies of pleasure; and did not find him. Every day he sent out messengers to all ships and boats; but there was no news of Cacambo. "What!" said he to Martin, "I have had time to sail from Surinam to Bordeaux, to go from Bordeaux to Paris, from Paris to Dieppe, from Dieppe to Portsmouth, to sail along the coasts of Portugal and Spain, to cross the Mediterranean, to spend several months at Venice, and the fair Cunegonde has not yet arrived! Instead of her I have met only a jade and an abbé from Périgord! Cunegonde is certainly dead and the only thing left for me is to die too. Ah! It would have been better to stay in the Paradise of Eldorado instead of returning to this accursed Europe. How right you are, my dear Martin! Everything is illusion and calamity!"

He fell into a black melancholy and took no part in the opera *à la mode* or in the other carnival amusements; not a lady caused him the least temptation.

Martin said: "You are indeed simple-minded to suppose that a half-breed valet with five or six millions in his pocket will go and look for your mistress at the other end of the world and bring her to you at Venice. If he finds her, he will take her for himself; if he does not find her, he will take another. I advise you to forget your valet Cacambo and your mistress Cunegonde."

Martin was not consoling. Candide's melancholy increased, and Martin persisted in proving to him that there was little virtue and small happiness in the world except perhaps in Eldorado where nobody could go.

While arguing about this important subject and waiting for Cunegonde, Candide noticed a young Theatine monk in the Piazza San Marco, with a girl on his arm. The Theatine looked fresh, plump and vigorous; his eyes were bright, his air assured, his countenance firm, and his step lofty. The girl was very pretty and was singing; she gazed amorously at her Theatine and every now and then pinched his fat cheeks.

"At least you will admit," said Candide to Martin, "that those people are happy. Hitherto I have only found unfortunates in the whole habitable earth, except in Eldorado; but I wager that this girl and the Theatine are very happy creatures."

"I wager they are not," said Martin.

"We have only to ask them to dinner," said Candide, "and you will see whether I am wrong."

He immediately accosted them, paid his respects to them, and invited them to come to his hotel to eat macaroni, Lombardy partridges, and caviare, and to drink Montepulciano, Lacryma Christi, Cyprus and Samos wine. The young lady blushed, the Theatine accepted the invitation, and the girl followed, looking at Candide with surprise and confusion in her eyes which were filled with a few tears. Scarcely had they entered Candide's room when she said: "What! Monsieur Candide does not recognise Paquette!"

At these words Candide, who had not looked at her very closely because he was occupied entirely by Cunegonde, said to her: "Alas! my poor child, so it was you who put Dr. Pangloss into the fine state I saw him in?"

"Alas! sir, it was indeed," said Paquette. "I see you have heard all about it. I have heard of the terrible misfortunes which happened to Her Ladyship the Baroness's whole family and to the fair Cunegonde. I swear to you that my fate has been just as sad. I was very innocent when you knew me. A Franciscan friar who was my confessor easily seduced me. The results were dreadful; I was obliged to leave the castle shortly after His Lordship the Baron expelled you by kicking you hard and frequently in the backside. If a famous doctor had not taken pity on me I should have died. For some time I was the doctor's mistress from gratitude to him. His wife, who was madly jealous, beat me every day relentlessly; she was a fury. The doctor was the ugliest of men, and I was the most unhappy of all living creatures at being continually beaten on account of a man I did not love. You know, sir, how dangerous it is for a shrewish woman to be the wife of a doctor. One day, exasperated by his wife's behavior, he gave her some medicine for a little cold and it was so efficacious that she died two hours afterwards in horrible convulsions. The lady's relatives brought a criminal prosecution against the husband; he fled and I was put in prison. My innocence would not have saved me if I had not been rather pretty. The judge set me free on condition that he took the doctor's place. I was soon supplanted by a rival, expelled without a penny, and obliged to continue the abominable occupation which to you men seems so amusing and which to us is nothing but an abyss of misery. I came to Venice to practise this profession. Ah! sir, if you could imagine what it is to be forced to caress impartially an old tradesman, a lawyer, a monk, a gondolier, an abbé; to be exposed to every insult and outrage; to be reduced often to borrow a petticoat in order to go and find some disgusting man who will lift it; to be robbed by one of what one has earned with another, to be despoiled by the police, and to contemplate for the future nothing but a dreadful old age, a hospital and a dunghill, you would conclude that I am one of the most unfortunate creatures in the world."

Paquette opened her heart in this way to Candide in a side room, in the presence of Martin, who said to Candide: "You see, I have already won half my wager."

Friar Giroflée had remained in the dining room, drinking a glass while he waited for dinner.

"But," said Candide to Paquette, "when I met you, you looked so gay, so happy; you were singing, you were caressing the Theatine so naturally; you seemed to me to be as happy as you are unfortunate."

"Ah! sir," replied Paquette, "that is one more misery of our profession. Yesterday I was robbed and beaten by an officer, and today I must seem to be in a good humor to please a monk."

Candide wanted to hear no more; he admitted that Martin was right. They sat down to table with Paquette and the Theatine. The meal was quite amusing and towards the end they were talking with some confidence.

"Father," said Candide to the monk, "you seem to me to enjoy a fate which everybody should envy; the flower of health shines on your cheek, your face is radiant with happiness; you have a very pretty girl for your recreation and you appear to be very well pleased with your state of life as a Theatine."

"Faith, Sir," said Friar Giroflée, "I wish all the Theatines were at the bottom of the sea. A hundred times I have been tempted to set fire to the monastery and to go and be a Turk. My parents forced me at the age of fifteen to put on this detestable robe, in order that more money might be left to my cursed elder brother, whom God confound! Jealousy, discord, fury, inhabit the monastery. It is true, I have preached a few bad sermons which bring me in a little money, half of which is stolen from me by the prior; the remainder I spend on girls; but when I go back to the monastery in the evening I feel ready to smash my head against the dormitory walls, and all my colleagues are in the same state."

Martin turned to Candide and said with his usual calm: "Well, have I not won the whole wager?"

Candide gave two thousand piastres to Paquette and a thousand to Friar Giroflée. "I warrant," said he, "that they will be happy with that."

"I don't believe it in the very least," said Martin. "Perhaps you will make them still more unhappy with those piastres."

"That may be," said Candide, "but I am consoled by one thing; I see that we often meet people we thought we should never meet again; it may very well be that as I met my red sheep and Paquette, I may also meet Cunegonde again."

"I hope," said Martin, "that she will one day make you happy; but I doubt it very much."

"You are very hard," said Candide.

"*That's because I have lived,*" said Martin.

"But look at these gondoliers," said Candide, "they sing all day long."

"You do not see them at home, with their wives and their brats of children," said Martin. "The Doge has his troubles, the gondoliers have theirs. True, looking at it all round, a gondolier's lot is preferable to a Doge's; but I think the difference so slight that it is not worth examining."

"They talk," said Candide, "about Senator Pococurante who lives in that handsome palace on the Brenta and who is hospitable to foreigners. He is supposed to be a man who has never known a grief."

"I should like to meet so rare a specimen," said Martin.

Candide immediately sent a request to Lord Pococurante for permission to wait upon him next day.

CHAPTER XXV

VISIT TO THE NOBLE VENETIAN,
LORD POCOCURANTE

Candide and Martin took a gondola and rowed to the noble Pococurante's palace. The gardens were extensive and ornamented with fine marble statues; the architecture of the palace was handsome. The master of this establishment, a very wealthy man of about sixty, received the two visitors very politely but with very little cordiality, which disconcerted Candide but did not displease Martin. Two pretty and neatly dressed girls served them with very frothy chocolate. Candide could not refrain from praising their beauty, their grace and their skill.

"They are quite good creatures," said Senator Pococurante, "and I sometimes make them sleep in my bed, for I am very tired of the ladies of the town, with their coquetries, their jealousies, their quarrels, their humors, their meanness, their pride, their folly, and the sonnets one must write or have written for them; but, after all, I am getting very tired of these two girls."

After this collation, Candide was walking in a long gallery and was surprised by the beauty of the pictures. He asked what master had painted the two first.

"They are by Raphael," said the Senator. "Some years ago I bought them at a very high price out of mere vanity; I am told they are the finest in Italy, but they give me no pleasure; the color has gone very dark, the faces are not sufficiently rounded and do not stand out enough; the draperies have not the least resemblance to material; in short, whatever they may say, I do not consider them a true imitation of nature. I shall only like a picture when it makes me think it is nature itself; and there are none of that kind. I have a great many pictures, but I never look at them now."

While they waited for dinner, Pococurante gave them a concert. Candide thought the music delicious.

"This noise," said Pococurante, "is amusing for half an hour; but if it lasts any longer, it wearies everybody although nobody dares to say so. Music nowadays is merely the art of executing difficulties and in the end that which is only difficult ceases to please. Perhaps I should like the opera more, if they had not made it a monster which revolts me. Those who please may go to see bad tragedies set to music, where the scenes are only composed to bring in clumsily two or three ridiculous songs which show off an actress's voice; those who will or can, may swoon with pleasure when they see an eunuch humming the part of Cæsar and Cato as he awkwardly treads the boards; for my part, I long ago abandoned such trivialities, which nowadays are the glory of Italy and for which monarchs pay so dearly."

Candide demurred a little, but discreetly. Martin entirely agreed with the Senator.

They sat down to table and after an excellent dinner went into the library. Candide saw a magnificently bound Homer and complimented the Illustrissimo on his good taste. "That is the book," said he, "which so much delighted the great Pangloss, the greatest philosopher of Germany."

"It does not delight me," said Pococurante coldly; "formerly I was made to believe that I took pleasure in reading it; but this continual repetition of battles which are all alike, these gods who are perpetually active and achieve nothing decisive, this Helen who is the cause of the war and yet scarcely an actor in the piece, this Troy which is always besieged and never taken—all bore me extremely. I have sometimes asked learned men if they were as bored as I am by reading it; all who were sincere confessed that the book fell from their hands, but that it must be in every library, as a monument of antiquity, and like those rusty coins which cannot be put into circulation."

"Your Excellency has a different opinion of Virgil?" said Candide.

"I admit," said Pococurante, "that the second, fourth and sixth books of his Æneid are excellent, but as for his pious Æneas and the strong Cloanthes and the faithful Achates and the little Ascanius and the imbecile king Latinus and the middle-class Amata and the insipid Lavinia, I think there could be nothing more frigid and disagreeable. I prefer Tasso and the fantastic tales of Ariosto."

"May I venture to ask you, sir," said Candide, "if you do not take great pleasure in reading Horace?"

"He has some maxims," said Pococurante, "which might be useful to a man of the world, and which, being compressed in energetic verses, are more easily impressed upon the memory; but I care very little for his Journey to Brundisium, and his description of a Bad Dinner, and the street brawlers' quarrel between—what is his name?—Rupilius, whose words, he says, were full of pus, and another person whose words were all vinegar. I was extremely disgusted with his gross verses against old women and witches; and I cannot see there is any merit in his telling his friend Mæcenas that, if he is placed by him among the lyric poets, he will strike the stars with his lofty brow. Fools admire everything in a celebrated author. I only read to please myself, and I only like what suits me."

Candide, who had been taught never to judge anything for himself, was greatly surprised by what he heard; and Martin thought Pococurante's way of thinking quite reasonable.

"Oh! There is a Cicero," said Candide. "I suppose you are never tired of reading that great man?"

"I never read him," replied the Venetian. "What do I care that he pleaded for Rabirius or Cluentius. I have enough cases to judge myself; I could better have endured his philosophical works; but when I saw that he doubted everything, I concluded I knew as much as he and did not need anybody else in order to be ignorant."

"Ah! There are eighty volumes of the Proceedings of an Academy of Sciences," exclaimed Martin, "there might be something good in them."

"There would be," said Pococurante, "if a single one of

the authors of all that rubbish had invented even the art of making pins; but in all those books there is nothing but vain systems and not a single useful thing."

"What a lot of plays I see there," said Candide. "Italian, Spanish, and French!"

"Yes," said the Senator, "there are three thousand and not three dozen good ones. As for those collections of sermons, which all together are not worth a page of Seneca, and all those large volumes of theology you may well suppose that they are never opened by me or anybody else."

Martin noticed some shelves filled with English books. "I should think," he said, "that a republican would enjoy most of those works written with so much freedom."

"Yes," replied Pococurante, "it is good to write as we think; it is the privilege of man. In all Italy, we only write what we do not think; those who inhabit the country of the Cæsars and the Antonines dare not have an idea without the permission of a Dominican monk. I should applaud the liberty which inspires Englishmen of genius if passion and party spirit did not corrupt everything estimable in that precious liberty."

Candide, in noticing a Milton, asked him if he did not consider that author to be a very great man.

"Who?" said Pococurante. "That barbarian who wrote a long commentary on the first chapter of Genesis in ten books of harsh verses? That gross imitator of the Greeks, who disfigures the Creation, and who, while Moses represents the Eternal Being as producing the world by speech, makes the Messiah take a large compass from the heavenly cupboard in order to trace out his work? Should I esteem the man who spoiled Tasso's hell and devil; who disguises Lucifer sometimes as a toad, sometimes as a pigmy; who makes him repeat the same things a hundred times; makes him argue about theology; and imitates seriously Ariosto's comical invention of firearms by making the devils fire a cannon in Heaven? Neither I nor anyone else in Italy could enjoy such wretched extravagances. The marriage of Sin and Death and the snakes which sin brings forth nauseate any man of delicate taste, and his long description of a hospital would only please a gravedigger. This obscure, bizarre and disgusting poem was despised at its birth; I treat it today as it was treated by its contemporaries in its own country. But then I say what I think, and care very little whether others think as I do."

Candide was distressed by these remarks; he respected Homer and rather liked Milton.

"Alas!" he whispered to Martin, "I am afraid this man would have a sovereign contempt for our German poets."

"There wouldn't be much harm in that," said Martin.

"Oh! What a superior man!" said Candide under his breath. "What a great genius this Pococurante is! Nothing can please him."

After they had thus reviewed all his books they went down into the garden. Candide praised all its beauties.

"I have never met anything more tasteless," said the owner. "We have nothing but gewgaws; but tomorrow I shall begin to plant one on a more noble plan."

When the two visitors had taken farewell of his Excellency, Candide said to Martin: "Now you will admit that he is the happiest of men, for he is superior to everything he possesses."

"Do you not see," said Martin, "that he is disgusted with everything he possesses? Plato said long ago that the best stomachs are not those which refuse all food."

"But," said Candide, "is there not pleasure in criticising, in finding faults where other men think they see beauty?"

"That is to say," answered Martin, "that there is pleasure in not being pleased."

"Oh! Well," said Candide, "then there is no one happy except me—when I see Mademoiselle Cunegonde again."

"It is always good to hope," said Martin.

However, the days and weeks went by; Cacambo did not return and Candide was so much plunged in grief that he did not even notice that Paquette and Friar Giroflée had not once come to thank him.

CHAPTER XXVI

HOW CANDIDE AND MARTIN SUPPED
WITH SIX STRANGERS AND
WHO THEY WERE

One evening when Candide and Martin were going to sit down to table with the strangers who lodged in the same

hotel, a man with a face the color of soot came up to him
from behind and, taking him by the arm, said: "Get ready
to come with us, and do not fail."

He turned round and saw Cacambo. Only the sight of
Cunegonde could have surprised and pleased him more. He
was almost wild with joy. He embraced his dear friend.

"Cunegonde is here, of course? Where is she? Take me to
her, let me die of joy with her."

"Cunegonde is not here," said Cacambo. "She is in Constantinople."

"Heavens! In Constantinople! But, were she in China, I
would fly to her; let us start at once."

"We will start after supper," replied Cacambo. "I cannot
tell you any more; I am a slave, and my master is waiting for
me; I must go and serve him at table! Do not say anything;
eat your supper, and be in readiness."

Candide, torn between joy and grief, charmed to see his
faithful agent again, amazed to see him a slave, filled with
the idea of seeing his mistress again, with turmoil in his heart,
agitation in his mind, sat down to table with Martin (who
met every strange occurrence with the same calmness), and
with six strangers, who had come to spend the Carnival at
Venice.

Cacambo, who acted as butler to one of the strangers,
bent down to his master's head towards the end of the meal
and said: "Sire, your Majesty can leave when you wish, the
ship is ready." After saying this, Cacambo withdrew.

The guests looked at each other with surprise without saying a word, when another servant came up to his master and
said: "Sire, your Majesty's post chaise is at Padua, and the boat
is ready." The master made a sign and the servant departed.

Once more all the guests looked at each other, and the
general surprise was increased twofold. A third servant went
up to the third stranger and said: "Sire, believe me, your
Majesty cannot remain here any longer; I will prepare everything." And he immediately disappeared.

Candide and Martin had no doubt that this was a Carnival
masquerade. A fourth servant said to the fourth master:
"Your Majesty can leave when you wish." And he went out
like the others. The fifth servant spoke similarly to the fifth
master. But the sixth servant spoke differently to the sixth
stranger who was next to Candide, and said: "Faith, sire,
they will not give your Majesty any more credit nor me either,

and we may very likely be jailed tonight, both of us; I am
going to look to my own affairs, good bye."

When the servants had all gone, the six strangers, Candide
and Martin remained in profound silence. At last it was broken by Candide.

"Gentlemen," said he, "this is a curious jest. How is it
you are all kings? I confess that neither Martin nor I are
kings."

Cacambo's master then gravely spoke and said in Italian:
"I am not jesting, my name is Achmet III. For several years
I was Sultan; I dethroned my brother; my nephew dethroned
me; they cut off the heads of my viziers; I am ending my
days in the old seraglio; my nephew, Sultan Mahmoud, sometimes allows me to travel for my health, and I have come to
spend the Carnival at Venice."

A young man who sat next to Achmet spoke after him
and said: "My name is Ivan; I was Emperor of all the Rus-
sias; I was dethroned in my cradle; my father and mother
were imprisoned and I was brought up in prison; I sometimes have permission to travel, accompanied by those who
guard me, and I have come to spend the Carnival at Venice."

The third said: "I am Charles Edward, King of England;
my father gave up his rights to the throne to me and I fought
a war to assert them; the hearts of eight hundred of my
adherents were torn out and dashed in their faces. I have
been in prison; I am going to Rome to visit the King, my
father, who is dethroned like my grandfather and me; and I
have come to spend the Carnival at Venice."

The fourth then spoke and said: "I am the King of Poland;
the chance of war deprived me of my hereditary states; my
father endured the same reverse of fortune; I am resigned
to Providence like the Sultan Achmet, the Emperor Ivan and
King Charles Edward, to whom God grant long life; and I
have come to spend the Carnival at Venice."

The fifth said: "I also am the King of Poland, I have lost
my kingdom twice; but Providence has given me another
state in which I have been able to do more good than all the
kings of the Sarmatians together have been ever able to do
on the banks of the Vistula; I also am resigned to Providence
and I have come to spend the Carnival at Venice."

It was now for the sixth monarch to speak. "Gentlemen,"
said he, "I am not so eminent as you; but I have been a king
like anyone else. I am Theodore; I was elected King of Cor-

sica; I have been called Your Majesty and now I am barely called Sir. I have coined money and do not own a farthing; I have had two Secretaries of State and now have scarcely a valet; I have occupied a throne and for a long time lay on straw in a London prison. I am much afraid I shall be treated in the same way here, although I have come, like your Majesties, to spend the Carnival at Venice."

The five other kings listened to this speech with a noble compassion. Each of them gave King Theodore twenty sequins to buy clothes and shirts; Candide presented him with a diamond worth two thousand sequins.

"Who is this man," said the five kings, "who is able to give a hundred times as much as any of us, and who gives it?"

As they were leaving the table, there came to the same hotel four serene highnesses who had also lost their states in the chance of war, and who had come to spend the rest of the Carnival at Venice; but Candide did not even notice these newcomers, he could think of nothing but of going to Constantinople to find his dear Cunegonde.

CHAPTER XXVII

CANDIDE'S VOYAGE TO CONSTANTINOPLE

The faithful Cacambo had already spoken to the Turkish captain who was to take Sultan Achmet back to Constantinople and had obtained permission for Candide and Martin to come on board. They both entered this ship after having prostrated themselves before his miserable Highness.

On the way, Candide said to Martin: "So we have just supped with six dethroned kings! And among those six kings there was one to whom I gave charity. Perhaps there are many other princes still more unfortunate. Now, I have only lost a hundred sheep and I am hastening to Cunegonde's arms. My dear Martin, once more, Pangloss was right, all is well."

"I hope so," said Martin.

"But," said Candide, "this is a very singular experience we have just had at Venice. Nobody has ever seen or heard of six dethroned kings supping together in a tavern."

" 'Tis no more extraordinary," said Martin, "than most of the things which have happened to us. It is very common for kings to be dethroned; and as to the honor we have had of supping with them, 'tis a trifle not deserving our attention."

Scarcely had Candide entered the ship when he threw his arms round the neck of his old valet, of his friend Cacambo.

"Well!" said he, "what is Cunegonde doing? Is she still a marvel of beauty? Does she still love me? How is she? Of course you have bought her a palace in Constantinople?"

"My dear master," replied Cacambo, "Cunegonde is washing dishes on the banks of Propontis for a prince who possesses very few dishes; she is a slave in the house of a former sovereign named Ragotsky, who receives in his refuge three crowns a day from the Grand Turk; but what is even more sad is that she has lost her beauty and has become horribly ugly."

"Ah! beautiful or ugly," said Candide, "I am a man of honor and my duty is to love her always. But how can she be reduced to so abject a condition with the five or six millions you carried off?"

"Ah!" said Cacambo, "did I not have to give two millions to Señor Don Fernando d'Ibaraa y Figueora y Mascarenes y Lampourdos y Souza, Governor of Buenos Ayres, for permission to bring away Mademoiselle Cunegonde? And did not a pirate bravely strip us of all the rest? And did not this pirate take us to Cape Matapan, to Milo, to Nicaria, to Samos, to Petra, to the Dardanelles, to Marmora, to Scutari? Cunegonde and the old woman are servants to the prince I mentioned, and I am slave to the dethroned Sultan."

"What a chain of terrible calamities!" said Candide. "But after all, I still have a few diamonds; I shall easily deliver Cunegonde. What a pity she has become so ugly."

Then, turning to Martin, he said: "Who do you think is the most to be pitied, the Sultan Achmet, the Emperor Ivan, King Charles Edward, or me?"

"I do not know at all," said Martin. "I should have to be in your hearts to know."

"Ah!" said Candide, "if Pangloss were here he would know and would tell us."

"I do not know," said Martin, "what scales your Pangloss would use to weigh the misfortunes of men and to estimate their sufferings. All I presume is that there are millions of men on the earth a hundred times more to be pitied than King Charles Edward, the Emperor Ivan and the Sultan Achmet."

"That may very well be," said Candide.

In a few days they reached the Black Sea channel. Candide began by paying a high ransom for Cacambo and, without wasting time, he went on board a galley with his companions bound for the shores of Propontis, in order to find Cunegonde however ugly she might be. Among the galley slaves were two convicts who rowed very badly and from time to time the Levantine captain applied several strokes of a bull's pizzle to their naked shoulders. From a natural feeling of pity Candide watched them more attentively than the other galley slaves and went up to them. Some features of their disfigured faces appeared to him to have some resemblance to Pangloss and the wretched Jesuit, the Baron, Mademoiselle Cunegonde's brother. This idea disturbed and saddened him. He looked at them still more carefully. "Truly," said he to Cacambo, "if I had not seen Dr. Pangloss hanged, and if I had not been so unfortunate as to kill the Baron, I should think they were rowing in this galley."

At the words Baron and Pangloss, the two convicts gave a loud cry, stopped on their seats and dropped their oars. The Levantine captain ran up to them and the lashes with the bull's pizzle were redoubled.

"Stop! Stop, sir!" cried Candide. "I will give you as much money as you want."

"What! Is it Candide?" said one of the convicts.

"What! Is it Candide?" said the other.

"Is it a dream?" said Candide. "Am I awake? Am I in this galley? Is that my Lord the Baron whom I killed? Is that Dr. Pangloss whom I saw hanged?"

"It is, it is," they replied.

"What! Is that the great philosopher?" said Martin.

"Ah! sir," said Candide to the Levantine captain, "how much money do you want for My Lord Thunder-ten-tronckh, one of the first Barons of the empire, and for Dr. Pangloss, the most profound metaphysician of Germany?"

"Dog of a Christian," replied the Levantine captain, "since these two dogs of Christian convicts are Barons and metaphysicians, which no doubt is a high rank in their country, you shall pay me fifty thousand sequins."

"You shall have them, sir. Row back to Constantinople like lightning and you shall be paid at once. But, no, take me to Mademoiselle Cunegonde."

The captain, at Candide's first offer, had already turned the bow towards the town, and rowed there more swiftly than a bird cleaves the air.

Candide embraced the Baron and Pangloss a hundred times. "How was it I did not kill you, my dear Baron? And, my dear Pangloss, how do you happen to be alive after having been hanged? And why are you both in a Turkish galley?"

"Is it really true that my dear sister is in this country?" said the Baron.

"Yes," replied Cacambo.

"So once more I see my dear Candide!" cried Pangloss.

Candide introduced Martin and Cacambo. They all embraced and all talked at the same time. The galley flew; already they were in the harbor. They sent for a Jew, and Candide sold him for fifty thousand sequins a diamond worth a hundred thousand, for which he swore by Abraham he could not give any more. The ransom of the Baron and Pangloss was immediately paid. Pangloss threw himself at the feet of his liberator and bathed them with tears; the other thanked him with a nod and promised to repay the money at the first opportunity. "But is it possible that my sister is in Turkey?" said he.

"Nothing is so possible," replied Cacambo, "since she washes up the dishes of a prince of Transylvania."

They immediately sent for two Jews; Candide sold some more diamonds; and they all set out in another galley to rescue Cunegonde.

CHAPTER XXVIII

WHAT HAPPENED TO CANDIDE, TO CUNEGONDE, TO PANGLOSS, TO MARTIN, ETC.

"Pardon once more," said Candide to the Baron, "pardon me, reverend father, for having thrust my sword through your body."

"Let us say no more about it," said the Baron. "I admit I was a little too sharp; but since you wish to know how it was

you saw me in a galley, I must tell you that after my wound
was healed by the brother apothecary of the college, I was attacked and carried off by a Spanish raiding party; I was imprisoned in Buenos Ayres at the time when my sister had just
left. I asked to return to the Vicar-General in Rome. I was
ordered to Constantinople to act as almoner to the Ambas-
sador of France. A week after I had taken up my office I
met towards evening a very handsome young page of the Sultan. It was very hot; the young man wished to bathe; I took
the opportunity to bathe also. I did not know that it was a
most serious crime for a Christian to be found naked with a
young Mahometan. A cadi sentenced me to a hundred strokes
on the soles of my feet and condemned me to the galley. I
do not think a more horrible injustice has ever been committed. But I should very much like to know why my sister is
in the kitchen of a Transylvanian sovereign living in exile
among the Turks."

"But, my dear Pangloss," said Candide, "how does it happen
that I see you once more?"

"It is true," said Pangloss, "that you saw me hanged; and in
the natural course of events I should have been burned. But
you remember, it poured with rain when they were going
to roast me; the storm was so violent that they despaired of
lighting the fire; I was hanged because they could do nothing
better; a surgeon bought my body, carried me home and
dissected me. He first made a crucial incision in me from the
navel to the collarbone. Nobody could have been worse
hanged than I was. The executioner of the holy Inquisition,
who was a sub-deacon, was marvellously skilful in burning
people, but he was not accustomed to hang them; the rope
was wet and did not slide easily and it was knotted; in short,
I still breathed. The crucial incision caused me to utter so
loud a scream that the surgeon fell over backwards and,
thinking he was dissecting the devil, fled away in terror and
fell down the staircase in his flight. His wife ran in from another room at the noise; she saw me stretched out on the
table with my crucial incision; she was still more frightened
than her husband, fled, and fell on top of him. When they
had recovered themselves a little, I heard the surgeon's wife
say to the surgeon: 'My dear, what were you thinking of, to
dissect a heretic? Don't you know the devil always possesses
them? I will go and get a priest at once to exorcise him.'

"At this I shuddered and collected the little strength I had
left to shout: 'Have pity on me!' At last the Portuguese bar-

ber grew bolder; he sewed up my skin; his wife even took care of me, and at the end of a fortnight I was able to walk again. The barber found me a situation and made me lackey to a Knight of Malta who was going to Venice; but, as my master had no money to pay me wages, I entered the service of a Venetian merchant and followed him to Constantinople.

"One day I took it into my head to enter a mosque; there was nobody there except an old Imam and a very pretty young devotee who was reciting her prayers; her breasts were entirely uncovered; between them she wore a bunch of tulips, roses, anemones, ranunculus, hyacinths and auriculas; she dropped her bunch of flowers; I picked it up and returned it to her with a most respectful alacrity. I was so long putting them back that the Imam grew angry and, seeing I was a Christian, called for help. I was taken to the cadi, who sentenced me to receive a hundred strokes on the soles of my feet and sent me to the galleys. I was chained on the same seat and in the same galley as My Lord the Baron. In this galley there were four young men from Marseilles, five Neapolitan priests and two monks from Corfu, who assured us that similar accidents occurred every day. His Lordship the Baron claimed that he had suffered a greater injustice than I; and I claimed that it was much more permissible to replace a bunch of flowers between a woman's breasts than to be naked with one of the Sultan's pages. We argued continually, and every day received twenty strokes of the bull's pizzle, when the chain of events of this universe led you to our galley and you ransomed us."

"Well! my dear Pangloss," said Candide, "when you were hanged, dissected, stunned with blows and made to row in the galleys, did you always think that everything was for the best in this world?"

"I am still of my first opinion," replied Pangloss, "for after all I am a philosopher; and it would be unbecoming for me to recant, since Leibnitz could not be in the wrong and pre-established harmony is the finest thing imaginable like the plenum and subtle matter."

CHAPTER XXIX

HOW CANDIDE FOUND CUNEGONDE AND THE OLD WOMAN AGAIN

While Candide, the Baron, Pangloss, Martin and Cacambo were relating their adventures, reasoning upon contingent or non-contingent events of the universe, arguing about effects and causes, moral and physical evil, free will and necessity, and the consolation to be found in the Turkish galleys, they came to the house of the Transylvanian prince on the shores of Propontis.

The first objects which met their sight were Cunegonde and the old woman hanging out towels to dry on the line. At this sight the Baron grew pale. Candide, that tender lover, seeing his fair Cunegonde sunburned, blear-eyed, flat-breasted, with wrinkles round her eyes and red, chapped arms, recoiled three paces in horror, and then advanced from mere politeness. She embraced Candide and her brother. They embraced the old woman; Candide bought them both.

In the neighborhood was a little farm; the old woman suggested that Candide should buy it, until some better fate befell the group. Cunegonde did not know that she had become ugly, for nobody had told her so; she reminded Candide of his promises in so peremptory a tone that the good Candide dared not refuse her. He therefore informed the Baron that he was about to marry his sister.

"Never," said the Baron, "will I endure such baseness on her part and such insolence on yours; nobody shall ever reproach me with this infamy; my sister's children could never enter the chapters of Germany. No, my sister shall never marry anyone but a Baron of the Empire."

Cunegonde threw herself at his feet and bathed them in tears; but he was inflexible.

"Madman," said Candide, "I rescued you from the galleys, I paid your ransom and your sister's; she was washing dishes here, she is ugly, I am so kind as to make her my wife, and you pretend to oppose me! I should re-kill you if I listened to my anger."

"You may kill me again," said the Baron, "but you shall never marry my sister while I am alive."

CHAPTER XXX

CONCLUSION

At the bottom of his heart Candide had not the least wish to marry Cunegonde. But the Baron's extreme impertinence determined him to complete the marriage, and Cunegonde urged it so warmly that he could not retract. He consulted Pangloss, Martin and the faithful Cacambo. Pangloss wrote an excellent memorandum by which he proved that the Baron had no rights over his sister and that by all the laws of the empire she could make a left-handed marriage with Candide. Martin advised that the Baron should be thrown into the sea; Cacambo decided that he should be returned to the Levantine captain and sent back to the galleys, after which he would be returned by the first ship to the Vicar-General at Rome. This was thought to be very good advice; the old woman approved it; they said nothing to the sister; the plan was carried out with the aid of a little money and they had the pleasure of duping a Jesuit and punishing the pride of a German Baron.

It would be natural to suppose that when, after so many disasters, Candide was married to his mistress, and living with the philosopher Pangloss, the Philosopher Martin, the prudent Cacambo and the old woman, having brought back so many diamonds from the country of the ancient Incas, he would lead the most pleasant life imaginable. But he was so cheated by the Jews that he had nothing left but his little farm; his wife, growing uglier every day, became shrewish and unendurable; the old woman was ailing and even more bad tempered than Cunegonde. Cacambo, who worked in the garden and then went to Constantinople to sell vegetables, was overworked and cursed his fate. Pangloss was in despair because he did not shine in some German university.

As for Martin, he was firmly convinced that people are equally uncomfortable everywhere; he accepted things patiently. Candide, Martin and Pangloss sometimes argued about metaphysics and morals. From the windows of the farm they often watched the ships going by, filled with effendis, pashas, and cadis, who were being exiled to Lemnos, to Mitylene and Erzerum. They saw other cadis, other pashas and other effendis coming back to take the place of the exiles and to be exiled in their turn. They saw the neatly impaled heads which were taken to the Sublime Porte. These sights redoubled their discussions; and when they were not arguing, the boredom was so excessive that one day the old woman dared to say to them: "I should like to know which is worse, to be raped a hundred times by negro pirates, to have a buttock cut off, to run the gauntlet among the Bulgarians, to be whipped and flogged in an *auto-da-fé*, to be dissected, to row in a galley, in short, to endure all the miseries through which we have passed, or to remain here doing nothing?"

" 'Tis a great question," said Candide.

These remarks led to new reflections, and Martin especially concluded that man was born to live in the convulsions of distress or in the lethargy of boredom. Candide did not agree, but he asserted nothing. Pangloss confessed that he had always suffered horribly; but, having once maintained that everything was for the best, he had continued to maintain it without believing it.

One thing confirmed Martin in his destestable principles, made Candide hesitate more than ever, and embarrassed Pangloss. And it was this. One day there came to their farm Paquette and Friar Giroflée, who were in the most extreme misery; they had soon wasted their three thousand piastres, had left each other, made it up, quarrelled again, been put in prison, escaped, and finally Friar Giroflée had turned Turk. Paquette continued her occupation everywhere and now earned nothing by it.

"I foresaw," said Martin to Candide, "that your gifts would soon be wasted and would only make them the more miserable. You and Cacambo were once bloated with millions of piastres and you are no happier than Friar Giroflée and Paquette."

"Ah! Ha!" said Pangloss to Paquette, "so Heaven brings you back to us, my dear child? Do you know that you cost me the end of my nose, an eye and an ear! What a plight you are in! Ah! What a world this is!"

This new occurrence caused them to philosophise more than ever. In the neighborhood there lived a very famous Dervish, who was supposed to be the best philosopher in

Turkey; they went to consult him; Pangloss was the spokesman and said: "Master, we have come to beg you to tell us why so strange an animal as man was ever created."

"What has it to do with you?" said the Dervish. "Is it your business?"

"But, reverend father," said Candide, "there is a horrible amount of evil in the world."

"What does it matter," said the Dervish, "whether there is evil or good? When his highness sends a ship to Egypt, does he worry about the comfort or discomfort of the rats in the ship?"

"Then what should we do?" said Pangloss.

"Hold your tongue," said the Dervish.

"I flattered myself," said Pangloss, "that I should discuss with you effects and causes, this best of all possible worlds, the origin of evil, the nature of the soul and pre-established harmony."

At these words the Dervish slammed the door in their faces.

During this conversation the news went round that at Constantinople two viziers and the mufti had been strangled and several of their friends impaled. This catastrophe made a prodigious noise everywhere for several hours. As Pangloss, Candide and Martin were returning to their little farm, they came upon an old man who was taking the air under a bower of orange trees at his door. Pangloss, who was as curious as he was argumentative, asked him what was the name of the mufti who had just been strangled.

"I do not know," replied the old man. "I have never known the name of any mufti or of any vizier. I am entirely ignorant of the occurrence you mention; I presume that in general those who meddle with public affairs sometimes perish miserably and that they deserve it; but I never inquire what is going on in Constantinople; I content myself with sending there for sale the produce of the garden I cultivate."

Having spoken thus, he took the strangers into his house. His two daughters and his two sons presented them with several kinds of sherbet which they made themselves, caymac flavored with candied citron peel, oranges, lemons, limes, pineapples, dates, pistachios and Mocha coffee which had not been mixed with the bad coffee of Batavia and the Isles. After which this good Mussulman's two daughters perfumed the beards of Candide, Pangloss and Martin.

"You must have a vast and magnificent estate?" said Candide to the Turk.

"I have only twenty acres," replied the Turk. "I cultivate them with my children; and work keeps at bay three great evils; boredom, vice and need."

As Candide returned to his farm he reflected deeply on the Turk's remarks. He said to Pangloss and Martin: "That good old man seems to me to have chosen an existence preferable by far to that of the six kings with whom we had the honor to sup."

"Exalted rank," said Pangloss, "is very dangerous, according to the testimony of all philosophers; for Eglon, King of the Moabites, was murdered by Ehud; Absalom was hanged by the hair and pierced by three darts; King Nadab, son of Jeroboam, was killed by Baasha; King Elah by Zimri; Ahaziah by Jehu; Athaliah by Jehoiada; the Kings Jehoiakim, Jeconiah and Zedekiah were made slaves. You know in what manner died Crœsus, Astyages, Darius, Denys of Syracuse, Pyrrhus, Perseus, Hannibal, Jugurtha, Ariovistus, Cæsar, Pompey, Nero, Otho, Vitellius, Domitian, Richard II of England, Edward II, Henry VI, Richard III, Mary Stuart, Charles I, the three Henrys of France, the Emperor Henry IV. You know . . ."

"I also know," said Candide, "that we should cultivate our gardens."

"You are right," said Pangloss, "for, when man was placed in the Garden of Eden, he was placed there *ut operaretur eum,* to dress it and to keep it; which proves that man was not born for idleness."

"Let us work without theorizing," said Martin; " 'tis the only way to make life endurable."

The whole small fraternity entered into this praiseworthy plan, and each started to make use of his talents. The little farm yielded well. Cunegonde was indeed very ugly, but she became an excellent pastry cook; Paquette embroidered; the old woman took care of the linen. Even Friar Giroflée performed some service; he was a very good carpenter and even became a man of honor; and Pangloss sometimes said to Candide: "All events are linked up in this best of all possible worlds; for, if you had not been expelled from the noble castle, by hard kicks in your backside for love of Mademoiselle Cunegonde, if you had not been clapped into the Inquisition, if you had not wandered about America on foot, if you had not stuck your sword in the Baron, if you had not lost all your sheep from the land of Eldorado, you would not be eating candied citrons and pistachios here."

" 'Tis well said," replied Candide, "but we must cultivate our gardens."

First Love

BY IVAN TURGENEV
(1818-1883)

Speaking at Turgenev's funeral, Ernest Renan said, "No man has been as much as he the incarnation of a whole race: generations of ancestors, lost in the sleep of centuries, speechless, came through him to life and utterance." It is a significant comment because Turgenev's finest works were written when he lived outside his native Russia. Son of wealthy landowners in Orel, he received his university education in Moscow and Berlin. Despite his wealthy background, Turgenev felt deep sympathy for the Russian peasants; his A Sportman's Sketches *(started in 1847, published in book form in 1852) did much to bring about the end of serfdom. About 1850 he left Russia, and when his masterpiece,* Fathers and Sons *(1861), was badly received by the Russian critics and public, he decided to remain in Paris. Turgenev's characteristic clarity and graciousness of style is obvious in* First Love *(1860), which many critics consider the finest story in Russian literature.*

First Love

The guests had long since departed. The clock had struck half-past twelve. There remained in the room only the host, Sergyei Nikolaevitch, and Vladimir Petrovitch.

The host rang and ordered the remains of the supper to be removed.—"So then, the matter is settled," he said, ensconcing himself more deeply in his arm-chair, and lighting a cigar:—"each of us is to narrate the history of his first love. 'Tis your turn, Sergyei Nikolaevitch."

Sergyei Nikolaevitch, a rather corpulent man, with a plump, fair-skinned face, first looked at the host, then raised his eyes to the ceiling.—"I had no first love,"—he began at last:—"I began straight off with the second."

"How was that?"

"Very simply. I was eighteen years of age when, for the first time, I dangled after a very charming young lady; but I courted her as though it were no new thing to me: exactly as I courted others afterward. To tell the truth, I fell in love, for the first and last time, at the age of six, with my nurse;—but that is a very long time ago. The details of our relations have been erased from my memory; but even if I remembered them, who would be interested in them?"

"Then what are we to do?"—began the host.—"There was nothing very startling about my first love either; I never fell in love with anyone before Anna Ivanovna, now my wife; and everything ran as though on oil with us; our fathers made up the match, we very promptly fell in love with each other, and entered the bonds of matrimony without delay. My story can be told in two words. I must confess, gentlemen, that in raising the question of first love, I set my hopes on you, I will not say old, but yet no longer young bachelors. Will not you divert us with something, Vladimir Petrovitch?"

"My first love belongs, as a matter of fact, not altogether

to the ordinary category,"—replied, with a slight hesitation, Vladimir Petrovitch, a man of forty, whose black hair was sprinkled with grey.

"Ah!" said the host and Sergyei Nikolaevitch in one breath.—"So much the better. . . . Tell us."

"As you like . . . or no: I will not narrate; I am no great hand at telling a story; it turns out dry and short, or long-drawn-out and artificial. But if you will permit me, I will write down all that I remember in a note-book, and will read it aloud to you."

At first the friends would not consent, but Vladimir Petrovitch insisted on having his own way. A fortnight later they came together again, and Vladimir Petrovitch kept his promise.

This is what his note-book contained.

I

I was sixteen years old at the time. The affair took place in the summer of 1833.

I was living in Moscow, in my parents' house. They had hired a villa near the Kaluga barrier, opposite the Neskutchny Park.[1]—I was preparing for the university, but was working very little and was not in a hurry.

No one restricted my freedom. I had done whatever I pleased ever since I had parted with my last French governor, who was utterly unable to reconcile himself to the thought that he had fallen "like a bomb (*comme une bombe*) into Russia, and with a stubborn expression on his face, wallowed in bed for whole days at a time. My father treated me in an indifferently affectionate way; my mother paid hardly any attention to me, although she had no children except me: other cares engrossed her. My father, still a young man and very handsome, had married her from calculation; she was ten years older than he. My mother led a melancholy life; she was incessantly in a state of agitation, jealousy, and wrath—but not in the presence of my father; she was very much afraid of him, and he maintained a stern, cold, and distant

---

[1] The finest of the public parks in Moscow, situated near the famous Sparrow Hills, is called "Neskutchny"—"Not Tiresome," generally rendered "Sans Souci." It contains an imperial residence, the Alexander Palace, used as an official summer home by the Governor-General of Moscow.—TRANSLATOR.

manner . . . I have never seen a man more exquisitely calm, self-confident, and self-controlled.

I shall never forget the first weeks I spent at the villa. The weather was magnificent; we had left town the ninth of May, on St. Nicholas's day. I rambled,—sometimes in the garden of our villa, sometimes in Neskutchny Park, sometimes beyond the city barriers; I took with me some book or other,—a course of Kaidanoff,—but rarely opened it, and chiefly recited aloud poems, of which I knew a great many by heart. The blood was fermenting in me, and my heart was aching—so sweetly and absurdly; I was always waiting for something, shrinking at something, and wondering at everything, and was all ready for anything at a moment's notice. My fancy was beginning to play, and hovered swiftly ever around the selfsame image, as martins hover round a belfry at sunset. But even athwart my tears and athwart the melancholy, inspired now by a melodious verse, now by the beauty of the evening, there peered forth, like grass in springtime, the joyous sensation of young, bubbling life.

I had a saddle-horse; I was in the habit of saddling it myself, and when I rode off alone as far as possible, in some direction, launching out at a gallop and fancying myself a knight at a tourney—how blithely the wind whistled in my ears!—Or, turning my face skyward, I welcomed its beaming light and azure into my open soul.

I remember, at that time, the image of woman, the phantom of woman's love, almost never entered my mind in clearly defined outlines; but in everything I thought, in everything I felt, there lay hidden the half-conscious, shamefaced presentiment of something new, inexpressibly sweet, feminine. . . .

This presentiment, this expectation permeated my whole being; I breathed it, it coursed through my veins in every drop of blood . . . it was fated to be speedily realized.

Our villa consisted of a wooden manor-house with columns, and two tiny outlying wings; in the wing to the left a tiny factory of cheap wallpapers was installed. . . . More than once I went thither to watch how half a score of gaunt, dishevelled young fellows in dirty smocks and with tipsy faces were incessantly galloping about at the wooden levers which jammed down the square blocks of the press, and in that manner, by the weight of their puny bodies, printed the motley-hued patterns of the wallpapers. The wing on the right stood empty and was for rent. One day—three weeks after the ninth of May—the shutters on the windows of this wing were opened, and women's faces made their appearance in them; some family or other had moved into it. I remember how, that same day at dinner, my mother inquired of the butler who our new neighbors were, and on hearing the name of Princess Zasyekin, said at first, not without some respect:—"Ah! a Princess" . . . and then she added:—"She must be some poor person!"

"They came in three hired carriages, ma'am,"—remarked the butler, as he respectfully presented a dish. "They have no carriage of their own, ma'am, and their furniture is of the very plainest sort."

"Yes,"—returned my mother,—"and nevertheless; it is better so."

My father shot a cold glance at her; she subsided into silence.

As a matter of fact, Princess Zasyekin could not be a wealthy woman: the wing she had hired was so old and tiny and low-roofed that people in the least well-to-do would not have been willing to inhabit it.—However, I let this go in at one ear and out at the other. The princely title had little effect on me: I had recently been reading Schiller's "The Brigands."

II

I had a habit of prowling about our garden every evening, gun in hand, and standing guard against the crows.—I had long cherished a hatred for those wary, rapacious and crafty birds. On the day of which I have been speaking, I went into the garden as usual, and, after having fruitlessly made the round of all the alleys (the crows recognized me from afar, and merely cawed spasmodically at a distance), I accidentally approached the low fence which separated *our* territory from the narrow strip of garden extending behind the right-hand wing and appertaining to it. I was walking along with drooping head. Suddenly I heard voices: I glanced over the fence—and was petrified. . . . A strange spectacle presented itself to me.

A few paces distant from me, on a grass-plot between green raspberry-bushes, stood a tall, graceful young girl, in a striped, pink frock and with a white kerchief on her head; around her pressed four young men, and she was tapping them in turn on the brow with those small grey flowers, the

name of which I do not know, but which are familiar to children; these little flowers form tiny sacs, and burst with a pop
when they are struck against anything hard. The young
men offered their foreheads to her so willingly, and in the
girl's movements (I saw her form in profile) there was something so bewitching, caressing, mocking, and charming, that
I almost cried aloud in wonder and pleasure; and I believe I
would have given everything in the world if those lovely little
fingers had only consented to tap me on the brow. My gun
slid down on the grass, I forgot everything, I devoured with
my eyes that slender waist, and the neck and the beautiful
arms, and the slightly ruffled fair hair, the intelligent eyes and
those lashes, and the delicate cheek beneath them. . . .

"Young man, hey there, young man!"—suddenly spoke up
a voice near me:—"Is it permissible to stare like that at
strange young ladies?"

I trembled all over, I was stupefied. . . . Beside me, on
the other side of the fence, stood a man with closely clipped
black hair, gazing ironically at me. At that same moment,
the young girl turned toward me. . . . I beheld huge grey
eyes in a mobile, animated face—and this whole face suddenly began to quiver, and to laugh, and the white teeth
gleamed from it, the brows elevated themselves in an amusing way. . . . I flushed, picked up my gun from the ground,
and, pursued by ringing but not malicious laughter, I ran to
my own room, flung myself on the bed, and covered my
face with my hands. My heart was fairly leaping within me;
I felt very much ashamed and very merry: I experienced an
unprecedented emotion.

After I had rested awhile, I brushed my hair, made myself
neat and went down-stairs to tea. The image of the young
girl floated in front of me; my heart had ceased to leap, but
ached in an agreeable sort of way.

"What ails thee?"—my father suddenly asked me:—"hast
thou killed a crow?"

I was on the point of telling him all, but refrained and only
smiled to myself. As I was preparing for bed, I whirled round
thrice on one foot, I know not why, pomaded my hair, got
into bed and slept all night like a dead man. Toward morning
I awoke for a moment, raised my head, cast a glance of rapture around me—and fell asleep again.

III

"How am I to get acquainted with them?" was my first thought, as soon as I awoke in the morning. I went out into the garden before tea, but did not approach too close to the fence, and saw no one. After tea I walked several times up and down the street in front of the villa, and cast a distant glance at the windows. . . . I thought I descried *her* face behind the curtains, and retreated with all possible despatch. "But I must get acquainted,"—I thought, as I walked with irregular strides up and down the sandy stretch which extends in front of the Neskutchny Park . . . "but how? that is the question." I recalled the most trifling incidents of the meeting on the previous evening; for some reason, her manner of laughing at me presented itself to me with particular clearness. . . . But while I was fretting thus and constructing various plans, Fate was already providing for me.

During my absence, my mother had received a letter from her new neighbor on grey paper sealed with brown wax, such as is used only on postal notices, and on the corks of cheap wine. In this letter, written in illiterate language, and with a slovenly chirography, the Princess requested my mother to grant her her protection: my mother, according to the Princess's words, was well acquainted with the prominent people on whom the fortune of herself and her children depended, as she had some extremely important law-suits: "I apeal tyou,"—she wrote,—"as a knoble woman to a knoble woman, and moarover, it is agriable to me to makeus of this opportunity." In conclusion, she asked permission of my mother to call upon her. I found my mother in an unpleasant frame of mind: my father was not at home, and she had no one with whom to take counsel. It was impossible not to reply to a "knoble woman," and to a Princess into the bargain; but how to reply perplexed my mother. It seemed to her ill-judged to write a note in French, and my mother was not strong in Russian orthography herself—and was aware of the fact—and did not wish to compromise herself. She was delighted at my arrival, and immediately ordered me to go to the Princess and explain to her verbally that my mother was always ready, to the extent of her ability, to be of service to Her Radiance[1] and begged that she would call upon her about one o'clock.

[1] Princes, princesses, counts, and countesses have the title of *Siyatelstvo* (*siyam*— to shine, to be radiant); generally translated "Illustrious Highness" or "Serenity."—TRANSLATOR.

This unexpectedly swift fulfillment of my secret wishes both delighted and frightened me; but I did not betray the emotion which held possession of me, and preliminarily betook myself to my room for the purpose of donning a new neck-cloth and coat; at home I went about in a round-jacket and turn-over collars, although I detested them greatly.

IV

In the cramped and dirty anteroom of the wing, which I entered with an involuntary trembling of my whole body, I was received by a grey-haired old serving-man with a face the hue of dark copper, pig-like, surly little eyes, and such deep wrinkles on his forehead as I had never seen before in my life. He was carrying on a platter the gnawed spinal bone of a herring, and, pushing to with his foot the door which led into the adjoining room, he said abruptly:—"What do you want?"

"Is Princess Zasyekin at home?"—I inquired.

"Vonifaty!"—screamed a quavering female voice on the other side of the door.

The servant silently turned his back on me, thereby displaying the badly worn rear of his livery with its solitary, rusted, armouried button, and went away, leaving the platter on the floor.

"Hast thou been to the police-station?"—went on that same feminine voice. The servant muttered something in reply.—"Hey? . . . Someone has come?"—was the next thing audible. . . . "The young gentleman from next door? —Well, ask him in."

"Please come into the drawing-room, sir,"—said the servant, making his appearance again before me, and picking up the platter from the floor. I adjusted my attire and entered the "drawing-room."

I found myself in a tiny and not altogether clean room, with shabby furniture which seemed to have been hastily set in place. At the window, in an easy-chair with a broken arm, sat a woman of fifty, with uncovered hair[1] and plain-featured, clad in an old green gown, and with a variegated

---

[1] The custom still prevails in Russia, to a great extent, for all elderly women to wear caps. In the peasant class it is considered as extremely indecorous to go "simple-haired," as the expression runs. —TRANSLATOR.

worsted kerchief round her neck. Her small black eyes fairly bored into me.

I went up to her and made my bow.

"I have the honor of speaking to Princess Zasyekin?"

"I am Princess Zasyekin: and you are the son of Mr. B—?"

"Yes, madam. I have come to you with a message from my mother."

"Pray be seated. Vonifaty! where are my keys? Hast thou seen them?"

I communicated to Madame Zasyekin my mother's answer to her note. She listened to me, tapping the window-pane with her thick, red fingers, and when I had finished she riveted her eyes on me once more.

"Very good; I shall certainly go,"—said she at last.—"But how young you are still! How old are you, allow me to ask?"

"Sixteen,"—I replied with involuntary hesitation.

The Princess pulled out of her pocket some dirty, written documents, raised them up to her very nose and began to sort them over.

" 'Tis a good age,"—she suddenly articulated, turning and fidgeting in her chair.—"And please do not stand on ceremony. We are plain folks."

"Too plain,"—I thought, with involuntary disgust taking in with a glance the whole of her homely figure.

At that moment, the other door of the drawing-room was swiftly thrown wide open, and on the threshold appeared the young girl whom I had seen in the garden the evening before. She raised her hand and a smile flitted across her face.

"And here is my daughter,"—said the Princess, pointing at her with her elbow.—"Zinotchka, the son of our neighbor, Mr. B—. What is your name, permit me to inquire?"

"Vladimir,"—I replied, rising and lisping with agitation.

"And your patronymic?"

"Petrovitch."

"Yes! I once had an acquaintance, a chief of police, whose name was Vladimir Petrovich also. Vonifaty! don't hunt for the keys; the keys are in my pocket."

The young girl continued to gaze at me with the same smile as before, slightly puckering up her eyes and bending her head a little on one side.

"I have already seen M'sieu Voldemar,"—she began. (The silvery-tone of her voice coursed through me like a sweet chill.)—"Will you permit me to call you so?"

"Pray do, madam,"—I lisped.

"Where was that?"—asked the Princess.

The young Princess did not answer her mother.

"Are you busy now?"—she said, without taking her eyes off me.

"Not in the least, madam."

"Then will you help me to wind some wool? Come hither, to me."

She nodded her head at me and left the drawing-room. I followed her.

In the room which we entered the furniture was a little better and was arranged with great taste.—But at that moment I was almost unable to notice anything; I moved as though in a dream and felt a sort of intense sensation of well-being verging on stupidity throughout my frame.

The young Princess sat down, produced a knot of red wool, and pointing me to a chair opposite her, she carefully unbound the skein and placed it on my hands. She did all this in silence, with a sort of diverting deliberation, and with the same brilliant and crafty smile on her slightly parted lips. She began to wind the wool upon a card doubled together, and suddenly illumined me with such a clear, swift glance, that I involuntarily dropped my eyes. When her eyes, which were generally half closed, opened to their full extent her face underwent a complete change; it was as though light had inundated it.

"What did you think of me yesterday, M'sieu Voldemar?"—she asked, after a brief pause.—"You certainly must have condemned me?"

"I . . . Princess . . . I thought nothing . . . how can I . . ." I replied, in confusion.

"Listen,"—she returned.—"You do not know me yet; I want people always to speak the truth to me. You are sixteen, I heard, and I am twenty-one; you see that I am a great deal older than you, and therefore you must always speak the truth to me . . . and obey me,"—she added.—"Look at me; why don't you look at me?"

I became still more confused; but I raised my eyes to hers, nevertheless. She smiled, only not in her former manner, but with a different, an approving smile.—"Look at me,"—she said, caressingly lowering her voice:—"I don't like that. . . . Your face pleases me; I foresee that we shall be friends. And do you like me?"—she added slyly.

"Princess . . ." I was beginning. . . .

"In the first place, call me Zinaida Alexandrovna; and in the second place,—what sort of a habit is it for children"—(she corrected herself)—"for young men—not to say straight out what they feel? You do like me, don't you?"

Although it was very pleasant to me to have her talk so frankly to me, still I was somewhat nettled. I wanted to show her that she was not dealing with a small boy, and, assuming as easy and serious a mien as I could, I said:—"Of course I like you very much, Zinaida Alexandrovna; I have no desire to conceal the fact."

She shook her head, pausing at intervals.—"Have you a governor?"—she suddenly inquired.

"No, I have not had a governor this long time past."

I lied: a month had not yet elapsed since I had parted with my Frenchman.

"Oh, yes, I see: you are quite grown up."

She slapped me lightly on the fingers.—"Hold your hands straight!"—And she busied herself diligently with winding her ball.

I took advantage of the fact that she did not raise her eyes, and set to scrutinizing her, first by stealth, then more and more boldly. Her face seemed to me even more charming than on the day before: everything about it was so delicate, intelligent and lovely. She was sitting with her back to the window, which was hung with a white shade; a ray of sunlight making its way through that shade inundated with a flood of light her fluffy golden hair, her innocent neck, sloping shoulders, and calm, tender bosom.—I gazed at her—and how near and dear she became to me! It seemed to me both that I had known her for a long time and that I had known nothing and had not lived before she came. . . . She wore a rather dark, already shabby gown, with an apron; I believe I would willingly have caressed every fold of that gown and of that apron. The tips of her shoes peeped out from under her gown; I would have bowed down to those little boots. . . . "And here I sit, in front of her,"—I thought.—"I have become acquainted with her . . . what happiness, my God!" I came near bouncing out of my chair with rapture, but I merely dangled my feet to and fro a little, like a child who is enjoying dainties.

I felt as much at my ease as a fish does in water, and I would have liked never to leave that room again as long as I lived.

Her eyelids slowly rose, and again her brilliant eyes beamed caressingly before me, and again she laughed.

"How you stare at me!"—she said slowly, shaking her finger at me.

I flushed scarlet. . . . "She understands all, she sees all," —flashed through my head. "And how could she fail to see and understand all?"

Suddenly there was a clattering in the next room, and a sword clanked.

"Zina!"—screamed the old Princess from the drawing-room.—"Byelovzoroff has brought thee a kitten."

"A kitten!"—cried Zinaida, and springing headlong from her chair, she flung the ball on my knees and ran out.

I also rose, and, laying the skein of wool on the window-sill, went into the drawing-room, and stopped short in amazement. In the centre of the room lay a kitten with outstretched paws: Zinaida was kneeling in front of it, and carefully raising its snout. By the side of the young Princess, taking up nearly the entire wallspace between the windows, was visible a fair-complexioned, curly-haired young man, a hussar, with a rosy face and protruding eyes.

"How ridiculous!"—Zinaida kept repeating:—"and its eyes are not grey, but green, and what big ears it has! Thank you, Viktor Egoritch! you are very kind."

The hussar, in whom I recognized one of the young men whom I had seen on the preceding evening, smiled and bowed, clicking his spurs and clanking the links of his sword as he did so.

"You were pleased to say yesterday that you wished to possess a striped kitten with large ears . . . so I have got it, madam. Your word is my law."—And again he bowed.

The kitten mewed faintly, and began to sniff at the floor.

"He is hungry!"—cried Zinaida.—"Vonifaty! Sonya! bring some milk."

The chambermaid, in an old yellow gown and with a faded kerchief on her head, entered with a saucer of milk in her hand, and placed it in front of the kitten. The kitten quivered, blinked, and began to lap.

"What a rosy tongue it has,"—remarked Zinaida, bending her head down almost to the floor, and looking sideways at it, under its very nose.

The kitten drank its fill, and began to purr, affectedly contracting and relaxing its paws. Zinaida rose to her feet, and turning to the maid, said indifferently:—"Take it away."

"Your hand—in return for the kitten,"—said the hussar, displaying his teeth, and bending over the whole of his huge body, tightly confined in a new uniform.

"Both hands,"—replied Zinaida, offering him her hands. While he was kissing them, she gazed at me over his shoulder.

I stood motionless on one spot, and did not know whether to laugh or to say something, or to hold my peace. Suddenly, through the open door of the anteroom, the figure of our footman, Feodor, caught my eye. He was making signs to me. I mechanically went out to him.

"What dost thou want?"—I asked.

"Your mamma has sent for you,"—he said in a whisper.—"She is angry because you do not return with an answer."

"Why, have I been here long?"

"More than an hour."

"More than an hour!"—I repeated involuntarily, and returning to the drawing-room, I began to bow and scrape my foot.

"Where are you going?"—the young Princess asked me, with a glance at the hussar.

"I must go home, madam. So I am to say,"—I added, addressing the old woman,—"that you will call upon us at two o'clock."

"Say that, my dear fellow."

The old Princess hurriedly drew out her snuff-box, and took a pinch so noisily that I fairly jumped.—"Say that,"—she repeated, tearfully blinking and grunting.

I bowed once more, turned and left the room with the same sensation of awkwardness in my back which a very young man experiences when he knows that people are staring after him.

"Look here, M'sieu Voldemar, you must drop in to see us,"—called Zinaida, and again burst out laughing.

"What makes her laugh all the time?" I thought, as I wended my way home accompanied by Feodor, who said nothing to me, but moved along disapprovingly behind me. My mother reproved me, and inquired, with surprise, "What could I have been doing so long at the Princess's?" I made her no answer, and went off to my own room. I had suddenly grown very melancholy. . . . I tried not to weep. . . . I was jealous of the hussar.

V

The Princess, according to her promise, called on my mother, and did not please her. I was not present at their meeting, but at table my mother narrated to my father that that Princess Zasyekin seemed to her a *femme très vulgaire;* that she had bored her immensely with her requests that she would intervene on her behalf with Prince Sergyei; that she was always having such law-suits and affairs,—*de vilaines affaires d'argent,*—and that she must be a great rogue. But my mother added that she had invited her with her daughter to dine on the following day (on hearing the words "with her daughter," I dropped my nose into my plate),—because, notwithstanding, she was a neighbor, and with a name. Thereupon my father informed my mother that he now recalled who the lady was: that in his youth he had known the late Prince Zasyekin, a capitally-educated but flighty and captious man; that in society he was called *"le Parisien,"* because of his long residence in Paris; that he had been very wealthy, but had gambled away all his property—and, no one knew why, though probably it had been for the sake of the money,—"although he might have made a better choice,"—added my father, with a cold smile,—he had married the daughter of some clerk in a chancellery, and after his marriage had gone into speculation, and ruined himself definitively.

"'Tis a wonder she did not try to borrow money,"—remarked my mother.

"She is very likely to do it,"—said my father, calmly.— "Does she speak French?"

"Very badly."

"M-m-m. However, that makes no difference. I think thou saidst that thou hadst invited her daughter; some one assured me that she is a very charming and well-educated girl."

"Ah! Then she does not take after her mother."

"Nor after her father,"—returned my father.—"He was also well educated, but stupid."

My mother sighed, and became thoughtful. My father relapsed into silence. I felt very awkward during the course of that conversation.

After dinner I betook myself to the garden, but without my gun. I had pledged my word to myself that I would not go near the "Zasyekin garden"; but an irresistible force drew me thither, and not in vain. I had no sooner approached the fence than I caught sight of Zinaida. This time she was alone. She was holding a small book in her hands and strolling slowly along the path. She did not notice me. I came near letting her slip past; but suddenly caught myself up and coughed.

She turned round but did not pause, put aside with one hand the broad blue ribbon of her round straw hat, looked at me, smiled quietly, and again riveted her eyes on her book. I pulled off my cap, and after fidgeting about a while on one spot, I went away with a heavy heart. *"Que suis-je pour elle?"*—I thought (God knows why) in French.

Familiar footsteps resounded behind me; I glanced round and beheld my father advancing toward me with swift, rapid strides.

"Is that the young Princess?"—he asked me.

"Yes."

"Dost thou know her?"

"I saw her this morning at the Princess her mother's."

My father halted and, wheeling abruptly round on his heels, retraced his steps. As he came on a level with Zinaida he bowed courteously to her. She bowed to him in return, not without some surprise on her face, and lowered her book. I saw that she followed him with her eyes. My father always dressed very elegantly, originally and simply; but his figure had never seemed to me more graceful, never had his grey hat sat more handsomely on his curls, which were barely beginning to grow thin.

I was on the point of directing my course toward Zinaida, but she did not even look at me, but raised her book once more and walked away.

VI

I spent the whole of that evening and the following day in a sort of gloomy stupor. I remember that I made an effort to work, and took up Kaidanoff; but in vain did the large-printed lines and pages of the famous text-book flit before my eyes. Ten times in succession I read the words: "Julius Cæsar was distinguished for military daring," without understanding a word, and I flung aside my book. Before dinner I pomaded my hair again, and again donned my frock-coat and neckerchief.

"What's that for?"—inquired my mother.—"Thou are not a student yet, and God knows whether thou wilt pass thy examination. And thy round-jacket was made not very long ago. Thou must not discard it!"

"There are to be guests,"—I whispered, almost in despair.

"What nonsense! What sort of guests are they?"

I was compelled to submit. I exchanged my coat for my round-jacket, but did not remove my neckerchief. The Princess and her daughter made their appearance half an hour before dinner; the old woman had thrown a yellow shawl over her green gown, with which I was familiar, and had donned an old-fashioned mob-cap with ribbons of a fiery hue. She immediately began to talk about her notes of hand, to sigh and to bewail her poverty, and to "importune," but did not stand in the least upon ceremony; and she took snuff noisily and fidgeted and wriggled in her chair as before. It never seemed to enter her head that she was a Princess. On the other hand, Zinaida bore herself very stiffly, almost haughtily, like a real young Princess. Cold impassivity and dignity had made their appearance on her countenance, and I did not recognize her,—did not recognize her looks or her smile, although in this new aspect she seemed to me very beautiful. She wore a thin barège gown with pale-blue figures; her hair fell in long curls along her cheeks, in the English fashion: this coiffure suited the cold expression of her face.

My father sat beside her during dinner, and with the exquisite and imperturbable courtesy which was characteristic of him, showed attention to his neighbor. He glanced at her from time to time, and she glanced at him now and then, but in such a strange, almost hostile, manner. Their conversation proceeded in French;—I remember that I was surprised at the purity of Zinaida's accent. The old Princess, as before, did not restrain herself in the slightest degree during dinner, but ate a great deal and praised the food. My mother evidently found her wearisome, and answered her with a sort of sad indifference; my father contracted his brows in a slight frown from time to time. My mother did not like Zinaida either.

"She's a haughty young sprig,"—she said the next day.— "And when one comes to think of it, what is there for her to be proud of?—*avec sa mine de grisette!*"

"Evidently, thou hast not seen any grisettes,"—my father remarked to her.

"Of course I haven't, God be thanked! . . . Only, how art thou capable of judging of them?"

Zinaida paid absolutely no attention whatever to me. Soon after dinner the old Princess began to take her leave.

"I shall rely upon your protection, Marya Nikolaevna and Piotr Vasilievitch,"—she said, in a sing-song tone, to my father and mother.—"What is to be done! I have seen prosperous days, but they are gone. Here am I a Radiance,"—she added, with an unpleasant laugh,—"but what's the good of an honor when you've nothing to eat?"—My father bowed respectfully to her and escorted her to the door of the anteroom. I was standing there in my round-jacket, and staring at the floor, as though condemned to death. Zinaida's behavior toward me had definitively annihilated me. What, then, was my amazement when, as she passed me, she whispered to me hastily, and with her former affectionate expression in her eyes:—"Come to us at eight o'clock, do you hear? without fail. . . ." I merely threw my hands apart in amazement;—but she was already retreating, having thrown a white scarf over her head.

VII

Precisely at eight o'clock I entered the tiny wing inhabited by the Princess, clad in my coat, and with my hair brushed up into a crest on top of my head. The old servant glared surlily at me, and rose reluctantly from his bench. Merry voices resounded in the drawing-room. I opened the door and retreated a pace in astonishment. In the middle of the room, on a chair, stood the young Princess, holding a man's hat in front of her; around the chair thronged five men. They were trying to dip their hands into the hat, but she kept raising it on high and shaking it violently. On catching sight of me she exclaimed:—

"Stay, stay! Here's a new guest; he must be given a ticket," —and springing lightly from the chair, she seized me by the lapel of my coat.—"Come along,"—said she;—"why do you stand there? Messieurs, allow me to make you acquainted: this is Monsieur Voldemar, the son of our neighbor. And this," —she added, turning to me, and pointing to the visitors in turn,—"is Count Malevsky, Doctor Lushin, the poet Maidanoff, retired Captain Nirmatzky, and Byelovzoroff the hussar, whom you have already seen. I beg that you will love and favor each other."

I was so confused that I did not even bow to any one; in Doctor Lushin I recognized that same swarthy gentleman who had so ruthlessly put me to shame in the garden; the others were strangers to me.

"Count!"—pursued Zinaida,—"write a ticket for M'sieu Voldemar."

"That is unjust,"—returned the Count, with a slight accent,—a very handsome and foppishly-attired man, with a dark complexion, expressive brown eyes, a thin, white little nose, and a slender moustache over his tiny mouth.—"He has not been playing at forfeits with us."

" 'Tis unjust,"—repeated Byelovzoroff and the gentleman who had been alluded to as the retired Captain,—a man of forty, horribly pock-marked, curly-haired as a negro, round-shouldered, bow-legged, and dressed in a military coat without epaulets, worn open on the breast.

"Write a ticket, I tell you,"—repeated the Princess.—"What sort of a rebellion is this? M'sieu Voldemar is with us for the first time, and to-day no law applies to him. No grumbling—write; I will have it so."

The Count shrugged his shoulders, but submissively bowing his head, he took a pen in his white, ring-decked hand, tore off a scrap of paper and began to write on it.

"Permit me at least to explain to M'sieu Voldemar what it is all about,"—began Lushin, in a bantering tone;—"otherwise he will be utterly at a loss. You see, young man, we are playing at forfeits; the Princess must pay a fine, and the one who draws out the lucky ticket must kiss her hand. Do you understand what I have told you?"

I merely glanced at him and continued to stand as though in a fog, while the Princess again sprang upon the chair and again began to shake the hat. All reached up to her—I among the rest.

"Maidanoff,"—said the Princess to the tall young man with a gaunt face, tiny mole-like eyes and extremely long, black hair,—"you, as a poet, ought to be magnanimous and surrender your ticket to M'sieu Voldemar, so that he may have two chances instead of one."

But Maidanoff shook his head in refusal and tossed his hair. I put in my hand into the hat after all the rest, drew out and unfolded a ticket. . . . O Lord! what were my sensations when I beheld on it, "Kiss!"

"Kiss!"—I cried involuntarily.

"Bravo! He has won,"—chimed in the Princess.—"How

delighted I am!"—She descended from the chair and gazed into my eyes so clearly and sweetly that my heart fairly laughed with joy.—"And are you glad?"—she asked me.

"I?" . . . I stammered.

"Sell me your ticket,"—suddenly blurted out Byelovzoroff, right in my ear.—"I'll give you one hundred rubles for it."

I replied to the hussar by such a wrathful look that Zinaida clapped her hands, and Lushin cried:—"That's a gallant fellow!"

"But,"—he went on,—"in my capacity of master of cere-monies, I am bound to see that all the regulations are car-ried out. M'sieu Voldemar, get down on one knee. That is our rule."

Zinaida stood before me with her head bent a little to one side, as though the better to scrutinize me, and offered me her hand with dignity. Things grew dim before my eyes; I tried to get down on one knee, plumped down on both knees, and applied my lips to Zinaida's fingers in so awkward a man-ner that I scratched the tip of my nose slightly on her nails.

"Good!"—shouted Lushin, and helped me to rise.

The game of forfeits continued. Zinaida placed me beside her. What penalties they did invent! Among other things, she had to impersonate a "statue"—and she selected as a pedestal the monstrously homely Nirmatzky, ordering him to lie flat on the floor, and to tuck his face into his breast. The laughter did not cease for a single moment. All this noise and up-roar, this unceremonious, almost tumultuous merriment, these unprecedented relations with strangers, fairly flew to my head; for I was a boy who had been reared soberly, and in solitude, and had grown up in a stately home of gentry. I be-came simply intoxicated, as though with wine. I began to shout with laughter and chatter more loudly than the rest, so that even the old Princess, who was sitting in the adjoin-ing room with some sort of pettifogger from the Iversky Gate[1] who had been summoned for a conference, came out to take a look at me. But I felt so happy that, as the saying is, I didn't care a farthing for anybody's ridicule, or anybody's oblique glances.

Zinaida continued to display a preference for me and never let me leave her side. In one forfeit I was made to sit

[1] The famous gate from the "White town" into the "China town," in Moscow, where there is a renowned holy picture of the Iberian Virgin, in a chapel. Evidently the lawyers' quarter was in this vicinity.—TRANSLATOR.

by her, covered up with one and the same silk kerchief: I was bound to tell her *my secret*. I remember how our two heads found themselves suddenly in choking, semitransparent, fragrant gloom; how near and softly her eyes sparkled in that gloom, and how hotly her parted lips breathed; and her teeth were visible, and the tips of her hair tickled and burned me. I maintained silence. She smiled mysteriously and slyly, and at last whispered to me: "Well, what is it?" But I merely flushed and laughed, and turned away, and could hardly draw my breath. We got tired of forfeits, and began to play "string." Good heavens! what rapture I felt when, forgetting myself with gaping, I received from her a strong, sharp rap on my fingers; and how afterward I tried to pretend that I was yawning with inattention, but she mocked at me and did not touch my hands, which were awaiting the blow!

But what a lot of other pranks we played that same evening! We played on the piano, and sang, and danced, and represented a gipsy camp. We dressed Nirmatzky up like a bear, and fed him with water and salt. Count Malevsky showed us several card tricks, and ended by stacking the cards and dealing himself all the trumps at whist; upon which Lushin "had the honor of congratulating him." Maidanoff declaimed to us fragments from his poem, "The Murderer" (this occurred in the very thick of romanticism), which he intended to publish in a black binding, with the title in letters of the color of blood. We stole his hat from the knees of the pettifogger from the Iversky Gate, and made him dance the kazak dance by way of redeeming it. We dressed old Vonifaty up in a mob-cap, and the young Princess put on a man's hat. . . . It is impossible to recount all we did. Byelovzoroff alone remained most of the time in a corner, angry and frowning. . . . Sometimes his eyes became suffused with blood, he grew scarlet all over and seemed to be on the very point of swooping down upon all of us and scattering us on all sides, like chips; but the Princess glanced at him, menaced him with her finger, and again he retired into his corner.

We were completely exhausted at last. The old Princess was equal to anything, as she put it,—no shouts disconcerted her,—but she felt tired and wished to rest. At midnight supper was served, consisting of a bit of old, dry cheese and a few cold patties filled with minced ham, which seemed to us more savory than any pasty; there was only one bottle of wine, and that was rather queer:—dark, with a swollen neck, and the wine in it left an aftertaste of pinkish dye:

however, no one drank it. Weary and happy to exhaustion, I emerged from the wing; a thunder-storm seemed to be brewing; the black storm-clouds grew larger and crept across the sky, visibly altering their smoky outlines. A light breeze was uneasily quivering in the dark trees, and somewhere beyond the horizon the thunder was growling angrily and dully, as though to itself.

I made my way through the back door to my room. My nurse-valet was sleeping on the floor and I was obliged to step over him; he woke up, saw me, and reported that my mother was angry with me, and had wanted to send after me again, but that my father had restrained her. I never went to bed without having bidden my mother good night and begged her blessing. There was no help for it! I told my valet that I would undress myself and go to bed unaided,—and extinguished the candle. But I did not undress and I did not go to bed.

I seated myself on a chair and sat there for a long time, as though enchanted. That which I felt was so new and so sweet . . . I sat there, hardly looking around me and without moving, breathing slowly, and only laughing silently now, as I recalled, now inwardly turning cold at the thought that I was in love, that here it was, that love. Zinaida's face floated softly before me in the darkness—floated, but did not float away; her lips still smiled as mysteriously as ever, her eyes gazed somewhat askance at me, interrogatively, thoughtfully and tenderly . . . as at the moment when I had parted from her. At last I rose on tiptoe, stepped to my bed and cautiously, without undressing, laid my head on the pillow, as though endeavoring by the sharp movement to frighten off that wherewith I was filled to overflowing. . . .

I lay down, but did not even close an eye. I speedily perceived that certain faint reflections kept constantly falling into my room. . . . I raised myself and looked out of the window. Its frame was distinctly defined from the mysteriously and confusedly whitened panes. " 'Tis the thunderstorm,"—I thought,—and so, in fact, there was a thunderstorm; but it had passed very far away, so that even the claps of thunder were not audible; only in the sky long, indistinct, branching flashes of lightning, as it were, were uninterruptedly flashing up. They were not flashing up so much as they were quivering and twitching, like the wing of a dying bird. I rose, went to the window, and stood there until morning. . . . The lightning-flashes never ceased for a mo-

ment; it was what is called a pitch-black night. I gazed at the
dumb, sandy plain, at the dark mass of the Neskutchny Park,
at the yellowish façades of the distant buildings, which also
seemed to be trembling at every faint flash. . . . I gazed,
and could not tear myself away; those dumb lightning-flashes,
those restrained gleams, seemed to be responding to the
dumb and secret outbursts which were flaring up within me
also. Morning began to break; the dawn started forth in scarlet patches. With the approach of the sun the lightning-
flashes grew paler and paler; they quivered more and more
infrequently, and vanished at last, drowned in the sobering
and unequivocal light of the breaking day.

And my lightning-flashes vanished within me also. I felt
great fatigue and tranquillity . . . but Zinaida's image continued to hover triumphantly over my soul. Only it, that
image, seemed calm; like a flying swan from the marshy
sedges, it separated itself from the other ignoble figures which
surrounded it, and as I fell asleep, I bowed down before it for
the last time in farewell and confiding adoration. . . .

Oh, gentle emotions, soft sounds, kindness and calming of
the deeply-moved soul, melting joy of the first feelings of
love,—where are ye, where are ye?

VIII

On the following morning, when I went downstairs to tea,
my mother scolded me,—although less than I had anticipated,—and made me narrate how I had spent the preceding evening. I answered her in few words, omitting many particulars and endeavoring to impart to my narrative the most
innocent of aspects.

"Nevertheless, they are not people *comme il faut,*" —remarked my mother;—"and I do not wish thee to run after
them, instead of preparing thyself for the examination,
and occupying thyself."

As I knew that my mother's anxiety was confined to these
few words, I did not consider it necessary to make her any
reply; but after tea my father linked his arm in mine, and be-
taking himself to the garden with me, made me tell him
everything I had done and seen at the Zasyekins'.

My father possessed a strange influence over me, and
our relations were strange. He paid hardly any attention to
my education, but he never wounded me; he respected my
liberty—he was even, if I may so express it, courteous to me

. . . only, he did not allow me to get close to him. I loved him, I admired him; he seemed to me a model man; and great heavens! how passionately attached to him I should have been, had I not constantly felt his hand warding me off! On the other hand, when he wished, he understood how to evoke in me, instantaneously, with one word, one movement, unbounded confidence in him. My soul opened, I chatted with him as with an intelligent friend, as with an indulgent preceptor . . . then, with equal suddenness, he abandoned me, and again his hand repulsed me, caressingly and softly, but repulsed nevertheless.

Sometimes a fit of mirth came over him, and then he was ready to frolic and play with me like a boy (he was fond of every sort of energetic bodily exercise); once—only once —did he caress me with so much tenderness that I came near bursting into tears. . . . But his mirth and tenderness also vanished without leaving a trace, and what had taken place between us gave me no hopes for the future; it was just as though I had seen it all in a dream. I used to stand and scrutinize his clever, handsome, brilliant face . . . and my heart would begin to quiver, and my whole being would yearn toward him, . . . and he would seem to feel what was going on within me, and would pat me on the cheek in passing— and either go away, or begin to occupy himself with something, or suddenly freeze all over,—as he alone knew how to freeze,—and I would immediately shrivel up and grow frigid also. His rare fits of affection for me were never called forth by my speechless but intelligible entreaties; they always came upon him without warning. When meditating, in after years, upon my father's character, I came to the conclusion that he did not care for me or for family life; he loved something different, and enjoyed that other thing to the full. "Seize what thou canst thyself, and do not give thyself into any one's power; the whole art of life consists in belonging to one's self,"—he said to me once. On another occasion I, in my capacity of a young democrat, launched out in his presence into arguments about liberty (he was what I called "kind" that day; at such times one could say whatever one liked to him).—"Liberty,"—he repeated,—"but dost thou know what can give a man liberty?"

"What?"

"Will, his own will, and the power which it gives is better than liberty. Learn to will, and thou wilt be free, and wilt command."

My father wished, first of all and most of all, to enjoy life—and he did enjoy life. . . . Perhaps he had a presentiment that he was not fated long to take advantage of the "art" of living: he died at the age of forty-two.

I described to my father in detail my visit to the Zasyekins. He listened to me half-attentively, half-abstractedly, as he sat on the bench and drew figures on the sand with the tip of his riding-whip. Now and then he laughed, glanced at me in a brilliant, amused sort of way, and spurred me on by brief questions and exclamations. At first I could not bring myself even to utter Zinaida's name, but I could not hold out, and began to laud her. My father still continued to laugh. Then he became thoughtful, dropped his eyes and rose to his feet.

I recalled the fact that, as he came out of the house, he had given orders that his horse should be saddled. He was a capital rider, and knew much better how to tame the wildest horses than did Mr. Rarey.

"Shall I ride with thee, papa?"—I asked him.

"No,"—he replied, and his face assumed its habitual indifferently-caressing expression.—"Go alone, if thou wishest; but tell the coachman that I shall not go."

He turned his back on me and walked swiftly away. I followed him with my eyes, until he disappeared beyond the gate. I saw his hat moving along the fence; he went into the Zasyekins' house.

He remained with them no more than an hour, but immediately thereafter went off to town and did not return home until evening.

After dinner I went to the Zasyekins' myself. I found no one in the drawing-room but the old Princess. When she saw me, she scratched her head under her cap with the end of her knitting-needle, and suddenly asked me: would I copy a petition for her?

"With pleasure,"—I replied, and sat down on the edge of a chair.

"Only look out, and see that you make the letters as large as possible,"—said the Princess, handing me a sheet of paper scrawled over in a slovenly manner:—"and couldn't you do it today, my dear fellow?"

"I will copy it this very day, madam."

The door of the adjoining room opened a mere crack and Zinaida's face showed itself in the aperture,—pale, thoughtful, with hair thrown carelessly back. She stared at me with her large, cold eyes, and softly shut the door.

"Zina,—hey there, Zina!"—said the old woman. Zinaida did not answer. I carried away the old woman's petition, and sat over it the whole evening.

IX

My "passion" began with that day. I remember that I then felt something of that which a man must feel when he enters the service: I had already ceased to be a young lad; I was in love. I have said that my passion dated from that day; I might have added that my sufferings also dated from that day. I languished when absent from Zinaida; my mind would not work, everything fell from my hands; I thought intently of her for days together. . . . I languished . . . but in her presence I was no more at ease. I was jealous, I recognized my insignificance, I stupidly sulked and stupidly fawned; and nevertheless, an irresistible force drew me to her and every time I stepped across the threshold of her room, it was with an involuntary thrill of happiness. Zinaida immediately divined that I had fallen in love with her, and I never thought of concealing the fact; she mocked at my passion, played tricks on me, petted and tormented me. It is sweet to be the sole source, the autocratic and irresponsible cause of the greatest joys and the profoundest woe to another person, and I was like soft wax in Zinaida's hands. However, I was not the only one who was in love with her; all the men who were in the habit of visiting her house were crazy over her, and she kept them all in a leash at her feet. It amused her to arouse in them now hopes, now fears, to twist them about at her caprice—(she called it, "knocking people against one another"),—and they never thought of resisting, and willingly submitted to her. In all her vivacious and beautiful being there was a certain peculiarly bewitching mixture of guilefulness and heedlessness, of artificiality and simplicity, of tranquillity and playfulness; over everything she did or said, over her every movement, hovered a light, delicate charm, and an original sparkling force made itself felt in everything. And her face was incessantly changing and sparkling also; it expressed almost simultaneously derision, pensiveness, and passion. The most varied emotions, light, fleeting as the shadows of the clouds on a sunny, windy day, kept flitting over her eyes and lips.

Every one of her adorers was necessary to her. Byelovzoroff, whom she sometimes called "my wild beast," and sometimes simply "my own," would gladly have flung himself into the fire for her; without trusting to his mental capacities and other merits, he kept proposing that he should marry her, and hinting that the others were merely talking idly. Maidanoff responded to the poetical chords of her soul: a rather cold man, as nearly all writers are, he assured her with intense force—and perhaps himself also—that he adored her. He sang her praises in interminable verses and read them to her with an unnatural and a genuine sort of enthusiasm. And she was interested in him and jeered lightly at him; she did not believe in him greatly, and after listening to his effusions she made him read Pushkin, in order, as she said, to purify the air. Lushin, the sneering doctor, who was cynical in speech, knew her best of all and loved her best of all, although he abused her to her face and behind her back. She respected him, but would not let him go, and sometimes, with a peculiar, malicious pleasure, made him feel that he was in her hands. "I am a coquette, I am heartless. I have the nature of an actress," she said to him one day in my presence; "and 'tis well! So give me your hand and I will stick a pin into it, and you will feel ashamed before this young man, and it will hurt you; but nevertheless, Mr. Upright Man, you will be so good as to laugh." Lushin flushed crimson, turned away and bit his lips, but ended by putting out his hand. She pricked it, and he actually did break out laughing . . . and she laughed also, thrusting the pin in pretty deeply and gazing into his eyes while he vainly endeavored to glance aside. . . .

I understood least of all the relations existing between Zinaida and Count Malevsky. That he was handsome, adroit, and clever even I felt, but the presence in him of some false, dubious element, was palpable even to me, a lad of sixteen, and I was amazed that Zinaida did not notice it. But perhaps she did detect that false element and it did not repel her. An irregular education, strange acquaintances, the constant presence of her mother, the poverty and disorder in the house—all this, beginning with the very freedom which the young girl enjoyed, together with the consciousness of her own superiority to the people who surrounded her, had developed in her a certain half-scornful carelessness and lack of exaction. No matter what happened—whether Vonifaty came to report that there was no sugar, or some wretched bit of gossip came to light, or the visitors got into a quarrel among themselves, she merely shook her curls, and said: "Nonsense!"—and grieved very little over it.

On the contrary, all my blood would begin to seethe when Malevsky would approach her, swaying his body cunningly like a fox, lean elegantly over the back of her chair and begin to whisper in her ear with a conceited and challenging smile, while she would fold her arms on her breast, gaze attentively at him and smile also, shaking her head the while.

"What possesses you to receive Malevsky?"—I asked her one day.

"Why, he has such handsome eyes,"—she replied.—"But that is no business of yours."

"You are not to think that I am in love with him,"—she said to me on another occasion.—"No; I cannot love people upon whom I am forced to look down. I must have some one who can subdue me. . . . And I shall not hit upon such an one, for God is merciful! I shall not spare any one who falls into my paws—no, no!"

"Do you mean to say that you will never fall in love?"

"And how about you? Don't I love you?"—she said, tapping me on the nose with the tip of her glove.

Yes, Zinaida made great fun of me. For the space of three weeks I saw her every day; and what was there that she did not do to me! She came to us rarely, but I did not regret that; in our house she was converted into a young lady, a Princess,—and I avoided her. I was afraid of betraying myself to my mother; she was not at all well disposed toward Zinaida, and kept a disagreeable watch on us. I was not so much afraid of my father; he did not appear to notice me, and talked little with her, but that little in a peculiarly clever and significant manner. I ceased to work, to read; I even ceased to stroll about the environs and to ride on horseback. Like a beetle tied by the leg, I hovered incessantly around the beloved wing; I believe I would have liked to remain there forever . . . but that was impossible. My mother grumbled at me, and sometimes Zinaida herself drove me out. On such occasions I shut myself up in my own room, or walked off to the very end of the garden, climbed upon the sound remnant of a tall stone hothouse, and dangling my legs over the wall, I sat there for hours and stared,—stared without seeing anything. White butterflies lazily flitted among the nettles beside me; an audacious sparrow perched not far off on the half-demolished red bricks and twittered in an irritating manner, incessantly twisting his whole body about and spreading out his tail; the still distrustful crows now and then emitted a caw, as they sat high, high above me on the naked crest of a birch-tree; the sun and the wind played softly through its sparse branches; the chiming of the bells, calm and melancholy, at the Don Monastery was wafted to me now and then,—and I sat on, gazing and listening, and became filled with a certain nameless sensation which embraced everything: sadness and joy, and a presentiment of the future, and the desire and the fear of life. But I understood nothing at the time of all that which was fermenting within me, or I would have called it all by one name, the name of Zinaida.

But Zinaida continued to play with me as a cat plays with a mouse. Now she coquetted with me, and I grew agitated and melted with emotion; now she repulsed me, and I dared not approach her, dared not look at her.

I remember that she was very cold toward me for several days in succession and I thoroughly quailed, and when I timidly ran to the wing to see them, I tried to keep near the old Princess, despite the fact that she was scolding and screaming a great deal just at that time: her affairs connected with her notes of hand were going badly, and she had also had two scenes with the police-captain of the precinct.

One day I was walking through the garden, past the familiar fence, when I caught sight of Zinaida. Propped up on both arms, she was sitting motionless on the grass. I tried to withdraw cautiously, but she suddenly raised her head and made an imperious sign to me. I became petrified on the spot; I did not understand her the first time. She repeated her sign. I immediately sprang over the fence and ran joyfully to her; but she stopped me with a look and pointed to the path a couple of paces from her. In my confusion, not knowing what to do, I knelt down on the edge of the path. She was so pale, such bitter grief, such profound weariness were revealed in her every feature, that my heart contracted within me, and I involuntarily murmured: "What is the matter with you?"

Zinaida put out her hand, plucked a blade of grass, bit it, and tossed it away as far as she could.

"Do you love me very much?"—she inquired suddenly.— "Yes?"

I made no answer,—and what answer was there for me to make?

"Yes,"—she repeated, gazing at me as before.—"It is so.

They are the same eyes,"—she added, becoming pensive, and covering her face with her hands.—"Everything has become repulsive to me,"—she whispered;—"I would like to go to the end of the world; I cannot endure this, I cannot reconcile myself. . . . And what is in store for me? . . . Akh, I am heavy at heart . . . my God, how heavy at heart!"

"Why?"—I timidly inquired

Zinaida did not answer me and merely shrugged her shoulders. I continued to kneel and to gaze at her with profound melancholy. Every word of hers fairly cut me to the heart. At that moment, I think I would willingly have given my life to keep her from grieving. I gazed at her, and nevertheless, not understanding why she was heavy at heart, I vividly pictured to myself how, in a fit of uncontrollable sorrow, she had suddenly gone into the garden, and had fallen on the earth, as though she had been mowed down. All around was bright and green; the breeze was rustling in the foliage of the trees, now and then rocking a branch of raspberry over Zinaida's head. Doves were cooing somewhere and the bees were humming as they flew low over the scanty grass. Overhead the sky shone blue,—but I was so sad. . . .

"Recite some poetry to me,"—said Zinaida in a low voice, leaning on her elbow.—"I like to hear you recite verses. You make them go in a sing-song, but that does not matter, it is youthful. Recite to me: 'On the Hills of Georgia.'—Only, sit down first."

I sat down and recited, "On the Hills of Georgia."

" 'That it is impossible not to love,' "—repeated Zinaida. —"That is why poetry is so nice; it says to us that which does not exist, and which is not only better than what does exist, but even more like the truth. . . . 'That it is impossible not to love'?—I would like to, but cannot!"—Again she fell silent for a space, then suddenly started and rose to her feet. —"Come along, Maidanoff is sitting with mamma; he brought his poem to me, but I left him. He also is embittered now . . . how can it be helped? Some day you will find out . . . but you must not be angry with me!"

Zinaida hastily squeezed my hand, and ran on ahead. We returned to the wing. Maidanoff set to reading us his poem of "The Murderer," which had only just been printed, but I did not listen. He shrieked out his four-footed iambics in a sing-song voice; the rhymes alternated and jingled like sleigh-bells, hollow and loud; but I kept staring all the while at Zinaida, and striving to understand the meaning of her strange words.

> *"Or, perchance, a secret rival*
> *Has unexpectedly subjugated thee?"*

suddenly exclaimed Maidanoff through his nose—and my eyes and Zinaida's met. She dropped hers and blushed faintly. I saw that she was blushing, and turned cold with fright. I had been jealous before, but only at that moment did the thought that she had fallen in love flash through my mind. "My God! She is in love!"

X

My real tortures began from that moment. I cudgelled my brains, I pondered and pondered again, and watched Zinaida importunately, but secretly, as far as possible. A change had taken place in her, that was evident. She took to going off alone to walk, and walked a long while. Sometimes she did not show herself to her visitors; she sat for hours together in her chamber. This had not been her habit hitherto. Suddenly I became—or it seemed to me that I became—extremely penetrating. "Is it he? Or is it not he?"—I asked myself, as in trepidation I mentally ran from one of her admirers to another. Count Malevsky (although I felt ashamed to admit it for Zinaida's sake) privately seemed to me more dangerous than the others.

My powers of observation extended no further than the end of my own nose, and my dissimulation probably failed to deceive any one; at all events, Doctor Lushin speedily saw through me. Moreover, he also had undergone a change of late; he had grown thin, he laughed as frequently as ever, but somehow it was in a duller, more spiteful, a briefer way; —an involuntary, nervous irritability had replaced his former light irony and feigned cynicism.

"Why are you forever tagging on here, young man?"— he said to me one day, when he was left alone with me in the Zasyekins' drawing-room. (The young Princess had not yet returned from her stroll and the shrill voice of the old Princess was resounding in the upper story; she was wrangling with her maid.)—"You ought to be studying your lessons, working while you are young;—but instead of that, what are you doing?"

"You cannot tell whether I work at home,"—I retorted not without arrogance, but also not without confusion.

"Much work you do! That's not what you have in your head. Well, I will not dispute . . . at your age, that is in the natural order of things. But your choice is far from a happy one. Can't you see what sort of a house this is?"

"I do not understand you,"—I remarked.

"You don't understand me? So much the worse for you. I regard it as my duty to warn you. Fellows like me, old bachelors, may sit here: what harm will it do us? We are a hardened lot. You can't pierce our hide, but your skin is still tender; the air here is injurious for you,—believe me, you may become infected."

"How so?"

"Because you may. Are you healthy now? Are you in a normal condition? Is what you are feeling useful to you, good for you?"

"But what am I feeling?"—said I;—and in my secret soul I admitted that the doctor was right.

"Eh, young man, young man,"—pursued the doctor, with an expression as though something extremely insulting to me were contained in those two words;—"there's no use in your dissimulating, for what you have in your soul you still show in your face, thank God! But what's the use of arguing? I would not come hither myself, if . . ." (the doctor set his teeth) . . . "if I were not such an eccentric fellow. Only this is what amazes me—how you, with your intelligence, can fail to see what is going on around you."

"But what is going on?"—I interposed, pricking up my ears.

The doctor looked at me with a sort of sneering compassion.

"A nice person I am,"—said he, as though speaking to himself.—"What possessed me to say that to him. In a word,"—he added, raising his voice,—"I repeat to you: the atmosphere here is not good for you. You find it pleasant here, and no wonder! And the scent of a hot-house is pleasant also—but one cannot live in it! Hey! hearken to me,—set to work again on Kadianoff."

The old Princess entered and began to complain to the doctor of toothache. Then Zinaida made her appearance.

"Here,"—added the old Princess,—"scold her, doctor, do. She drinks iced water all day long; is that healthy for her, with her weak chest?"

"Why do you do that?"—inquired Lushin.

"But what result can it have?"

"What result? You may take cold and die."

"Really? Is it possible? Well, all right—that just suits me!"

"You don't say so!"—growled the doctor. The old Princess went away.

"I do say so,"—retorted Zinaida.—"Is living such a cheerful thing? Look about you . . . Well—is it nice? Or do you think that I do not understand it, do not feel it? It affords me pleasure to drink iced water, and you can seriously assure me that such a life is worth too much for me to imperil it for a moment's pleasure—I do not speak of happiness."

"Well, yes,"—remarked Lushin:—"caprice and independence. . . . Those two words sum you up completely; your whole nature lies in those two words."

Zinaida burst into a nervous laugh.

"You're too late by one mail, my dear doctor. You observe badly; you are falling behind.—Put on your spectacles.—I am in no mood for caprices now; how jolly to play pranks on you or on myself!—and as for independence. . . . M'sieu Voldemar,"—added Zinaida, suddenly stamping her foot,—"don't wear a melancholy face. I cannot endure to have people commiserating me."—She hastily withdrew.

"This atmosphere is injurious, injurious to you, young man,"—said Lushin to me once more.

XI

On the evening of that same day the customary visitors assembled at the Zasyekins'; I was among the number.

The conversation turned on Maidanoff's poem; Zinaida candidly praised it.—"But do you know what?" she said:—"If I were a poet, I would select other subjects. Perhaps this is all nonsense, but strange thoughts sometimes come into my head, especially when I am wakeful toward morning, when the sky is beginning to turn pink and grey.—I would, for example . . . You will not laugh at me?"

"No! No!"—we all exclaimed with one voice.

"I would depict,"—she went on, crossing her arms on her breast, and turning her eyes aside,—"a whole company of young girls, by night, in a big boat, on a tranquil river. The moon is shining, and they are all in white and wear garlands of white flowers, and they are singing, you know, something in the nature of a hymn."

"I understand, I understand, go on,"—said Maidanoff significantly and dreamily.

"Suddenly there is a noise—laughter, torches, tambourines on the shore. . . . It is a throng of bacchantes running with songs and outcries. It is your business to draw the picture, Mr. Poet . . . only I would like to have the torches red and very smoky, and that the eyes of the bacchantes should gleam beneath their wreaths, and that the wreaths should be dark. Don't forget also tiger-skins and cups—and gold, a great deal of gold."

"But where is the gold to be?" inquired Maidanoff, tossing back his lank hair and inflating his nostrils.

"Where? On the shoulders, the hands, the feet, everywhere. They say that in ancient times women wore golden rings on their ankles.—The bacchantes call the young girls in the boat to come to them. The girls have ceased to chant their hymn,—they cannot go on with it,—but they do not stir; the river drifts them to the shore. And now suddenly one of them rises quietly. . . . This must be well described: how she rises quietly in the moonlight, and how startled her companions are. . . . She has stepped over the edge of the boat, the bacchantes have surrounded her, they have dashed off into the night, into the gloom. . . . Present at this point smoke in clouds; and everything has become thoroughly confused. Nothing is to be heard but their whimpering, and her wreath has been left lying on the shore."

Zinaida ceased speaking. "Oh, she is in love!"—I thought again.

"Is that all?"—asked Maidanoff.

"That is all,"—she replied.

"That cannot be made the subject of an entire poem,"—he remarked pompously,—"but I will utilize your idea for some lyrical verses."

"In the romantic vein?"—asked Malevsky.

"Of course, in the romantic vein—in Byron's style."

"But in my opinion, Hugo is better than Byron,"—remarked the young Count, carelessly:—"he is more interesting."

"Hugo is a writer of the first class,"—rejoined Maidanoff, "and my friend Tonkosheeff, in his Spanish romance, 'El Trovador' . . ."

"Ah, that's the book with the question-marks turned upside down?"—interrupted Zinaida.

"Yes. That is the accepted custom among the Spaniards. I was about to say that Tonkosheeff. . . ."

"Come now! You will begin to wrangle again about classi-

cism and romanticism,"—Zinaida interrupted him again.—
"Let us rather play . . ."

"At forfeits?"—put in Lushin.

"No, forfeits is tiresome; but at comparisons." (This game
had been invented by Zinaida herself; some object was
named, and each person tried to compare it with something
or other, and the one who matched the thing with the best
comparison received a prize.) She went to the window. The
sun had just set; long, crimson clouds hung high aloft in
the sky.

"What are those clouds like?"—inquired Zinaida and, without waiting for our answers, she said:—"I think that they
resemble those crimson sails which were on Cleopatra's
golden ship, when she went to meet Antony. You were telling me about that not long ago, do you remember, Maidanoff?"

All of us, like Polonius in "Hamlet," decided that the
clouds reminded us precisely of those sails, and that none of
us could find a better comparison.

"And how old was Antony at that time?"—asked Zinaida.

"He was assuredly still a young man,"—remarked Malevsky.

"Yes, he was young,"—assented Maidanoff confidently.

"Excuse me,"—exclaimed Lushin,—"he was over forty
years of age."

"Over forty years of age,"—repeated Zinaida, darting a
swift glance at him. . . .

I soon went home.—"She is in love," my lips whispered involuntarily. . . . "But with whom?"

XII

The days passed by. Zinaida grew more and more strange,
more and more incomprehensible. One day I entered her
house and found her sitting on a straw-bottomed chair, with
her head pressed against the sharp edge of a table. She
straightened up . . . her face was again all bathed in tears.

"Ah! It's you!"—she said, with a harsh grimace.—"Come
hither."

I went up to her: she laid her hand on my head and, suddenly seizing me by the hair, began to pull it.

"It hurts" . . . I said at last.

"Ah! It hurts! And doesn't it hurt me? Doesn't it hurt
me?"—she repeated.

"Ai!"—she suddenly cried, perceiving that she had pulled out a small tuft of my hair.—"What have I done? Poor M'sieu Voldemar!" She carefully straightened out the hairs she had plucked out, wound them round her finger, and twisted them into a ring.

"I will put your hair in my locket and wear it,"—she said, and tears glistened in her eyes.—"Perhaps that will comfort you a little . . . but now, good-bye."

I returned home and found an unpleasant state of things there. A scene was in progress between my father and my mother; she was upbraiding him for something or other, while he, according to his wont, was maintaining a cold, polite silence—and speedily went away. I could not hear what my mother was talking about, neither did I care to know: I remember only, that, at the conclusion of the scene, she ordered me to be called to her boudoir, and expressed herself with great dissatisfaction about my frequent visits at the house of the old Princess, who was, according to her assertions, *une femme capable de tout.* I kissed her hand (I always did that when I wanted to put an end to the conversation), and went off to my own room. Zinaida's tears had completely discomfited me; I positively did not know what to think, and was ready to cry myself: I was still a child, in spite of my sixteen years. I thought no more of Malevsky, although Byelovzoroff became more and more menacing every day, and glared at the shifty Count like a wolf at a sheep; but I was not thinking of anything or of anybody. I lost myself in conjectures and kept seeking isolated spots. I took a special fancy to the ruins of the hothouse. I could clamber up on the high wall, seat myself, and sit there such an unhappy, lonely, and sad youth that I felt sorry for myself—and how delightful those mournful sensations were, how I gloated over them! . . .

One day, I was sitting thus on the wall, gazing off into the distance and listening to the chiming of the bells . . . when suddenly something ran over me—not a breeze exactly, not a shiver, but something resembling a breath, the consciousness of some one's proximity. . . . I dropped my eyes. Below me, in a light grey gown, with a pink parasol on her shoulder, Zinaida was walking hastily along the road. She saw me, halted, and, pushing up the brim of her straw hat, raised her velvety eyes to mine.

"What are you doing there, on such a height?"—she asked me, with a strange sort of smile.—"There now,"—she went on,—"you are always declaring that you love me—jump down to me here on the road if you really do love me."

Before the words were well out of Zinaida's mouth I had flown down, exactly as though some one had given me a push from behind. The wall was about two fathoms high. I landed on the ground with my feet, but the shock was so violent that I could not retain my balance; I fell, and lost consciousness for a moment. When I came to myself I felt, without opening my eyes, that Zinaida was by my side.—"My dear boy,"—she was saying, as she bent over me—and tender anxiety was audible in her voice—"how couldst thou do that, how couldst thou obey? . . . I love thee . . . rise."

Her breast was heaving beside me, her hands were touching my head, and suddenly—what were my sensations then! —her soft, fresh lips began to cover my whole face with kisses . . . they touched my lips. . . . But at this point Zinaida probably divined from the expression of my face that I had already recovered consciousness, although I still did not open my eyes—and swiftly rising to her feet, she said:— "Come, get up, you rogue, you foolish fellow! Why do you lie there in the dust?"—I got up.

"Give me my parasol,"—said Zinaida.—"I have thrown it somewhere; and don't look at me like that . . . what nonsense is this? You are hurt? You have burned yourself with the nettles, I suppose. Don't look at me like that, I tell you. . . . Why, he understands nothing, he doesn't answer me," —she added, as though speaking to herself. . . . "Go home, M'sieu Voldemar, brush yourself off, and don't dare to follow me—if you do I shall be very angry, and I shall never again . . .."

She did not finish her speech and walked briskly away, while I sat down by the roadside . . . my legs would not support me. The nettles had stung my hands, my back ached, and my head was reeling; but the sensation of beatitude which I then experienced has never since been repeated in my life. It hung like a sweet pain in all my limbs and broke out at last in rapturous leaps and exclamations. As a matter of fact, I was still a child.

XIII

I was so happy and proud all that day; I preserved so vividly on my visage the feeling of Zinaida's kisses; I recalled her every word with such ecstasy; I so cherished my unexpected happiness that I even became frightened; I did not even wish to see her who was the cause of those new sensations. It seemed to me that I could ask nothing more of Fate, that now I must "take and draw a deep breath for the last time, and die." On the other hand, when I set off for the wing next day, I felt a great agitation, which I vainly endeavored to conceal beneath the discreet facial ease suitable for a man who wishes to let it be understood that he knows how to keep a secret. Zinaida received me very simply, without any emotion, merely shaking her finger at me and asking: Had I any bruises? All my discreet ease of manner and mysteriousness instantly disappeared, and along with them my agitation. Of course I had not expected anything in particular, but Zinaida's composure acted on me like a dash of cold water. I understood that I was a child in her eyes—and my heart waxed very heavy! Zinaida paced to and fro in the room, smiling swiftly every time she glanced at me; but her thoughts were far away, I saw that clearly. . . . "Shall I allude to what happened yesterday myself,"—I thought;—"shall I ask her where she was going in such haste, in order to find out, definitively?" . . . but I merely waved my hand in despair and sat down in a corner.

Byelovzoroff entered; I was delighted to see him.

"I have not found you a gentle saddle-horse,"—he began in a surly tone;—"Freitag vouches to me for one—but I am not convinced. I am afraid."

"Of what are you afraid, allow me to inquire?" asked Zinaida.

"Of what? Why, you don't know how to ride. God forbid that any accident should happen! And what has put that freak into your head?"

"Come, that's my affair, M'sieu my wild beast. In that case, I will ask Piotr Vasilievitch" . . . (My father was called Piotr Vasilievitch . . . I was amazed that she should mention his name so lightly and freely, exactly as though she were convinced of his readiness to serve her.)

"You don't say so!"—retorted Byelovzoroff.—"Is it with him that you wish to ride?"

"With him or some one else,—that makes no difference to you. Only not with you."

"Not with me,"—said Byelovzoroff.—"As you like. What does it matter? I will get you the horse."

"But see to it that it is not a cow-like beast. I warn you in advance that I mean to gallop."

"Gallop, if you wish. . . . But is it with Malevsky that you are going to ride?"

"And why shouldn't I ride with him, warrior? Come, quiet down. I'll take you too. You know that for me Malevsky is now—fie!"—She shook her head.

"You say that just to console me,"—growled Byelovzoroff.

Zinaida narrowed her eyes.—"Does that console you? . . . oh . . . oh . . . oh . . . warrior!"—she said at last, as though unable to find any other word.—"And would you like to ride with us, M'sieu Voldemar?"

"I'm not fond of riding . . . in a large party," . . . I muttered without raising my eyes.

"You prefer a *tête-à-tête?* . . . Well, everyone to his taste,"—she said, with a sigh.—"But go, Byelovzoroff, make an effort. I want the horse for tomorrow."

"Yes; but where am I to get the money?"—interposed the old Princess.

Zinaida frowned.

"I am not asking any from you; Byelovzoroff will trust me."

"He will, he will," . . . grumbled the old Princess—and suddenly screamed at the top of her voice:—"Dunyashka!"

"*Maman*, I made you a present of a bell,"—remarked the young Princess.

"Dunyashka!"—repeated the old woman.

Byelovzoroff bowed himself out; I went out with him. Zinaida did not detain me.

XIV

I rose early the next morning, cut myself a staff, and went off beyond the city barrier. "I'll have a walk and banish my grief,"—I said to myself. It was a beautiful day, brilliant but not too hot; a cheerful, fresh breeze was blowing over the earth and rustling and playing moderately, keeping in constant motion and agitating nothing. For a long time I roamed about on the hills and in the forests. I did not feel happy; I had left home with the intention of surrendering myself to melancholy;—but youth, the fine weather, the fresh air, the diversion of brisk pedestrian exercise, the delight of lying in solitude on the thick grass, produced their effect; the memory of those unforgettable words, of those kisses, again thrust themselves into my soul. It was pleasant to me to think that

Zinaida could not, nevertheless, fail to do justice to my decision, to my heroism. . . . "Others are better for her than I,"—I thought:—"so be it! On the other hand, the others only say what they will do, but I have done it! And what else am I capable of doing for her?"—My imagination began to ferment. I began to picture to myself how I would save her from the hands of enemies; how, all bathed in blood, I would wrest her out of prison; how I would die at her feet. I recalled a picture which hung in our drawing-room of Malek-Adel carrying off Matilda—and thereupon became engrossed in the appearance of a big, speckled woodpecker which was busily ascending the slender trunk of a birch-tree, and uneasily peering out from behind it, now on the right, now on the left, like a musician from behind the neck of his bass-viol.

Then I began to sing: "Not the white snows,"—and ran off into the romance which was well known at that period, "I will await thee when the playful breeze"; then I began to recite aloud Ermak's invocation to the stars in Khomyakoff's tragedy; I tried to compose something in a sentimental vein; I even thought out the line wherewith the whole poem was to conclude: "Oh, Zinaida! Zinaida!"—But it came to nothing. Meanwhile, dinner-time was approaching. I descended into the valley; a narrow, sandy path wound through it and led toward the town. I strolled along that path. . . . The dull trampling of horses' hoofs resounded behind me. I glanced round, involuntarily came to a standstill and pulled off my cap. I beheld my father and Zinaida. They were riding side by side. My father was saying something to her, bending his whole body toward her, and resting his hand on the neck of her horse; he was smiling. Zinaida was listening to him in silence, with her eyes severely downcast and lips compressed. At first I saw only them; it was not until several moments later that Byelovzoroff made his appearance from round a turn in the valley, dressed in hussar uniform with pelisse, and mounted on a foam-flecked black horse. The good steed was tossing his head, snorting and curvetting; the rider was both reining him in and spurring him on. I stepped aside. My father gathered up his reins and moved away from Zinaida; she slowly raised her eyes to his—and both set off at a gallop. . . . Byelovzoroff dashed headlong after them with clanking sword. "He is as red as a crab,"—I thought,—"and she. . . . Why is she so pale? She has been riding the whole morning—and yet she is pale?"

I redoubled my pace and managed to reach home just

before dinner. My father was already sitting, re-dressed, well-washed and fresh, beside my mother's arm-chair, and reading aloud to her in his even, sonorous voice, the feuilleton of the *Journal des Débats* but my mother was listening to him inattentively and, on catching sight of me, inquired where I had been all day, adding, that she did not like to have me prowling about God only knew where and God only knew with whom. "But I have been walking alone,"—I was on the point of replying; but I glanced at my father and for some reason or other held my peace.

XV

During the course of the next five or six days I hardly saw Zinaida; she gave it out that she was ill, which did not, however prevent the habitual visitors from presenting themselves at the wing—"to take their turn in attendance,"—as they expressed it;—all except Maidanoff, who immediately became dispirited as soon as he had no opportunity to go into raptures. Byelovzoroff sat morosely in a corner, all tightly buttoned up and red in the face; on Count Malevsky's delicate visage hovered constantly a sort of evil smile; he really had fallen into disfavor with Zinaida and listened with particular pains to the old Princess, and drove with her to the Governor-General's in a hired carriage. But this trip proved unsuccessful and even resulted in an unpleasantness for Malevsky: he was reminded of some row with certain Puteisk officers, and was compelled, in self-justification, to say that he was inexperienced at the time. Lushin came twice a day, but did not remain long. I was somewhat afraid of him after our last explanation and, at the same time, I felt a sincere attachment for him. One day he went for a stroll with me in the Neskutchny Park, was very good-natured and amiable, imparted to me the names and properties of various plants and flowers, and suddenly exclaimed—without rhyme or reason, as the saying is—as he smote himself on the brow: "And I, like a fool, thought she was a coquette! Evidently, it is sweet to sacrifice one's self—for some people!"

"What do you mean to say by that?"—I asked.

"I don't mean to say anything to you,"—returned Lushin, abruptly.

Zinaida avoided me; my appearance—I could not but perceive the fact—produced an unpleasant impression on her.

She involuntarily turned away from me . . . involuntarily; that was what was bitter, that was what broke my heart! But there was no help for it and I tried to keep out of her sight and only stand guard over her from a distance, in which I was not always successful. As before, something incomprehensible was taking place with her; her face had become different—she was altogether a different person. I was particularly struck by the change which had taken place in her on a certain warm, tranquil evening. I was sitting on a low bench under a wide-spreading elder-bush; I loved that little nook; the window of Zinaida's chamber was visible thence. I was sitting there; over my head, in the darkened foliage, a tiny bird was rummaging fussily about; a great cat with outstretched back had stolen into the garden, and the first beetles were booming heavily in the air, which was still transparent although no longer light. I sat there and stared at the window, and waited to see whether some one would not open it: and, in fact, it did open, and Zinaida made her appearance in it. She wore a white gown, and she herself—her face, her shoulders and her hands—was pale to whiteness. She remained for a long time motionless, and for a long time stared without moving, straight in front of her from beneath her contracted brows. I did not recognize that look in her. Then she clasped her hands very, very tightly, raised them to her lips, to her forehead—and suddenly, unlocking her fingers, pushed her hair away from her ears, shook it back and, throwing her head downward from above with a certain decisiveness, she shut the window with a bang.

Two days later she met me in the park. I tried to step aside, but she stopped me.

"Give me your hand,"—she said to me, with her former affection.—"It is a long time since you and I have had a chat."

I looked at her; her eyes were beaming softly and her face was smiling, as though athwart a mist.

"Are you still ailing?"—I asked her.

"No, everything has passed off now,"—she replied, breaking off a small, red rose.—"I am a little tired, but that will pass off also."

"And will you be once more the same as you used to be?" —I queried.

Zinaida raised the rose to her face, and it seemed to me as though the reflection of the brilliant petals fell upon her cheeks.—"Have I changed?"—she asked me.

"Yes, you have changed,"—I replied in a low voice.

"I was cold toward you,—I know that,"—began Zinaida; —"but you must not pay any heed to that. . . . I could not do otherwise. . . . Come, what's the use of talking about that?"

"You do not want me to love you—that's what!" I exclaimed gloomily, with involuntary impetuosity.

"Yes, love me, but not as before."

"How then?"

"Let us be friends,—that is how!"—Zinaida allowed me to smell of the rose.—"Listen; I am much older than you, you know—I might be your aunt, really; well, if not your aunt, then your elder sister. While you . . ."

"I am a child to you," I interrupted her.

"Well, yes, you are a child, but a dear, good, clever child, of whom I am very fond. Do you know what? I will appoint you to the post of my page from this day forth; and you are not to forget that pages must not be separated from their mistress. Here is a token of your new dignity for you,"—she added, sticking the rose into the button-hole of my round-jacket; "a token of our favor toward you."

"I have received many favors from you in the past,"—I murmured.

"Ah!"—said Zinaida, and darting a sidelong glance at me. —"What a memory you have! Well? And I am ready now also . . ."

And bending toward me, she imprinted on my brow a pure, calm kiss.

I only stared at her—but she turned away and, saying,— "Follow me, my page,"—walked to the wing. I followed her —and was in a constant state of bewilderment.—"Is it possible,"—I thought,—"that this gentle, sensible young girl is that same Zinaida whom I used to know?"—And her very walk seemed to me more quiet, her whole figure more majestic, more graceful. . . .

And, my God! with what fresh violence did love flame up within me!

XVI

After dinner the visitors were assembled again in the wing, and the young Princess came out to them. The whole company was present, in full force, as on that first evening, never

to be forgotten by me: even Nirmatzky had dragged himself thither. Maidanoff had arrived earlier than all the rest; he had brought some new verses. The game of forfeits began again, but this time without the strange sallies, without pranks and uproar; the gipsy element had vanished. Zinaida gave a new mood to our gathering. I sat beside her, as a page should. Among other things, she proposed that the one whose forfeit was drawn should narrate his dream but this was not a success. The dreams turned out to be either uninteresting (Byelovzoroff had dreamed that he had fed his horse on carp, and that it had a wooden head), or unnatural, fictitious. Maidanoff regaled us with a complete novel; there were sepulchres and angels with harps, and burning lights and sounds wafted from afar. Zinaida did not allow him to finish. "If it is a question of invention,"—said she,—"then let each one relate something which is positively made up."
—Byelovzoroff had to speak first.

The young hussar became confused.—"I cannot invent anything!"—he exclaimed.

"What nonsense!"—interposed Zinaida.—"Come, imagine, for instance, that you are married, and tell us how you would pass the time with your wife. Would you lock her up?"

"I would."

"And would you sit with her yourself?"

"I certainly would sit with her myself."

"Very good. Well, and what if that bored her, and she betrayed you?"

"I would kill her."

"Just so. Well, now supposing that I were your wife, what would you do then?"

Byelovzoroff made no answer for a while.—"I would kill myself . . ."

Zinaida burst out laughing.—"I see that there's not much to be got out of you."

The second forfeit fell to Zinaida's share. She raised her eyes to the ceiling and meditated.—"See here,"—she began at last,—"this is what I have devised. . . . Imagine to yourselves a magnificent palace, a summer night, and a marvelous ball. This ball is given by the young Queen. Everywhere there are gold, marble, silk, lights, diamonds, flowers, the smoke of incense—all the whims of luxury."

"Do you love luxury?"—interrupted Lushin.

"Luxury is beautiful,"—she returned;—"I love everything that is beautiful."

"More than what is fine?"—he asked.

"That is difficult; somehow I don't understand. Don't bother me. So then, there is a magnificent ball. There are many guests, they are all young, very handsome, brave; all are desperately in love with the Queen."

"Are there no women among the guests?"—inquired Malevsky.

"No—or stay—yes, there are."

"Also very handsome?"

"Charming. But the men are all in love with the Queen. She is tall and slender; she wears a small gold diadem on her black hair."

I looked at Zinaida—and at that moment she seemed so far above us, her white forehead and her impassive eyebrows exhaled so much clear intelligence and such sovereignty, that I said to myself: "Thou thyself art that Queen!"

"All throng around her,"—pursued Zinaida;—"all lavish the most flattering speeches on her."

"And is she fond of flattery?"—asked Lushin.

"How intolerable! He is continually interrupting . . . Who does not like flattery?"

"One more final question,"—remarked Malevsky:—"Has the Queen a husband?"

"I have not thought about that. No, why should she have a husband?"

"Of course,"—assented Malevsky;—"why should she have a husband?"

"Silence!"—exclaimed, in English, Maidanoff, who spoke French badly.

"*Merci*,"—said Zinaida to him.—"So then, the Queen listens to those speeches, listens to the music, but does not look at a single one of the guests. Six windows are open from top to bottom, from ceiling to floor, and behind them are the dark sky with great stars and the dark garden with huge trees. The Queen gazes into the garden. There, near the trees is a fountain: it gleams white athwart the gloom—long, as long as a spectre. The Queen hears the quiet plashing of its waters in the midst of the conversation and the music. She gazes and thinks: 'All of you gentlemen are noble, clever, wealthy; you are all ready to die at my feet, I rule over you; . . . but yonder, by the side of the fountain, by the side of that plashing water, there is standing and waiting for me the man whom I love, who rules over me. He wears no rich garments, nor precious jewels; no one knows him; but he is waiting for me, and is convinced that I shall come—and I shall come, and there is no power in existence which can stop me when I wish to go to him and remain with him and lose myself with him yonder, in the gloom of the park, beneath the rustling of the trees, beneath the plashing of the fountain . . .' "

Zinaida ceased speaking.

"Is that an invention?"—asked Malevsky slyly.

Zinaida did not even glance at him.

"But what should we do, gentlemen,"—suddenly spoke up Lushin,—"if we were among the guests and knew about that lucky man by the fountain?"

"Stay, stay,"—interposed Zinaida:—"I myself will tell you what each one of you would do. You, Byelovzoroff, would challenge him to a duel; you, Maidanoff, would write an epigram on him. . . . But no—you do not know how to write epigrams; you would compose a long iambic poem on him, after the style of Barbier, and would insert your production in the *Telegraph*. You Nirmatzky, would borrow from him . . . no, you would lend him money on interest; you, doctor . . ." She paused. . . . "I really do not know about you, —what you would do."

"In my capacity of Court-physician," replied Lushin, "I would advise the Queen not to give balls when she did not feel in the mood for guests . . ."

"Perhaps you would be in the right. And you, Count?"

"And I?"—repeated Malevsky, with an evil smile.

"And you would offer him some poisoned sugar-plums."

Malevsky's face writhed a little and assumed for a moment a Jewish expression; but he immediately burst into a guffaw.

"As for you, M'sieu Voldemar . . ." went on Zinaida,— "but enough of this; let us play at some other game."

"M'sieu Voldemar, in his capacity of page to the Queen, would hold up her train when she ran off into the park,"— remarked Malevsky viciously.

I flared up, but Zinaida swiftly laid her hand on my shoulder and rising, said in a slightly tremulous voice:—"I have never given Your Radiance the right to be insolent, and therefore I beg that you will withdraw."—She pointed him to the door.

"Have mercy, Princess,"—mumbled Malevsky, turning pale all over.

"The Princess is right,"—exclaimed Byelovzoroff, rising to his feet also.

"By God! I never in the least expected this,"—went on Malevsky:—"I think there was nothing in my words which . . . I had no intention of offending you. . . . Forgive me."

Zinaida surveyed him with a cold glance, and smiled coldly.—"Remain, if you like,"—she said, with a careless wave of her hand.—"M'sieu Voldemar and I have taken offence without cause. You find it merry to jest. . . . I wish you well."

"Forgive me,"—repeated Malevsky once more; and I, recalling Zinaida's movement, thought again that a real queen could not have ordered an insolent man out of the room with more majesty.

The game of forfeits did not continue long after this little scene; all felt somewhat awkward, not so much in consequence of the scene itself as from another, not entirely defined, but oppressive sensation. No one alluded to it, but each one was conscious of its existence within himself and in his neighbor. Maidanoff recited to us all his poems—and Malevsky lauded them with exaggerated warmth.

"How hard he is trying to appear amiable now,"—Lushin whispered to me.

We soon dispersed. Zinaida had suddenly grown pensive; the old Princess sent word that she had a headache; Nirmatzky began to complain of his rheumatism. . . .

For a long time I could not get to sleep; Zinaida's narrative had impressed me.—"Is it possible that it contains a hint?"— I asked myself:—"and at whom was she hinting? And if there really is some one to hint about . . . what must I decide to do? No, no, it cannot be,"—I whispered, turning over from one burning cheek to the other. . . . But I called to mind the expression of Zinaida's face during her narration. . . . I called to mind the exclamation which had broken from Lushin in the Neskutchny Park, the sudden changes in her treatment of me—and lost myself in conjectures. "Who is he?" Those three words seemed to stand in front of my eyes, outlined in the darkness; a low-lying, ominous cloud seemed to be hanging over me—and I felt its pressure—and waited every moment for it to burst. I had grown used to many things of late; I had seen many things at the Zasyekins'; their disorderliness, tallow candle-ends, broken knives and forks, gloomy Vonifaty, the shabby maids, the manners of the old Princess herself,—all that strange life no longer surprised me. . . . But to that which I now dimly felt in

Zinaida I could not get used . . . "An adventuress,"—my mother had one day said concerning her. An adventuress—she, my idol, my divinity! That appellation seared me; I tried to escape from it by burrowing into my pillow; I raged—and at the same time, to what would not I have agreed, what would not I have given, if only I might be that happy mortal by the fountain! . . .

My blood grew hot and seethed within me. "A garden . . . a fountain," . . . I thought . . . "I will go into the garden." I dressed myself quickly and slipped out of the house. The night was dark, the trees were barely whispering; a quiet chill was descending from the sky, an odor of fennel was wafted from the vegetable-garden. I made the round of all the alleys; the light sound of my footsteps both disconcerted me and gave me courage; I halted, waiting and listening to hear how my heart was beating quickly and violently. At last I approached the fence and leaned against a slender post. All at once—or was it only my imagination?—a woman's figure flitted past a few paces distant from me. . . . I strained my eyes intently on the darkness; I held my breath. What was this? Was it footsteps that I heard or was it the thumping of my heart again?—"Who is here?"—I stammered in barely audible tones. What was that again? A suppressed laugh? . . . or a rustling in the leaves? . . . or a sigh close to my very ear? I was terrified. . . . "Who is here?"—I repeated, in a still lower voice.

The breeze began to flutter for a moment; a fiery band flashed across the sky; a star shot down.—"Is it Zinaída?"—I tried to ask, but the sound died on my lips. And suddenly everything became profoundly silent all around, as often happens in the middle of the night. . . . Even the katydids ceased to shrill in the trees; only a window rattled somewhere. I stood and stood, then returned to my chamber, to my cold bed. I felt a strange agitation—exactly as though I had gone to a tryst, and had remained alone, and had passed by someone else's happiness.

XVII

The next day I caught only a glimpse of Zinaída; she drove away somewhere with the old Princess in a hired carriage. On the other hand, I saw Lushin—who, however, barely deigned to bestow a greeting on me—and Malévsky. The young Count grinned and entered into conversation with me in friendly wise. Among all the visitors to the wing he alone had managed to effect an entrance to our house, and my mother had taken a fancy to him. My father did not favor him and treated him politely to the point of insult.

"Ah, *monsieur le page*,"—began Malevsky,—"I am very glad to meet you. What is your beauteous queen doing?"

His fresh, handsome face was so repulsive to me at that moment, and he looked at me with such a scornfully-playful stare, that I made him no answer whatsoever.

"Are you still in a bad humor?"—he went on.—"There is no occasion for it. It was not I, you know, who called you a page; and pages are chiefly with queens. But permit me to observe to you that you are fulfilling your duties badly."

"How so?"

"Pages ought to be inseparable from their sovereigns; pages ought to know everything that they do; they ought even to watch over them,"—he added, lowering his voice,— "day and night."

"What do you mean by that?"

"What do I mean? I think I have expressed myself plainly. Day—and night. It does not matter so much about the day; by day it is light and there are people about; but by night— that's exactly the time to expect a catastrophe. I advise you not to sleep o' nights and to watch, watch with all your might. Remember—in a garden, by night, near the fountain—that's where you must keep guard. You will thank me for this."

Malevsky laughed and turned his back on me. He did not, in all probability, attribute any special importance to what he had said to me; he bore the reputation of being a capital hand at mystification, and was renowned for his cleverness in fooling people at the masquerades, in which that almost un-conscious disposition to lie, wherewith his whole being was permeated, greatly aided him. . . . He had merely wished to tease me; but every word of his trickled like poison through all my veins.—The blood flew to my head.

"Ah! so that's it!"—I said to myself:—"good! So it was not for nothing that I felt drawn to the garden! That shall not be!" I exclaimed, smiting myself on the breast with my fist; although I really did not know what it was that I was determined not to permit.—"Whether Malevsky himself comes into the garden,"—I thought (perhaps he had blurted out a secret; he was insolent enough for that),—"or some-one else,"—(the fence of our vegetable-garden was very low and it cost no effort to climb over it)—"at any rate, it will be all the worse for the person whom I catch! I would not advise anyone to encounter me! I'll show the whole world and her, the traitress,"—(I actually called her a traitress)— "that I know how to avenge myself!"

I returned to my own room, took out of my writing-table a recently purchased English knife, felt of the sharp blade, and, knitting my brows, thrust it into my pocket with a cold and concentrated decision, exactly as though it was nothing remarkable for me to do such deeds, and this was not the first occasion. My heart swelled angrily within me and grew stony; I did not unbend my brows until nightfall and did not relax my lips, and kept striding back and forth, clutching the knife which had grown warm in my pocket, and preparing myself in advance for something terrible. These new, unprecedented emotions so engrossed and even cheered me, that I thought very little about Zinaida herself. There kept constantly flitting through my head Aleko, the young gipsy: [1]— "Where art thou going, handsome youth?—Lie down . . ." and then: "Thou'rt all with blood bespattered! . . . Oh, what is't that thou hast done? . . . Nothing!" With what a harsh smile I repeated that: that "Nothing!"

My father was not at home; but my mother, who for some time past had been in a state of almost constant, dull irritation, noticed my baleful aspect at supper, and said to me:— "What art thou sulking at, like a mouse at groats?"—I merely smiled patronisingly at her by way of reply and thought to myself: "If they only knew!"—The clock struck eleven; I went to my own room but did not undress; I was waiting for midnight; at last it struck.—" 'Tis time!"—I hissed between my teeth, and buttoning my coat to the throat and even turning up my sleeves I betook myself to the garden.

I had selected a place beforehand where I meant to stand on guard. At the end of the garden, at the spot where the fence, which separated our property from the Zasyekins', abutted on the party-wall, grew a solitary spruce-tree. Standing beneath its low, thick branches, I could see well, as far as the nocturnal gloom permitted, all that went on around; there also meandered a path which always seemed to me mysterious; like a serpent it wound under the fence, which at that point bore traces of clambering feet, and led to an arbor of dense acacias. I reached the spruce-tree, leaned against its trunk and began my watch.

The night was as tranquil as the preceding one had been;

[1] In Pushkin's poem, "The Gipsies."—TRANSLATOR.

but there were fewer storm-clouds in the sky, and the outlines of the bushes, even of the tall flowers, were more
plainly discernible. The first moments of waiting were wearisome, almost terrible. I had made up my mind to everything;
I was merely considering how I ought to act. Ought I to thunder out: "Who goes there? Halt! Confess—or die!"—or simply smite . . . Every sound, every noise and rustling seemed
to me significant, unusual. . . . I made ready. . . . I bent
forward. . . . But half an hour, an hour, elapsed; my blood
quieted down and turned cold; the consciousness that I was
doing all this in vain, that I was even somewhat ridiculous,
that Malevsky had been making fun of me, began to steal into
my soul. I abandoned my ambush and made the round of the
entire garden. As though expressly, not the slightest sound
was to be heard anywhere; everything was at rest; even our
dog was asleep, curled up in a ball at the gate. I climbed up
on the ruin of the hothouse, beheld before me the distant
plain, recalled my meeting with Zinaida, and became im-
mersed in meditation. . . .

I started. . . . I thought I heard the creak of an opening
door, then the light crackling of a broken twig. In two bounds
I had descended from the ruin—and stood petrified on the
spot. Swift, light but cautious footsteps were plainly audible
in the garden. They were coming toward me. "Here he is.
. . . Here he is, at last!"—darted through my heart. I convulsively jerked the knife out of my pocket, convulsively
opened it—red sparks whirled before my eyes, the hair stood
up on my head with fright and wrath. . . . The steps were
coming straight toward me—I bent over, and went to meet
them. . . . A man made his appearance. . . . My God! It
was my father!

I recognized him instantly, although he was all enveloped
in a dark cloak,—and had pulled his hat down over his face.
He went past me on tip-toe. He did not notice me although
nothing concealed me; but I had so contracted myself and
shrunk together that I think I must have been on a level with
the ground. The jealous Othello, prepared to murder, had
suddenly been converted into the school-boy. . . . I was so
frightened by the unexpected apparition of my father that I
did not even take note, at first, in what direction he was going
and where he had disappeared. I merely straightened up at
the moment and thought: "Why is my father walking in the
garden by night?"—when everything around had relapsed
into silence. In my alarm I had dropped my knife in the grass,

but I did not even try to find it; I felt very much ashamed. I became sobered on the instant. But as I wended my way home, I stepped up to my little bench under the elderbush and cast a glance at the little window of Zinaida's chamber. The small, somewhat curved panes of the little window gleamed dully blue in the faint light which fell from the night sky. Suddenly their color began to undergo a change. . . . Behind them—I saw it, saw it clearly,—a whitish shade was lowered, descended to the sill,—and there remained motionless.

"What is the meaning of that?"—I said aloud, almost involuntarily, when I again found myself in my own room.— "Was it a dream, an accident, or. . . ." The surmises which suddenly came into my head were so new and strange that I dared not even yield to them.

XVIII

I rose in the morning with a headache. My agitation of the night before had vanished. It had been replaced by an oppressive perplexity and a certain, hitherto unknown sadness, —exactly as though something had died in me.

"What makes you look like a rabbit which has had half of its brain removed?"—said Lushin, who happened to meet me. At breakfast I kept casting covert glances now at my father, now at my mother; he was calm, as usual; she, as usual, was secretly irritated. I waited to see whether my father would address me in a friendly way, as he sometimes did. . . . But he did not even caress me with his cold everyday affection.—"Shall I tell Zinaida all?"—I thought. . . . "For it makes no difference now—everything is over between us." I went to her, but I not only did not tell her anything,— I did not even get a chance to talk to her as I would have liked. The old Princess's son, a cadet aged twelve, had come from Petersburg to spend his vacation with her; Zinaida immediately confided her brother to me.—"Here, my dear Volodya,"—said she (she called me so for the first time), "is a comrade for you. His name is Volodya also. Pray, like him; he's a wild little fellow still, but he has a good heart. Show him Neskutchny Park, walk with him, take him under your protection. You will do that, will you not? You, too, are such a good fellow!"—She laid both hands affectionately on my shoulder—and I was reduced to utter confusion. The arrival of that boy turned me into a boy. I stared in silence at the cadet, who riveted his eyes in corresponding silence on me. Zinaida burst out laughing and pushed us toward each other. —"Come, embrace, children!"—We embraced.—"I'll take you into the garden if you wish,—shall I?"—I asked the cadet.

"Certainly, sir,"—he replied, in a hoarse, genuine cadet voice. Again Zinaida indulged in a burst of laughter. . . . I managed to notice that never before had she had such charming color in her face. The cadet and I went off together. In our garden stood an old swing. I seated him on the thin little board and began to swing him. He sat motionless in his new little uniform of thick cloth with broad gold galloon, and clung tightly to the ropes.

"You had better unhook your collar,"—I said to him.

"Never mind, sir,[1] we are used to it, sir"—he said, and cleared his throat.

He resembled his sister; his eyes were particularly suggestive of her. It was pleasant to me to be of service to him; and, at the same time, that aching pain kept quietly gnawing at my heart. "Now I really am a child," I thought; "but last night. . . ." I remembered where I had dropped my knife and found it. The cadet asked me to lend it to him, plucked a thick stalk of lovage, cut a whistle from it, and began to pipe. Othello piped also.

But in the evening, on the other hand, how he did weep, that same Othello, over Zinaida's hands when, having sought him out in a corner of the garden, she asked him what made him so melancholy. My tears streamed with such violence that she was frightened.—"What is the matter with you? What is the matter with you, Volodya?"—she kept repeating, and seeing that I made her no reply, she took it into her head to kiss my wet cheek. But I turned away from her and whispered through my sobs:—"I know everything: why have you trifled with me? . . . . Why did you want my love?"

"I am to blame toward you, Volodya". . . . said Zinaida. —"Akh, I am very much to blame" . . . she said, and clenched her hands.—"How much evil, dark, sinful, there is in me! . . . But I am not trifling with you now, I love you— you do not suspect why and how. . . . But what is it you know?"

What could I say to her? She stood before me and gazed at me—and I belonged to her wholly, from head to foot, as

[1] The respectful "s," which is an abbreviation of "sir" or "madam." —TRANSLATOR.

soon as she looked at me. . . . A quarter of an hour later I was running a race with the cadet and Zinaida; I was not weeping; I was laughing, although my swollen eyelids dropped tears from laughing; on my neck, in place of a tie, was bound a ribbon of Zinaida's, and I shouted with joy when I succeeded in seizing her around the waist. She did with me whatsoever she would.

XIX

I should be hard put to it, if I were made to narrate in detail all that went on within me in the course of the week which followed my unsuccessful nocturnal expedition. It was a strange, feverish time, a sort of chaos in which the most opposite emotions, thoughts, suspicions, hopes, joys, and sufferings revolved in a whirlwind; I was afraid to look into myself, if a sixteen-year-old can look into himself; I was afraid to account to myself for anything whatsoever; I simply made haste to live through the day until the evening; on the other hand, at night I slept . . . childish giddiness helped me. I did not want to know whether I was beloved, and would not admit to myself that I was not beloved; I shunned my father—but could not shun Zinaida. . . . I burned as with fire in her presence, . . . but what was the use of my knowing what sort of fire it was wherewith I burned and melted—seeing that it was sweet to me to burn and melt! I surrendered myself entirely to my impressions, and dealt artfully with myself, turned away from my memories and shut my eyes to that of which I had a presentiment in the future. . . . This anguish probably would not have continued long . . . a thunder-clap put an instantaneous end to everything and hurled me into a new course.

On returning home one day to dinner from a rather long walk, I learned with surprise that I was to dine alone; that my father had gone away, while my mother was ill, did not wish to dine and had shut herself up in her bedroom. From the footmen's faces I divined that something unusual had taken place. . . . I dared not interrogate them, but I had a friend, the young butler Philipp, who was passionately fond of poetry and an artist on the guitar; I applied to him. From him I learned that a frightful scene had taken place between my father and mother (for in the maids' room everything was audible, to the last word; a great deal had been said in French, but the maid Masha had lived for five years with a

dressmaker from Paris and understood it all); that my
mother had accused my father of infidelity, of being intimate
with the young lady our neighbor; that my father had first
defended himself, then had flared up and in his turn had
made some harsh remark "seemingly about her age," which
had set my mother to crying; that my mother had also re-
ferred to a note of hand, which appeared to have been given
to the old Princess, and expressed herself very vilely about
her, and about the young lady as well; and that then my
father had threatened her.—"And the whole trouble arose,"
—pursued Philipp, "out of an anonymous letter; but who
wrote it no one knows;—otherwise there was no reason why
this affair should have come out."

"But has there been anything?"—I enunciated with difficulty, while my hands and feet turned cold, and something
began to quiver in the very depths of my breast.

Philipp winked significantly.—"There has. You can't conceal such doings, cautious as your papa has been in this case;
—still, what possessed him, for example, to hire a carriage,
or to . . . for you can't get along without people there
also."

I dismissed Philipp, and flung myself down on my bed. I
did not sob, I did not give myself up to despair; I did not ask
myself when and how all this had taken place; I was not
surprised that I had not guessed it sooner, long before—I did
not even murmur against my father. . . . That which I had
learned was beyond my strength; this sudden discovery had
crushed me. . . . All was over. All my flowers had been
plucked up at one blow and lay strewn around me, scattered
and trampled under foot.

XX

On the following day my mother announced that she was
going to remove to town. My father went into her bedroom
in the morning and sat there a long time alone with her. No
one heard what he said to her, but my mother did not weep
any more; she calmed down and asked for something to eat,
but did not show herself and did not alter her intention. I
remember that I wandered about all day long, but did not go
into the garden and did not glance even once at the wing—
and in the evening I was the witness of an amazing occurrence; my father took Count Malevsky by the arm and led
him out of the hall into the anteroom and, in the presence

of a lackey, said coldly to him: "Several days ago Your Radiance was shown the door in a certain house. I shall not enter into explanations with you now, but I have the honor to inform you that if you come to my house again I shall fling you through the window. I don't like your handwriting." The Count bowed, set his teeth, shrank together, and disappeared.

Preparations began for removing to town, on the Arbat,[1] where our house was situated. Probably my father himself no longer cared to remain in the villa; but it was evident that he had succeeded in persuading my mother not to make a row. Everything was done quietly, without haste; my mother even sent her compliments to the old Princess and expressed her regret that, owing to ill-health, she would be unable to see her before her departure. I prowled about like a crazy person, and desired but one thing,—that everything might come to an end as speedily as possible. One thought never quitted my head: how could she, a young girl,—well, and a princess into the bargain,—bring herself to such a step, knowing that my father was not a free man while she had the possibility of marrying Byelovzoroff at least, for example? What had she hoped for? How was it that she had not been afraid to ruin her whole future?—"Yes,"—I thought,—"that's what love is,—that is passion,—that is devotion," . . . and I recalled Lushin's words to me: "Self-sacrifice is sweet—for some people." Once I happened to catch sight of a white spot in one of the windows of the wing. . . . "Can that be Zinaida's face?"—I thought, . . . and it really was her face. I could not hold out. I could not part from her without bidding her a last farewell. I seized a convenient moment and betook myself to the wing.

In the drawing-room the old Princess received me with her customary, slovenly-careless greeting.

"What has made your folks uneasy so early, my dear fellow?"—she said, stuffing snuff up both her nostrils. I looked at her, and a weight was removed from my heart. The word "note of hand" uttered by Philipp tormented me. She suspected nothing . . . so it seemed to me then, at least. Zinaida made her appearance from the adjoining room in a black gown, pale, with hair out of curl; she silently took me by the hand and led me away to her room.

"I heard your voice,"—she began,—"and came out at once. And did you find it so easy to desert us, naughty boy?"

"I have come to take leave of you, Princess,"—I replied,

[1] A square in Moscow.—TRANSLATOR.

—"probably forever. You may have heard we are going away."

Zinaida gazed intently at me.

"Yes, I have heard. Thank you for coming. I was beginning to think that I should not see you.—Think kindly of me. I have sometimes tormented you; but nevertheless I am not the sort of person you think I am."

She turned away and leaned against the window-casing.

"Really, I am not that sort of person. I know that you have a bad opinion of me."

"I?"

"Yes, you . . . you."

"I?"—I repeated sorrowfully, and my heart began to quiver as of old, beneath the influence of the irresistible, inexpressible witchery.—"I? Believe me, Zinaida Alexandrovna, whatever you may have done, however you may have tormented me, I shall love and adore you until the end of my life."

She turned swiftly toward me and opening her arms widely, she clasped my head, and kissed me heartily and warmly. God knows whom that long, farewell kiss was seeking, but I eagerly tasted its sweetness. I knew that it would never more be repeated.—"Farewell, farewell!" I kept saying. . . .

She wrenched herself away and left the room. And I withdrew also. I am unable to describe the feeling with which I retired. I should not wish ever to have it repeated; but I should consider myself unhappy if I had never experienced it.

We removed to town. I did not speedily detach myself from the past, I did not speedily take up my work. My wound healed slowly; but I really had no evil feeling toward my father. On the contrary, he seemed to have gained in stature in my eyes . . . let the psychologists explain this contradiction as best they may. One day I was walking along the boulevard when, to my indescribable joy, I encountered Lushin. I liked him for his straightforward, sincere character; and, moreover, he was dear to me in virtue of the memories which he awakened in me. I rushed at him.

"Aha!"—he said, with a scowl.—"Is it you, young man? Come, let me have a look at you. You are still all sallow, and yet there is not the olden trash in your eyes. You look like a man, not like a lap-dog. That's good. Well, and how are you? Are you working?"

I heaved a sigh. I did not wish to lie, and I was ashamed to tell the truth.

"Well, never mind,"—went on Lushin,—"don't be afraid. The principal thing is to live in normal fashion and not to yield to impulses. Otherwise, where's the good? No matter whither the wave bears one—'tis bad; let a man stand on a stone if need be, but on his own feet. Here I am croaking . . . but Byelovzoroff—have you heard about him?"

"What about him? No."

"He has disappeared without leaving a trace; they say he has gone to the Caucasus. A lesson to you, young man. And the whole thing arises from not knowing how to say good-bye,—to break bonds in time. You, now, seem to have jumped out successfully. Look out, don't fall in again. Farewell."

"I shall not fall in,"—I thought. . . . "I shall see her no more." But I was fated to see Zinaida once more.

XXI

My father was in the habit of riding on horseback every day; he had a splendid red-roan English horse, with a long, slender neck and long legs, indefatigable and vicious. Its name was Electric. No one could ride it except my father. One day he came to me in a kindly frame of mind, which had not happened with him for a long time: he was preparing to ride, and had donned his spurs. I began to entreat him to take me with him.

"Let us, rather, play at leap-frog,"—replied my father,— "for thou wilt not be able to keep up with me on thy cob."

"Yes, I shall; I will put on spurs also."

"Well, come along."

We set out. I had a shaggy, black little horse, strong on its feet and fairly spirited; it had to gallop with all its might, it is true, when Electric was going at a full trot; but nevertheless I did not fall behind. I have never seen such a horseman as my father. His seat was so fine and so carelessly-adroit that the horse under him seemed to be conscious of it and to take pride in it. We rode the whole length of all the boulevards, reached the Maidens' Field,[1] leaped over several enclosures (at first I was afraid to leap, but my father despised timid people,

---

[1] A great plain situated on the outskirts of the town. So called because (says tradition) it was here that annually were assembled the young girls who were sent, in addition to the money tribute, to the Khan, during the Tatar period in the thirteenth and fourteenth centuries.—TRANSLATOR.

and I ceased to be afraid), crossed the Moscow river twice;—and I was beginning to think that we were on our way homeward, the more so as my father remarked that my horse was tired, when suddenly he turned away from me in the direction of the Crimean Ford, and galloped along the shore. —I dashed after him. When he came on a level with a lofty pile of old beams which lay heaped together, he sprang nimbly from Electric, ordered me to alight and, handing me the bridle of his horse, told me to wait for him on that spot, near the beams; then he turned into a narrow alley and disappeared. I began to pace back and forth along the shore, leading the horses after me and scolding Electric, who as he walked kept incessantly twitching his head, shaking himself, snorting and neighing; when I stood still, he alternately pawed the earth with his hoof, and squealed and bit my cob on the neck; in a word, behaved like a spoiled darling, *pur sang*. My father did not return. A disagreeable humidity was wafted from the river; a fine rain set in and mottled the stupid, grey beams, around which I was hovering and of which I was so heartily tired, with tiny, dark spots. Anxiety took possession of me, but still my father did not come. A Finnish sentry, also all grey, with a huge, old-fashioned shako, in the form of a pot, on his head, and armed with a halberd (why should there be a sentry, I thought, on the shores of the Moscow river?), approached me, and turning his elderly, wrinkled face to me, he said:

"What are you doing here with those horses, my little gentleman? Hand them over to me; I'll hold them."

I did not answer him; he asked me for some tobacco. In order to rid myself of him (moreover, I was tortured by impatience), I advanced a few paces in the direction in which my father had retreated; then I walked through the alley to the very end, turned a corner, and came to a standstill. On the street, forty paces distant from me, in front of the open window of a small wooden house, with his back to me, stood my father; he was leaning his breast on the windowsill, while in the house, half concealed by the curtain, sat a woman in a dark gown talking with my father: the woman was Zinaida.

I stood rooted to the spot in amazement. I must confess that I had in nowise expected this. My first impulse was to flee. "My father will glance round," I thought,—"and then I am lost." . . . But a strange feeling—a feeling more powerful than curiosity, more powerful even than jealousy, more powerful than fear,—stopped me. I began to stare, I tried to hear. My father appeared to be insisting upon something. Zinaida would not consent. I seem to see her face now—sad, serious, beautiful, and with an indescribable imprint of adoration, grief, love, and a sort of despair. She uttered monosyllabic words, did not raise her eyes, and only smiled—submissively and obstinately. From that smile alone I recognized my former Zinaida. My father shrugged his shoulders, and set his hat straight on his head—which was always a sign of impatience with him. . . . Then the words became audible: "*Vous devez vous séparer de cette.*" . . . Zinaida drew herself up and stretched out her hand. . . . Suddenly, before my very eyes, an incredible thing came to pass:—all at once, my father raised the riding-whip, with which he had been lashing the dust from his coat-tails,—and the sound of a sharp blow on that arm, which was bare to the elbow, rang out. I could hardly keep from shrieking, but Zinaida started, gazed in silence at my father, and slowly raising her arm to her lips, kissed the mark which glowed scarlet upon it.

My father hurled his riding-whip from him, and running hastily up the steps of the porch, burst into the house. . . . Zinaida turned round, and stretching out her arms, and throwing back her head, she also quitted the window.

My heart swooning with terror, and with a sort of alarmed perplexity, I darted backward; and dashing through the alley, and almost letting go of Electric, I returned to the bank of the river . . . I could understand nothing. I knew that my cold and self-contained father was sometimes seized by fits of wild fury; and yet I could not in the least comprehend what I had seen. . . . But I immediately felt that no matter how long I might live, it would be impossible for me ever to forget that movement, Zinaida's glance and smile; that her image, that new image which had suddenly been presented to me, had forever imprinted itself on my memory. I stared stupidly at the river and did not notice that my tears were flowing. "She is being beaten,"—I thought. . . . "She is being beaten . . . beaten . . ."

"Come, what ails thee?—Give me my horse!"—rang out my father's voice behind me.

I mechanically gave him the bridle. He sprang upon Electric . . . the half-frozen horse reared on his hind legs and leaped forward half a fathom . . . but my father speedily got him under control; he dug his spurs into his flanks and beat him on the neck with his fist. . . . "Ekh, I have no whip,"—he muttered.

I remembered the recent swish through the air and the blow of that same whip, and shuddered.

"What hast thou done with it?"—I asked my father, after waiting a little.

My father did not answer me and galloped on. I dashed after him. I was determined to get a look at his face.

"Didst thou get bored in my absence?"—he said through his teeth.

"A little. But where didst thou drop thy whip?"—I asked him again.

My father shot a swift glance at me.—"I did not drop it," —he said,—"I threw it away."—He reflected for a space and dropped his head . . . and then, for the first and probably for the last time, I saw how much tenderness and compunction his stern features were capable of expressing.

He set off again at a gallop, and this time I could not keep up with him; I reached home a quarter of an hour after him.

"That's what love is,"—I said to myself again, as I sat at night before my writing-table, on which copy-books and text-books had already begun to make their appearance,—"that is what passion is! . . . How is it possible not to revolt, how is it possible to endure a blow from any one whomsoever . . . even from the hand that is most dear? But evidently it can be done if one is in love. . . . And I . . . I imagined . . ."

The last month had aged me greatly, and my love, with all its agitations and sufferings, seemed to me like something very petty and childish and wretched in comparison with that other unknown something at which I could hardly even guess, and which frightened me like a strange, beautiful but menacing face that one strives, in vain, to get a good look at in the semi-darkness. . . .

That night I had a strange and dreadful dream. I thought I was entering a low, dark room. . . . My father was standing there, riding-whip in hand, and stamping his feet; Zinaida was crouching in one corner and had a red mark, not on her arm, but on her forehead . . . and behind the two rose up Byelovzoroff, all bathed in blood, with his pale lips open, and wrathfully menacing my father.

Two months later I entered the university, and six months afterward my father died (of an apoplectic stroke) in Petersburg, whither he had just removed with my mother and myself. A few days before his death my father had received a letter from Moscow which had agitated him extremely.

. . . He went to beg something of my mother and, I was told, even wept,—he, my father! On the very morning of the day on which he had the stroke, he had begun a letter to me in the French language: "My son,"—he wrote to me,— "fear the love of women, fear that happiness, that poison . . ." After his death my mother sent a very considerable sum of money to Moscow.

XXII

Four years passed. I had but just left the university, and did not yet quite know what to do with myself, at what door to knock; in the meanwhile, I was lounging about without occupation. One fine evening I encountered Maidanoff in the theatre. He had contrived to marry and enter the government service; but I found him unchanged. He went into unnecessary raptures, just as of old, and became low-spirited as suddenly as ever.

"You know,"—he said to me,—"by the way, that Madame Dolsky is here."

"What Madame Dolsky?"

"Is it possible that you have forgotten? The former Princess Zasyekin, with whom we were all in love, you included. At the villa, near Neskutchny Park, you remember?"

"Did she marry Dolsky?"

"Yes."

"And is she here in the theatre?"

"No, in Petersburg; she arrived here a few days ago; she is preparing to go abroad."

"What sort of a man is her husband?"—I asked.

"A very fine young fellow and wealthy. He's my comrade in the service, a Moscow man. You understand—after that scandal . . . you must be well acquainted with all that . . ." (Maidanoff smiled significantly), "it was not easy for her to find a husband; there were consequences . . . but with her brains everything is possible. Go to her; she will be delighted to see you. She is handsomer than ever."

Maidanoff gave me Zinaida's address. She was stopping in the Hotel Demuth. Old memories began to stir in me. . . . I promised myself that I would call upon my former "passion" the next day. But certain affairs turned up: a week elapsed, and when, at last, I betook myself to the Hotel Demuth and inquired for Madame Dolsky I learned that she had died four days previously, almost suddenly, in childbirth.

Something seemed to deal me a blow in the heart. The thought that I might have seen her but had not, and that I should never see her,—that bitter thought seized upon me with all the force of irresistible reproach. "Dead!" I repeated, staring dully at the door-porter, then quietly made my way to the street and walked away, without knowing whither. The whole past surged up at one blow and stood before me. And now this was the way it had ended, this was the goal of that young, fiery, brilliant life? I thought that—I pictured to myself those dear features, those eyes, those curls in the narrow box, in the damp, underground gloom,—right there, not far from me, who was still alive, and, perchance, only a few paces from my father. . . . I thought all that, I strained my imagination, and yet—

From a mouth indifferent I heard the news of death,
And with indifference did I receive it—

resounded through my soul. O youth, youth! Thou carest for nothing: thou possessest, as it were, all the treasures of the universe; even sorrow comforts thee, even melancholy becomes thee; thou are self-confident and audacious; thou sayest: "I alone live—behold!"—But the days speed on and vanish without a trace and without reckoning, and everything vanishes in thee, like wax in the sun, like snow. . . . And perchance the whole secret of thy charm consists not in the power to do everything, but in the possibility of thinking that thou wilt do everything—consists precisely in the fact that thou scatterest to the winds thy powers which thou hast not understood how to employ in any other way,—in the fact that each one of us seriously regards himself as a prodigal, seriously assumes that he has a right to say: "Oh, what could I not have done, had I not wasted my time!"

And I myself . . . what did I hope for, what did I expect, what rich future did I foresee, when I barely accompanied with a single sigh, with a single mournful emotion, the spectre of my first love which had arisen for a brief moment?

And what has come to pass of all for which I hoped? Even now, when the shades of evening are beginning to close in upon my life, what is there that has remained for me fresher, more precious than the memory of that morning spring thunder-storm which sped so swiftly past?

But I calumniate myself without cause. Even then, at that frivolous, youthful epoch, I did not remain deaf to the sorrowful voice which responded within me to the triumphant

sound which was wafted to me from beyond the grave. I remember that a few days after I learned of Zinaida's death
I was present, by my own irresistible longing, at the death-
bed of a poor old woman who lived in the same house with
us. Covered with rags, with a sack under her head, she died
heavily and with difficulty. Her whole life had been passed in
a bitter struggle with daily want; she had seen no joy, she
had not tasted the honey of happiness—it seemed as though
she could not have failed to rejoice at death, at her release,
her repose. But nevertheless, as long as her decrepit body
held out, as long as her breast heaved under the icy hand
which was laid upon it, until her last strength deserted her,
the old woman kept crossing herself and whispering:—"O
Lord, forgive my sins,"—and only with the last spark of consciousness did there vanish from her eyes the expression of
fear and horror at her approaching end. And I remember
that there, by the bedside of that poor old woman, I felt terrified for Zinaida, and felt like praying for her, for my father
—and for myself.

1860 A.D.

[Translated by Isabel F. Hapgood.]

Benito Cereno

BY HERMAN MELVILLE
(1819-1891)

In 1851, Herman Melville published Moby Dick, *one of the greatest novels in American literature. In* Benito Cereno, *published five years later, Melville utilized the same technique that he had developed as he wrote his masterpiece: an exciting adventure story infused with metaphysical meaning through the use of symbolism. He based his story upon a chapter of Amasa Delano's* Voyages and Travels, *an autobiography of a Massachusetts sea captain; but Melville knew the sea and the life of the seaman from firsthand experience. He had gone to sea at an early age following the death of his father, who had left the family in destitute circumstances. After his first voyage, he tried schoolteaching, then shipped out aboard a whaler. He tired of whaling after eighteen months and jumped ship at the Marquesas Islands in the South Seas. For a month he was held captive by the savages in the valley of Typee. After several more trips he returned to New York. His early novels, which attracted a wide following, were fictional accounts of his adventures. After publishing* The Piazza Tales (1856), *the volume in which* Benito Cereno *appeared, Melville wrote only two more prose works:* The Confidence Man (1857) *and* Billy Budd, *which was not published until many years after his death. During the final years of his life, he devoted himself to poetry, living upon small earnings as a customs inspector in New York.*

Benito Cereno

1855

In the year 1799, Captain Amasa Delano, of Duxbury, in Massachusetts, commanding a large sealer and general trader, lay at anchor, with a valuable cargo, in the harbour of St. Maria—a small, desert, uninhabited island towards the southern extremity of the long coast of Chili. There he had touched for water.

On the second day, not long after dawn, while lying in his berth, his mate came below, informing him that a strange sail was coming into the bay. Ships were then not so plenty in those waters as now. He rose, dressed, and went on deck.

The morning was one peculiar to that coast. Everything was mute and calm; everything grey. The sea, though undulated into long roods of swells, seemed fixed, and was sleeked at the surface like waved lead that has cooled and set in the smelters' mould. The sky seemed a grey mantle. Flights of troubled grey fowl, kith and kin with flights of troubled grey vapours among which they were mixed, skimmed low and fitfully over the waters, as swallows over meadows before storms. Shadows present, foreshadowing deeper shadows to come.

To Captain Delano's surprise, the stranger, viewed through the glass, showed no colours; though to do so upon entering a haven, however uninhabited in its shores, where but a single other ship might be lying, was the custom among peaceful seamen of all nations. Considering the lawlessness and loneliness of the spot, and the sort of stories, at that day, associated with those seas, Captain Delano's surprise might have deepened into some uneasiness had he not been a person of a singularly undistrustful good nature, not liable, except on extraordinary and repeated excitement, and hardly then, to indulge in personal alarms, any way involving the imputation of malign evil in man. Whether, in view of what humanity is capable, such a trait implies, along with a benevolent heart, more than ordinary quickness and accuracy of intellectual perception, may be left to the wise to determine.

But whatever misgivings might have obtruded on first seeing the stranger, would almost, in any seaman's mind, have been dissipated by observing that, the ship, in navigating into the harbour, was drawing too near the land, for her own safety's sake, owing to a sunken reef making out off her bow. This seemed to prove her a stranger, indeed, not only to the sealer, but the island; consequently, she could be no wonted freebooter on that ocean. With no small interest, Captain Delano continued to watch her—a proceeding not much facilitated by the vapours partly mantling the hull, through which the far matin light from her cabin streamed equivocally enough; much like the sun—by this time crescented on the rim of the horizon, and apparently, in company with the strange ship, entering the harbour—which, wimpled by the same low, creeping clouds, showed not unlike a Lima intriguante's one sinister eye peering across the Plaza from the Indian loop-hole of her dusk *saya-y-manta*.

It might have been but a deception of the vapours, but, the longer the stranger was watched, the more singular appeared her manœuvres. Ere long it seemed hard to decide whether she meant to come in or no—what she wanted, or what she was about. The wind, which had breezed up a little during the night, was now extremely light and baffling, which the more increased the apparent uncertainty of her movements.

Surmising, at last, that it might be a ship in distress, Captain Delano ordered his whale-boat to be dropped, and, much to the wary opposition of his mate, prepared to board her, and, at the least, pilot her in. On the night previous, a fishing-party of the seamen had gone a long distance to some detached rocks out of sight from the sealer, and, an hour or two before day-break, had returned, having met with no small success. Presuming that the stranger might have been long off soundings, the good captain put several baskets of the fish, for presents, into his boat, and so pulled away. From her continuing too near the sunken reef, deeming her in danger, calling to his men, he made all haste to apprise those on board of their situation. But, some time ere the boat came up, the wind, light though it was, having shifted, had headed the vessel off, as well as partly broken the vapours from about her.

Upon gaining a less remote view, the ship, when made signally visible on the verge of the leaden-hued swells, with the shreds of fog here and there raggedly furring her, appeared like a white-washed monastery after a thunder-storm, seen perched upon some dun cliff among the Pyrenees. But it was no purely fanciful resemblance which now, for a moment, almost led Captain Delano to think that nothing less than a ship-load of monks was before him. Peering over the bulwarks were what really seemed, in the hazy distance, throngs of dark cowls; while fitfully revealed through the open port-holes, other dark moving figures were dimly descried, as of Black Friars pacing the cloisters.

Upon a still nigher approach, this appearance was modified, and the true character of the vessel was plain—a Spanish merchantman of the first class; carrying negro slaves, amongst other valuable freight, from one colonial port to another. A very large, and, in its time, a very fine vessel, such as in those days were at intervals encountered along that main; sometimes superseded Acapulco treasure-ships, or retired frigates of the Spanish king's navy, which, like superannuated Italian palaces, still, under a decline of masters, preserved signs of former state.

As the whale-boat drew more and more nigh, the cause of the peculiar pipe-clayed aspect of the stranger was seen in the slovenly neglect pervading her. The spars, ropes, and great part of the bulwarks, looked woolly, from long unacquaintance with the scraper, tar, and the brush. Her keel seemed laid, her ribs put together, and she launched, from Ezekiel's Valley of Dry Bones.

In the present business in which she was engaged, the ship's general model and rig appeared to have undergone no material change from their original warlike and Froissart pattern. However, no guns were seen.

The tops were large, and were railed about with what had once been octagonal net-work, all now in sad disrepair. These tops hung overhead like three ruinous aviaries, in one of which was seen perched, on a ratlin, a white noddy, a strange fowl, so called from its lethargic somnambulistic character, being frequently caught by hand at sea. Battered and mouldy, the castellated forecastle seemed some ancient turret, long ago taken by assault, and then left to decay. Towards the stern, two high-raised quarter galleries—the balus-

trades here and there covered with dry, tindery sea-moss—
opening out from the unoccupied state-cabin, whose dead
lights, for all the mild weather, were hermetically closed and
caulked—these tenantless balconies hung over the sea as if it
were the grand Venetian canal. But the principal relic of faded
grandeur was the ample oval of the shield-like stern-piece,
intricately carved with the arms of Castile and Leon, medal-
lioned about by groups of mythological or symbolical devices;
uppermost and central of which was a dark satyr in a mask,
holding his foot on the prostrate neck of a writhing figure,
likewise masked.

Whether the ship had a figure-head, or only a plain beak,
was not quite certain, owing to canvas wrapped about that
part, either to protect it while undergoing a refurbishing, or
else decently to hide its decay. Rudely painted or chalked, as
in a sailor freak, along the forward side of a sort of pedestal
below the canvas, was the sentence, *"Seguid vuestro jefe,"*
(follow your leader); while upon the tarnished headboards,
near by, appeared, in stately capitals, once gilt, the ship's
name, "SAN DOMINICK," each letter streakingly corroded
with tricklings of copper-spike rust; while, like mourning
weeds, dark festoons of sea-grass slimily swept to and fro
over the name, with every hearse-like roll of the hull.

As at last the boat was hooked from the bow along toward
the gangway amidship, its keel, while yet some inches separated from the hull, harshly grated as on a sunken coral reef.
It proved a huge bunch of conglobated barnacles adhering
below the water to the side like a wen; a token of baffling airs
and long calms passed somewhere in those seas.

Climbing the side, the visitor was at once surrounded by
a clamorous throng of whites and blacks, but the latter out-
numbering the former more than could have been expected,
negro transportation-ship as the stranger in port was. But,
in one language, and as with one voice, all poured out a
common tale of suffering; in which the negresses, of whom
there were not a few, exceeded the others in their dolorous
vehemence. The scurvy, together with a fever, had swept
off a great part of their number, more especially the Spaniards. Off Cape Horn, they had narrowly escaped shipwreck;
then, for days together, they had lain tranced without wind;
their provisions were low; their water next to none; their lips
that moment were baked.

While Captain Delano was thus made the mark of all eager

tongues, his one eager glance took in all the faces, with every other object about him.

Always upon first boarding a large and populous ship at sea, especially a foreign one, with a nondescript crew such as Lascars or Manilla men, the impression varies in a peculiar way from that produced by first entering a strange house with strange inmates in a strange land. Both house and ship, the one by its walls and blinds, the other by its high bulwarks like ramparts, hoard from view their interiors till the last moment; but in the case of the ship there is this addition: that the living spectacle it contains, upon its sudden and complete disclosure, has, in contrast with the blank ocean which zones it, something of the effect of enchantment. The ship seems unreal; these strange costumes, gestures, and faces, but a shadowy tableau just emerged from the deep, which directly must receive back what it gave.

Perhaps it was some such influence as above is attempted to be described which, in Captain Delano's mind, heightened whatever, upon a staid scrutiny, might have seemed unusual; especially the conspicuous figures of four elderly grizzled negroes, their heads like black, doddered willow tops, who, in venerable contrast to the tumult below them, were couched sphynx-like, one on the starboard cathead, another on the larboard, and the remaining pair face to face on the opposite bulwarks above the main-chains. They each had bits of unstranded old junk in their hands, and, with a sort of stoical self-content, were picking the junk into oakum, a small heap of which lay by their sides. They accompanied the task with a continuous, low, monotonous chant; droning and drooling away like so many grey-headed bag-pipers playing a funeral march.

The quarter-deck rose into an ample elevated poop, upon the forward verge of which, lifted, like the oakum-pickers, some eight feet above the general throng, sat along in a row, separated by regular spaces, the cross-legged figures of six other blacks; each with a rusty hatchet in his hand, which, with a bit of brick and a rag, he was engaged like a scullion in scouring; while between each two was a small stack of hatchets, their rusted edges turned forward awaiting a like operation. Though occasionally the four oakum-pickers would briefly address some person or persons in the crowd below, yet the six hatchet-polishers neither spoke to others, nor breathed a whisper among themselves, but sat intent upon their task, except at intervals, when, with the peculiar love in negroes of uniting industry with pastime, two-and-two they sideways clashed their hatchets together, like cymbals, with a barbarous din. All six, unlike the generality, had the raw aspect of unsophisticated Africans.

But that first comprehensive glance which took in those ten figures, with scores less conspicuous, rested but an instant upon them, as, impatient of the hubbub of voices, the visitor turned in quest of whomsoever it might be that commanded the ship.

But as if not unwilling to let nature make known her own case among his suffering charge, or else in despair of restraining it for the time, the Spanish captain, a gentlemanly, reserved-looking, and rather young man to a stranger's eye, dressed with singular richness, but bearing plain traces of recent sleepless cares and disquietudes, stood passively by, leaning against the main-mast, at one moment casting a dreary, spiritless look upon his excited people, at the next an unhappy glance toward his visitor. By his side stood a black of small stature, in whose rude face, as occasionally, like a shepherd's dog, he mutely turned it up into the Spaniard's, sorrow and affection were equally blended.

Struggling through the throng, the American advanced to the Spaniard, assuring him of his sympathies, and offering to render whatever assistance might be in his power. To which the Spaniard returned, for the present, but grave and ceremonious acknowledgments, his national formality dusked by the saturnine mood of ill health.

But losing no time in mere compliments, Captain Delano returning to the gangway, had his baskets of fish brought up; and as the wind still continued light, so that some hours at least must elapse ere the ship could be brought to the anchorage, he bade his men return to the sealer, and fetch back as much water as the whaleboat could carry, with whatever soft bread the steward might have, all the remaining pumpkins on board, with a box of sugar, and a dozen of his private bottles of cider.

Not many minutes after the boat's pushing off, to the vexation of all, the wind entirely died away, and the tide turning, began drifting back the ship helplessly seaward. But trusting this would not long last, Captain Delano sought with good hopes to cheer up the strangers, feeling no small satisfaction that, with persons in their condition he could—thanks to his frequent voyages along the Spanish main—converse with some freedom in their native tongue.

While left alone with them, he was not long in observing some things tending to heighten his first impressions; but surprise was lost in pity, both for the Spaniards and blacks, alike evidently reduced from scarcity of water and provisions; while long-continued suffering seemed to have brought out the less good-natured qualities of the negroes, besides, at the same time, impairing the Spaniard's authority over them. But, under the circumstances, precisely this condition of things was to have been anticipated. In armies, navies, cities, or families—in nature herself—nothing more relaxes good order than misery. Still, Captain Delano was not without the idea, that had Benito Cereno been a man of greater energy, misrule would hardly have come to the present pass. But the debility, constitutional or induced by the hardships, bodily and mental, of the Spanish captain, was too obvious to be overlooked. A prey to settled dejection, as if long mocked with hope he would not now indulge it, even when it had ceased to be a mock, the prospect of that day or evening at furthest, lying at anchor, with plenty of water for his people, and a brother captain to counsel and befriend, seemed in no perceptible degree to encourage him. His mind appeared unstrung, if not still more seriously affected. Shut up in these oaken walls, chained to one dull round of command, whose unconditionality cloyed him, like some hypochondriac abbot he moved slowly about, at times suddenly pausing, starting, or staring, biting his lip, biting his fingernails, flushing, paling, twitching his beard, with other symptoms of an absent or moody mind. This distempered spirit was lodged, as before hinted, in as distempered a frame. He was rather tall, but seemed never to have been robust, and now with nervous suffering was almost worn to a skeleton. A tendency to some pulmonary complaint appeared to have been lately confirmed. His voice was like that of one with lungs half gone, hoarsely suppressed, a husky whisper. No wonder that, as in this state he tottered about, his private servant apprehensively followed him. Sometimes the negro gave his master his arm, or took his handkerchief out of his pocket for him; performing these and similar offices with that affectionate zeal which transmutes into something filial or fraternal acts in themselves but menial; and which has gained for the negro the repute of making the most pleasing body servant in the world; one, too, whom a master need be on no stiffly superior terms with, but may treat with familiar trust; less a servant than a devoted companion.

Marking the noisy indocility of the blacks in general, as well as what seemed the sullen inefficiency of the whites, it was not without humane satisfaction that Captain Delano witnessed the steady good conduct of Babo.

But the good conduct of Babo, hardly more than the ill-behaviour of others, seemed to withdraw the half-lunatic Don Benito from his cloudy languor. Not that such precisely was the impression made by the Spaniard on the mind of his visitor. The Spaniard's individual unrest was, for the present, but noted as a conspicuous feature in the ship's general affliction. Still, Captain Delano was not a little concerned at what he could not help taking for the time to be Don Benito's unfriendly indifference toward himself. The Spaniard's manner, too, conveyed a sort of sour and gloomy disdain, which he seemed at no pains to disguise. But this the American in charity ascribed to the harassing effects of sickness, since, in former instances, he had noted that there are peculiar natures on whom prolonged physical suffering seems to cancel every social instinct of kindness; as if forced to black bread themselves, they deemed it but equity that each person coming nigh them should, indirectly, by some slight or affront, be made to partake of their fare.

But ere long Captain Delano bethought him that, indulgent as he was at the first, in judging the Spaniard, he might not, after all, have exercised charity enough. At bottom it was Don Benito's reserve which displeased him; but the same reserve was shown toward all but his personal attendant. Even the formal reports which, according to sea-usage, were at stated times made to him by some petty underling (either a white, mulatto or black), he hardly had patience enough to listen to, without betraying contemptuous aversion. His manner upon such occasions was, in its degree, not unlike that which might be supposed to have been his imperial countryman's, Charles V., just previous to the anchoritish retirement of that monarch from the throne.

This splenetic disrelish of his place was evinced in almost every function pertaining to it. Proud as he was moody, he condescended to no personal mandate. Whatever special orders were necessary, their delivery was delegated to his body-servant, who in turn transferred them to their ultimate destination, through runners, alert Spanish boys or slave boys, like pages or pilot-fish within easy call continually hovering round Don Benito. So that to have beheld this undemonstrative invalid gliding about, apathetic and mute, no landsman could have dreamed that in him was lodged a dictatorship beyond which, while at sea, there was no earthly appeal.

Thus, the Spaniard, regarded in his reserve, seemed as the involuntary victim of mental disorder. But, in fact, his reserve might, in some degree, have proceeded from design. If so, then in Don Benito was evinced the unhealthy climax of that icy though conscientious policy, more or less adopted by all commanders of large ships, which, except in signal emergencies, obliterates alike the manifestation of sway with every trace of sociality; transforming the man into a block, or rather into a loaded cannon, which, until there is call for thunder, has nothing to say.

Viewing him in this light, it seemed but a natural token of the perverse habit induced by a long course of such hard self-restraint, that, notwithstanding the present condition of his ship, the Spaniard should still persist in a demeanour, which, however harmless—or it may be, appropriate—in a well-appointed vessel, such as the *San Dominick* might have been at the outset of the voyage, was anything but judicious now. But the Spaniard perhaps thought that it was with captains as with gods: reserve, under all events, must still be their cue. But more probably this appearance of slumbering dominion might have been but an attempted disguise to conscious imbecility—not deep policy, but shallow device. But be all this as it might, whether Don Benito's manner was designed or not, the more Captain Delano noted its pervading reserve, the less he felt uneasiness at any particular manifestation of that reserve toward himself.

Neither were his thoughts taken up by the captain alone. Wonted to the quiet orderliness of the sealer's comfortable family of a crew, the noisy confusion of the *San Dominick's* suffering host repeatedly challenged his eye. Some prominent breaches not only of discipline but of decency were observed. These Captain Delano could not but ascribe, in the main, to the absence of those subordinate deck-officers to whom, along with higher duties, is entrusted what may be styled the police department of a populous ship. True, the old oakum-pickers appeared at times to act the part of monitorial constables to their countrymen, the blacks; but though occasionally succeeding in allaying trifling outbreaks now and then between man and man, they could do little or nothing toward establishing general quiet. The *San Dominick* was in the condition of a transatlantic emigrant ship, among whose multitude of living freight are some individuals, doubtless,

as little troublesome as crates and bales; but the friendly remonstrances of such with their ruder companions are of not
so much avail as the unfriendly arm of the mate. What the
San Dominick wanted was, what the emigrant ship has, stern
superior officers. But on these decks not so much as a fourth
mate was to be seen.

The visitor's curiosity was roused to learn the particulars
of those mishaps which had brought about such absenteeism,
with its consequences; because, though deriving some inkling
of the voyage from the wails which at the first moment had
greeted him, yet of the details no clear understanding had
been had. The best account would, doubtless, be given by the
captain. Yet at first the visitor was loth to ask it, unwilling
to provoke some distant rebuff. But plucking up courage, he
at last accosted Don Benito, renewing the expression of his
benevolent interest, adding, that did he (Captain Delano)
but know the particulars of the ship's misfortunes, he would,
perhaps, be better able in the end to relieve them. Would Don
Benito favour him with the whole story?

Don Benito faltered; then, like some somnambulist suddenly interfered with, vacantly stared at his visitor, and ended
by looking down on the deck. He maintained this posture so
long, that Captain Delano, almost equally disconcerted, and
involuntarily almost as rude, turned suddenly from him,
walking forward to accost one of the Spanish seamen for the
desired information. But he had hardly gone five paces, when
with a sort of eagerness Don Benito invited him back, re-
gretting his momentary absence of mind, and professing
readiness to gratify him.

While most part of the story was being given, the two captains stood on the after part of the main-deck, a privileged
spot, no one being near but the servant.

"It is now a hundred and ninety days," began the
Spaniard, in his husky whisper, "that this ship, well officered
and well manned, with several cabin passengers—some fifty
Spaniards in all—sailed from Buenos Ayres bound to Lima,
with a general cargo, Paraguay tea and the like—and," pointing forward, "that parcel of negroes, now not more than a
hundred and fifty, as you see, but then numbering over three
hundred souls. Off Cape Horn we had heavy gales. In one
moment, by night, three of my best officers, with fifteen sailors, were lost, with the main-yard; the spar snapping under
them in the slings, as they sought, with heavers, to beat
down the icy sail. To lighten the hull, the heavier sacks of

mata were thrown into the sea, with most of the water-pipes lashed on deck at the time. And this last necessity it was, combined with the prolonged detentions afterwards experienced, which eventually brought about our chief causes of suffering. When—"

Here there was a sudden fainting attack of his cough, brought on, no doubt, by his mental distress. His servant sustained him, and drawing a cordial from his pocket placed it to his lips. He a little revived. But unwilling to leave him unsupported while yet imperfectly restored, the black with one arm still encircled his master, at the same time keeping his eye fixed on his face, as if to watch for the first sign of complete restoration, or relapse, as the event might prove.

The Spaniard proceeded, but brokenly and obscurely, as one in a dream.

—"Oh, my God! rather than pass through what I have, with joy I would have hailed the most terrible gales; but—"

His cough returned and with increased violence; this subsiding, with reddened lips and closed eyes he fell heavily against his supporter.

"His mind wanders. He was thinking of the plague that followed the gales," plaintively sighed the servant; "my poor, poor master!" wringing one hand, and with the other wiping the mouth. "But be patient, Señor," again turning to Captain Delano, "these fits do not last long; master will soon be himself."

Don Benito reviving, went on; but as this portion of the story was very brokenly delivered, the substance only will here be set down.

It appeared that after the ship had been many days tossed in storms off the Cape, the scurvy broke out, carrying off numbers of the whites and blacks. When at last they had worked round into the Pacific, their spars and sails were so damaged, and so inadequately handled by the surviving mariners, most of whom were become invalids, that, unable to lay her northerly course by the wind, which was powerful, the unmanageable ship for successive days and nights was blown northwestward, where the breeze suddenly deserted her, in unknown waters, to sultry calms. The absence of the water-pipes now proved as fatal to life as before their presence had menaced it. Induced, or at least aggravated, by the more than scanty allowance of water, a malignant fever followed the scurvy; with the excessive heat of the lengthened calm, making such short work of it as to sweep away, as by billows, whole families of the Africans, and a yet larger number, proportionably, of the Spaniards, including, by a luckless fatality, every officer on board. Consequently, in the smart west winds eventually following the calm, the already rent sails having to be simply dropped, not furled, at need, had been gradually reduced to the beggar's rags they were now. To procure substitutes for his lost sailors, as well as supplies of water and sails, the captain at the earliest opportunity had made for Baldivia, the southernmost civilized port of Chili and South America; but upon nearing the coast the thick weather had prevented him from so much as sighting that harbour. Since which period, almost without a crew, and almost without canvas and almost without water, and at intervals giving its added dead to the sea, the *San Dominick* had been battle-dored about by contrary winds, inveigled by currents, or grown weedy in calms. Like a man lost in woods, more than once she had doubled upon her own track.

"But throughout these calamities," huskily continued Don Benito, painfully turning in the half embrace of his servant, "I have to thank those negroes you see, who, though to your inexperienced eyes appearing unruly, have, indeed, conducted themselves with less of restlessness than even their owner could have thought possible under such circumstances."

Here he again fell faintly back. Again his mind wandered: but he rallied, and less obscurely proceeded.

"Yes, their owner was quite right in assuring me that no fetters would be needed with his blacks; so that while, as is wont in this tranportation, those negroes have always remained upon deck—not thrust below, as in the Guineamen—they have, also from the beginning, been freely permitted to range within given bounds at their pleasure."

Once more the faintness returned—his mind roved—but, recovering, he resumed:

"But it is Babo here to whom, under God, I owe not only my own preservation, but likewise to him, chiefly, the merit is due, of pacifying his more ignorant brethren, when at intervals tempted to murmurings."

"Ah, master," sighed the black, bowing his face, "don't speak of me; Babo is nothing; what Babo has done was but duty."

"Faithful fellow!" cried Captain Delano. "Don Benito, I envy you such a friend; slave I cannot call him."

As master and man stood before him, the black upholding the white, Captain Delano could not but bethink him of the beauty of that relationship which could present such a spectacle of fidelity on the one hand and confidence on the other. The scene was heightened by the contrast in dress, denoting their relative positions. The Spaniard wore a loose Chili jacket of dark velvet; white small clothes and stockings, with silver buckles at the knee and instep; a high-crowned sombrero, of fine grass; a slender sword, silver mounted, hung from a knot in his sash; the last being an almost invariable adjunct, more for utility than ornament, of a South American gentleman's dress to this hour. Excepting when his occasional nervous contortions brought about disarray, there was a certain precision in his attire, curiously at variance with the unsightly disorder around; especially in the belittered Ghetto, forward of the main-mast, wholly occupied by the blacks.

The servant wore nothing but wide trousers, apparently, from their coarseness and patches, made out of some old topsail; they were clean, and confined at the waist by a bit of unstranded rope, which, with his composed, deprecatory air at times, made him look something like a begging friar of St. Francis.

However unsuitable for the time and place, at least in the blunt-thinking American's eyes, and however strangely surviving in the midst of all his afflictions, the toilette of Don Benito might not, in fashion at least, have gone beyond the style of the day among South Americans of his class. Though on the present voyage sailing from Buenos Ayres, he had avowed himself a native and resident of Chili, whose inhabitants had not so generally adopted the plain coat and once plebeian pantaloons; but, with a becoming modification, adhered to their provincial costume, picturesque as any in the world. Still, relatively to the pale history of the voyage, and his own pale face, there seemed something so incongruous in the Spaniard's apparel, as almost to suggest the image of an invalid courtier tottering about London streets in the time of the plague.

The portion of the narrative which, perhaps, most excited interest, as well as some surprise, considering the latitudes in question, was the long calms spoken of, and more particularly the ship's so long drifting about. Without communicating the opinion, of course, the American could not but impute at least part of the detentions both to clumsy seamanship and faulty navigation. Eyeing Don Benito's small, yellow hands, he easily inferred that the young captain had not got into command at the hawse-hole but the cabin-window, and if so, why wonder at incompetence, in youth, sickness, and aristocracy united? Such was his democratic conclusion.

But drowning criticism in compassion, after a fresh repetition of his sympathies, Captain Delano having heard out his story, not only engaged, as in the first place, to see Don Benito and his people supplied in their immediate bodily needs, but, also, now further promised to assist him in procuring a large permanent supply of water, as well as some sails and rigging; and, though it would involve no small embarrassment to himself, yet he would spare three of his best seamen for temporary deck officers; so that without delay the ship might proceed to Concepcion, there fully to refit for Lima, her destined port.

Such generosity was not without its effect, even upon the invalid. His face lighted up; eager and hectic, he met the honest glance of his visitor. With gratitude he seemed overcome.

"This excitement is bad for master," whispered the servant, taking his arm, and with soothing words gently drawing him aside.

When Don Benito returned, the American was pained to observe that his hopefulness, like the sudden kindling in his cheek, was but febrile and transient.

Ere long, with a joyless mien, looking up toward the poop, the host invited his guest to accompany him there, for the benefit of what little breath of wind might be stirring.

As during the telling of the story, Captain Delano had once or twice started at the occasional cymballing of the hatchet-polishers, wondering why such an interruption should be allowed, especially in that part of the ship, and in the ears of an invalid; and, moreover, as the hatchets had anything but an attractive look, and the handlers of them still less so, it was, therefore, to tell the truth, not without some lurking reluctance, or even shrinking, it may be, that Captain Delano, with apparent complaisance, acquiesced in his host's invitation. The more so, since with an untimely caprice of punctilio, rendered distressing by his cadaverous aspect, Don Benito, with Castilian bows, solemnly insisted upon his guest's preceding him up the ladder leading to the elevation; where, one on each side of the last step, sat four armorial supporters and sentries, two of the ominous file. Gingerly enough stepped good Captain Delano between them, and in the instant of leaving them behind, like one running the gant-let, he felt an apprehensive twitch in the calves of his legs.

But when, facing about, he saw the whole file, like so many organ-grinders, still stupidly intent on their work, unmindful of everything beside, he could not but smile at his late fidget-ing panic.

Presently, while standing with Don Benito, looking for-ward upon the decks below, he was struck by one of those instances of insubordination previously alluded to. Three black boys, with two Spanish boys, were sitting together on the hatches, scraping a rude wooden platter, in which some scanty mess had recently been cooked. Suddenly, one of the black boys, enraged at a word dropped by one of his white companions, seized a knife, and though called to forbear by one of the oakum-pickers, struck the lad over the head, in-flicting a gash from which blood flowed.

In amazement, Captain Delano inquired what this meant. To which the pale Benito dully muttered, that it was merely the sport of the lad.

"Pretty serious sport, truly," rejoined Captain Delano. "Had such a thing happened on board the *Bachelor's Delight,* instant punishment would have followed."

At these words the Spaniard turned upon the American one of his sudden, staring, half-lunatic looks; then, relapsing into his torpor, answered, "Doubtless, doubtless, Señor."

Is it, thought Captain Delano, that this helpless man is one of those paper captains I've known, who by policy wink at what by power they cannot put down? I know no sadder sight than a commander who has little of command but the name.

"I should think, Don Benito," he now said, glancing to-ward the oakum-picker who had sought to interfere with the boys, "that you would find it advantageous to keep all your blacks employed, especially the younger ones, no matter at what useless task, and no matter what happens to the ship. Why, even with my little band, I find such a course indispen-sable. I once kept a crew on my quarter-deck thrumming mats for my cabin, when, for three days, I had given up my ship —mats, men, and all—for a speedy loss, owing to the vio-lence of a gale in which we could do nothing but helplessly drive before it."

"Doubtless, doubtless," muttered Don Benito.

"But," continued Captain Lelano, again glancing upon

the oakum-pickers and then at the hatchet-polishers, near by, "I see you keep some at least of your host employed."

"Yes," was again the vacant response.

"Those old men there, shaking their pows from their pulpits," continued Captain Delano, pointing to the oakum-pickers, "seem to act the part of old dominies to the rest, little heeded as their admonitions are at times. Is this voluntary on their part, Don Benito, or have you appointed them shepherds to your flock of black sheep?"

"What posts they fill, I appointed them," rejoined the Spaniard in an acrid tone, as if resenting some supposed satiric reflection.

"And these others, these Ashantee conjurors here," continued Captain Delano, rather uneasily eyeing the brandished steel of the hatchet-polishers, where in spots it had been brought to a shine, "this seems a curious business they are at, Don Benito?"

"In the gales we met," answered the Spaniard, "what of our general cargo was not thrown overboard was much damaged by the brine. Since coming into calm weather, I have had several cases of knives and hatchets daily brought up for overhauling and cleaning."

"A prudent idea, Don Benito. You are part owner of ship and cargo, I presume; but not of the slaves, perhaps?"

"I am owner of all you see," impatiently returned Don Benito, "except the main company of blacks, who belonged to my late friend, Alexandro Aranda."

As he mentioned this name, his air was heart-broken, his knees shook; his servant supported him.

Thinking he divined the cause of such unusual emotion, to confirm his surmise, Captain Delano, after a pause, said, "And may I ask, Don Benito, whether—since awhile ago you spoke of some cabin passengers—the friend, whose loss so afflicts you, at the outset of the voyage accompanied his blacks?"

"Yes."

"But died of the fever?"

"Died of the fever.—Oh, could I but—"

Again quivering, the Spaniard paused.

"Pardon me," said Captain Delano slowly, "but I think that, by a sympathetic experience, I conjecture, Don Benito, what it is that gives the keener edge to your grief. It was once my hard fortune to lose at sea a dear friend, my own brother, then supercargo. Assured of the welfare of his spirit, its departure I could have borne like a man; but that honest eye, that honest hand—both of which had so often met mine—and that warm heart; all, all—like scraps to the dogs!—to throw all to the sharks! It was then I vowed never to have for fellow-voyager a man I loved, unless, unbeknown to him, I had provided every requisite, in case of a fatality, for embalming his mortal part for interment on shore. Were your friend's remains now on board this ship, Don Benito, not thus strangely would the mention of his name affect you."

"On board this ship?" echoed the Spaniard. Then, with horrified gestures, as directed against some spectre, he unconsciously fell into the ready arms of his attendant, who, with a silent appeal toward Captain Delano, seemed beseeching him not again to broach a theme so unspeakably distressing to his master.

This poor fellow now, thought the pained American, is the victim of that sad superstition which associates goblins with the deserted body of man, as ghosts with an abandoned house. How unlike are we made! What to me, in like case, would have been a solemn satisfaction, the bare suggestion, even, terrifies the Spaniard into this trance. Poor Alexandro Aranda! what would you say could you here see your friend—who, on former voyages, when you for months were left behind, has, I dare say, often longed, and longed, for one peep at you—now transported with terror at the least thought of having you anyway nigh him.

At this moment, with a dreary graveyard toll, betokening a flaw, the ship's forecastle bell, smote by one of the grizzled oakum-pickers, proclaimed ten o'clock through the leaden calm; when Captain Delano's attention was caught by the moving figure of a gigantic black, emerging from the general crowd below, and slowly advancing toward the elevated poop. An iron collar was about his neck, from which depended a chain, thrice wound round his body; the terminating links padlocked together at a broad band of iron, his girdle.

"How like a mute Atufal moves," murmured the servant.

The black mounted the steps of the poop, and, like a brave prisoner, brought up to receive sentence, stood in unquailing muteness before Don Benito, now recovered from his attack.

At the first glimpse of his approach, Don Benito had started, a resentful shadow swept over his face; and, as with the sudden memory of bootless rage, his white lips glued together.

This is some mulish mutineer, thought Captain Delano,

surveying, not without a mixture of admiration, the colossal form of the negro.

"See, he waits your question, master," said the servant.

Thus reminded, Don Benito, nervously averting his glance, as if shunning, by anticipation, some rebellious response, in a disconcerted voice, thus spoke:

"Atufal, will you ask my pardon now?"

The black was silent.

"Again, master," murmured the servant, with bitter upbraiding eyeing his countryman; "Again, master; he will bend to master yet."

"Answer," said Don Benito, still averting his glance, "say but the one word *pardon*, and your chains shall be off."

Upon this, the black, slowly raising both arms, let them lifelessly fall, his links clanking, his head bowed; as much as to say, "No, I am content."

"Go," said Don Benito, with inkept and unknown emotion.

Deliberately as he had come, the black obeyed.

"Excuse me, Don Benito," said Captain Delano, "but this scene surprises me; what means it, pray?"

"It means that that negro alone, of all the band, has given me peculiar cause of offence. I have put him in chains; I—"

Here he paused; his hand to his head, as if there were a swimming there, or a sudden bewilderment of memory had come over him; but meeting his servant's kindly glance seemed reassured, and proceeded:

"I could not scourge such a form. But I told him he must ask my pardon. As yet he has not. At my command, every two hours he stands before me."

"And how long has this been?"

"Some sixty days."

"And obedient in all else? And respectful?"

"Yes."

"Upon my conscience, then," exclaimed Captain Delano, impulsively, "he has a royal spirit in him, this fellow."

"He may have some right to it," bitterly returned Don Benito; "he says he was king in his own land."

"Yes," said the servant, entering a word, "those slits in Atufal's ears once held wedges of gold; but poor Babo here, in his own land, was only a poor slave; a black man's slave was Babo, who now is the white's."

Somewhat annoyed by these conversational familiarities, Captain Delano turned curiously upon the attendant, then glanced inquiringly at his master; but, as if long wonted to these little informalities, neither master nor man seemed to understand him.

"What, pray, was Atufal's offence, Don Benito?" asked Captain Delano; "if it was not something very serious, take a fool's advice, and, in view of his general docility, as well as in some natural respect for his spirit, remit his penalty."

"No, no, master never will do that," here murmured the servant to himself, "proud Atufal must first ask master's pardon. The slave there carries the padlock, but master here carries the key."

His attention thus directed, Captain Delano now noticed for the first time that, suspended by a slender silken cord, from Don Benito's neck hung a key. At once, from the servant's muttered syllables divining the key's purpose, he smiled and said: "So, Don Benito—padlock and key—significant symbols, truly."

Biting his lip, Don Benito faltered.

Though the remark of Captain Delano, a man of such native simplicity as to be incapable of satire or irony, had been dropped in playful allusion to the Spaniard's singularly evidenced lordship over the black; yet the hypochondriac seemed in some way to have taken it as a malicious reflection upon his confessed inability thus far to break down, at least, on a verbal summons, the entrenched will of the slave. Deploring this supposed misconception, yet despairing of correcting it, Captain Delano shifted the subject; but finding his companion more than ever withdrawn, as if still slowly digesting the lees of the presumed affront above-mentioned, by-and-by Captain Delano likewise became less talkative, oppressed, against his own will, by what seemed the secret vindictiveness of the morbidly sensitive Spaniard. But the good sailor himself, of a quite contrary disposition, refrained, on his part, alike from the appearance as from the feeling of resentment, and if silent, was only so from contagion.

Presently the Spaniard, assisted by his servant, somewhat discourteously crossed over from Captain Delano; a procedure which, sensibly enough, might have been allowed to pass for idle caprice of ill-humour, had not master and man, lingering round the corner of the elevated skylight, begun whispering together in low voices. This was unpleasing. And more: the moody air of the Spaniard, which at times had not been without a sort of valetudinarian stateliness, now seemed anything but dignified; while the menial familiarity of the servant lost its original charm of simple-hearted attachment.

In his embarrassment, the visitor turned his face to the other side of the ship. By so doing, his glance accidentally fell on a young Spanish sailor, a coil of rope in his hand, just stepped from the deck to the first round of the mizzen-rigging. Perhaps the man would not have been particularly noticed, were it not that, during his ascent to one of the yards, he with a sort of covert intentness, kept his eye fixed on Captain Delano, from whom, presently, it passed, as if by a natural sequence, to the two whisperers.

His own attention thus redirected to that quarter, Captain Delano gave a slight start. From something in Don Benito's manner just then, it seemed as if the visitor had, at least partly, been the subject of the withdrawn consultation going on—a conjecture as little agreeable to the guest as it was little flattering to the host.

The singular alternations of courtesy and ill-breeding in the Spanish captain were unaccountable, except on one of two suppositions—innocent lunacy, or wicked imposture.

But the first idea, though it might naturally have occurred to an indifferent observer, and, in some respects, had not hitherto been wholly a stranger to Captain Delano's mind, yet, now that, in an incipient way, he began to regard the stranger's conduct something in the light of an intentional affront, of course the idea of lunacy was virtually vacated. But if not a lunatic, what then? Under the circumstances, would a gentleman, nay, any honest boor, act the part now acted by his host? The man was an impostor. Some low-born adventurer, masquerading as an oceanic grandee; yet so ignorant of the first requisites of mere gentlemanhood as to be betrayed into the present remarkable indecorum. That strange ceremoniousness, too, at other times evinced, seemed not uncharacteristic of one playing a part above his real level. Benito Cereno—Don Benito Cereno—a sounding name. One, too, at that period, not unknown, in the surname, to super-cargoes and sea captains trading along the Spanish Main, as belonging to one of the most enterprising and extensive mercantile families in all those provinces; several members of it having titles; a sort of Castilian Rothschild, with a noble brother, or cousin, in every great trading town of South America. The alleged Don Benito was in early manhood, about twenty-nine or thirty. To assume a sort of roving cadet-ship in the maritime affairs of such a house, what more likely scheme for a young knave of talent and spirit? But the Spaniard was a pale invalid. Never mind. For even to the degree of simulating mortal disease, the craft of some tricksters had been known to attain. To think that, under the aspect of infantile weakness, the most savage energies might be couched—those velvets of the Spaniard but the velvet paw to his fangs.

From no train of thought did these fancies come; not from within, but from without; suddenly, too, and in one throng, like hoar frost; yet as soon to vanish as the mild sun of Captain Delano's good-nature regained its meridian.

Glancing over once again toward Don Benito—whose side-face, revealed above the skylight, was now turned toward him—Captain Delano was struck by the profile, whose clearness of cut was refined by the thinness incident to ill-health, as well as ennobled about the chin by the beard. Away with suspicion. He was a true off-shoot of a true hidalgo Cereno.

Relieved by these and other better thoughts, the visitor, lightly humming a tune, now began indifferently pacing the poop, so as not to betray to Don Benito that he had at all mistrusted incivility, much less duplicity; for such mistrust would yet be proved illusory, and by the event; though, for the present, the circumstance which had provoked that distrust remained unexplained. But when that little mystery should have been cleared up, Captain Delano thought he might extremely regret it, did he allow Don Benito to become aware that he had indulged in ungenerous surmises. In short, to the Spaniard's blackletter text, it was best, for a while, to leave open margin.

Presently, his pale face twitching and overcast, the Spaniard, still supported by his attendant, moved over toward his guest, when, with even more than his usual embarrassment, and a strange sort of intriguing intonation in his husky whisper, the following conversation began:

"Señor, may I ask how long you have lain at this isle?"

"Oh, but a day or two, Don Benito."

"And from what port are you last?"

"Canton."

"And there, Señor, you exchanged your seal-skins for teas and silks, I think you said?"

"Yes. Silks, mostly."

"And the balance you took in specie, perhaps?"

Captain Delano, fidgeting a little, answered—

"Yes; some silver; not a very great deal, though."

"Ah—well. May I ask how many men have you on board, Señor?"

Captain Delano slightly started, but answered:

"About five-and-twenty, all told."

"And at present, Señor, all on board, I suppose?"

"All on board, Don Benito," replied the captain now with satisfaction.

"And will be to-night, Señor?"

At this last question, following so many pertinacious ones, for the soul of him Captain Delano could not but look very earnestly at the questioner, who, instead of meeting the glance, with every token of craven discomposure dropped his eyes to the deck; presenting an unworthy contrast to his servant; who, just then, was kneeling at his feet adjusting a loose shoe-buckle; his disengaged face meantime, with humble curiosity, turned openly up into his master's downcast one.

The Spaniard, still with a guilty shuffle, repeated his question:

"And—and will be to-night, Señor?"

"Yes, for aught I know," returned Captain Delano,—"but nay," rallying himself into fearless truth, "some of them talked of going off on another fishing party about midnight."

"Your ships generally go—go more or less armed, I believe, Señor?"

"Oh, a six-pounder or two, in case of emergency," was the intrepidly indifferent reply, "with a small stock of muskets, sealing-spears, and cutlasses, you know."

As he thus responded, Captain Delano again glanced at Don Benito, but the latter's eyes were averted; while abruptly and awkwardly shifting the subject, he made some peevish allusion to the calm, and then, without apology, once more, with his attendant, withdrew to the opposite bulwarks, where the whispering was resumed.

At this moment, and ere Captain Delano could cast a cool thought upon what had just passed, the young Spanish sailor before mentioned was seen descending from the rigging. In act of stooping over to spring inboard to the deck, his voluminous, unconfined frock, or shirt, of coarse woollen, much spotted with tar, opened out far down the chest, revealing a soiled under-garment of what seemed the finest linen, edged, about the neck, with a narrow blue ribbon, sadly faded and worn. At this moment the young sailor's eye was again fixed on the whisperers, and Captain Delano thought he observed a lurking significance in it, as if silent signs of some freemason sort had that instant been interchanged.

This once more impelled his own glance in the direction of Don Benito, and, as before, he could not but infer that himself formed the subject of the conference. He paused. The sound of the hatchet-polishing fell on his ears. He cast another swift side-look at the two. They had the air of conspirators. In connection with the late questionings, and the incident of the young sailor, these things now begat such return of involuntary suspicion, that the singular guilelessness of the American could not endure it. Plucking up a gay and humorous expression, he crossed over to the two rapidly, saying: "Ha, Don Benito, your black here seems high in your trust; a sort of privy-counsellor, in fact."

Upon this, the servant looked up with a good-natured grin, but the master started as from a venomous bite. It was a moment or two before the Spaniard sufficiently recovered himself to reply; which he did, at last, with cold constraint: "Yes, Señor, I have trust in Babo."

Here Babo, changing his previous grin of mere animal humour into an intelligent smile, not ungratefully eyed his master.

Finding that the Spaniard now stood silent and reserved, as if involuntarily, or purposely giving hint that his guest's proximity was inconvenient just then, Captain Delano, unwilling to appear uncivil even to incivility itself, made some trivial remark and moved off; again and again turning over in his mind the mysterious demeanour of Don Benito Cereno.

He had descended from the poop, and, wrapped in thought, was passing near a dark hatchway, leading down into the steerage, when, perceiving motion there, he looked to see what moved. The same instant there was a sparkle in the shadowy hatchway, and he saw one of the Spanish sailors, prowling there, hurriedly placing his hand in the bosom of his frock, as if hiding something. Before the man could have been certain who it was that was passing, he slunk below out of sight. But enough was seen of him to make it sure that he was the same young sailor before noticed in the rigging.

What was that which so sparkled? thought Captain Delano. It was no lamp—no match—no live coal. Could it have been a jewel? But how come sailors with jewels?—or with silk-trimmed undershirts either? Has he been robbing the trunks of the dead cabin passengers? But if so, he would hardly wear one of the stolen articles on board ship here. Ah, ah— if now that was, indeed, a secret sign I saw passing between this suspicious fellow and his captain awhile since; if I could only be certain that in my uneasiness my senses did not deceive me, then—

Here, passing from one suspicious thing to another, his mind revolved the point of the strange questions put to him concerning his ship.

By a curious coincidence, as each point was recalled, the black wizards of Ashantee would strike up with their hatchets, as in ominous comment on the white stranger's thoughts. Pressed by such enigmas and portents, it would have been almost against nature, had not, even into the least distrustful heart, some ugly misgivings obtruded.

Observing the ship now helplessly fallen into a current, with enchanted sails, drifting with increased rapidity seaward; and noting that, from a lately intercepted projection of the land, the sealer was hidden, the stout mariner began to quake at thoughts which he barely durst confess to himself. Above all, he began to feel a ghostly dread of Don Benito. And yet when he roused himself, dilated his chest, felt himself strong on his legs, and coolly considered it—what did all these phantoms amount to?

Had the Spaniard any sinister scheme, it must have reference not so much to him (Captain Delano) as to his ship (the *Bachelor's Delight*). Hence the present drifting away of the one ship from the other, instead of favouring any such possible scheme, was, for the time at least, opposed to it. Clearly any suspicion, combining such contradictions, must need be delusive. Besides, was it not absurd to think of a vessel in distress—a vessel by sickness almost dismanned of her crew—a vessel whose inmates were parched for water—was it not a thousand times absurd that such a craft should, at present, be of a piratical character; or her commander, either for himself or those under him, cherish any desire but for speedy relief and refreshment? But then, might not general distress, and thirst in particular, be affected? And might not that same undiminished Spanish crew, alleged to have perished off to a remnant, be at that very moment lurking in the hold? On heartbroken pretence of entreating a cup of cold water, fiends in human form had got into lonely dwellings, nor retired until a dark deed had been done. And among the Malay pirates, it was no unusual thing to lure ships after them into their treacherous harbours, or entice boarders from a declared enemy at sea, by the spectacle of thinly manned or vacant decks, beneath which prowled a hundred spears with yellow arms ready to upthrust them through the mats. Not that Captain Delano had entirely credited such things. He had heard of them—and now, as stories, they recurred. The present destination of the ship was the anchorage. There she would be near his own vessel. Upon gaining that vicinity, might not the *San Dominick*, like a slumbering volcano, suddenly let loose energies now hid?

He recalled the Spaniard's manner while telling his story. There was a gloomy hesitancy and subterfuge about it. It was just the manner of one making up his tale for evil purposes, as he goes. But if that story was true, what was the truth? That the ship had unlawfully come into the Spaniard's possession? But in many of its details, especially in reference to the more calamitous parts, such as the fatalities among the seamen, the consequent prolonged beating about, the past sufferings from obstinate calms, and still continued suffering from thirst; in all these points, as well as others, Don Benito's story had corroborated not only the wailing ejaculations of the indiscriminate multitude, white and black, but likewise—what seemed impossible to be counterfeit—by the very expression and play of every human feature, which Captain Delano saw. If Don Benito's story was throughout an invention, then every soul on board, down to the youngest negress, was his carefully drilled recruit in the plot: an incredible inference. And yet, if there was ground for mistrusting the Spanish captain's veracity, that inference was a legitimate one.

In short, scarce an uneasiness entered the honest sailor's mind but, by a subsequent spontaneous act of good sense, it was ejected. At last he began to laugh at these forebodings; and laugh at the strange ship for, in its aspect someway siding with them, as it were; and laugh, too, at the odd-looking blacks, particularly those old scissors-grinders, the Ashantees; and those bed-ridden old knitting-women, the oakum-pickers; and in a human way, he almost began to laugh at the dark Spaniard himself, the central hobgoblin of all.

For the rest, whatever in a serious way seemed enigmatical, was now good-naturedly explained away by the thought that, for the most part, the poor invalid scarcely knew what he was about; either sulking in black vapours, or putting random questions without sense or object. Evidently, for the present, the man was not fit to be entrusted with the ship. On some benevolent plea withdrawing the command from him, Captain Delano would yet have to send her to Concepcion in charge of his second mate, a worthy person and good navigator—a plan which would prove no wiser for the *San Dominick* than for Don Benito; for—relieved from all anxiety, keeping wholly to his cabin—the sick man, under the good nursing of his servant, would probably, by the end of the passage, be in a measure restored to health and with that he should also be restored to authority.

Such were the American's thoughts. They were tranquillizing. There was a difference between the idea of Don Benito's darkly pre-ordaining Captain Delano's fate, and Captain Delano's lightly arranging Don Benito's. Nevertheless, it was not without something of relief that the good seaman presently perceived his whale-boat in the distance. Its absence had been prolonged by unexpected detention at the sealer's side, as well as its returning trip lengthened by the continual recession of the goal.

The advancing speck was observed by the blacks. Their shouts attracted the attention of Don Benito, who, with a return of courtesy, approaching Captain Delano, expressed satisfaction at the coming of some supplies, slight and temporary as they must necessarily prove.

Captain Delano responded; but while doing so, his attention was drawn to something passing on the deck below: among the crowd climbing the landward bulwarks, anxiously watching the coming boat, two blacks, to all appearances accidentally incommoded by one of the sailors, flew out against him with horrible curses, which the sailor someway resenting, the two blacks dashed him to the deck and jumped upon him, despite the earnest cries of the oakumpickers.

"Don Benito," said Captain Delano quickly, "do you see what is going on there? Look!"

But, seized by his cough, the Spaniard staggered, with both hands to his face, on the point of falling. Captain Delano would have supported him, but the servant was more alert, who, with one hand sustaining his master, with the other applied the cordial. Don Benito, restored, the black withdrew his support, slipping aside a little, but dutifully remaining within call of a whisper. Such discretion was here evinced as quite wiped away, in the visitor's eyes, any blemish of impropriety which might have attached to the attendant, from the indecorous conferences before mentioned; showing, too, that if the servant were to blame, it might be more the master's fault than his own, since when left to himself he could conduct thus well.

His glance thus called away from the spectacle of disorder to the more pleasing one before him, Captain Delano could not avoid again congratulating Don Benito upon possessing such a servant, who, though perhaps a little too forward now and then, must upon the whole be invaluable to one in the invalid's situation.

"Tell me, Don Benito," he added, with a smile—"I should like to have your man here myself—what will you take for him? Would fifty doubloons be any object?"

"Master wouldn't part with Babo for a thousand doubloons," murmured the black, overhearing the offer, and taking it in earnest, and, with the strange vanity of a faithful slave appreciated by his master, scorning to hear so paltry a valuation put upon him by a stranger. But Don Benito, apparently hardly yet completely restored, and again interrupted by his cough, made but some broken reply.

Soon his physical distress became so great, affecting his mind, too, apparently, that, as if to screen the sad spectacle, the servant gently conducted his master below.

Left to himself, the American, to while away the time till his boat should arrive, would have pleasantly accosted some one of the few Spanish seamen he saw; but recalling something that Don Benito had said touching their ill conduct, he refrained, as a ship-master indisposed to countenance cowardice or unfaithfulness in seamen.

While, with these thoughts, standing with eye directed forward toward that handful of sailors—suddenly he thought that some of them returned the glance and with a sort of meaning. He rubbed his eyes, and looked again; but again seemed to see the same thing. Under a new form, but more obscure than any previous one, the old suspicions recurred, but, in the absence of Don Benito, with less of panic than before. Despite the bad account given of the sailors, Captain Delano resolved forthwith to accost one of them. Descending the poop, he made his way through the blacks, his movement drawing a queer cry from the oakum-pickers, prompted by whom the negroes, twitching each other aside, divided before him; but, as if curious to see what was the object of this deliberate visit to their Ghetto, closing in behind, in tolerable order, followed the white stranger up. His progress thus proclaimed as by mounted kings-at-arms, and escorted as by a Caffre guard of honour, Captain Delano, assuming a good-humoured, off-hand air, continued to advance; now and then saying a blithe word to the negroes, and his eye curiously surveying the white faces, here and there sparsely mixed in with the blacks, like stray white pawns venturously involved in the ranks of the chessmen opposed.

While thinking which of them to select for his purpose, he chanced to observe a sailor seated on the deck engaged in tarring the strap of a large block, with a circle of blacks squatted round him inquisitively eyeing the process.

The mean employment of the man was in contrast with something superior in his figure. His hand, black with continually thrusting it into the tar-pot held for him by a negro, seemed not naturally allied to his face, a face which would have been a very fine one but for its haggardness. Whether this haggardness had aught to do with criminality could not be determined; since, as intense heat and cold, though unlike, produce like sensations, so innocence and guilt, when, through casual association with mental pain, stamping any visible impress, use one seal—a hacked one.

Not again that this reflection occurred to Captain Delano at the time, charitable man as he was. Rather another idea. Because observing so singular a haggardness to be combined with a dark eye, averted as in trouble and shame, and then, however illogically, uniting in his mind his own private suspicions of the crew with the confessed ill-opinion on the part of their captain, he was insensibly operated upon by certain general notions, which, while disconnecting pain and abashment from virtue, as invariably link them with vice.

If, indeed, there be any wickedness on board this ship, thought Captain Delano, be sure that man there has fouled his hand in it, even as now he fouls it in the pitch. I don't like to accost him. I will speak to this other, this old Jack here on the windlass.

He advanced to an old Barcelona tar, in ragged red breeches and dirty night-cap, cheeks trenched and bronzed, whiskers dense as thorn hedges. Seated between two sleepy-looking Africans, this mariner, like his younger shipmate, was employed upon some rigging—splicing a cable—the sleepy-looking blacks performing the inferior function of holding the outer parts of the ropes for him.

Upon Captain Delano's approach, the man at once hung his head below its previous level; the one necessary for business.

It appeared as if he desired to be thought absorbed, with more than common fidelity, in his task. Being addressed, he glanced up, but with what seemed a furtive, diffident air, which sat strangely enough on his weatherbeaten visage, much as if a grizzly bear, instead of growling and biting, should simper and cast sheep's eyes. He was asked several questions concerning the voyage—questions purposely referring to several particulars in Don Benito's narrative—not previously corroborated by those impulsive cries greeting the visitor on first coming on board. The questions were briefly answered, confirming all that remained to be confirmed of the story. The negroes about the windlass joined in with the old sailor, but, as they became talkative, he by degrees became mute, and at length quite glum, seemed morosely unwilling to answer more questions, and yet, all the while, this ursine air was somehow mixed with his sheepish one.

Despairing of getting into unembarrassed talk with such a centaur, Captain Delano, after glancing round for a more promising countenance, but seeing none, spoke pleasantly to the blacks to make way for him; and so, amid various grins and grimaces, returned to the poop, feeling a little strange at first, he could hardly tell why, but upon the whole with regained confidence in Benito Cereno.

How plainly, thought he, did that old whiskerando yonder betray a consciousness of ill-desert. No doubt, when he saw me coming, he dreaded lest I, apprised by his captain of the crew's general misbehaviour, came with sharp words for him, and so down with his head. And yet—and yet, now that I think of it, that very old fellow, if I err not, was one of those who seemed so earnestly eyeing me here awhile since. Ah, these currents spin one's head round almost as much as they do the ship. Ha, there now's a pleasant sort of sunny sight; quite sociable, too.

His attention had been drawn to a slumbering negress, partly disclosed through the lace-work of some rigging, lying, with youthful limbs carelessly disposed, under the lee of the bulwarks, like a doe in the shade of a woodland rock. Sprawling at her lapped breasts was her wide-awake fawn, stark naked, its black little body half lifted from the deck, crosswise with its dam's; its hands, like two paws, clambering upon her; its mouth and nose ineffectually rooting to get at the mark; and meantime giving a vexatious half-grunt, blending with the composed snore of the negress.

The uncommon vigour of the child at length roused the mother. She started up, at distance facing Captain Delano. But, as if not at all concerned at the attitude in which she had been caught, delightedly she caught the child up, with maternal transports, covering it with kisses.

There's naked nature, now; pure tenderness and love, thought Captain Delano, well pleased.

This incident prompted him to remark the other negresses more particularly than before. He was gratified with their manners; like most uncivilized women, they seemed at once tender of heart and tough of constitution; equally ready to die for their infants or fight for them. Unsophisticated as leopardesses; loving as doves. Ah! thought Captain Delano, these perhaps are some of the very women whom Mungo Park saw in Africa, and gave such a noble account of.

These natural sights somehow insensibly deepened his confidence and ease. At last he looked to see how his boat was getting on; but it was still pretty remote. He turned to see if Don Benito had returned; but he had not.

To change the scene, as well as to please himself with a leisurely observation of the coming boat, stepping over into the mizzen-chains he clambered his way into the starboard quarter-gallery; one of those abandoned Venetian-looking water-balconies previously mentioned; retreats cut off from the deck. As his foot pressed the half-damp, half-dry sea-mosses matting the place, and a chance phantom cat's-paw —an islet of breeze, unheralded, unfollowed—as this ghostly cat's-paw came fanning his cheek, as his glance fell upon the row of small, round dead-lights—all closed like coppered eyes of the coffined—and the state-cabin door, once connecting with the gallery, even as the deadlights had once looked out upon it, but now caulked fast like a sarcophagus lid; and to a purple-black, tarred-over panel, threshold, and post; and he bethought him of the time, when that state-cabin and this state-balcony had heard the voices of the Spanish king's officers, and the forms of the Lima viceroy's daughters had perhaps leaned where he stood—as these and other images flitted through his mind, as the cat's-paw through the calm, gradually he felt rising a dreamy inquietude, like that of one who alone on the prairie feels unrest from the repose of the noon.

He leaned against the carved balustrade, again looking off toward his boat; but found his eye falling upon the ribboned grass, trailing along the ship's water-line, straight as a border

of green box; and parterres of sea-weed, broad ovals and
crescents, floating nigh and far, with what seemed long formal alleys between, crossing the terraces of swells, and
sweeping round as if leading to the grottoes below. And overhanging all was the balustrade by his arm, which, partly
stained with pitch and partly embossed with moss, seemed the
charred ruins of some summer-house in a grand garden long
running to waste.

Trying to break one charm, he was but becharmed anew.
Though upon the wide sea, he seemed in some far inland
country; prisoner in some deserted château, left to stare at
empty grounds, and peer out at vague roads, where never
wagon or wayfarer passed.

But these enchantments were a little disenchanted as his
eye fell on the corroded main-chains. Of an ancient style,
massy and rusty in link, shackle and bolt, they seemed even
more fit for the ship's present business than the one for which
probably she had been built.

Presently he thought something moved nigh the chains.
He rubbed his eyes, and looked hard. Groves of rigging were
about the chains; and there, peering from behind a great
stay, like an Indian from behind a hemlock, a Spanish sailor,
a marlingspike in his hand, was seen, who made what
seemed an imperfect gesture toward the balcony—but immediately, as if alarmed by some advancing step along the
deck within, vanished into the recesses of the hempen forest,
like a poacher.

What meant this? Something the man had sought to com-
municate unbeknown to any one, even to his captain. Did
the secret involve aught unfavourable to his captain? Were
those previous misgivings of Captain Delano's about to be
verified? Or, in his haunted mood at the moment, had some
random, unintentional motion of the man, while busy with
the stay, as if repairing it, been mistaken for a significant
beckoning?

Not unbewildered, again he gazed off for his boat. But it
was temporarily hidden by a rocky spur of the isle. As with
some eagerness he bent forward, watching for the first shoot-
ing view of its beak, the balustrade gave way before him like
charcoal. Had he not clutched an outreaching rope he would
have fallen into the sea. The crash, though feeble, and the
fall, though hollow, of the rotten fragments, must have been
overheard. He glanced up. With sober curiosity peering down
upon him was one of the old oakum-pickers, slipped from his

perch to an outside boom; while below the old negro—and, invisible to him, reconnoitring from a port-hole like a fox from the mouth of its den—crouched the Spanish sailor again. From something suddenly suggested by the man's air, the mad idea now darted into Captain Delano's mind; that Don Benito's plea of indisposition, in withdrawing below, was but a pretence: that he was engaged there maturing some plot, of which the sailor, by some means gaining an inkling, had a mind to warn the stranger against; incited, it may be, by gratitude for a kind word on first boarding the ship. Was it from foreseeing some possible interference like this, that Don Benito had, beforehand, given such a bad character of his sailors, while praising the negroes; though, indeed, the former seemed as docile as the latter the contrary? The whites, too, by nature, were the shrewder race. A man with some evil design, would not he be likely to speak well of that stupidity which was blind to his depravity, and malign that intelligence from which it might not be hidden? Not unlikely, perhaps. But if the whites had dark secrets concerning Don Benito, could then Don Benito be any way in complicity with the blacks? But they were too stupid. Besides, who ever heard of a white so far a renegade as to apostatize from his very species almost, by leaguing in against it with negroes? These difficulties recalled former ones. Lost in their mazes, Captain Delano, who had now regained the deck, was uneasily advancing along it, when he observed a new face; an aged sailor seated cross-legged near the main hatchway. His skin was shrunk up with wrinkles like a pelican's empty pouch; his hair frosted; his countenance grave and composed. His hands were full of ropes, which he was working into a large knot. Some blacks were about him obligingly dipping the strands for him, here and there, as the exigencies of the operation demanded.

Captain Delano crossed over to him, and stood in silence surveying the knot; his mind, by a not uncongenial transition, passing from its own entanglements to those of the hemp. For intricacy such a knot he had never seen in an American ship, or indeed any other. The old man looked like an Egyptian priest, making gordian knots for the temple of Ammon. The knot seemed a combination of double-bow-line-knot, treble-crown-knot, back-handed-well-knot, knot-in-and-out-knot, and jamming-knot.

At last, puzzled to comprehend the meaning of such a knot, Captain Delano addressed the knotter:—

"What are you knotting there, my man?"

"The knot," was the brief reply, without looking up.

"So it seems; but what is it for?"

"For some one else to undo," muttered back the old man, plying his fingers harder than ever, the knot being now nearly completed.

While Captain Delano stood watching him, suddenly the old man threw the knot toward him, and said in broken English,—the first heard in the ship,—something to this effect —"Undo it, cut it, quick." It was said lowly, but with such condensation of rapidity, that the long, slow words in Spanish, which had preceded and followed, almost operated as covers to the brief English between.

For a moment, knot in hand, and knot in head, Captain Delano stood mute; while, without further heeding him, the old man was now intent upon other ropes. Presently there was a slight stir behind Captain Delano. Turning, he saw the chained negro, Atufal, standing quietly there. The next moment the old sailor rose, muttering, and, followed by his subordinate negroes, removed to the forward part of the ship, where in the crowd he disappeared.

An elderly negro, in a clout like an infant's, and with a pepper and salt head, and a kind of attorney air, now approached Captain Delano. In tolerable Spanish, and with a good-natured, knowing wink, he informed him that the old knotter was simple-witted, but harmless; often playing his old tricks. The negro concluded by begging the knot, for of course the stranger would not care to be troubled with it. Unconsciously, it was handed to him. With a sort of congé, the negro received it, and turning his back ferreted into it like a detective Custom House officer after smuggled laces. Soon, with some African word, equivalent to pshaw, he tossed the knot overboard.

All this is very queer now, thought Captain Delano, with a qualmish sort of emotion; but as one feeling incipient seasickness, he strove, by ignoring the symptoms, to get rid of the malady. Once more he looked off for his boat. To his delight, it was now again in view, leaving the rocky spur astern.

The sensation here experienced, after at first relieving his uneasiness, with unforeseen efficiency, soon began to remove it. The less distant sight of that well-known boat—showing it, not as before, half blended with the haze, but with outline defined, so that its individuality, like a man's, was manifest; that boat, *Rover* by name, which, though now in strange seas, had often pressed the beach of Captain Delano's home, and, brought to its threshold for repairs, had familiarly lain there, as a Newfoundland dog; the sight of that household boat evoked a thousand trustful associations, which, contrasted with previous suspicions, filled him not only with lightsome confidence, but somehow with half humorous self-reproaches at his former lack of it.

"What, I, Amasa Delano—Jack of the Beach, as they called me when a lad—I, Amasa; the same that, duck-satchel in hand, used to paddle along the waterside to the schoolhouse made from the old hulk;—I, little Jack of the Beach, that used to go berrying with cousin Nat and the rest; I to be murdered here at the ends of the earth, on board a haunted pirate-ship by a horrible Spaniard?—Too nonsensical to think of! Who would murder Amasa Delano? His conscience is clean. There is some one above. Fie, fie, Jack of the Beach! you are a child indeed; a child of the second childhood, old boy; you are beginning to dote and drule, I'm afraid."

Light of heart and foot, he stepped aft, and there was met by Don Benito's servant, who, with a pleasing expression, responsive to his own present feelings, informed him that his master had recovered from the effects of his coughing fit, and had just ordered him to go present his compliments to his good guest, Don Amasa, and say that he (Don Benito) would soon have the happiness to rejoin him.

There now, do you mark that? again thought Captain Delano, walking the poop. What a donkey I was. This kind gentleman who here sends me his kind compliments, he, but ten minutes ago, dark-lantern in hand, was dodging round some old grind-stone in the hold, sharpening a hatchet for me, I thought. Well, well; these long calms have a morbid effect on the mind, I've often heard, though I never believed it before. Ha! glancing toward the boat; there's *Rover;* a good dog; a white bone in her mouth. A pretty big bone though, seems to me.—What? Yes, she has fallen afoul of the bubbling tide-rip there. It sets her the other way, too, for the time. Patience.

It was now about noon, though, from the greyness of everything, it seemed to be getting toward dusk.

The calm was confirmed. In the far distance, away from the influence of land, the leaden ocean seemed laid out and leaded up, its course finished, soul gone, defunct. But the current from landward, where the ship was, increased; silently sweeping her further and further toward the tranced waters beyond.

Still, from his knowledge of those latitudes, cherishing hopes of a breeze, and a fair and fresh one, at any moment, Captain Delano, despite present prospects, buoyantly counted upon bringing the *San Dominick* safely to anchor ere night. The distance swept over was nothing; since, with a good wind, ten minutes' sailing would retrace more than sixty minutes' drifting. Meantime, one moment turning to mark "Rover" fighting the tide-rip, and the next to see Don Benito approaching, he continued walking the poop.

Gradually he felt a vexation arising from the delay of his boat; this soon merged into uneasiness; and at last, his eye falling continually, as from a stage-box into the pit, upon the strange crowd before and below him, and by-and-by recognizing there the face—now composed to indifference—of the Spanish sailor who had seemed to beckon from the main chains, something of his old trepidations returned.

Ah, thought he—gravely enough—this is like the ague: because it went off, it follows not that it won't come back.

Though ashamed of the relapse, he could not altogether subdue it; and so, exerting his good nature to the utmost, insensibly he came to a compromise.

Yes, this is a strange craft; a strange history, too, and strange folks on board. But—nothing more.

By way of keeping his mind out of mischief till the boat should arrive, he tried to occupy it with turning over and over, in a purely speculative sort of way, some lesser peculiarities of the captain and crew. Among others, four curious points recurred.

First, the affair of the Spanish lad assailed with a knife by the slave boy; an act winked at by Don Benito. Second, the tyranny in Don Benito's treatment of Atufal, the black; as if a child should lead a bull of the Nile by the ring in his nose. Third, the trampling of the sailor by the two negroes; a piece of insolence passed over without so much as a reprimand. Fourth, the cringing submission to their master of all the ship's underlings, mostly blacks; as if by the least inadvertence they feared to draw down his despotic displeasure.

Coupling these points, they seemed somewhat contradictory. But what then, thought Captain Delano, glancing toward his now nearing boat,—what then? Why, this Don Benito is a very capricious commander. But he is not the first of the sort I have seen; though it's true he rather exceeds any other. But as a nation—continued he in his reveries—these Spaniards are all an odd set; the very word Spaniard has a curious, conspirator, Guy-Fawkish twang to it. And yet, I dare say, Spaniards in the main are as good folks as any in Duxbury, Massachusetts. Ah, good! At last "Rover" has come.

As, with its welcome freight, the boat touched the side, the oakum-pickers, with venerable gestures, sought to restrain the blacks, who, at the sight of three gurried water-casks in its bottom, and a pile of wilted pumpkins in its bow, hung over the bulwarks in disorderly raptures.

Don Benito with his servant now appeared; his coming, perhaps, hastened by hearing the noise. Of him Captain Delano sought permission to serve out the water, so that all might share alike, and none injure themselves by unfair excess. But sensible, and, on Don Benito's account, kind as this offer was, it was received with what seemed impatience; as if aware that he lacked energy as a commander, Don Benito, with the true jealousy of weakness, resented as an affront any interference. So, at least, Captain Delano inferred.

In another moment the casks were being hoisted in, when some of the eager negroes accidentally jostled Captain Delano, where he stood by the gangway; so that, unmindful of Don Benito, yielding to the impulse of the moment, with good-natured authority he bade the blacks stand back; to enforce his words making use of a half-mirthful, half-menacing gesture. Instantly the blacks paused, just where they were, each negro and negress suspended in his or her posture, exactly as the word had found them—for a few seconds continuing so—while, as between the responsive posts of a telegraph, an unknown syllable ran from man to man among the perched oakum-pickers. While Captain Delano's attention was fixed by this scene, suddenly the hatchet-polishers half rose, and a rapid cry came from Don Benito.

Thinking that at the signal of the Spaniard he was about to be massacred, Captain Delano would have sprung for his boat, but paused, as the oakum-pickers, dropping down into the crowd with earnest exclamations, forced every white and every negro back, at the same moment, with gestures friendly and familiar, almost jocose, bidding him, in substance, not be a fool. Simultaneously the hatchet-polishers resumed their seats, quietly as so many tailors, and at once, as if nothing had happened, the work of hoisting in the casks was resumed, whites and blacks singing at the tackle.

Captain Delano glanced toward Don Benito. As he saw his

meagre form in the act of recovering itself from reclining in the servant's arms, into which the agitated invalid had fallen, he could not but marvel at the panic by which himself had been surprised on the darting supposition that such a commander, who upon a legitimate occasion, so trivial, too, as it now appeared, could lose all self-command, was, with energetic iniquity, going to bring about his murder.

The casks being on deck, Captain Delano was handed a number of jars and cups by one of the steward's aides, who, in the name of Don Benito, entreated him to do as he had proposed: dole out the water. He complied, with republican impartiality as to this republican element, which always seeks one level, serving the oldest white no better than the youngest black; excepting, indeed, poor Don Benito, whose condition, if not rank, demanded an extra allowance. To him, in the first place, Captain Delano presented a fair pitcher of the fluid; but, thirsting as he was for fresh water, Don Benito quaffed not a drop until after several grave bows and salutes: a reciprocation of courtesies which the sight-loving Africans hailed with clapping of hands.

Two of the less wilted pumpkins being reserved for the cabin table, the residue were minced up on the spot for the general regalement. But the soft bread, sugar, and bottled cider, Captain Delano would have given the Spaniards alone, and in chief Don Benito; but the latter objected; which disinterestedness, on his part, not a little pleased the American; and so mouthfuls all around were given alike to whites and blacks; excepting one bottle of cider, which Babo insisted upon setting aside for his master.

Here it may be observed that as, on the first visit of the boat, the American had not permitted his men to board the ship, neither did he now; being unwilling to add to the confusion of the decks.

Not uninfluenced by the peculiar good humour at present prevailing, and for the time oblivious of any but benevolent thoughts, Captain Delano, who from recent indications counted upon a breeze within an hour or two at furthest, despatched the boat back to the sealer with orders for all the hands that could be spared immediately to set about rafting casks to the watering-place and filling them. Likewise he bade word be carried to his chief officer, that if against present expectation the ship was not brought to anchor by sunset, he need be under no concern, for as there was to be a full moon that night, he (Captain Delano) would remain on board ready to play the pilot, should the wind come soon or late.

As the two captains stood together, observing the departing boat—the servant as it happened having just spied a spot on his master's velvet sleeve, and silently engaged in rubbing it out—the American expressed his regrets that the *San Dominick* had no boats; none, at least, but the unseaworthy old hulk of the long-boat, which, warped as a camel's skeleton in the desert, and almost as bleached, lay potwise inverted amidships, one side a little tipped, furnishing a subterraneous sort of den for family groups of the blacks, mostly women and small children; who, squatting on old mats below, or perched above in the dark dome, on the elevated seats, were descried, some distance within, like a social circle of bats, sheltering in some friendly cave; at intervals, ebon flights of naked boys and girls, three or four years old, darting in and out of the den's mouth.

"Had you three or four boats now, Don Benito," said Captain Delano, "I think that, by tugging at the oars, your negroes here might help along matters some.—Did you sail from port without boats, Don Benito?"

"They were stove in the gales, Señor."

"That was bad. Many men, too, you lost then. Boats and men.—Those must have been hard gales, Don Benito."

"Past all speech," cringed the Spaniard.

"Tell me, Don Benito," continued his companion with increased interest, "tell me, were these gales immediately off the pitch of Cape Horn?"

"Cape Horn?—who spoke of Cape Horn?"

"Yourself did, when giving me an account of your voyage," answered Captain Delano with almost equal astonishment at this eating of his own words, even as he ever seemed eating his own heart, on the part of the Spaniard. "You yourself, Don Benito, spoke of Cape Horn," he emphatically repeated.

The Spaniard turned, in a sort of stooping posture, pausing an instant, as one about to make a plunging exchange of elements, as from air to water.

At this moment a messenger-boy, a white, hurried by, in the regular performance of his function carrying the last expired half-hour forward to the forecastle, from the cabin time-piece, to have it struck at the ship's large bell.

"Master," said the servant, discontinuing his work on the coat sleeve, and addressing the rapt Spaniard with a sort of timid apprehensiveness, as one charged with a duty, the discharge of which, it was foreseen, would prove irksome to the very person who had imposed it, and for whose benefit it was intended, "master told me never mind where he was, or how engaged, always to remind him, to a minute, when shaving-time comes. Miguel has gone to strike the half-hour afternoon. It is *now*, master. Will master go into the cuddy?"

"Ah—yes," answered the Spaniard, starting, somewhat as from dreams into realities; then turning upon Captain Delano, he said that ere long he would resume the conversation.

"Then if master means to talk more to Don Amasa," said the servant, "why not let Don Amasa sit by master in the cuddy, and master can talk, and Don Amasa can listen, while Babo here lathers and strops."

"Yes," said Captain Delano, not unpleased with this sociable plan, "yes, Don Benito, unless you had rather not, I will go with you."

"Be it so, Señor."

As the three passed aft, the American could not but think it another strange instance of his host's capriciousness, this being shaved with such uncommon punctuality in the middle of the day. But he deemed it more than likely that the servant's anxious fidelity had something to do with the matter; inasmuch as the timely interruption served to rally his master from the mood which had evidently been coming upon him.

The place called the cuddy was a light deck-cabin formed by the poop, a sort of attic to the large cabin below. Part of it had formerly been the quarters of the officers; but since their death all the partitionings had been thrown down, and the whole interior converted into one spacious and airy marine hall; for absence of fine furniture and picturesque disarray, of odd appurtenances, somewhat answering to the wide, cluttered hall of some eccentric bachelor-squire in the country, who hangs his shooting-jacket and tobacco-pouch on deer antlers, and keeps his fishing-rod, tongs, and walking-stick in the same corner.

The similitude was heightened, if not originally suggested, by glimpses of the surrounding sea; since, in one aspect, the country and the ocean seem cousins-german.

The floor of the cuddy was matted. Overhead, four or five old muskets were stuck into horizontal holes along the beams. On one side was a claw-footed old table lashed to the deck; a thumbed missal on it, and over it a small, meagre crucifix attached to the bulkhead. Under the table lay a dented cutlass or two, with a hacked harpoon, among some melancholy old rigging, like a heap of poor friar's girdles. There were also two long, sharp-ribbed settees of malacca cane, black with age, and uncomfortable to look at as inquisitors' racks, with a large, misshapen arm-chair, which, furnished with a rude barber's crutch at the back, working with a screw, seemed some grotesque Middle Age engine of torment. A flag locker was in one corner, exposing various coloured bunting, some rolled up, others half unrolled, still others tumbled. Opposite was a cumbrous washstand, of black mahogany, all of one block, with a pedestal, like a font, and over it a railed shelf, containing combs, brushes, and other implements of the toilet. A torn hammock of stained grass swung near; the sheets tossed, and the pillow wrinkled up like a brow, as if whoever slept here slept but silly, with alternate visitations of sad thoughts and bad dreams.

The further extremity of the cuddy, overhanging the ship's stern, was pierced with three openings, windows or port holes, according as men or cannon might peer, socially or unsocially, out of them. At present neither men nor cannon were seen, though huge ring-bolts and other rusty iron fixtures of the wood-work hinted of twenty-four-pounders.

Glancing toward the hammock as he entered, Captain Delano said, "You sleep here, Don Benito?"

"Yes, Señor, since we got into mild weather."

"This seems a sort of dormitory, sitting-room, sail-loft, chapel, armoury, and private closet together, Don Benito," added Captain Delano, looking round.

"Yes, Señor; events have not been favourable to much order in my arrangements."

Here the servant, napkin on arm, made a motion as if waiting his master's good pleasure. Don Benito signified his readiness, when, seating him in the malacca arm-chair, and for the guest's convenience drawing opposite it one of the settees, the servant commenced operations by throwing back his master's collar and loosening his cravat.

There is something in the negro which, in a peculiar way, fits him for avocations about one's person. Most negroes are natural valets and hair-dressers; taking to the comb and brush congenially as to the castanets, and flourishing them apparently with almost equal satisfaction. There is, too, a smooth tact about them in this employment, with a marvelous, noiseless, gliding briskness, not ungraceful in its way, singularly pleasing to behold, and still more so to be the manipulated subject of. And above all is the great gift of good humour. Not the mere grin or laugh is here meant. Those were unsuitable. But a certain easy cheerfulness, harmonious in every glance and gesture; as though God had set the whole negro to some pleasant tune.

When to all this is added the docility arising from the unaspiring contentment of a limited mind, and that susceptibility of blind attachment sometimes inhering in indisputable inferiors, one readily perceives why those hypochondriacs, Johnson and Byron—it may be something like the hypochondriac, Benito Cereno—took to their hearts, almost to the exclusion of the entire white race, their serving men, the negroes, Barber and Fletcher. But if there be that in the negro which exempts him from the inflicted sourness of the morbid or cynical mind, how, in his most prepossessing aspects, must he appear to a benevolent one? When at ease with respect to exterior things, Captain Delano's nature was not only benign, but familiarly and humourously so. At home, he had often taken rare satisfaction in sitting in his door, watching some free man of colour at his work or play. If on a voyage he chanced to have a black sailor, invariably he was on chatty, and half-gamesome terms with him. In fact, like most men of a good, blithe heart, Captain Delano took to negroes, not philanthropically, but genially, just as other men to Newfoundland dogs.

Hitherto the circumstances in which he found the *San Dominick* had repressed the tendency. But in the cuddy, relieved from his former uneasiness, and, for various reasons, more sociably inclined than at any previous period of the day, and seeing the coloured servant, napkin on arm, so debonair about his master, in a business so familiar as that of shaving, too, all his old weakness for negroes returned.

Among other things, he was amused with an odd instance of the African love of bright colours and fine shows, in the black's informally taking from the flag-locker a great piece of bunting of all hues, and lavishly tucking it under his master's chin for an apron.

The mode of shaving among the Spaniards is a little different from what it is with other nations. They have a basin, specially called a barber's basin, which on one side is scooped out, so as accurately to receive the chin, against which it is closely held in lathering; which is done, not with a brush, but with soap dipped in the water of the basin and rubbed on the face.

In the present instance salt-water was used for lack of better; and the parts lathered were only the upper lip, and low down under the throat, all the rest being cultivated beard.

These preliminaries being somewhat novel to Captain Delano he sat curiously eyeing them, so that no conversation took place, nor for the present did Don Benito appear disposed to renew any.

Setting down his basin, the negro searched among the razors, as for the sharpest, and having found it, gave it an additional edge by expertly stropping it on the firm, smooth, oily skin of his open palm; he then made a gesture as if to begin, but midway stood suspended for an instant, one hand elevating the razor, the other professionally dabbling among the bubbling suds on the Spaniard's lank neck. Not unaffected by the close sight of the gleaming steel, Don Benito nervously shuddered, his usual ghastliness was heightened by the lather, which lather, again, was intensified in its hue by the contrasting sootiness of the negro's body. Altogether the scene was somewhat peculiar, at least to Captain Delano, nor, as he saw the two thus postured, could he resist the vagary, that in the black he saw a headsman, and in the white, a man at the block. But this was one of those antic conceits, appearing and vanishing in a breath, from which, perhaps, the best regulated mind is not free.

Meantime the agitation of the Spaniard had a little loosened the bunting from around him, so that one broad fold swept curtain-like over the chair-arm to the floor, revealing, amid a profusion of armorial bars and ground-colours—black, blue and yellow—a closed castle in a blood-red field diagonal with a lion rampant in a white.

"The castle and the lion," exclaimed Captain Delano— "why, Don Benito, this is the flag of Spain you use here. It's well it's only I and not the King, that sees this," he added with a smile, "but"—turning toward the black,—"it's all one, I suppose, so the colours be gay," which playful remark did not fail somewhat to tickle the negro.

"Now, master," he said, readjusting the flag, and pressing the head gently further back into the crotch of the chair; "now master," and the steel glanced nigh the throat.

Again Don Benito faintly shuddered.

"You must not shake so, master.—See, Don Amasa, master always shakes when I shave him. And yet master knows I never yet have drawn blood, though it's true, if master will shake so, I may some of these times. Now, master," he continued. "And now, Don Amasa, please go on with your talk about the gale, and all that, master can hear, and between times master can answer."

"Ah yes, these gales," said Captain Delano; "but the more I think of your voyage, Don Benito, the more I wonder, not at the gales, terrible as they must have been, but at the disastrous interval following them. For here, by your account, have you been these two months and more getting from Cape Horn to St. Maria, a distance which I myself, with a good wind, have sailed in a few days. True, you had calms, and long ones, but to be becalmed for two months, that is, at least, unusual. Why, Don Benito, had almost any other gentleman told me such a story, I should have been half disposed to a little incredulity."

Here an involuntary expression came over the Spaniard, similar to that just before on the deck, and whether it was the start he gave, or a sudden gawky roll of the hull in the calm, or a momentary unsteadiness of the servant's hand; however it was, just then the razor drew blood, spots of which stained the creamy lather under the throat; immediately the black barber drew back his steel, and remaining in his professional attitude, back to Captain Delano, and face to Don Benito, held up the trickling razor, saying, with a sort of half humorous sorrow, "See, master,—you shook so— here's Babo's first blood."

No sword drawn before James the First of England, no assassination in that timid King's presence, could have produced a more terrified aspect than was now presented by Don Benito.

Poor fellow, thought Captain Delano, so nervous he can't even bear the sight of barber's blood; and this unstrung, sick man, is it credible that I should have imagined he meant to spill all my blood, who can't endure the sight of one little drop of his own? Surely, Amasa Delano, you have been beside yourself this day. Tell it not when you get home, sappy Amasa. Well, well, he looks like a murderer, doesn't he? More like as if himself were to be done for. Well, well, this day's experience shall be a good lesson.

Meantime, while these things were running through the honest seaman's mind, the servant had taken the napkin from his arm, and to Don Benito had said: "But answer Don Amasa, please, master, while I wipe this ugly stuff off the razor, and strop it again."

As he said the words, his face was turned half round, so as to be alike visible to the Spaniard and the American, and seemed by its expression to hint, that he was desirous, by getting his master to go on with the conversation, considerately to withdraw his attention from the recent annoying accident. As if glad to snatch the offered relief, Don Benito resumed, rehearsing to Captain Delano, that not only were the calms of unusual duration, but the ship had fallen in with obstinate currents and other things he added, some of which were but repetitions of former statements, to explain how it came to pass that the passage from Cape Horn to St. Maria had been so exceedingly long, now and then mingling with his words, incidental praises, less qualified than before, to the blacks for their general good conduct.

These particulars were not given consecutively, the servant now and then using his razor, and so, between the intervals of shaving, the story and panegyric went on with more than usual huskiness.

To Captain Delano's imagination, now again not wholly at rest, there was something so hollow in the Spaniard's manner, with apparently some reciprocal hollowness in the servant's dusky comment of silence, that the idea flashed across him, that possibly master and man, for some unknown purpose, were acting out, both in word and deed, nay, to the very tremor of Don Benito's limbs, some juggling play before him. Neither did the suspicion of collusion lack apparent support, from the fact of those whispered conferences before mentioned. But then, what could be the object of enacting this play of the barber before him? At last, regarding the notion as a whimsy, insensibly suggested, perhaps, by the theatrical aspect of Don Benito in his harlequin ensign, Captain Delano speedily banished it.

The shaving over, the servant bestirred himself with a small bottle of scented waters, pouring a few drops on the head, and then diligently rubbing; the vehemence of the exercise causing the muscles of his face to twitch rather strangely.

His next operation was with comb, scissors and brush; going round and round, smoothing a curl here, clipping an unruly whisker-hair there, giving a graceful sweep to the temple-lock, with other impromptu touches evincing the hand of a master; while, like any resigned gentleman in barber's hands, Don Benito bore all, much less uneasily, at least, than he had done the razoring; indeed, he sat so pale and rigid now, that the negro seemed a Nubian sculptor finishing off a white statue-head.

All being over at last, the standard of Spain removed,

tumbled up, and tossed back into the flag-locker, the negro's warm breath blowing away any stray hair which might have lodged down his master's neck; collar and cravat readjusted; a speck of lint whisked off the velvet lapel; all this being done; backing off a little space, and pausing with an expression of subdued self-complacency, the servant for a moment surveyed his master, as, in toilet at least, the creature of his own tasteful hands.

Captain Delano playfully complimented him upon his achievement; at the same time congratulating Don Benito.

But neither sweet waters, nor shampooing, nor fidelity, nor sociality, delighted the Spaniard. Seeing him relapsing into forbidding gloom, and still remaining seated, Captain Delano, thinking that his presence was undesired just then, withdrew, on pretence of seeing whether, as he had prophesied, any signs of a breeze were visible.

Walking forward to the mainmast, he stood awhile thinking over the scene, and not without some undefined misgivings, when he heard a noise near the cuddy, and turning, saw the negro, his hand to his cheek. Advancing, Captain Delano perceived that the cheek was bleeding. He was about to ask the cause, when the negro's wailing soliloquy enlightened him.

"Ah, when will master get better from his sickness; only the sour heart that sour sickness breeds made him serve Babo so; cutting Babo with the razor, because, only by accident, Babo had given master one little scratch; and for the first time in so many a day, too. Ah, ah, ah," holding his hand to his face.

Is it possible, thought Captain Delano; was it to wreak in private his Spanish spite against this poor friend of his, that Don Benito, by his sullen manner, impelled me to withdraw? Ah, this slavery breeds ugly passions in man! Poor fellow!

He was about to speak in sympathy to the negro, but with a timid reluctance he now re-entered the cuddy.

Presently master and man came forth; Don Benito leaning on his servant as if nothing had happened.

But a sort of love-quarrel, after all, thought Captain Delano.

He accosted Don Benito, and they slowly walked together. They had gone but a few paces, when the steward—a tall, rajah-looking mulatto, orientally set off with a pagoda turban formed by three or four Madras handkerchiefs wound about his head, tier on tier—approaching with a salaam, announced lunch in the cabin.

On their way thither, the two captains were preceded by the mulatto, who, turning round as he advanced, with continual smiles and bows, ushered them in, a display of elegance which quite completed the insignificance of the small bare-headed Babo, who, as if not unconscious of inferiority, eyed askance the graceful steward. But in part, Captain Delano imputed his jealous watchfulness to that peculiar feeling which the full-blooded African entertains for the adulterated one. As for the steward, his manner, if not bespeaking much dignity of self-respect, yet evidenced his extreme desire to please; which is doubly meritorious, at once Christian and Chesterfieldian.

Captain Delano observed with interest that while the complexion of the mulatto was hybrid, his physiognomy was European; classically so.

"Don Benito," whispered he, "I am glad to see this usher-of-the-golden-rod of yours; the sight refutes an ugly remark once made to me by a Barbados planter that when a mulatto has a regular European face, look out for him; he is a devil. But see, your steward here has features more regular than King George's of England; and yet there he nods, and bows, and smiles; a king, indeed—the king of kind hearts and polite fellows. What a pleasant voice he has, too?"

"He has, Señor."

"But, tell me, has he not, so far as you have known him, always proved a good, worthy fellow?" said Captain Delano, pausing, while with a final genuflexion the steward disappeared into the cabin; "come, for the reason just mentioned, I am curious to know."

"Francesco is a good man," rather sluggishly responded Don Benito, like a phlegmatic appreciator, who would neither find fault nor flatter.

"Ah, I thought so. For it were strange indeed, and not very creditable to us white-skins, if a little of our blood mixed with the African's, should, far from improving the latter's quality, have the sad effect of pouring vitriolic acid into black broth; improving the hue, perhaps, but not the wholesomeness."

"Doubtless, doubtless, Señor, but"—glancing at Babo—"not to speak of negroes, your planter's remark I have heard applied to the Spanish and Indian intermixtures in our provinces. But I know nothing about the matter," he listlessly added.

And here they entered the cabin.

The lunch was a frugal one. Some of Captain Delano's fresh fish and pumpkins, biscuit and salt beef, the reserved bottle of cider, and the *San Dominick's* last bottle of Canary.

As they entered, Francesco, with two or three coloured aids, was hovering over the table giving the last adjustments. Upon perceiving their master they withdrew, Francesco making a smiling congé, and the Spaniard, without condescending to notice it, fastidiously remarking to his companion that he relished not superfluous attendance.

Without companions, host and guest sat down, like a childless married couple, at opposite ends of the table, Don Benito waving Captain Delano to his place, and, weak as he was, insisting upon that gentleman being seated before himself.

The negro placed a rug under Don Benito's feet, and a cushion behind his back, and then stood behind, not his master's chair, but Captain Delano's. At first, this a little surprised the latter. But it was soon evident that, in taking his position, the black was still true to his master; since by facing him he could the more readily anticipate his slightest want.

"This is an uncommonly intelligent fellow of yours, Don Benito," whispered Captain Delano across the table.

"You say true, Señor."

During the repast, the guest again reverted to parts of Don Benito's story, begging further particulars here and there. He inquired how it was that the scurvy and fever should have committed such wholesale havoc upon the whites, while destroying less than half of the blacks. As if this question reproduced the whole scene of plague before the Spaniard's eyes, miserably reminding him of his solitude in a cabin where before he had had so many friends and officers round him, his hand shook, his face became hueless, broken words escaped; but directly the sane memory of the past seemed replaced by insane terrors of the present. With starting eyes he stared before him at vacancy. For nothing was to be seen but the hand of his servant pushing the Canary over toward him. At length a few sips served partially to restore him. He made random reference to the different constitutions of races, enabling one to offer more resistance to certain maladies than another. The thought was new to his companion.

Presently Captain Delano, intending to say something to his host concerning the pecuniary part of the business he had undertaken for him, especially—since he was strictly accountable to his owners—with reference to the new suit of sails, and other things of that sort; and naturally preferring to conduct such affairs in private, was desirous that the servant should withdraw; imagining that Don Benito for a few minutes could dispense with his attendance. He, however, waited awhile; thinking that, as the conversation proceeded, Don Benito, without being prompted, would perceive the propriety of the step.

But it was otherwise. At last catching his host's eye, Captain Delano, with a slight backward gesture of his thumb, whispered, "Don Benito, pardon me, but there is an interference with the full expression of what I have to say to you."

Upon this the Spaniard changed countenance; which was imputed to his resenting the hint, as in some way a reflection upon his servant. After a moment's pause, he assured his guest that the black's remaining with him could be of no disservice; because since losing his officers he had made Babo (whose original office, it now appeared, had been captain of the slaves) not only his constant attendant and companion, but in all things his confidant.

After this, nothing more could be said; though, indeed, Captain Délano could hardly avoid some little tinge of irritation upon being left ungratified in so inconsiderable a wish, by one, too, for whom he intended such solid services. But it is only his querulousness, thought he; and so filling his glass he proceeded to business.

The price of the sails and other matters was fixed upon. But while this was being done, the American observed that, though his original offer of assistance had been hailed with hectic animation, yet now when it was reduced to a business transaction, indifference and apathy were betrayed. Don Benito, in fact, appeared to submit to hearing the details more out of regard to common propriety, than from any impression that weighty benefit to himself and his voyage was involved.

Soon, this manner became still more reserved. The effort was vain to seek to draw him into social talk. Gnawed by his splenetic mood, he sat twitching his beard, while to little purpose the hand of his servant, mute as that on the wall, slowly pushed over the Canary.

Lunch being over, they sat down on the cushioned transom; the servant placing a pillow behind his master. The long continuance of the calm had now affected the atmosphere. Don Benito sighed heavily, as if for breath.

"Why not adjourn to the cuddy," said Captain Delano; "there is more air there." But the host sat silent and motionless.

Meantime his servant knelt before him, with a large fan of feathers. And Francesco, coming in on tiptoes, handed the negro a little cup of aromatic waters, with which at intervals he chafed his master's brow, smoothing the hair along the temples as a nurse does a child's. He spoke no word. He only rested his eye on his master's, as if, amid all Don Benito's distress, a little to refresh his spirit by the silent sight of fidelity.

Presently the ship's bell sounded two o'clock; and through the cabin-windows a slight rippling of the sea was discerned; and from the desired direction.

"There," exclaimed Captain Delano, "I told you so, Don Benito, look!"

He had risen to his feet, speaking in a very animated tone, with a view the more to rouse his companion. But though the crimson curtain of the stern-window near him that moment fluttered against his pale cheek, Don Benito seemed to have even less welcome for the breeze than the calm.

Poor fellow, thought Captain Delano, bitter experience has taught him that one ripple does not make a wind, any more than one swallow a summer. But he is mistaken for once. I will get his ship in for him, and prove it.

Briefly alluding to his weak condition, he urged his host to remain quietly where he was, since he (Captain Delano) would with pleasure take upon himself the responsibility of making the best use of the wind.

Upon gaining the deck, Captain Delano started at the unexpected figure of Atufal, monumentally fixed at the threshold, like one of those sculptured porters of black marble guarding the porches of Egyptian tombs.

But this time the start was, perhaps, purely physical. Atufal's presence, singularly attesting docility even in sullenness, was contrasted with that of the hatchet-polishers, who in patience evinced their industry; while both spectacles showed, that lax as Don Benito's general authority might be, still, whenever he chose to exert it, no man so savage or colossal but must, more or less, bow.

Snatching a trumpet which hung from the bulwarks, with a free step Captain Delano advanced to the forward edge of the poop, issuing his orders in his best Spanish. The few sail-

ors and many negroes, all equally pleased, obediently set
about heading the ship toward the harbour.

While giving some directions about setting a lower stu'n'-
sail, suddenly Captain Delano heard a voice faithfully repeating his orders. Turning, he saw Babo, now for the time acting, under the pilot, his original part of captain of the slaves.
This assistance proved valuable. Tattered sails and warped
yards were soon brought into some trim. And no brace or
halyard was pulled but to the blithe songs of the inspirited
negroes.

Good fellows, thought Captain Delano, a little training
would make fine sailors of them. Why see, the very women
pull and sing, too. These must be some of those Ashantee
negresses that make such capital soldiers, I've heard. But
who's at the helm? I must have a good hand there.

He went to see.

The *San Dominick* steered with a cumbrous tiller, with
large horizontal pullies attached. At each pulley-end stood a
subordinate black, and between them, at the tiller-head, the
responsible post, a Spanish seaman, whose countenance
evinced his due share in the general hopefulness and confidence at the coming of the breeze.

He proved the same man who had behaved with so shamefaced an air on the windlass.

"Ah,—it is you, my man," exclaimed Captain Delano—
"well, no more sheep's-eyes now;—look straightforward and
keep the ship so. Good hand, I trust? And want to get into
the harbour, don't you?"

"Sí Señor," assented the man with an inward chuckle,
grasping the tiller-head firmly. Upon this, unperceived by
the American, the two blacks eyed the sailor askance.

Finding all right at the helm, the pilot went forward to
the forecastle, to see how matters stood there.

The ship now had way enough to breast the current. With
the approach of evening, the breeze would be sure to freshen.

Having done all that was needed for the present, Captain
Delano, giving his last orders to the sailors, turned aft to
report affairs to Don Benito in the cabin; perhaps addition-
ally incited to rejoin him by the hope of snatching a moment's private chat while his servant was engaged upon deck.

From opposite sides, there were, beneath the poop, two
approaches to the cabin; one further forward than the
other, and consequently communicating with a longer passage. Marking the servant still above, Captain Delano, taking

the nighest entrance—the one last named, and at whose porch Atufal still stood—hurried on his way, till, arrived at the cabin threshold, he paused an instant, a little to recover from his eagerness. Then, with the words of his intended business upon his lips, he entered. As he advanced toward the Spaniard, on the transom, he heard another footstep, keeping time with his. From the opposite door, a salver in hand, the servant was likewise advancing.

"Confound the faithful fellow," thought Captain Delano; "what a vexatious coincidence."

Possibly, the vexation might have been something different, were it not for the buoyant confidence inspired by the breeze. But even as it was, he felt a slight twinge, from a sudden involuntary association in his mind of Babo with Atufal.

"Don Benito," said he, "I give you joy; the breeze will hold, and will increase. By the way, your tall man and time-piece, Atufal, stands without. By your order, of course?"

Don Benito recoiled, as if at some bland satirical touch, delivered with such adroit garnish of apparent good-breeding as to present no handle for retort.

He is like one flayed alive, thought Captain Delano; where may one touch him without causing a shrink?

The servant moved before his master, adjusting a cushion; recalled to civility, the Spaniard stiffly replied: "You are right. The slave appears where you saw him, according to my command; which is, that if at the given hour I am below, he must take his stand and abide my coming."

"Ah now, pardon me, but that is treating the poor fellow like an ex-king denied. Ah, Don Benito," smiling, "for all the license you permit in some things, I fear lest, at bottom, you are a bitter hard master."

Again Don Benito shrank; and this time, as the good sailor thought, from a genuine twinge of his conscience.

Conversation now became constrained. In vain Captain Delano called attention to the now perceptible motion of the keel gently cleaving the sea; with lack-lustre eye, Don Benito returned words few and reserved.

By-and-by, the wind having steadily risen, and still blowing right into the harbour, bore the *San Dominick* swiftly on. Rounding a point of land, the sealer at distance came into open view.

Meantime Captain Delano had again repaired to the deck, remaining there some time. Having at last altered the ship's course, so as to give the reef a wide berth, he returned for a few moments below.

I will cheer up my poor friend, this time, thought he.

"Better and better, Don Benito," he cried as he blithely reentered; "there will soon be an end to your cares, at least for awhile. For when, after a long, sad voyage, you know, the anchor drops into the haven, all its vast weight seems lifted from the captain's heart. We are getting on famously, Don Benito. My ship is in sight. Look through this sidelight here; there she is; all a-taunt-o! The *Bachelor's Delight,* my good friend. Ah, how this wind braces one up. Come, you must take a cup of coffee with me this evening. My old steward will give you as fine a cup as ever any sultan tasted. What say you, Don Benito, will you?"

At first, the Spaniard glanced feverishly up, casting a longing look toward the sealer, while with mute concern his servant gazed into his face. Suddenly the old ague of coldness returned, and dropping back to his cushions he was silent.

"You do not answer. Come, all day you have been my host; would you have hospitality all on one side?"

"I cannot go," was the response.

"What? It will not fatigue you. The ships will lie together as near as they can, without swinging foul. It will be little more than stepping from deck to deck; which is but as from room to room. Come, come, you must not refuse me."

"I cannot go," decisively and repulsively repeated Don Benito.

Renouncing all but the last appearance of courtesy, with a sort of cadaverous sullenness, and biting his thin nails to the quick, he glanced, almost glared, at his guest; as if impatient that a stranger's presence should interfere with the full indulgence of his morbid hour. Meantime the sound of the parted waters came more and more gurglingly and merrily in at the windows; as reproaching him for his dark spleen; as telling him that, sulk as he might, and go mad with it, nature cared not a jot; since, whose fault was it, pray?

But the foul mood was now at its depth, as the fair wind at its height.

There was something in the man so far beyond any mere unsociality or sourness previously evinced, that even the forbearing good-nature of his guest could no longer endure it. Wholly at a loss to account for such demeanour, and deeming sickness with eccentricity, however extreme, no adequate excuse, well satisfied, too, that nothing in his own conduct could justify it, Captain Delano's pride began to be roused. Himself became reserved. But all seemed one to the Spaniard. Quitting him, therefore, Captain Delano once more went to the deck.

The ship was now within less than two miles of the sealer. The whale-boat was seen darting over the interval.

To be brief, the two vessels, thanks to the pilot's skill, ere long in neighborly style lay anchored together.

Before returning to his own vessel, Captain Delano had intended communicating to Don Benito the practical details of the proposed services to be rendered. But, as it was, unwilling anew to subject himself to rebuffs, he resolved, now that he had seen the *San Dominick* safely moored, immediately to quit her, without further allusion to hospitality or business. Indefinitely postponing his ulterior plans, he would regulate his future actions according to future circumstances. His boat was ready to receive him; but his host still tarried below. Well, thought Captain Delano, if he has little breeding, the more need to show mine. He descended to the cabin to bid a ceremonious, and, it may be, tacitly rebukeful adieu. But to his great satisfaction, Don Benito, as if he began to feel the weight of that treatment with which his slighted guest had, not indecorously, retaliated upon him, now supported by his servant, rose to his feet, and grasping Captain Delano's hand, stood tremulous; too much agitated to speak. But the good augury hence drawn was suddenly dashed, by his resuming all his previous reserve, with augmented gloom, as, with half-averted eyes, he silently reseated himself on his cushions. With a corresponding return to his own chilled feelings, Captain Delano bowed and withdrew.

He was hardly midway in the narrow corridor, dim as a tunnel, leading from the cabin to the stairs, when a sound, as of the tolling for execution in some jail-yard, fell on his ears. It was the echo of the ship's flawed bell, striking the hour, drearily reverberated in this subterranean vault. Instantly, by a fatality not to be withstood, his mind, responsive to the portent, swarmed with superstitious suspicions. He paused. In images far swifter than these sentences, the minutest details of all his former distrusts swept through him.

Hitherto, credulous good-nature had been too ready to furnish excuses for reasonable fears. Why was the Spaniard, so superfluously punctilious at times, now heedless of common propriety in not accompanying to the side his departing guest? Did indisposition forbid? Indisposition had not forbidden more irksome exertion that day. His last equivocal demeanour recurred. He had risen to his feet, grasped his guest's hand, motioned toward his hat; then, in an instant, all was eclipsed in sinister muteness and gloom. Did this imply one brief, repentant relenting at the final moment, from some iniquitous plot, followed by remorseless return to it? His last glance seemed to express a calamitous, yet acquiescent farewell to Captain Delano for ever. Why decline the invitation to visit the sealer that evening? Or was the Spaniard less hardened than the Jew, who refrained not from supping at the board of Him whom the same night he meant to betray? What imported all those day-long enigmas and contradictions, except they were intended to mystify, preliminary to some stealthy blow? Atufal, the pretended rebel, but punctual shadow, that moment lurked by the threshold without. He seemed a sentry, and more. Who, by his own confession, had stationed him there? Was the negro now lying in wait?

The Spaniard behind—his creature before: to rush from darkness to light was the involuntary choice.

The next moment, with clenched jaw and hand, he passed Atufal, and stood unarmed in the light. As he saw his trim ship lying peacefully at her anchor, and almost within ordinary call; as he saw his household boat, with familiar faces in it, patiently rising and falling on the short waves by the *San Dominick's* side; and then, glancing about the decks where he stood, saw the oakum-pickers still gravely plying their fingers; and heard the low, buzzing whistle and industrious hum of the hatchet-polishers, still bestirring themselves over their endless occupation; and more than all, as he saw the benign aspect of Nature, taking her innocent repose in the evening; the screened sun in the quiet camp of the west shining out like the mild light from Abraham's tent; as his charmed eye and ear took in all these, with the chained figure of the black, the clenched jaw and hand relaxed. Once again he smiled at the phantoms which had mocked him, and felt something like a tinge of remorse, that, by indulging them even for a moment, he should, by implication, have betrayed an almost atheist doubt of the everwatchful Providence above.

There was a few minutes' delay, while, in obedience to his orders, the boat was being hooked along to the gangway. During this interval, a sort of saddened satisfaction stole over

Captain Delano, at thinking of the kindly offices he had that day discharged for a stranger. Ah, thought he, after good actions one's conscience is never ungrateful, however much so the benefited party may be.

Presently, his foot, in the first act of descent into the boat, pressed the first round of the side-ladder, his face presented inward upon the deck. In the same moment, he heard his name courteously sounded; and, to his pleased surprise, saw Don Benito advancing—an unwonted energy in his air, as if, at the last moment, intent upon making amends for his recent discourtesy. With instinctive good feeling, Captain Delano, revoking his foot, turned and reciprocally advanced. As he did so, the Spaniard's nervous eagerness increased, but his vital energy failed; so that, the better to support him, the servant, placing his master's hand on his naked shoulder, and gently holding it there, formed himself into a sort of crutch.

When the two captains met, the Spaniard again fervently took the hand of the American, at the same time casting an earnest glance into his eyes, but, as before, too much overcome to speak.

I have done him wrong, self-reproachfully thought Captain Delano; his apparent coldness has deceived me; in no instance has he meant to offend.

Meantime, as if fearful that the continuance of the scene might too much unstring his master, the servant seemed anxious to terminate it. And so, still presenting himself as a crutch, and walking between the two captains, he advanced with them toward the gangway; while still, as if full of kindly contrition, Don Benito would not let go the hand of Captain Delano, but retained it in his, across the black's body.

Soon they were standing by the side, looking over into the boat, whose crew turned up their curious eyes. Waiting a moment for the Spaniard to relinquish his hold, the now embarrassed Captain Delano lifted his foot, to overstep the threshold of the open gangway; but still, Don Benito would not let go his hand. And yet, with an agitated tone, he said, "I can go no further; here I must bid you adieu. Adieu, my dear, dear Don Amasa. Go—go!" suddenly tearing his hand loose, "go, and God guard you better than me, my best friend."

Not unaffected, Captain Delano would now have lingered; but catching the meekly admonitory eye of the servant, with a hasty farewell he descended into his boat, followed by the continual adieus of Don Benito, standing rooted in the gangway.

Seating himself in the stern, Captain Delano, making a last salute, ordered the boat shoved off. The crew had their oars on end. The bowsman pushed the boat a sufficient distance for the oars to be lengthwise dropped. The instant that was done, Don Benito sprang over the bulwarks, falling at the feet of Captain Delano; at the same time, calling towards his ship, but in tones so frenzied, that none in the boat could understand him. But, as if not equally obtuse, three Spanish sailors, from three different and distant parts of the ship, splashed into the sea, swimming after their captain, as if intent upon his rescue.

The dismayed officer of the boat eagerly asked what this meant. To which, Captain Delano, turning a disdainful smile upon the unaccountable Benito Cereno, answered that, for his part, he neither knew nor cared; but it seemed as if the Spaniard had taken it into his head to produce the impression among his people that the boat wanted to kidnap him. "Or else—give way for your lives," he wildly added, starting at a clattering hubbub in the ship, above which rang the tocsin of the hatchet-polishers; and seizing Don Benito by the throat he added, "this plotting pirate means murder!" Here, in apparent verification of the words, the servant, a dagger in his hand, was seen on the rail overhead, poised, in the act of leaping, as if with desperate fidelity to befriend his master to the last; while, seemingly to aid the black, the three Spanish sailors were trying to clamber into the hampered bow. Meantime, the whole host of negroes, as if inflamed at the sight of their jeopardized captain, impended in one sooty avalanche over the bulwarks.

All this, with what preceded, and what followed, occurred with such involutions of rapidity, that past, present, and future seemed one.

Seeing the negro coming, Captain Delano had flung the Spaniard aside, almost in the very act of clutching him, and, by the unconscious recoil, shifting his place, with arms thrown up, so promptly grappled the servant in his descent, that with dagger presented at Captain Delano's heart, the black seemed of purpose to have leaped there as to his mark. But the weapon was wrenched away, and the assailant dashed down into the bottom of the boat, which now, with disentangled oars, began to speed through the sea.

At this juncture, the left hand of Captain Delano, on one

side, again clutched the half-reclined Don Benito, heedless that he was in a speechless faint, while his right foot, on the other side, ground the prostrate negro; and his right arm pressed for added speed on the after oar, his eye bent forward, encouraging his men to their utmost.

But here, the officer of the boat, who had at last succeeded in beating off the towing Spanish sailors, and was now, with face turned aft, assisting the bowsman at his oar, suddenly called to Captain Delano, to see what the black was about; while a Portuguese oarsman shouted to him to give heed to what the Spaniard was saying.

Glancing down at his feet, Captain Delano saw the freed hand of the servant aiming with a second dagger—a small one, before concealed in his wool—with this he was snakishly writhing up from the boat's bottom, at the heart of his master, his countenance lividly vindictive, expressing the centred purpose of his soul; while the Spaniard, half-choked, was vainly shrinking away, with husky words, incoherent to all but the Portuguese.

That moment, across the long benighted mind of Captain Delano, a flash of revelation swept, illuminating in unanticipated clearness Benito Cereno's whole mysterious demeanour, with every enigmatic event of the day, as well as the entire past voyage of the *San Dominick*. He smote Babo's hand down, but his own heart smote him harder. With infinite pity he withdrew his hold from Don Benito. Not Captain Delano, but Don Benito, the black, in leaping into the boat, had intended to stab.

Both the black's hands were held, as, glancing up toward the *San Dominick*, Captain Delano, now with the scales dropped from his eyes, saw the negroes, not in misrule, not in tumult, not as if frantically concerned for Don Benito, but with mask torn away, flourishing hatchets and knives, in ferocious piratical revolt. Like delirious black dervishes, the six Ashantees danced on the poop. Prevented by their foes from springing into the water, the Spanish boys were hurrying up to the topmost spars, while such of the few Spanish sailors, not already in the sea, less alert, were descried, helplessly mixed in, on deck, with the blacks.

Meantime Captain Delano hailed his own vessel, ordering the ports up, and the guns run out. But by this time the cable of the *San Dominick* had been cut; and the fag-end, in lashing out, whipped away the canvas shroud about the beak, suddenly revealing, as the bleached hull swung round toward the open ocean, death for the figurehead, in a human skeleton; chalky comment on the chalked words below, *"Follow your leader."*

At the sight, Don Benito, covering his face, wailed out: " 'Tis he, Aranda! my murdered, unburied friend!"

Upon reaching the sealer, calling for ropes, Captain Delano bound the negro, who made no resistance, and had him hoisted to the deck. He would then have assisted the now almost helpless Don Benito up the side; but Don Benito, wan as he was, refused to move, or be moved, until the negro should have been first put below out of view. When, presently assured that it was done, he no more shrank from the ascent.

The boat was immediately despatched back to pick up the three swimming sailors. Meantime, the guns were in readiness, though, owing to the *San Dominick* having glided somewhat astern of the sealer, only the aftermost one could be brought to bear. With this, they fired six times; thinking to cripple the fugitive ship by bringing down her spars. But only a few inconsiderable ropes were shot away. Soon the ship was beyond the guns' range, steering broad out of the bay; the blacks thickly clustering round the bowsprit, one moment with taunting cries toward the whites, the next with upthrown gestures hailing the now dusky expanse of ocean —cawing crows escaped from the hand of the fowler.

The first impulse was to slip the cables and give chase. But, upon second thought, to pursue with whale-boat and yawl seemed more promising.

Upon inquiring of Don Benito what firearms they had on board the *San Dominick,* Captain Delano was answered that they had none that could be used; because, in the earlier stages of the mutiny, a cabin-passenger, since dead, had secretly put out of order the locks of what few muskets there were. But with all his remaining strength, Don Benito entreated the American not to give chase, either with ship or boat; for the negroes had already proved themselves such desperadoes, that, in case of a present assault, nothing but a total massacre of the whites could be looked for. But, regarding this warning as coming from one whose spirit had been crushed by misery, the American did not give up his design.

The boats were got ready and armed. Captain Delano ordered twenty-five men into them. He was going himself when Don Benito grasped his arm.

"What! have you saved my life, Señor, and are you now going to throw away your own?"

The officers also, for reasons connected with their interests and those of the voyage, and a duty owing to the owners, strongly objected against their commander's going. Weighing their remonstrances a moment, Captain Delano felt bound to remain; appointing his chief mate—an athletic and resolute man, who had been a privateer's man, and, as his enemies whispered, a pirate—to head the party. The more to encourage the sailors, they were told, that the Spanish captain considered his ship as good as lost; that she and her cargo, including some gold and silver, were worth upwards of ten thousand doubloons. Take her, and no small part should be theirs. The sailors replied with a shout.

The fugitives had now almost gained an offing. It was nearly night; but the moon was rising. After hard, prolonged pulling, the boats came up on the ship's quarters, at a suitable distance laying upon their oars to discharge their muskets. Having no bullets to return, the negroes sent their yells. But, upon the second volley, Indian-like, they hurtled their hatchets. One took off a sailor's fingers. Another struck the whaleboat's bow, cutting off the rope there, and remaining stuck in the gunwale, like a woodman's axe. Snatching it, quivering from its lodgment, the mate hurled it back. The returned gauntlet now stuck in the ship's broken quarter-gallery, and so remained.

The negroes giving too hot a reception, the whites kept a more respectful distance. Hovering now just out of reach of the hurtling hatchets, they, with a view to the close encounter which must soon come, sought to decoy the blacks into entirely disarming themselves of their most murderous weapons in a hand-to-hand fight, by foolishly flinging them, as missiles, short of the mark, into the sea. But ere long perceiving the stratagem, the negroes desisted, though not before many of them had to replace their lost hatchets with handspikes; an exchange which, as counted upon, proved in the end favourable to the assailants.

Meantime, with a strong wind, the ship still clove the water; the boats alternately falling behind, and pulling up, to discharge fresh volleys.

The fire was mostly directed toward the stern, since there, chiefly, the negroes, at present, were clustering. But to kill or maim the negroes was not the object. To take them, with the ship, was the object. To do it, the ship must be boarded;

which could not be done by boats while she was sailing so fast.

A thought now struck the mate. Observing the Spanish boys still aloft, high as they could get, he called to them to descend to the yards, and cut adrift the sails. It was done. About this time, owing to causes hereafter to be shown, two Spaniards, in the dress of sailors and conspicuously showing themselves, were killed; not by volleys, but by deliberate marksman's shots; while, as it afterwards appeared, during one of the general discharges, Atufal, the black, and the Spaniard at the helm likewise were killed. What now, with the loss of the sails, and loss of leaders, the ship became unmanageable to the negroes.

With creaking masts she came heavily round to the wind; the prow slowly swinging into view of the boats, its skeleton gleaming in the horizontal moonlight, and casting a gigantic ribbed shadow upon the water. One extended arm of the ghost seemed beckoning the whites to avenge it.

"Follow your leader!" cried the mate; and, one on each bow, the boats boarded. Scaling-spears and cutlasses crossed hatchets and handspikes. Huddled upon the long-boat amidships, the negresses raised a wailing chant, whose chorus was the clash of the steel.

For a time, the attack wavered; the negroes wedging themselves to beat it back; the half-repelled sailors, as yet unable to gain a footing, fighting as troopers in the saddle, one leg sideways flung over the bulwarks, and one without, plying their cutlasses like carters' whips. But in vain. They were almost overborne, when, rallying themselves into a squad as one man, with a huzza, they sprang inboard; where, entangled, they involuntarily separated again. For a few breaths' space there was a vague, muffled, inner sound as of submerged sword-fish rushing hither and thither through shoals of black-fish. Soon, in a reunited band, and joined by the Spanish seamen, the whites came to the surface, irresistibly driving the negroes toward the stern. But a barricade of casks and sacks, from side to side, had been thrown up by the mainmast. Here the negroes faced about, and though scorning peace or truce, yet fain would have had a respite. But, without pause, overleaping the barrier, the unflagging sailors again closed. Exhausted, the blacks now fought in despair. Their red tongues lolled, wolf-like, from their black mouths. But the pale sailors' teeth were set; not a word was spoken; and, in five minutes more, the ship was won.

Nearly a score of the negroes were killed. Exclusive of those by the balls, many were mangled; their wounds—mostly inflicted by the long-edged scaling-spears—resembling those shaven ones of the English at Preston Pans, made by the poled scythes of the Highlanders. On the other side, none were killed, though several were wounded; some severely, including the mate. The surviving negroes were temporarily secured, and the ship, towed back into the harbour at midnight, once more lay anchored.

Omitting the incidents and arrangements ensuing, suffice it that, after two days spent in refitting, the two ships sailed in company for Concepcion in Chili, and thence for Lima in Peru; where, before the vice-regal courts, the whole affair, from the beginning, underwent investigation.

Though, midway on the passage, the ill-fated Spaniard, relaxed from constraint, showed some signs of regaining health with free-will; yet, agreeably to his own foreboding, shortly before arriving at Lima, he relapsed, finally becoming so reduced as to be carried ashore in arms. Hearing of his story and plight, one of the many religious institutions of the City of Kings opened an hospitable refuge to him, where both physician and priest were his nurses, and a member of the order volunteered to be his one special guardian and consoler, by night and by day.

The following extracts, translated from one of the official Spanish documents, will, it is hoped, shed light on the preceding narrative, as well as, in the first place, reveal the true port of departure and true history of the San Dominick's voyage, down to the time of her touching at the island of Santa Maria.

But, ere the extracts come, it may be well to preface them with a remark.

The document selected, from among many others, for partial translation, contains the deposition of Benito Cereno; the first taken in the case. Some disclosures therein were, at the time, held dubious for both learned and natural reasons. The tribunal inclined to the opinion that the deponent, not undisturbed in his mind by recent events, raved of some things which could never have happened. But subsequent depositions of the surviving sailors, bearing out the revelations of their captain in several of the strangest particulars, gave credence to the rest. So that the tribunal, in its final decision, rested its capital sentences upon statements which, had they lacked confirmation, it would have deemed it but duty to reject.

I, DON JOSÉ DE ABOS AND PADILLA, His Majesty's Notary for the Royal Revenue, and Register of this Province, and Notary Public of the Holy Crusade of this Bishopric, etc.

Do certify and declare, as much as is requisite in law, that, in the criminal cause commenced the twenty-fourth of the month of September, in the year seventeen hundred and ninety-nine, against the Senegal negroes of the ship *San Dominick*, the following declaration before me was made.

Declaration of the first witness, DON BENITO CERENO.

The same day, and month, and year, His Honour Doctor Juan Martinez de Dozas, Councillor of the Royal Audience of this Kingdom, and learned in the law of this Intendancy, ordered the captain of the ship *San Dominick*, Don Benito Cereno, to appear; which he did in his litter, attended by the monk Infelez; of whom he received, before Don José de Abos and Padilla, Notary Public of the Holy Crusade, the oath, which he took by God, our Lord, and a sign of the Cross; under which he promised to tell the truth of whatever he should know and should be asked;—and being interrogated agreeably to the tenor of the act commencing the process, he said, that on the twentieth of May last, he set sail with his ship from the port of Valparaiso, bound to that of Callao; loaded with the produce of the country and one hundred and sixty blacks, of both sexes, mostly belonging to Don Alexandro Aranda, gentleman, of the city of Mendoza; that the crew of the ship consisted of thirty-six men, beside the persons who went as passengers; that the negroes were in part as follows:

[*Here, in the original, follows a list of some fifty names, descriptions, and ages, compiled from certain recovered documents of Aranda's, and also from recollections of the deponent, from which portions only are extracted.*]

—One, from about eighteen to nineteen years, named José, and this was the man that waited upon his master, Don Alexandro, and who speaks well the Spanish, having served him four or five years; . . . a mulatto, named Francesco, the cabin steward, of a good person and voice, having sung

in the Valparaiso churches, native of the province of Buenos
Ayres, aged about thirty-five years. . . . A smart negro,
named Dago, who had been for many years a grave-digger
among the Spaniards, aged forty-six years. . . . Four old
negroes, born in Africa, from sixty to seventy, but sound,
caulkers by trade, whose names are as follows:—the first was
named Muri, and he was killed (as was also his son named
Diamelo); the second, Nacta; the third, Yola, likewise killed;
the fourth, Ghofan; and six full-grown negroes, aged from
thirty to forty-five, all raw, and born among the Ashantees—
Martiniqui, Yan, Lecbe, Hapenda, Yambaio, Akim; four of
whom were killed; . . . a powerful negro named Atufal,
who, being supposed to have been a chief in Africa, his owners set great store by him. . . . And a small negro of Senegal, but some years among the Spaniards, aged about thirty,
which negro's name was Babo; . . . that he does not remember the names of the others, but that still expecting the
residue of Don Alexandro's papers will be found, will then
take due account of them all, and remit to the court; . . .
and thirty-nine women and children of all ages.

[*After the catalogue, the deposition goes on as follows:*]

. . . That all the negroes slept upon deck, as is customary
in this navigation, and none wore fetters, because the owner,
his friend Aranda, told him that they were all tractable;
. . . that on the seventh day after leaving port, at three
o'clock in the morning, all the Spaniards being asleep except
the two officers on the watch, who were the boatswain, Juan
Robles, and the carpenter, Juan Bautista Gayete, and the
helmsman and his boy, the negroes revolted suddenly,
wounded dangerously the boatswain and the carpenter, and
successively killed eighteen men of those who were sleeping
upon deck, some with handspikes and hatchets, and others
by throwing them alive overboard, after tying them; that of
the Spaniards upon deck, they left about seven, as he thinks,
alive and tied, to manœuvre the ship and three or four more
who hid themselves, remained also alive. Although in the act
of revolt the negroes made themselves masters of the hatchway, six or seven wounded went through it to the cockpit,
without any hindrance on their part; that in the act of revolt,
the mate and another person, whose name he does not recollect, attempted to come up through the hatchway, but having
been wounded at the onset, they were obliged to return to

the cabin; that the deponent resolved at break of day to come up the companionway, where the negro Babo was, being the ringleader, and Atufal, who assisted him, and having spoken to them, exhorted them to cease committing such atrocities, asking them, at the same time, what they wanted and intended to do, offering, himself, to obey their commands; that, notwithstanding this, they threw, in his presence, three men, alive and tied, overboard; that they told the deponent to come up, and that they would not kill him; which having done, the negro Babo asked him whether there were in those seas any negro countries where they might be carried, and he answered them, no; that the negro Babo afterwards told him to carry them to Senegal, or to the neighbouring islands of St. Nicholas; and he answered, that this was impossible, on account of the great distance, the necessity involved of rounding Cape Horn, the bad condition of the vessel, the want of provisions, sails, and water; but that the negro Babo replied to him he must carry them in any way; that they would do and conform themselves to everything the deponent should require as to eating and drinking; that after a long conference, being absolutely compelled to please them, for they threatened him to kill all the whites if they were not, at all events, carried to Senegal, he told them that what was most wanting for the voyage was water; that they would go near the coast to take it, and hence they would proceed on their course; that the negro Babo agreed to it; and the deponent steered toward the intermediate ports, hoping to meet some Spanish or foreign vessel that would save them; that within ten or eleven days they saw the land, and continued their course by it in the vicinity of Nasca; that the deponent observed that the negroes were now restless and mutinous, because he did not effect the taking in of water, the negro Babo having required, with threats, that it should be done, without fail, the following day; he told him he saw plainly that the coast was steep, and the rivers designated in the maps were not to be found, with other reasons suitable to the circumstances; that the best way would be to go to the island of Santa Maria, where they might water and victual easily, it being a desert island, as the foreigners did; that the deponent did not go to Pisco, that was near, nor make any other port of the coast, because the negro Babo had intimated to him several times, that he would kill all the whites the very moment he should perceive any city, town, or settlement of any kind on the shores to which they should

be carried: that having determined to go to the island
of Santa Maria, as the deponent had planned, for the purpose
of trying whether, in the passage or in the island itself, they
could find any vessel that should favour them, or whether he
could escape from it in a boat to the neighbouring coast of
Arruco; to adopt the necessary means he immediately
changed his course, steering for the island; that the negroes
Babo and Atufal held daily conferences, in which they discussed what was necessary for their design of returning to
Senegal, whether they were to kill all the Spaniards, and
particularly the deponent; that eight days after parting from
the coast of Nasca, the deponent being on the watch a little
after day-break, and soon after the negroes had their meeting, the negro Babo came to the place where the deponent
was, and told him that he had determined to kill his master,
Don Alexandro Aranda, both because he and his companions
could not otherwise be sure of their liberty, and that, to keep
the seamen in subjection, he wanted to prepare a warning of
what road they should be made to take did they or any of
them oppose him; and that, by means of the death of Don
Alexandro, that warning would best be given; but, that what
this last meant, the deponent did not at the time comprehend, nor could not, further than that the death of Don
Alexandro was intended; and moreover, the negro Babo proposed to the deponent to call the mate Raneds, who was sleeping in the cabin, before the thing was done, for fear, as the
deponent understood it, that the mate, who was a good navigator, should be killed with Don Alexandro and the rest;
that the deponent, who was the friend from youth of Don
Alexandro, prayed and conjured, but all was useless; for the
negro Babo answered him that the thing could not be prevented, and that all the Spaniards risked their death if they
should attempt to frustrate his will in this matter, or
any other; that, in this conflict, the deponent called the mate,
Raneds, who was forced to go apart, and immediately the
negro Babo commanded the Ashantee Martinqui and the
Ashantee Lecbe to go and commit the murder; that those two
went down with hatchets to the berth of Don Alexandro;
that, yet half alive and mangled, they dragged him on deck;
that they were going to throw him overboard in that state,
but the negro Babo stopped them, bidding the murder be completed on the deck before him, which was done, when, by
his orders, the body was carried below, forward; that nothing more was seen of it by the deponent for three days; . . .

that Don Alonzo Sidonia, an old man, long resident at Valparaiso, and lately appointed to a civil office in Peru, whither he had taken passage, was at the time sleeping in the berth opposite Don Alexandro's; that, awakening at his cries, surprised by them, and at the sight of the negroes with their bloody hatchets in their hands, he threw himself into the sea through a window which was near him, and was drowned, without it being in the power of the deponent to assist to take him up; . . . that, a short time after killing Aranda, they brought upon deck his german-cousin, of middle-age, Don Francisco Masa, of Mendoza, and the young Don Joaquin, Marques de Aramboalaza, then lately from Spain, with his Spanish servant Ponce, and the three young clerks of Aranda, José Mozairi, Lorenzo Bargas, and Hermenegildo Gandix, all of Cadiz; that Don Joaquin and Hermenegildo Gandix, the negro Babo for purposes hereafter to appear, preserved alive; but Don Francisco Masa, José Mozairi, and Lorenzo Bargas, with Ponce, the servant, beside the boatswain, Juan Robles, the boatswain's mates, Manuel Viscaya and Roderigo Hurta, and four of the sailors, the negro Babo ordered to be thrown alive into the sea, although they made no resistance, nor begged for anything else but mercy; that the boatswain, Juan Robles, who knew how to swim, kept the longest above water, making acts of contrition, and, in the last words he uttered, charged this deponent to cause mass to be said for his soul to our Lady of Succour: . . . that, during the three days which followed, the deponent, uncertain what fate had befallen the remains of Don Alexandro, frequently asked the negro Babo where they were, and, if still on board, whether they were to be preserved for interments ashore, entreating him so to order it; that the negro Babo answered nothing till the fourth day, when at sunrise, the deponent coming on deck, the negro Babo showed him a skeleton, which had been substituted for the ship's proper figure-head, the image of Christopher Colon, the discoverer of the New World; that the negro Babo asked him whose skeleton that was, and whether, from its whiteness, he should not think it a white's; that, upon his covering his face, the negro Babo, coming close, said words to this effect: "Keep faith with the blacks from here to Senegal, or you shall in spirit, as now in body, follow your leader," pointing to the prow; . . . that the same morning the negro Babo took by succession each Spaniard forward, and asked him whose skeleton that was, and whether, from its whiteness, he should not think it a white's;

that each Spaniard covered his face; that then to each the
negro Babo repeated the words in the first place said to the
deponent; . . . that they (the Spaniards), being then assembled aft, the negro Babo harangued them, saying that he
had now done all; that the deponent (as navigator for the
negroes) might pursue his course, warning him and all of
them that they should, soul and body, go the way of Don
Alexandro if he saw them (the Spaniards) speak or plot anything against them (the negroes)—a threat which was repeated every day; that, before the events last mentioned,
they had tied the cook to throw him overboard, for it is not
known what thing they heard him speak, but finally the
negro Babo spared his life, at the request of the deponent;
that a few days after, the deponent, endeavouring not to
omit any means to preserve the lives of the remaining whites,
spoke to the negroes peace and tranquillity, and agreed
to draw up a paper, signed by the deponent and the sailors
who could write, as also by the negro Babo, for himself and
all the blacks, in which the deponent obliged himself to carry
them to Senegal, and they not to kill any more, and he for-
mally to make over to them the ship, with the cargo, with
which they were for that time satisfied and quieted. . . .
But the next day, the more surely to guard against the sailors' escape, the negro Babo commanded all the boats to be
destroyed but the long-boat, which was unseaworthy, and
another, a cutter in good condition, which, knowing it would
yet be wanted for lowering the water casks, he had it lowered
down into the hold.

[*Various particulars of the prolonged and perplexed navigation ensuing here follow, with incidents of a calamitous
calm, from which portion one passage is extracted, to wit:*]

—That on the fifth day of the calm, all on board suffering
much from the heat, and want of water, and five having died
in fits, and mad, the negroes became irritable, and for a
chance gesture, which they deemed suspicious—though it
was harmless—made by the mate, Raneds, to the deponent, in
the act of handing a quadrant, they killed him; but that for
this they afterwards were sorry, the mate being the only remaining navigator on board, except the deponent.

—That omitting other events, which daily happened, and
which can only serve uselessly to recall past misfortunes and

conflicts, after seventy-three days' navigation, reckoned from the time they sailed from Nasca, during which they navigated under a scanty allowance of water, and were afflicted with the calms before mentioned, they at last arrived at the island of Santa Maria, on the seventeenth of the month of August, at about six o'clock in the afternoon, at which hour they cast anchor very near the American ship, *Bachelor's Delight,* which lay in the same bay, commanded by the generous Captain Amasa Delano; but at six o'clock in the morning, they had already descried the port, and the negroes became uneasy, as soon as at distance they saw the ship, not having expected to see one there; that the negro Babo pacified them, assuring them that no fear need be had; that straightway he ordered the figure on the bow to be covered with canvas, as for repairs, and had the decks a little set in order; that for a time the negro Babo and the negro Atufal conferred; that the Negro Atufal was for sailing away, but the negro Babo would not, and by himself, cast about what to do; that at last he came to the deponent, proposing to him to say and do all that the deponent declares to have said and done to the American captain; . . . that the negro Babo warned him that if he varied in the least, or uttered any word, or gave any look that should give the least intimation of the past events or present state, he would instantly kill him, with all his companions, showing a dagger, which he carried hid, saying something which, as he understood it, meant that that dagger would be alert as his eye; that the negro Babo then announced the plan to all his companions, which pleased them; that he then, the better to disguise the truth, devised many expedients, in some of them uniting deceit and defence; that of this sort was the device of the six Ashantees before named, who were his bravos; that them he stationed on the break of the poop, as if to clean certain hatchets (in cases, which were part of the cargo), but in reality to use them, and distribute them at need, and at a given word he told them that, among other devices, was the device of presenting Atufal, his righthand man, as chained, though in a moment the chains could be dropped; that in every particular he informed the deponent what part he was expected to enact in every device, and what story he was to tell on every occasion, always threatening him with instant death if he varied in the least: that, conscious that many of the negroes would be turbulent, the negro Babo appointed the four aged negroes, who were caulkers, to keep what domestic order they could on the decks; that again and again he harangued the Spaniards and his companions, informing them of his intent, and of his devices, and of the invented story that this deponent was to tell, charging them lest any of them varied from that story; that these arrangements were made and matured during the interval of two or three hours, between their first sighting the ship and the arrival on board of Captain Amasa Delano; that this happened at about half-past seven in the morning, Captain Amasa Delano coming in his boat, and all gladly receiving him; that the deponent, as well as he could force himself, acting then the part of principal owner, and a free captain of the ship, told Captain Amasa Delano, when called upon, that he came from Buenos Ayres, bound to Lima, with three hundred negroes; that off Cape Horn, and in a subsequent fever, many negroes had died; that also, by similar casualties, all the sea officers and the greatest part of the crew had died.

[*And so the deposition goes on, circumstantially recounting the fictitious story dictated to the deponent by Babo, and through the deponent imposed upon Captain Delano; and also recounting the friendly offers of Captain Delano, with other things, but all of which is here omitted. After the fictitious, strange story, etc., the deposition proceeds:*]

—That the generous Captain Amasa Delano remained on board all the day, till he left the ship anchored at six o'clock in the evening, deponent speaking to him always of his pretended misfortunes, under the fore-mentioned principles, without having had it in his power to tell a single word, or give him the least hint, that he might know the truth and state of things; because the negro Babo, performing the office of an officious servant with all the appearance of submission of the humble slave, did not leave the deponent one moment; that this was in order to observe the deponent's actions and words, for the negro Babo understands well the Spanish; and besides, there were thereabout some others who were constantly on the watch, and likewise understood the Spanish; . . . that upon one occasion, while deponent was standing on the deck conversing with Amasa Delano, by a secret sign the negro Babo drew him (the deponent) aside, the act appearing as if originating with the deponent; that then, he being drawn aside, the negro Babo proposed to him to gain from Amasa Delano full particulars about his ship and crew, and arms; that the deponent asked "For what?" that the negro Babo answered he might conceive; that, grieved at the prospect of what might overtake the generous Captain Amasa Delano, the deponent at first refused to ask the desired questions, and used every argument to induce the negro Babo to give up this new design; that the negro Babo showed the point of his dagger; that, after the information had been obtained, the negro Babo again drew him aside, telling him that that very night he (the deponent) would be captain of two ships instead of one, for that, great part of the American's ship's crew going to be absent fishing, the six Ashantees, without any one else, would easily take it; that at this time he said other things to the same purpose; that no entreaties availed; that before Amasa Delano's coming on board, no hint had been given touching the capture of the American ship: that to prevent this project the deponent was powerless; . . . —that in some things his memory is confused, he cannot distinctly recall every event; . . . —that as soon as they had cast anchor at six of the clock in the evening, as has before been stated, the American captain took leave to return to his vessel; that upon a sudden impulse, which the deponent believes to have come from God and his angels, he, after the farewell had been said, followed the generous Captain Amasa Delano as far as the gunwale, where he stayed, under the pretence of taking leave, until Amasa Delano should have been seated in his boat; that on shoving off, the deponent sprang from the gunwale, into the boat, and fell into it, he knows not how, God guarding him; that—

[*Here, in the original, follows the account of what further happened at the escape, and how the "San Dominick" was retaken, and of the passage to the coast; including in the recital many expressions of "eternal gratitude" to the "generous Captain Amasa Delano." The deposition then proceeds with recapitulatory remarks, and a partial renumeration of the negroes, making record of their individual part in the past events, with a view to furnishing, according to command of the court, the data whereon to found the criminal sentences to be pronounced. From this portion is the following:*]

—That he believes that all the negroes, though not in the first place knowing to the design of revolt, when it was ac-

complished, approved it. . . . That the negro, José, eighteen
years old, and in the personal service of Don Alexandro, was
the one who communicated the information to the negro
Babo, about the state of things in the cabin, before the revolt; that this is known, because, in the preceding midnight,
he used to come from his berth, which was under his
master's, in the cabin, to the deck where the ringleader and
his associates were, and had secret conversations with the
negro Babo, in which he was several times seen by the mate;
that, one night, the mate drove him away twice; . . . that
this same negro José, was the one who, without being commanded to do so by the negro Babo, as Lecbe and Martinqui
were, stabbed his master, Don Alexandro, after he had been
dragged half-lifeless to the deck; . . . that the mulatto
steward, Francesco, was of the first band of revolters, that
he was, in all things, the creature and tool of the negro Babo;
that, to make his court, he, just before a repast in the cabin,
proposed, to the negro Babo, poisoning a dish for the generous Captain Amasa Delano; this is known and believed,
because the negroes have said it; but that the negro Babo,
having another design, forbade Francesco; . . . that the
Ashantee Lecbe was one of the worst of them; for that, on
the day the ship was retaken, he assisted in the defence of
her, with a hatchet in each hand, with one of which he
wounded, in the breast, the chief mate of Amasa Delano, in
the first act of boarding; this all knew; that, in sight of the
deponent, Lecbe struck, with a hatchet, Don Francisco Masa
when, by the negro Babo's orders, he was carrying him to
throw him overboard, alive; beside participating in the murder, before mentioned, of Don Alexandro Aranda, and
others of the cabin-passengers; that, owing to the fury with
which the Ashantees fought in the engagement with the
boats, but this Lecbe and Yan survived; that Yan was bad as
Lecbe; that Yan was the man who, by Babo's command,
willingly prepared the skeleton of Don Alexandro, in a way
the negroes afterwards told the deponent, but which he, so
long as reason is left him, can never divulge; that Yan and
Lecbe were the two who, in a calm by night, riveted
the skeleton to the bow; this also the negroes told him; that
the negro Babo was he who traced the inscription below it;
that the negro Babo was the plotter from first to last; he ordered every murder, and was the helm and keel of the revolt;
that Atufal was his lieutenant in all; but Atufal, with his own
hand, committed no murder; nor did the negro Babo; . . .

that Atufal was shot, being killed in the fight with the boats, ere boarding; . . . that the negresses, of age, were knowing to the revolt, and testified themselves satisfied at the death of their master, Don Alexandro; that, had the negroes not restrained them, they would have tortured to death, instead of simply killing, the Spaniards slain by command of the negro Babo; that the negresses used their utmost influence to have the deponent made away with; that, in the various acts of murder, they sang songs and danced—not gaily, but solemnly; and before the engagement with the boats, as well as during the action, they sang melancholy songs to the negroes, and that this melancholy tone was more inflaming than a different one would have been, and was so intended; that all this is believed, because the negroes have said it.—That of the thirty-six men of the crew—exclusive of the passengers (all of whom are now dead), which the deponent had knowledge of—six only remained alive, with four cabin-boys and ship-boys, not included with the crew; . . . —that the negroes broke an arm of one of the cabin-boys and gave him strokes with hatchets.

[*Then follow various random disclosures referring to various periods of time. The following are extracted:*]

—That during the presence of Captain Amasa Delano on board, some attempts were made by the sailors, and one by Hermenegildo Gandix, to convey hints to him of the true state of affairs; but that these attempts were ineffectual, owing to fear of incurring death, and furthermore owing to the devices which offered contradictions to the true state of affairs; as well as owing to the generosity and piety of Amasa Delano, incapable of sounding such wickedness; . . . that Luys Galgo, a sailor about sixty years of age, and formerly of the king's navy; was one of those who sought to convey tokens to Captain Amasa Delano; but his intent, though undiscovered, being suspected, he was, on a pretence, made to retire out of sight, and at last into the hold, and there was made away with. This the negroes have since said; . . . that one of the ship-boys feeling, from Captain Amasa Delano's presence, some hopes of release, and not having enough prudence, dropped some chance-word respecting his expectations, which being overheard and understood by a slave-boy with whom he was eating at the time, the latter struck him on the head with a knife, inflicting a bad wound, but of which the boy is now healing; that likewise, not long before the ship was brought to anchor, one of the seamen, steering at the time, endangered himself by letting the blacks remark a certain unconscious hopeful expression in his countenance, arising from some cause similar to the above; but this sailor, by his heedful after conduct, escaped; . . . that these statements are made to show the court that from the beginning to the end of the revolt, it was impossible for the deponent and his men to act otherwise than they did; . . . —that the third clerk, Hermenegildo Gandix, who before had been forced to live among the seamen, wearing a seaman's habit, and in all respects appearing to be one for the time; he, Gandix, was killed by a musket-ball fired through a mistake from the American boats before boarding; having in his fright run up the mizzen-rigging, calling to the boats —"don't board," lest upon their boarding the negroes should kill him; that this inducing the Americans to believe he some way favoured the cause of the negroes, they fired two balls at him, so that he fell wounded from the rigging, and was drowned in the sea; . . . —that the young Don Joaquin, Marques de Arambaolaza, like Hermenegildo Gandix, the third clerk, was degraded to the office and appearance of a common seaman; that upon one occasion, when Don Joaquin shrank, the negro Babo commanded the Ashantee Lecbe to take tar and heat it, and pour it upon Don Joaquin's hands; . . . —that Don Joaquin was killed owing to another mistake of the Americans, but one impossible to be avoided, as upon the approach of the boats, Don Joaquin, with a hatchet tied edge out and upright to his hand, was made by the negroes to appear on the bulwarks; whereupon, seen with arms in his hands and in a questionable attitude, he was shot for a renegade seaman; . . . —that on the person of Don Joaquin was found secreted a jewel, which, by papers that were discovered, proved to have been meant for the shrine of our Lady of Mercy in Lima; a votive offering, beforehand prepared and guarded, to attest his gratitude, when he should have landed in Peru, his last destination, for the safe conclusion of his entire voyage from Spain; . . . —that the jewel, with the other effects of the late Don Joaquin, is in the custody of the brethren of the Hospital de Sacerdotes, awaiting the decision of the honourable court; . . . —that, owing to the condition of the deponent, as well as the haste in which the boats departed for the attack, the Americans were not forewarned that there were, among the apparent crew, a passenger and one of the clerks disguised by the negro Babo; . . . —that, beside the negroes killed in the action, some were killed after the capture and reanchoring at night, when shackled to the ring-bolts on deck; that these deaths were committed by the sailors, ere they could be prevented. That so soon as informed of it, Captain Amasa Delano used all his authority, and, in particular with his own hand, struck down Martinez Gola, who, having found a razor in the pocket of an old jacket of his, which one of the shackled negroes had on, was aiming it at the negro's throat; that the noble Captain Amasa Delano also wrenched from the hand of Bartholomew Barlo, a dagger secreted at the time of the massacre of the whites, with which he was in the act of stabbing a shackled negro, who, the same day, with another negro, had thrown him down and jumped upon him; . . . —that, for all the events, befalling through so long a time, during which the ship was in the hands of the negro Babo, he cannot here give account; but that, what he has said is the most substantial of what occurs to him at present, and is the truth under the oath which he has taken; which declaration he affirmed and ratified, after hearing it read to him.

He said that he is twenty-nine years of age, and broken in body and mind; that when finally dismissed by the court, he shall not return home to Chili, but betake himself to the monastery on Mount Agonia without; and signed with his honour, and crossed himself, and, for the time, departed as he came, in his litter, with the monk Infelez, to the Hospital de Sacerdotes.   BENITO CERENO.

DOCTOR ROZAS.

If the deposition of Benito Cereno has served as the key to fit into the lock of the complications which preceded it, then, as a vault whose door has been flung back, the *San Dominick's* hull lies open to-day.

Hitherto the nature of this narrative, besides rendering the intricacies in the beginning unavoidable, has more or less required that many things, instead of being set down in the order of occurrence, should be retrospectively, or irregularly given; this last is the case with the following passages, which will conclude the account:

During the long, mild voyage to Lima, there was, as before hinted, a period during which Don Benito a little recovered his health, or, at least in some degree, his tranquillity. Ere the decided relapse which came, the two captains had many cordial conversations—their fraternal unreserve in singular contrast with former withdrawments.

Again and again, it was repeated, how hard it had been to enact the part forced on the Spaniard by Babo.

"Ah, my dear Don Amasa," Don Benito once said, "at those very times when you thought me so morose and un-grateful—nay, when, as you now admit, you half thought me plotting your murder—at those very times my heart was frozen; I could not look at you, thinking of what, both on board this ship and your own, hung, from other hands, over my kind benefactor. And as God lives, Don Amasa, I know not whether desire for my own safety alone could have nerved me to that leap into your boat, had it not been for the thought that, did you, unenlightened, return to your ship, you, my best friend, with all who might be with you, stolen upon, that night, in your hammocks, would never in this world have wakened again. Do but think how you walked this deck, how you sat in this cabin, every inch of ground mined into honey-combs under you. Had I dropped the least hint, made the least advance toward an understanding between us, death, explosive death—yours as mine—would have ended the scene."

"True, true," cried Captain Delano, starting, "you saved my life, Don Benito, more than I yours; saved it, too, against my knowledge and will."

"Nay, my friend," rejoined the Spaniard, courteous even to the point of religion, "God charmed your life, but you saved mine. To think of some things you did—those smilings and chattings, rash pointings and gesturings. For less than these, they slew my mate, Raneds; but you had the Prince of Heaven's safe conduct through all ambuscades."

"Yes, all is owing to Providence, I know; but the temper of my mind that morning was more than commonly pleas-ant, while the sight of so much suffering—more apparent than real—added to my good nature, compassion, and char-ity, happily interweaving the three. Had it been otherwise, doubtless, as you hint, some of my interferences with the blacks might have ended unhappily enough. Besides that, those feelings I spoke of enabled me to get the better of mo-mentary distrust, at times when acuteness might have cost me my life, without saving another's. Only at the end did my suspicions get the better of me, and you know how wide of the mark they then proved."

"Wide, indeed," said Don Benito, sadly; "you were with

me all day; stood with me, sat with me, talked with me, looked at me, ate with me, drank with me; and yet, your last act was to clutch for a villain, not only an innocent man, but the most pitiable of all men. To such degree may malign machinations and deceptions impose. So far may even the best men err, in judging the conduct of one with the recesses of whose condition he is not acquainted. But you were forced to it; and you were in time undeceived. Would that, in both respects, it was so ever, and with all men."

"I think I understand you; you generalize, Don Benito; and mournfully enough. But the past is passed; why moralize upon it? Forget it. See, yon bright sun has forgotten it all, and the blue sea, and the blue sky; these have turned over new leaves."

"Because they have no memory," he dejectedly replied; "because they are not human."

"But these mild trades that now fan your cheek, Don Benito, do they not come with a human-like healing to you? Warm friends, steadfast friends are the trades."

"With their steadfastness they but waft me to my tomb, Señor," was the foreboding response.

"You are saved, Don Benito," cried Captain Delano, more and more astonished and pained; "you are saved; what has cast such a shadow upon you?"

"The negro."

There was silence, while the moody man sat, slowly and unconsciously gathering his mantle about him, as if it were a pall.

There was no more conversation that day.

But if the Spaniard's melancholy sometimes ended in muteness upon topics like the above, there were others upon which he never spoke at all; on which, indeed, all his old reserves were piled. Pass over the worst and, only to elucidate, let an item or two of these be cited. The dress so precise and costly, worn by him on the day whose events have been narrated, had not willingly been put on. And that silver-mounted sword, apparent symbol of despotic command, was not, indeed, a sword, but the ghost of one. The scabbard, artificially stiffened, was empty.

As for the black—whose brain, not body, had schemed and led the revolt, with the plot—his slight frame, inadequate to that which it held, had at once yielded to the superior muscular strength of his captor, in the boat. Seeing all was over, he uttered no sound, and could not be forced to. His aspect seemed to say: since I cannot do deeds, I will not speak words. Put in irons in the hold, with the rest, he was carried to Lima. During the passage Don Benito did not visit him. Nor then, nor at any time after, would he look at him. Before the tribunal he refused. When pressed by the judges he fainted. On the testimony of the sailors alone rested the legal identity of Babo. And yet the Spaniard would, upon occasion, verbally refer to the negro, as has been shown; but look on him he would not, or could not.

Some months after, dragged to the gibbet at the tail of a mule, the black met his voiceless end. The body was burned to ashes; but for many days, the head, that hive of subtlety, fixed on a pole in the Plaza, met, unabashed, the gaze of the whites; and across the Plaza looked toward St. Bartholomew's church, in whose vaults slept then, as now, the recovered bones of Aranda; and across the Rimac bridge looked toward the monastery, on Mount Agonia without; where, three months after being dismissed by the court, Benito Cereno, borne on the bier, did, indeed, follow his leader.

Master and Man

BY LEO TOLSTOY
(1828-1910)

Leo Tolstoy, frequently acclaimed by writers and critics as the world's greatest novelist, was born on the family estate in the province of Tula, Russia. While still young he displayed an interest in the life and living conditions of the peasants. In his early twenties, he attempted to establish a school for the peasants on his large estate, Yasnaya Polyana, which he had inherited from his parents. The failure of the peasants to respond to his efforts discouraged him and he returned to the carefree life available to a wealthy young nobleman in Moscow and St. Petersburg. He began his writing career while serving in the army. After his marriage, he settled on his estate and wrote his great novels, War and Peace and Anna Karenina. About 1876, he underwent a period of spiritual turmoil. Master and Man (1895) reflects Tolstoy's disenchantment with materialistic values and his discovery of a Christian way of life in the simple existence of the peasants. Tolstoy practiced his convictions, leaving his family and his possessions to live the life of a peasant. By the time he died, devoted followers of his principles throughout Russia respected him as a sage and saint.

Master and Man

1895

CHAPTER I

It happened in the seventies, in winter, on the day after St.
Nicholas' Day.[1] There was a holiday in the parish, and the
village landowner and second-guild merchant, Vasili Andreyitch Brekhunof, could not be absent, as he had to attend
church—he was a churchwarden—and receive and entertain
friends and acquaintances at home.

But at last all the guests were gone, and Vasili Andreyitch
began preparations for a drive over to see a neighboring
landed proprietor about buying from him the forest for
which they had been bargaining this long while. He was in
great haste to go, so as to forestall the town merchants, who
might snatch away this profitable purchase.

The youthful landowner asked ten thousand rubles for
the forest, simply because Vasili Andreyitch offered seven
thousand. In reality, seven thousand was but a third of the
real worth of the forest. Vasili Andreyitch might, perhaps,
even now make the bargain, because the forest stood in his
district, and by an old standing agreement between him and
the other village merchants, no one of them competed in
another's territory. But Vasili Andreyitch had learned that
the timber-merchants from the capital town of the province
intended to bid for the Goryatchkin forest, and he decided
to go at once and conclude the bargain. Accordingly, as soon
as the feast was over, he took seven hundred rubles of his
own from the strong box, added to them twenty-three hundred belonging to the church, so as to make three thousand,

[1] Winter St. Nicholas' Day is December 6 (O.S.).

and, after carefully counting the whole, he put the money into his pocket-book and made haste to be gone.

Nikita, the laborer, the only one of Vasili Andreyitch's men who was not drunk that day, ran to harness the horse. He was not drunk on this occasion, because he had been a drunkard, and now since the last day before the fast, when he spent his coat and leather boots in drink, he had sworn off and for two months had not tasted liquor. He was not drinking even now, in spite of the temptation arising from the universal consumption of alcohol during the first two days of the holiday.

Nikita was a fifty-year-old peasant from a neighboring village; no manager, as folk said of him, but one who lived most of his life with other people, and not at his own home. He was esteemed everywhere for his industry, dexterity, and strength, and still more for his kindliness and pleasantness. But he never lived long in one place, because twice a year, or even oftener, he took to drinking; and at such times, besides spending all he had, he became turbulent and quarrelsome. Vasili Andreyitch had dismissed him several times, and afterward engaged him again; valuing his honesty and kindness to animals, but chiefly his cheapness. The merchant did not pay Nikita eighty rubles, the worth of such a man, but forty; and even that he paid without regular account, in small instalments, and mostly not in cash, but in high-priced goods from his own shop.

Nikita's wife, Marfa, a vigorous and once beautiful woman, carried on the home, with a boy almost fully grown and two girls. She never urged Nikita to live at home: first, because she had lived for about twenty years with a cooper, a peasant from another village, who lodged with them; and secondly, because, although she treated her husband as she pleased when he was sober, she feared him like fire when he was drinking.

Once, when drunk at home, Nikita, apparently to revenge himself for all the submissiveness he had shown his wife when sober, broke open her box, took her best clothes, and, seizing an ax, cut to shreds all her dresses and garments. All the wages Nikita earned went to his wife, and he made no objection to this arrangement. Thus it was that Marfa, two days before the holiday, came to Vasili Andreyitch, and got from him wheat flour, tea, sugar, and a pint of vodka,—about three rubles' worth in all,—and five rubles in cash; and she thanked him as for a special favor, although, at the lowest figure, Vasili Andreyitch owed twenty rubles.

"What agreement did I make with you?" said Vasili Andreyitch to Nikita. "If you want anything, take it; you will work it out. I am not like other folks, with their delays, and accounts, and fines. We are dealing straightforwardly. You work for me, and I'll stand by you."

Talking in this way, Vasili Andreyitch was honestly convinced of his beneficence to Nikita; and he was so plausible that all those who depended on him for their money, beginning with Nikita, confirmed him in this conviction that he was not only not cheating them, but was doing them a service.

"I understand, Vasili Andreyitch; I do my best, I try to do as I would for my own father. I understand all right," answered Nikita, though he understood very well that Vasili Andreyitch was cheating him; at the same time he felt that it was useless to try to get the accounts cleared up. While there was nowhere else to go, he must stay where he was, and take what he could get.

Now, on receiving his master's orders to put the horse in, Nikita, willingly and cheerfully as always, and with a firm and easy stride, stepped to the cart-shed, took down from the nail the heavy, tasseled leather bridle, and, jingling the rings of the bit, went to the closed stable where by himself stood the horse which Vasili Andreyitch had ordered harnessed.

"Well, silly, were you lonely?" said Nikita, in answer to the soft, welcoming whinny which greeted him from the stallion, a fairly good dark bay of medium height, with sloping quarters, who stood solitary in his stall. "No, no! Quiet, quiet, there's plenty of time! Let me give you a drink first," he went on, addressing the horse as if he were speaking to a creature which could understand human speech. With the skirt of his coat he swept down the horse's broad, double-ridged back, rough and dusty as it was; then he put the bridle on the handsome young head, arranged his ears and mane, and throwing off the rope, led him away to drink.

Picking his way out of the dung-cumbered stall, Mukhortui began to plunge, making play with his hind foot, pretending that he wanted to kick Nikita, who was hurrying him to the well.

"Now, then, behave yourself, you rogue," said Nikita, knowing how careful Mukhortui was that the hind foot should only just touch his greasy sheepskin coat, but do no hurt; and Nikita himself especially enjoyed this sport.

After drinking the cold water, the horse drew a deep sigh, and moved his wet, strong lips from which transparent drops fell into the trough; then, after standing a moment as if in thought, he suddenly gave a loud neigh.

"If you want no more, you needn't take it. Well, let it be at that; but don't ask again for more," said Nikita, with perfect seriousness, emphasizing to Mukhortui the consequences of his behavior. Then he briskly ran back to the shed, pulling the rein on the gay young horse, who lashed out all the way along the yard.

No other men were about, except a stranger to the place, the husband of the cook, who had come for the holiday.

"Go and ask, there's a good fellow, which sledge is wanted, the wide one or the little one," said Nikita to him.

The cook's husband went into the high-perched, iron-roofed house, and soon returned with the answer that the small one was ordered. By this time Nikita had put on the brass-studded saddle, and carrying in one hand the light, painted yoke, with the other hand he led the horse toward the two sledges which stood under the shed.

"All right, the small one it is," said he, backing into the shafts the intelligent horse, which all the time pretended to bite at him; and, with the help of the cook's husband, he began to harness.

When all was nearly ready, and only the reins needed attention, Nikita sent the cook's husband to the shed for straw and to the storehouse for some sacking.

"That's great! There, there; don't bristle up so!" said Nikita, squeezing into the sledge the freshly thrashed oat straw which the cook's husband had brought. "Now give me the sacking, while we spread it out, and put the cloth over it. That's all right, just the thing, comfortable to sit on," said he, doing that which he was talking about, and making the cloth tight over the straw all round.

"Thanks, my dear fellow," said Nikita to the cook's husband. "When two work, it's done quicker."

Then, disentangling the leather reins, the ends of which were brought together and tied on a ring, he took the driver's seat on the sledge, and shook up the good horse, who stirred himself, eager to make across the frozen refuse that littered the yard, toward the gate.

"Uncle Mikit, uncle!" came a shout behind him, from a

seven-year-old boy in a black fur cloak, new white, felt boots, and warm cap, who came hurrying out from the entrance-hall toward the yard. "Put me in?" he asked in a shrill voice, buttoning his little coat as he ran.

"All right, come, my dove," said Nikita; and, stopping the sledge, he put in the master's son, whose face grew radiant with joy, and drove out into the road.

It was three o'clock, and cold—about ten degrees of frost —gloomy and windy. Half the sky was shrouded by a low-hanging dark cloud. In the yard it seemed quiet, but in the street the wind was more noticeable. The snow blew down from the roof of the barn close by, and at the corner by the baths flew whirling round. Nikita had scarcely driven out and turned round by the front door, when Vasili Andreyitch, too, with a cigarette in his mouth, wearing a sheepskin overcoat tightly fastened by a girdle placed low, came out from the entrance-hall. He strode down the trampled snow of the high steps, which creaked under his leather-trimmed felt boots, and stopped. Drawing in one final puff of smoke, he flung down his cigarette and trampled it underfoot; then, breathing out the smoke through his mustaches and critically surveying the horse, he began to turn in the corners of his overcoat collar on both sides of his ruddy face, clean-shaven, except for a mustache, so as to keep the fur clear from the moisture of his breath.

"See there! What a funny little rascal! He's all ready!" said he, as he caught sight of his little pale, thin son in the sledge. Vasili Andreyitch was excited by the wine he had taken with his guests, and was therefore more than usually satisfied with everything which belonged to him, and with everything he did. The sight of his son, whom he always in his own mind thought of as his heir, now caused him great satisfaction. He looked at him, and as he did so he smirked and showed his long teeth.

His wife, a pale and meager woman, about to become a mother, stood behind him in the entrance-hall with a woolen shawl so wrapped about her head and shoulders that only her eyes could be seen.

"Would it not be better to take Nikita with you?" she asked, timidly stepping out from the door.

Vasili Andreyitch made no reply, but merely spat, scowling angrily at her words, which evidently were disagreeable to him.

"You have money with you," the wife continued, in the

same plaintive voice. "What if the weather should get worse! Be careful, for God's sake."

"Do you think I don't know the road, that I need a guide?" retorted Vasili Andreyitch, with that affected compression of the lips with which he ordinarily addressed dealers in the market, and bringing out every syllable with extraordinary precision, as if he valued his own speech.

"Really, I would take him. I beg of you, for God's sake!" repeated his wife, folding her shawl closer.

"Just listen! She sticks to it like a leaf in the bath! . . . Why, where must I take him to?"

"Well, Vasili Andreyitch, I'm ready," said Nikita, cheerfully. "If I'm away, there are only the horses to be fed," he added, turning to his mistress.

"I'll look after that, Nikitushka; I'll tell Semyon," answered the mistress.

"Well, then, shall I come, Vasili Andreyitch?" asked Nikita, waiting.

"It seems we must have some regard for the old woman. But if you come, go and put on something warmer," said Vasili Andreyitch, smiling once more, and winking at Nikita's sheepskin coat, which was torn under the arms and down the back, and soiled and patched and frayed into fringes round the skirts.

"Hey, dear soul, come and hold the horse awhile!" shouted Nikita to the cook's husband, in the yard.

"I'll hold him myself," said the little boy, taking his half-frozen red hands out of his pockets, and seizing the cold leather reins.

"Only don't be too long putting your best coat on! Be quick!" shouted Vasili Andreyitch, grinning at Nikita.

"In a moment, Father, Vasili Andreyitch!" said Nikita, and, with his trousers stuffed into his old patched felt boots, he swiftly ran down the yard to the laborers' quarters.

"Here, Arinushka, give me my coat off the oven. I have to go with the master!" said Nikita, hastening into the room, and taking his girdle down from the nail.

The cook, who had just finished her after-dinner nap, and was about to get ready the samovar for her husband, turned cheerily to Nikita, and, catching his haste, moved about quickly, just as he was doing, took the well-worn woolen khalat off the oven, where it was drying, and shook and rubbed it.

"There now, you'll have a chance to spread and have a

good time with your husband here," said Nikita to the cook; always, as part of his good-natured politeness, ready to say something to any one whom he came across.

Then, putting round himself the narrow shrunken girdle, he drew in his breath and tightened it about his spare body as much as he could.

"There," he said afterward, addressing himself, not to the cook, but to the girdle, while tucking the ends under his belt, "this way, you won't jump out." Then, working his shoulders up and down to get his arms loose, he put on the coat, again stretching his back to free his arms, and poked up under his sleeves and took his mittens from the shelf.

"Now, we're all right."

"You ought to change your boots," said the cook; "those boots are very bad."

Nikita stopped, as if remembering something.

"Yes, I ought. . . . But it will go as it is; it's not far."

And he ran out into the yard.

"Won't you be cold, Nikitushka?" said the mistress, as he came up to the sledge.

"Why should I be cold? It is quite warm," answered Nikita, arranging the straw in the fore part of the sledge, so as to bring it over his legs, and stowing under it the whip which the good horse would not need.

Vasili Andreyitch had already taken his place in the sledge, almost filling up the whole of the curved back with the bulk of his body wrapped in two shubas; and, taking up the reins, he started at once. Nikita jumped in, seating himself in front, to the left, and hanging one leg over the side.

CHAPTER II

The good stallion took the sledge along at a brisk pace over the smooth frozen road through the village, the runners creaking faintly as they went.

"Look at him there, hanging on! Give me the whip, Mikita," shouted Vasili Andreyitch, evidently enjoying the sight of his boy holding to the sledge-runners, behind. "I'll give it to you! Run to your mamma, you young dog!"

The boy jumped off. Mukhortui began to pace and then, getting his breath, broke into a trot.

Krestui, the village where Vasili Andreyitch lived, consisted of six houses. Scarcely had they passed the blacksmith's hut, the last in the village, when they suddenly remarked that the wind was much stronger than they had thought. The road was by this time scarcely visible. The tracks of the sledge were instantly covered with snow, and the road was to be distinguished only by the fact that it was higher than anything else. There was a whirl of snow over the fields, and the line where the earth and sky join could not be distinguished. The Telyatin forest, always plainly in sight, loomed dimly through the driving snow-dust. The wind came from the left hand, persistently blowing to one side the mane on Mukhortui's powerful neck, turning away even his knotted tail, and pressing Nikita's high collar—he sat on the windward side—against his face and nose.

"There is no chance of showing his speed, with this snow," said Vasili Andreyitch, proud of his good horse. "I once went to Pashutino with him, and we got there in half an hour."

"What?" said Nikita, who could not hear on account of his collar.

"Pashutino, I said; and he did it in half an hour," shouted Vasili Andreyitch.

"A good horse that, no question," said Nikita.

They became silent. But Vasili Andreyitch wanted to talk.

"Say, I suppose you told your wife not to give any drink to the cooper?" said Vasili Andreyitch in the same loud voice, being perfectly convinced that Nikita must feel flattered, talking with such an important and sensible man as himself, and he was so pleased with his jest that it never entered his head that the subject might be unpleasant to Nikita.

Again the man failed to catch his master's words, the voice being carried away by the wind.

Vasili Andreyitch, in his loud clear voice, repeated the jest about the cooper.

"God help them, Vasili Andreyitch, I don't meddle in these matters. I only hope that she does no harm to the lad; if she does—then God help her!"

"That is right," said Vasili Andreyitch. "Well, are you going to buy a horse in the spring?" Thus he began a new topic of conversation.

"Yes, I must buy one," answered Nikita, turning down his collar, and leaning toward his master. Now the conversation became interesting to him, and he did not wish to lose a word.

"My lad is grown up; he must plow for himself, but now he is hired out all the time," said he.

"Well, then, take the horse with the thin loins; the price will not be high," shouted Vasili Andreyitch, feeling himself excited and consequently eagerly entering into his favorite business of horse-dealing, to which he gave all his intellectual powers.

"You give me fifteen rubles, and I'll buy in the market," said Nikita, who knew that at the highest price the horse which Vasili Andreyitch called "Bezkostretchnui" and wanted to sell him, was not worth more than seven rubles, but would cost him at his master's hands twenty-five; and that meant half a year's wages gone.

"The horse is a good one. I treat you as I would myself. Conscientiously. Brekhunof injures no man. Let me stand the loss, and me only. Honestly," he shouted in the voice which he used in cheating his customers, "a genuine horse."

"As you think," said Nikita, sighing, and convinced that it was useless to listen further, he again drew the collar over his ear and face.

They drove in silence for about half an hour. The wind cut sharply into Nikita's side and arm, where his shuba was torn. He huddled himself up and breathed into his coat-collar, which covered his mouth, was not wholly cold!

"What do you think; shall we go through Karamuishevo, or keep the straight road?" said Vasili Andreyitch.

The road through Karamuishevo was more frequented and staked on both sides; but it was longer. The straight road was nearer, but it was little used, and either there were no stakes, or they were poor ones left standing covered with snow.

Nikita thought awhile.

"Through Karamuishevo is farther, but it is better going," he said.

"But straight on we have only to be careful not to lose the road in passing the little valley, and then the way is fairly good, sheltered by the forest," said Vasili Andreyitch, who favored the direct road.

"As you wish," replied Nikita, and again he rolled up his collar.

So Vasili Andreyitch took this way, and after driving about half a verst, he came to a place where there was a long oak stake which shook in the wind, and to which a few dry leaves were clinging, and there he turned to the left.

On turning, the wind blew almost directly against them,

and the snow showered from on high. Vasili Andreyitch stirred up his horse, and inflated his cheeks, blowing his breath upon his mustaches. Nikita dozed.

They drove thus silently for about ten minutes. Suddenly Vasili Andreyitch began to say something.

"What?" asked Nikita, opening his eyes.

Vasili Andreyitch did not answer, but bent himself about, looking behind them, and then ahead of the horse. The sweat had curled the animal's coat on the groin and neck, and he was going at a walk.

"I say, what's the matter?" repeated Nikita.

"What is the matter?" mocked Vasili Andreyitch, irritated. "I see no stakes. We must be off the road."

"Well, pull up then, and I will find the road," said Nikita and lightly jumping down, he drew out the whip from the straw and started off to the left, from his own side of the sledge.

The snow was not deep that season, so that one could travel anywhere, but in places it was up to one's knee, and got into Nikita's boots. He walked about, feeling with his feet and the whip, but no road was to be found.

"Well?" said Vasili Andreyitch, when Nikita returned to the sledge.

"There is no road on this side. I must try the other."

"There's something dark there in front. Go and see what it is," said Vasili Andreyitch.

Nikita walked ahead; got near the dark patch; and found it was black earth which the wind had strewn over the snow, from some fields of winter wheat. After searching to the right also, he returned to the sledge, shook the snow off himself, cleared his boots, and took his seat.

"We must go to the right," he said decidedly. "The wind was on our left before, now it is straight in my face. To the right," he repeated, with the same decision.

Vasili Andreyitch heeded him and turned to the right. But yet no road was found. He drove on in this direction for some time. The wind did not diminish, and the snow still fell.

"We seem to be astray altogether, Vasili Andreyitch," suddenly exclaimed Nikita, as if he were announcing some pleasant news. "What is that?" he said, pointing to some black potato-leaves, which thrust themselves through the snow.

Vasili Andreyitch stopped the horse, which by this time was in a heavy perspiration and stood with its deep sides heaving.

"What can it mean?" asked he.

"It means that we are on the Zakharovsky lands. Why, we are ever so far astray!"

"You lie!" remarked Vasili Andreyitch.

"I am not lying, Vasili Andreyitch; it is the truth," said Nikita. "You can feel that the sledge is moving over a potato-field, and there are the heaps of old leaves. It is the Zakharovsky factory-land."

"What a long way we are out!" said Vasili Andreyitch. "What are we to do?"

"Go straight ahead, that's all. We shall reach some place," said Nikita. "If we do not get to Zakharovka, we shall come out at the owner's farm."

Vasili Andreyitch assented, and let the horse go as Nikita had said. They drove in this way for a long while. At times they passed over winter wheat fields all bare, and the sledge creaked over the humps of frozen soil. Sometimes they passed a stubble-field, sometimes a corn-field, where they could see the upstanding wormwood and straw beaten by the wind; sometimes they drove into deep and even white snow on all sides, with nothing visible above it.

The snow whirled down from on high, and sometimes seemed to rise up from below. The horse was evidently tiring; his coat grew crisp and white with frozen sweat, and he walked. Suddenly he stumbled in some ditch or water-course, and went down. Vasili Andreyitch wanted to halt, but Nikita cried to him:—

"Why should we stop? We have gone astray, and we must find our road. Hey, old fellow, hey," he shouted in an encouraging voice to the horse; and he jumped from the sledge, sinking into the ditch.

The horse dashed forward, and quickly landed upon a frozen heap. Obviously it was a man-made ditch.

"Where are we, then?" said Vasili Andreyitch.

"We shall see," answered Nikita. "Go ahead, we shall get to somewhere."

"Is not that the Goryatchkin forest?" asked Vasili Andreyitch, pointing out a dark mass which showed across the snow in front of them.

"When we get nearer, we shall see what forest it is," said Nikita.

He noticed that from the side of the dark mass, long, dry willow leaves were fluttering toward them; and so he knew that it was no forest, but a settlement; yet he chose not to say so. And, in fact, they had scarcely gone twenty-five yards beyond the ditch, when they distinctly made out the trees, and heard a new and melancholy sound. Nikita was right; it was not a forest but a row of tall willow trees, whereon a few scattered leaves still shivered. The willows were evidently ranged along the ditch of a threshing-floor. Coming up to the trees, through which the wind moaned and sighed, the horse suddenly planted his forefeet above the height of the sledge, then drew up his hind legs after him, turned to the left and leaped, sinking up to his knees in the snow. It was a road.

"Here we are," said Nikita, "but I don't know where."

The horse without erring ran along the snow-covered road, and they had not gone eighty yards when they saw the straight strip of a wattled fence, from which the snow was flying in the wind. Passing under a deeply drifted roof of a granary, the road turned in the direction of the wind, and brought them upon a snowdrift. But ahead of them was a passage between two houses; the drift was merely blown across the road, and had to be crossed. Indeed, after passing the drift, they came into a village street. In front of the end house of the village, the wind was shaking desperately the frozen linen which hung there: shirts, one red, one white, some leg-cloths, and a skirt. The white shirt especially shook frantically, tugging at the sleeves.

"Look there, either a lazy woman or a dead one left her linen out over the holiday," said Nikita, seeing the fluttering shirts.

CHAPTER III

At the beginning of the street, the wind was still fierce, and the road was snow-covered; but well within the village, it was calm, warm, and cheerful. At one house a dog was barking; at another, a woman, with a sleeveless coat over her head, came running out from somewhere, and stopped at the door of an izba to see who was driving past. In the middle of the village could be heard the sound of girls singing.

Here, in the village, the wind and the snow and the frost seemed subdued.

"Why, this is Grishkino," said Vasili Andreyitch.

"It is," said Nikita.

Grishkino it was. So they had strayed eight versts too far to the left, and traveled out of their proper direction; still, they had got somewhat nearer to their destination. From Grishkino to Goryatchkino was about five versts more.

In the middle of the village they almost ran into a tall man, walking in the center of the road.

"Who is driving?" said this man, and he held the horse. Then, recognizing Vasili Andreyitch, he took hold of the shaft, and reached the sledge, where he sat himself on the driver's seat.

It was the peasant Isaï, well known to Vasili Andreyitch, and known throughout the district as the most notorious horse-thief.

"Ah, Vasili Andreyitch, where is God sending you?" said Isaï, from whom Nikita caught the smell of vodka.

"We are going to Goryatchkino."

"You've come a long way round! You should have gone through Malakhovo."

"'Should have' is right, but we got astray," said Vasili Andreyitch, pulling up.

"A good horse," said Isaï, examining him, and dexterously tightening the loosened knot in his thick tail. "Are you going to stay the night here?"

"No, friend, we must go on."

"Your business must be pressing. And who is that? Ah, Nikita Stepanuich!"

"Who else?" answered Nikita. "Look here, good friend, can you tell us how not to miss the road again?"

"How can you possibly miss it? Just turn back straight along the street, and then outside the houses; keep straight ahead. Don't go to the left. When you reach the highroad, then turn to the right."

"And which turning do we take out of the highroad—the summer or the winter road?" asked Nikita.

"The winter road. As soon as you get clear of the village there are some bushes, and opposite them is a way-mark, an oaken one, all branches. There is the road."

Vasili Andreyitch turned the horse back, and drove through the village.

"You had better stay the night," Isaï shouted after them. But Vasili Andreyitch did not answer, and started up the horse; five versts of smooth road, two versts of it through the forest, was easy enough to drive over, especially as the wind seemed quieter and the snow had apparently ceased falling.

After once more passing along the street, darkened and trodden with fresh horse-tracks, and after passing the house where the linen was hung out,—the white shirt was by this time torn, and hung by one frozen sleeve,—they came to the weirdly moaning and sighing willows, and then were again in the open country.

Not only had the snow-storm not ceased, but it seemed to have gained strength. The whole road was under snow, and only the stakes proved that they were keeping right. But even these signs of the road were difficult to make out, for the wind blew straight into their faces.

Vasili Andreyitch screwed up his eyes, and bent his head, examining the way-marks; but for the most part, he left the horse alone, trusting to his sagacity. And, in fact, the creature went truly, turning now to the left, now to the right, along the windings of the road which he sensed under his feet. So that in spite of the thickening snow and strengthening wind, the way-marks were still to be seen, now on the left, now on the right.

They had driven thus for ten minutes, when suddenly, straight in front of their horse, appeared a black object moving through the obliquely flying whirlwind of snow. It was a party of travelers. Mukhortui had overtaken them, and he struck his forefeet against the cross-bar of their sledge.

"Drive round! . . . a-a-r! . . . Go ahead!" cried voices from the sledge.

Vasili Andreyitch started to go round them. In the sledge were four peasants, three men and a woman, evidently returning from a festival visit. One of the men was whipping the snow-plastered rump of their little horse with a switch, while two of them, waving their arms from the fore part of the sledge, shouted out something. The woman, muffled up and covered with snow, sat quiet and rigid at the back.

"Where are you from?" asked Vasili Andreyitch.

"A-a-a-skiye!" was all that could be heard.

"I say, where are you from?"

"A-a-a-skiye!" shouted one of the peasants, with all his strength; but nevertheless it was impossible to make out the name.

"Go on! don't give up!" cried another, the one who kept beating his poor little horse.

"So you have come from the festival, have you?"

"Get on! get on! Up, Semka! drive round! Up, up!"

The sledges struck together, almost locked their sides, then fell apart, and the peasants' sledge began to drop behind.

The shaggy, snow-covered, big-bellied pony, laboriously breathing under the duga-bow, and evidently at the end of his strength in his vain efforts to escape from the switch belaboring him, staggered along on his short legs through the deep snow, which he trod down with difficulty. With distended nostrils, and ears set back in distress, and with his lower lip stuck out like a fish's, he kept his muzzle near Nikita's shoulder for a moment; then he began to fall behind.

"See what drink does," said Nikita. "They have tired that horse to death. What heathens!"

For a few minutes, the pantings of the tired-out horse could be heard, with the drunken shouts of the peasants. Then the pantings became inaudible, and the shouts, also. Again nothing could be heard round about except the wind whistling in their ears, and the occasional scrape of the sledge-runners on a bare spot of road.

This encounter enlivened and encouraged Vasili Andreyitch, and he drove more boldly, not examining the way-marks, and again trusting to his horse.

Nikita had nothing to occupy him, and dozed just as he always did in such circumstances, thus wasting much good daylight. Suddenly the horse stopped, and Nikita was jerked forward, knocking his nose against the front.

"It seems we are going wrong again," said Vasili Andreyitch.

"What is the matter?"

"The way-marks are not to be seen. We must be out of the road."

"Well, if we've lost the road, we must look for it," said Nikita, laconically; and again stepping easily in his great bark overshoes, he started out to explore the snow.

He walked for a long time, now out of sight, now reappearing, then disappearing; at last, he returned.

"There is no road here; it may be farther on," said he, sitting down in the sledge.

It was already beginning to grow dark. The storm was neither increasing, nor did it diminish.

"I should like to hear those peasants again," said Vasili Andreyitch.

"Yes, but they won't pass near us; we must be a good distance off the road. Maybe they are astray, too," said Nikita.

"Where shall we make for, then?"

"Leave the horse to himself. He will find his way. Give me the reins."

Vasili Andreyitch handed over the reins; the more willingly because his hands, in spite of his warm gloves, were beginning to freeze.

Nikita took the reins, and held them lightly, trying to give no pressure; he was glad to prove the good sense of his favorite. And in fact, the intelligent horse, turning one ear and then the other, first in this and then in that direction, presently began to wheel round.

"He just doesn't speak," said Nikita. "Look how he manages it! Go on, go on, that's good."

The wind was now at their backs; they felt warmer.

"Is he not wise?" continued Nikita, delighted with his horse. "A Kirghiz beast is strong, but stupid. But this one,— see what he does with his ears. There is no need of a telegraph-wire; he can feel through a mile."

Hardly half an hour had gone, when a forest, or a village, or something, loomed up in front; and, to their right, the way-marks again showed. Evidently they were on the road again.

"We are back at Grishkino, are we not?" exclaimed Nikita, suddenly.

Indeed, on the left hand rose the same granary, with the snow flying from it; and farther on was the same line with the frozen washing—the shirts and drawers, so fiercely shaken by the wind.

Again they drove through the street, again felt the quiet, warmth, and cheerfulness, again saw the road with the horse-tracks; heard voices, songs, the barking of a dog. It was now so dark that a few windows were lighted.

Halfway down the street, Vasili Andreyitch turned the horse toward a large two-storied brick house, and drew up at the steps.

Nikita went to the snow-dimmed window, in the light from which glittered the flitting flakes, and knocked with the handle of the whip.

"Who is there?" a voice answered to his knock.

"The Brekhunofs, from Krestui, my good man," answered Nikita. "Come out for a minute."

Some one moved from the window, and in about two minutes the door in the entrance-hall was heard to open, the latch of the front door clicked, and holding the door against the wind, there peeped out a tall, old, white-bearded muzhik, who had thrown a sheepskin coat over his white holiday shirt. Behind him was a young fellow in a red shirt and leather boots.

"What, is it you, Andreyitch?" said the old man.

"We have lost our road, friend," said Vasili Andreyitch. "We set out for Goryatchkino, and found ourselves here. Then we went on, but lost the road again."

"Why, how you've wandered!" answered the old man. "Petrushka, go, open the gates," he said to the young man in the red shirt.

"Of course I will," said the young fellow, cheerfully, as he ran off through the entrance-hall.

"We are not stopping for the night, friend," said Vasili Andreyitch.

"Where can you go in the night-time? You had better stop."

"Should be very glad to spend the night, but I must go on business, friend; it's impossible!"

"Well, then, at least warm yourself a little; the samovar is just ready," said the old man.

"Warm ourselves? We can do that," said Vasili Andreyitch. "It cannot get darker, and when the moon is up, it will be still lighter. Come, Mikit, let us go in and warm up a bit."

"Why, yes, let us warm ourselves," said Nikita, who was very cold, and whose great desire was to thaw out his benumbed limbs in a well-heated room.

Vasili Andreyitch went with the old man into the house. Nikita drove through the gates opened by Petrushka, by whose advice he stood the horse under the pent-roof of the shed, the floor of which was strewn with stable-litter. The high bow over the head of the horse caught the roof-beam, and the hens and a cock, already gone to roost up there, began to cackle angrily and scratch on the wood. Some startled sheep, pattering their feet on the frozen dung-heap, huddled themselves out of the way. A dog yelped desperately in fright, after the manner of young hounds, and barked fiercely at the stranger.

Nikita held conversation with them all. He begged pardon of the fowls, and calmed them with assurances that he would give them no more trouble; he reproved the sheep for being needlessly frightened; and while fastening up the horse, he kept on exhorting the little dog.

"That will do," said he, shaking the snow from himself. "Hear, how he is barking!" added he, for the dog's benefit. "That's quite enough for you, quite enough, stupid! That will do! Why do you bother yourself? There are no thieves or strangers about."

"It is like the tale of the Three Domestic Counselors," said the young man, thrusting the sledge under the shed with his strong arms.

"What about the counselors?"

"The tale is in Paulson. A thief sneaks up to a house; the dog barks,—that means 'Be on your guard'; the cock crows, —that means 'Get up'; the cat washes itself,—that means 'A welcome guest is coming, be ready for him,'" said the young man, with a smile.

Petrukha could read and write, and knew, almost by heart, the only book he possessed, which was Paulson's primer; and he liked, especially when, as now, he had been drinking a little too much, to quote from the book some saying which seemed appropriate to the occasion.

"Quite true," said Nikita.

"I suppose you are cold, uncle," said Petrukha.

"Yes, something that way," said Nikita. They both crossed the yard and entered the house.

CHAPTER IV

The house at which Vasili Andreyitch had drawn up was one of the richest in the village. The family had five allotments of land, and hired still more outside. Their establishment owned six horses, three cows, two yearling heifers, and twenty head of sheep. In the house lived twenty-two souls; four married sons, six grandchildren (of whom one, Petrukha, was married), two great-grandchildren, three orphans, and four daughters-in-law with their children. It was one of the few families, living together in one household; yet even here was that indefinable interior work of disintegration,—beginning, as usual, among the women,—infallibly bound to bring about speedy separation. Two sons were water-carriers in Moscow; one was in the army. At present, those at home were the old man, his wife, the second son who managed the household, the oldest son who had come from Moscow on a holiday, and all the women and children. Besides the family there was a guest, a neighbor, who was an intimate friend.

Over the table in the living-room hung a shaded lamp, which threw a bright light down on the tea-service, a bottle of vodka, and some eatables, and on the brick walls, where, in the "red corner," hung the ikons with pictures on each side of them.

At the head of the table sat Vasili Andreyitch, in his black fur coat, sucking his frozen mustaches, and scrutinizing the people and the room with his bulging, hawk-like eyes. Beside him at the table sat the white-bearded, bald, old father of the house, in a white homespun shirt; next him sat the son from Moscow, with his sturdy back and shoulders, clad in a thin cotton shirt; then the other son, the broad-shouldered eldest brother, who acted as head of the house; then a lean and red-haired muzhik—the visiting neighbor.

The peasants, having drunk and eaten, prepared to take tea, and the samovar was already boiling as it stood on the floor near the oven. The children were to be seen on the oven and on the bunks. On the wall bench sat a woman with a cradle beside her. The aged mother of the house, whose face was covered with a network of fine wrinkles even to the lips, waited on Vasili Andreyitch.

As Nikita entered the room, she was just filling a coarse glass with vodka, and handing it to Vasili Andreyitch.

"No harm done, Vasili Andreyitch, but you must wish our good health," said she. "Have a drink, dear!"

The sight and smell of vodka, especially in his cold and tired condition, greatly disturbed Nikita's mind. He frowned, and after shaking the snow from his coat and hat, stood before the holy images: without apparently seeing any one, he made the sign of the cross thrice, and bowed to the images; then, turning to the old man, he bowed to him first, afterward to all who sat at table, and again to the women beside the oven; and saying, "Good fortune to your feast," he began to take off his overcoat without looking at the table.

"Why, you are all over frost, uncle," said the eldest brother, looking at the snow which crowned Nikita's face, eyes, and beard.

Nikita took off his coat, shook it again, hung it near the oven, and came to the table. They offered him vodka also.

There was a moment's bitter struggle; he came very near taking the glass and pouring the fragrant, transparent liquid into his mouth, but he looked at Vasili Andreyitch, remembered his vow, remembered the lost boots, the cooper, his son for whom he had promised to buy a horse when the spring came; he sighed, and refused.

"I don't drink, thank you humbly," he said gloomily, and sat down on the bench, near the second window.

"Why not?" asked the eldest brother.

"I don't drink, that's all," said Nikita, not daring to raise his eyes, and looking at his thin beard and mustache, and at the thawing icicles clinging to them.

"It is not good for him," said Vasili Andreyitch, munching a biscuit after emptying his glass.

"Then have some tea," said the kindly old woman. "I dare say you are quite benumbed, good soul. How lazy you women are with the samovar!"

"It is ready," answered the youngest, and wiping round the samovar with an apron, she bore it heavily to the table, and set it down with a thud.

Meanwhile, Vasili Andreyitch told how they had gone astray and worked back twice to the same village; what mistakes they had made, and how they had met the drunken peasants. Their hosts expressed surprise, showed why and where they had missed the road, told them the names of the revelers they had met, and made plain how they ought to go.

"From here to Molchanovka, a child might go; the only thing is to make sure where to turn out of the highroad; you'll see a bush there. But yet you did not get there," said the neighbor.

"You ought to stop here. The women will make up a bed," said the old woman, persuasively.

"You would make a better start in the morning; much pleasanter, that," said the old man, affirming what his wife had said.

"Impossible, friend! Business!" said Vasili Andreyitch. "If you let an hour go, you may not be able to make it up in a year," added he, remembering the forest and the dealers who might do him out of his purchase. "We shall get there, shan't we?" he said, turning to Nikita.

"We may lose ourselves again," said Nikita, gloomily. He was gloomy, because of the intense longing he felt for the vodka; and the tea, the only thing which could quench that longing, had not yet been offered to him.

"We have only to reach the turning, and there is no more danger of losing the road, as it goes straight through the forest," said Vasili Andreyitch.

"Just as you say, Vasili Andreyitch; if you want to go, let us go," said Nikita, taking the glass of tea offered to him.

"Well, let us drink up our tea, and then forward march!"

Nikita said nothing, but shook his head; and carefully pouring the tea into the saucer, began to warm his hands and his swollen fingers over the steam. Then, taking a small bite of sugar in his mouth, he turned to their hosts, said, "Your health," and drank down the warming liquid.

"Couldn't some one come with us to the turning?" asked Vasili Andreyitch.

"Why not? Certainly," said the eldest son. "Petrukha will put in the horse, and go with you as far as the turning."

"Then put in your horse, and I shall be in your debt."

"My dear man," said the kindly old woman, "we are right glad to do it."

"Petrukha, go and put in the mare," said the eldest son.

"All right," said Petrukha, smiling; and, without delay, taking his cap from the nail, he hurried away to harness up.

While the harnessing was in progress, the talk turned back to the point where it stood when Vasili Andreyitch arrived. The old man had complained to his neighbor, the village-elder, about the conduct of his third son, who had sent him no present this holiday-time, though he had sent a French shawl to his wife.

"These young folk are getting worse and worse," said the old man.

"Very much worse!" said the neighbor. "They are unmanageable. They know too much. There's Demotchkin, now, who broke his father's arm. It all comes from too much learning."

Nikita listened, watched the faces, and it was evident that he, too, would like to have a share in the conversation, had he not been so busy with his tea; as it was, he only nodded his head approvingly. He emptied glass after glass, growing warmer and warmer, and more and more comfortable. The talk continued in one strain, all about the harm that comes from family division; and it was clearly no theoretical discussion, but concerned with a rupture in this very house, arising through the second son, who sat there in his place, morosely silent. The question was a painful one, and absorbed the whole family; but out of politeness they refrained from discussing their private affairs before strangers.

At last, however, the old man could endure it no longer. In a tearful voice, he began to say that there should be no break-up of the family while he lived; that the house had much to thank God for, but if they fell apart—they must become beggars.

"Just like the Matveyefs," said the neighbor. "There was plenty among them all, but when they broke up the family, there was nothing for any of them."

"That's just what you want to do," said the old man to his son.

The son answered nothing, and there was a painful pause. The silence was broken by Petrukha, who had by this time harnessed the horse and returned to the room, where he had been standing for a few minutes, smiling all the time.

"There is a tale in Paulson, just like this," said he. "A father gave his sons a broom to break. They could not break it while it was bound together, but they broke it easily by taking every switch by itself. That's the way here," he said, with his broad smile. "All's ready!" he added.

"Well, if we're ready, let us start," said Vasili Andreyitch. "As to this quarrel, don't you give in, grandfather. You got everything together, and you are the master. Apply to the magistrate; he will show you how to keep your authority."

"And he gives himself such airs, such airs," continued the old man, in his complaining voice. "There is no ordering him! It is as if Satan lived in him."

Meanwhile, Nikita, having drunk his fifth glass of tea, did not stand it upside down, in sign that he had finished, but laid it on its side, hoping they might fill it a sixth time. But there was no longer any water in the samovar, and the hostess did not fill up for him again, and then Vasili Andreyitch began to put on his things. There was no help; Nikita also rose, put back into the sugar-basin the little lump of sugar, which he had nibbled on all sides, wiped the moisture from his face with the skirt of his coat, and went to put on his overcoat.

After getting into the garment, he sighed heavily: then, having thanked their hosts and said good-by, he went out from the warm, bright room, and through the dark, cold entrance-hall, where the wind creaked the doors and drove the snow in at the chinks, into the dark yard.

Petrukha, in his sheepskin, stood in the center of the yard with the horse, and smiling, recited verses from Paulson:—

Storm-clouds veil the sky with darkness,
Swiftly whirl the snowblasts wild,
Now the storm roars like a wild beast,
Now it waileth like a child.

Nikita nodded appreciatively and arranged the reins.

The old man, coming out with Vasili Andreyitch, brought a lantern into the entry to show the way, but the wind put it out at once. Even in the inclosed yard, one could see that the storm had become much more violent.

"What weather!" thought Vasili Andreyitch. "I'm afraid we shall not get there. But it must be! Business! And then, I have put our friend to the trouble of harnessing his horse. God helping, we shall get there."

Their aged host also thought it better not to go; but he had offered his arguments already, and they had not listened to him. It was useless to ask them again.

"Maybe it is old age makes me overcautious; they will get there all right," thought he. "And we can all go to bed at proper time. It will be less bother."

As for Petrukha, he had no thought of danger: he knew the way so well and the whole region, and then besides, the lines about "the snowblasts wild" encouraged him, because they were a true description of what was going on out-of-doors. Nikita had no wish to go at all; but he was long used to follow other people's wishes, and to give up his own. Therefore no one withheld the travelers.

CHAPTER V

Vasili Andreyitch went over to his sledge, found it with some difficulty in the darkness, got in, and took the reins.

"Go ahead!" he shouted.

Petrukha, kneeling in his sledge, started the horse. Mukhortui, who had before been whinnying, aware of the mare's nearness, now dashed after her, and they drove out into the street. They rode once more through the village, down the same road, past the space where the frozen linen had hung, but was no longer to be seen; past the same barn, now snowed-up almost as high as the roof, from which the snow flew incessantly; past the moaning, whistling, and bending willows; and again they came to where the sea of snow raged from above and below. The wind was so violent that, taking the travelers sidewise when they were crossing its direction, it heeled the sledge over and pushed the horse aside. Petrukha drove his good mare in front, at an easy trot, giving her an occasional lively shout of encouragement. Mukhortui pressed after her.

After driving thus for about ten minutes, Petrukha turned around and called out something. But neither Vasili Andreyitch nor Nikita could hear for the wind, but they guessed that they had reached the turning. In fact, Petrukha had turned to the right; the wind which had been at their side again blew in their faces, and to the right, through the snow, loomed something black. It was the bush beside the turning.

"Well, good-by to you!"

"Thanks, Petrukha!"

" 'The storm-clouds veil the sky with darkness!' " shouted Petrukha, and disappeared.

"Quite a poet," said Vasili Andreyitch, and shook the reins.

"Yes, a fine young man, a genuine peasant," said Nikita.

They drove on.

Nikita, protecting his head by crouching it down between his shoulders, so that his short beard covered up his throat, sat silent, trying not to lose the warmth which the tea had given him. Before him, he saw the straight lines of the shafts, which to his eyes looked like the ruts of the road; he saw the shifting quarters of the horse, with the knotted tail blown off in one direction by the wind; beyond, he saw the high duga-bow between the shafts, and the horse's rocking head and neck, with the floating mane. From time to time he noticed the stakes, and knew that, thus far, they had kept to the road, and he need not concern himself.

Vasili Andreyitch drove on, trusting to the horse to keep to the road. But Mukhortui, although he had rested a little in the village, went unwillingly, and seemed to shirk from the road, so that Vasili Andreyitch had to press him at times.

"Here is a stake on the right, here's another, and there's a third," reckoned Vasili Andreyitch, "and here, in front, is the forest," he thought, examining a dark patch ahead. But that which he took for a forest was only a bush. They passed the bush, drove about fifty yards farther, and there was neither the fourth stake nor the forest.

"We must reach the forest soon," thought Vasili Andreyitch; and buoyed up by the vodka and the tea, he shook the reins. The good, obedient animal responded, and now at an

amble, now at an easy trot, made in the direction he was
sent, although he knew it was not the way in which he
should have been going. Ten minutes went by, still no forest.

"I'm afraid we are astray again!" said Vasili Andreyitch,
pulling up.

Nikita silently got out from the sledge, and holding with
his hand the flaps of his khalat, which now pressed against
him and then flew from him as he stood and turned in the
wind, began to tread the snow; first he went to one side, then
to the other. Three times he went out of sight altogether. At
last he returned, and took the reins from Vasili Andreyitch's
hands.

"We must go to the right," he said sternly and peremptorily;
and he turned the horse.

"Well, if it must be to the right, let us go to the right,"
said Vasili Andreyitch, passing over the reins and thrusting
his frozen hands into his sleeves.

Nikita did not answer.

"Now then, old fellow, stir yourself," he called to the
horse; but Mukhortui, in spite of the shake of the reins, went
on only slowly. In places the snow was knee-deep, and the
sledge jerked at every movement of the horse.

Nikita took the whip, which hung in front of the sledge,
and struck once. The good creature, unused to the knout,
sprang forward at a trot, but soon fell again to a slow amble,
and then began to walk. Thus they went for five minutes. All
was so dark, and so blurred with snow from above and below, that sometimes they could not make out the duga-bow.
At times it seemed as if the sledge was standing, and the
ground running back. Suddenly the horse stopped short, evidently perceiving something a little distance in front of him.
Nikita once more lightly jumped out, throwing down the reins,
and went in front to find out what was the matter. But hardly
had he taken a pace clear ahead, when his feet slipped, and
he went rolling down some steep place.

"Whoa, whoa, whoa!" he said to himself, falling and trying to stop his fall. There was nothing to seize hold of, and
he brought up only when his feet plunged into a deep bed
of snow which lay in the ravine.

The fringe of drifted snow which hung on the edge of the
ravine, disturbed by Nikita's fall, showered down on him,
and got into his neck.

"What a way of doing!" cried Nikita, reproachfully addressing the snow and the ravine, as he cleared out his coat-collar.

"Mikit, hey, Mikit," shouted Vasili Andreyitch, from above. But Nikita did not answer.

He was too much occupied in shaking away the snow, than in looking for the whip, which he had lost in rolling down the bank. Having found the whip, he started to climb up the bank where he had rolled down, but it was a perfect impossibility; he slipped back every time; so that he was compelled to go along the foot of the bank to find a way up. About ten yards from the place where he fell, he managed to struggle up again on all fours, and then he turned back along the bank toward the place where the horse should have been. He could not see horse or sledge; but by going with the wind, he heard Vasili Andreyitch's voice and Mukhortui's whinny calling him, before he saw them.

"I'm coming; I'm coming. What are you cackling for!" he said.

Only when he had approached quite near the sledge could he make out the horse and Vasili Andreyitch, who stood close by, and looked gigantic.

"Where the devil have you been hiding? We've got to drive back. We must get back to Grishkino anyway," the master began to rebuke him angrily.

"I should be glad to get there, Vasili Andreyitch, but how are we to do it? Here is a ravine where if we once get in, we shall never come out. I pitched in there in such a way that I could hardly get out."

"Well, assuredly we can't stay here; somewhere we must go," said Vasili Andreyitch.

Nikita made no answer. He sat down on the sledge with his back to the wind, took off his boots and emptied them of snow; then, with a little straw which he took from the sledge, he stopped from the inside a gap in the left boot.

Vasili Andreyitch was silent, as if leaving everything to Nikita alone. Having got his boots on, Nikita drew his feet into the sledge, put on his mittens again, took the reins, and turned the horse along the ravine. But they had not driven a hundred paces when the horse stopped again. Another ravine confronted him.

Nikita got out again and began to explore the snow. He was gone a long while. At last he reappeared on the side opposite to that on which he started.

"Andreyitch, are you alive?" he called.

"Here!" shouted Vasili Andreyitch. "What is the matter?"

"I can't make anything out, it is too dark; except some ravines. We must drive to windward again."

They set off once more; Nikita explored again, stumbling through the snow. Again he sat down, again he crept forward, and at last, out of breath, he stopped beside the sledge.

"How now?" asked Vasili Andreyitch.

"Well, I'm quite tired out. And the horse is done up."

"What are we to do?"

"Wait a minute."

Nikita moved off again, and soon returned.

"Follow me," he said, going in front of the horse.

Vasili Andreyitch no longer gave orders, but implicitly did what Nikita told him.

"Here, this way!" shouted Nikita, stepping quickly to the right. Seizing Mukhortui by the bridle, he turned him toward a snowdrift.

At first the horse resisted, then dashed forward, hoping to leap the drift, but failed, and sank in snow up to the hams.

"Get out!" called Nikita to Vasili Andreyitch, who still sat in the sledge; and taking hold of one shaft, he tried to push the sledge after the horse.

"It's a pretty hard job, brother," he said to Mukhortui, "but it can't be helped. Na! na! Stir yourself! Just a little!" he called out.

The horse leaped forward, once, twice, but failed to clear himself, and sat back again as if thinking out something.

"Well, friend, this is no good," urged Nikita to Mukhortui. "Now, once more!"

Nikita pulled on the shaft again; Vasili Andreyitch did the same on the opposite side. The horse lifted his head, and made a sudden dash.

"Nu! na! You won't sink; don't be afraid," shouted Nikita.

One plunge, a second, a third, and at last the horse was out from the snowdrift, and stood still, breathing heavily and shaking himself clear. Nikita wanted to lead him on farther, but Vasili Andreyitch, in his two shubas, had so lost his breath that he could walk no more, and dropped into the sledge.

"Let me get my breath a little," he said, unbinding the handkerchief with which, at the village, he had tied the collar of his coat.

"We are all right here; you might as well lie down," said

Nikita. "I'll lead him along"; and with Vasili Andreyitch in the sledge, he led the horse by the head about ten paces farther, then up a slight rise, and stopped.

The place where Nikita drew up was not in a hollow, where the snow, swept from the drifts and piled up, might perfectly shelter them; but nevertheless it was partly protected from the wind by the edge of the ravine.

There were moments when the wind seemed to become quieter; but these intervals did not last long, and after them the storm, as if to make up for such a rest, rushed on with tenfold vigor, and tore and whirled the more angrily.

Such a gust of wind swept past as Vasili Andreyitch, with recovered breath, got out of the sledge, and went up to Nikita to talk over the situation. They both instinctively bowed themselves, and waited until the stress should be over. Mukhortui laid back his ears and shook his head. When the blast had abated a little, Nikita took off his mittens, stuck them in his girdle, and having breathed a little on his hands, began to undo the strap from the shaft bow.

"Why are you doing that?" asked Vasili Andreyitch.

"I'm taking out the horse. What else can we do? I'm done up," said Nikita, as if apologizing.

"But couldn't we drive somewhere?"

"No, we could not. We should only do harm to the horse. The poor beast is worn out," said Nikita, pointing to the creature, who stood there, with heavily heaving sides, submissively waiting for whatever should come. "We must put up for the night here," he repeated, as if they were at their inn. He began to undo the collar-straps.

The buckles fell apart.

"But we shall be frozen, shan't we?" queried Vasili Andreyitch.

"Well, if we are, we cannot help it," said Nikita.

CHAPTER VI

In his two fur coats, Vasili Andreyitch was quite warm; especially after his exertion in the snowdrift. But a cold shiver ran down his back when he learned that they really had to spend the night where they were. To calm himself, he sat down in the sledge, and got out his cigarettes and matches.

Meanwhile Nikita went on taking out the horse. He undid

the belly-band, took away the reins and collar-strap, and removed the shaft-bow, continuing to encourage the horse by speaking to him.

"Now, come out, come out," he said, leading him clear of the shafts. "We must tie you here. I'll put a bit of straw for you, and take off your bridle," he went on, doing as he said. "After a bite, you'll feel ever so much better."

But Mukhortui was not calmed by Nikita's words; uneasily, he shifted his feet, pressed against the sledge, turned his back to the wind, and rubbed his head on Nikita's sleeve.

As if not wholly to reject the treat of straw which Nikita put under his nose, Mukhortui just once seized a wisp out of the sledge, but quickly deciding that there was more important business than to eat straw, he threw it down again, and the wind instantly tore it away and hid it in the snow.

"Now we must make a signal," said Nikita, turning the front of the sledge against the wind; and having tied the shafts together with a strap, he set them on end in front of the sledge. "If the snow covers us, the good folk will see the shafts, and dig us out," said Nikita, slapping his mittens together and pulling them on. "That's what old hands advise."

Vasili Andreyitch had meanwhile opened his coat, and making a shelter with its folds, he rubbed match after match on the steel box. But his hands trembled, and the kindled matches were blown out by the wind, one after another, some when just struck, others when he thrust them to the cigarette. At last one match burned fully, and lighted up for a moment the fur of his coat, his hand with the gold ring on the bent forefinger, and the snow-sprinkled straw which stuck out from under the sacking. The cigarette lighted. Twice he eagerly whiffed the smoke, swallowed it, blew it through his mustaches, and would have gone on, but the wind tore away the burning tobacco and sent it whirling after the straw. Even these few whiffs of tobacco-smoke cheered up Vasili Andreyitch.

"Well, we will stop here," he said authoritatively.

"Wait a minute, and I'll make a flag," he said, picking up the handkerchief which he had taken from round his collar and put down in the sledge. Drawing off his gloves, and reaching up, he tied the handkerchief tightly to the strap that held the shafts together.

The handkerchief at once began to beat about wildly; now clinging round a shaft, now streaming out, and cracking like a whip.

"That's a clever piece of work," said Vasili Andreyitch, pleased with what he had done, and getting into the sledge. "We should be warmer together, but there's not room for two," he said.

"I can find a place," said Nikita, "but the horse must be covered; he's sweating, the good fellow. Excuse me," he added, going to the sledge, and drawing the sacking from under Vasili Andreyitch. This he folded, and after taking off the saddle and breeching, covered Mukhortui with it.

"Anyway, it will be a bit warmer, silly," he said, putting the saddle and heavy breeching over the sacking.

"You won't need the cloth, will you? and give me a little straw," said Nikita, coming back to the sledge after he had finished his work.

Taking these from beneath Vasili Andreyitch, Nikita went behind the sledge, dug there a hole in the snow, stuffed in the straw, and pulling down his hat, wrapping his kaftan well around him, and covering himself with the coarse matting, sat down on the straw, leaning against the bark back of the sledge, which kept off the wind and snow.

Vasili Andreyitch shook his head disapprovingly at what Nikita was doing, as he usually found fault with the peasants' ignorance and stupidity; and he began to make his own arrangements for the night.

He smoothed the remaining straw and heaped it thicker under his side; then he thrust his hands into his sleeves, and settled his head in the corner of the sledge sheltered from the wind in front.

He did not feel sleepy. He lay and thought; thought about one thing only, which was the aim, reason, pleasure, and pride of his life:—about how much money he had made and might make, and how much other men whom he knew had made and possessed, and the means whereby they gained it and were gaining it; and how he, in like manner, might gain a good deal more. The purchase of the Goryatchkin forest was for him an affair of the utmost importance. He counted on making from this transaction as much as ten thousand! And he began mentally to estimate the value of the forest, which he had inspected in the autumn so carefully as to count all the trees on five acres.

"The oak will make sledge-runners. The small stuff will take care of itself. And there'll be thirty cords of wood to the acre," said he to himself. "At the very worst there'll be a little less than eighty rubles an acre. There are one hundred and fifty acres."

He reckoned it up mentally and saw that it amounted to about twelve thousand rubles; but without his abacus he could not calculate it exactly.

"But for all that, I won't pay ten thousand; say eight thousand; besides, one must allow for the bare spaces. I'll oil the surveyor,—a hundred rubles will do it,—a hundred and fifty, if necessary; he'll deduct about thirteen acres out of the forest. He is sure to sell for eight; three thousand down. Never fear; he will weaken at that," he thought, pressing his forearm on the pocket-book beneath.

"And how we lost our way after we left the turning, God only knows! The forest and the woodman's hut should be near by. I should like to hear the dogs, but they never bark when they're wanted, the cursed brutes."

He opened his collar a little from his ear and tried to listen; all he could hear was the same whistle of the wind, the flapping and cracking of the handkerchief on the shafts, and the pelting of the falling snow on the bark matting of the sledge.

He covered himself again.

"If one had only known this beforehand, we had better have stayed where we were. But no matter, we shall get there tomorrow. It is only a day lost. In this weather, the others won't get there either."

Then he remembered that on the twenty-first he had to receive the price for some gelded rams, from the butcher.

"I wanted to be there myself, for if he doesn't find me, my wife won't know how to receive the money. She's very inexperienced, she doesn't know about the right way of doing things," he continued to reflect, remembering how she had failed in her behavior towards a commissary of police, who had come to pay them a visit the day before, at the feast. "Just a woman, of course. What has she ever seen anywhere? In my father's time, what a house we had! Nothing out of the way, a well-to-do countryman's: a barn and an inn, and that was the whole property. And now in these fifteen years what have I done? A general store, two taverns, a flour-mill, a granary, two farms rented, a house and warehouse all iron-roofed," he remembered proudly. "Not as it was in father's time! Who is known over the whole place? Brekhunof.

"And why is this? Because I know my business, I look after things; not like others, who idle or waste their time in foolishness. I don't sleep at night. Storm or no storm, I start out.

And of course, the thing is done. People think it's fun making money. Not at all; you work and rack your brains. You spend your night this way outdoors, and go without sleep! The thoughts whirling in your head are as good as a cushion!" he exclaimed with pride. "They think men get on through luck. Look at the Mironofs, who have their millions, now. Why? They worked. Then God gives. If God only grants me health!"

And the idea that he, also, might become a millionaire like Mironof, who began with nothing, so excited Vasili Andreyitch that he suddenly felt a need to talk to some one. But there was no one. . . . If he could only have reached Goryatchkino, he might have talked with the landowner, and "put spectacles on him."

"Whew! how it blows! It will snow us up so that we can't get out in the morning," he thought, as he listened to the rush of the wind, which blew against the front of the sledge, bending it back, and lashed the snow against the bark matting. He lifted himself and looked out: in the white whirling darkness all he could see was Mukhortui's black head, and his back covered with the fluttering matting, and his thick twisted tail; all around, on every side, in front and behind, was the same monotonous white waving mist, occasionally appearing to grow a little lighter, then again growing thicker and denser.

"I was foolish enough yielding to Nikita," he thought. "We ought to have driven on, we should have come out somewhere. We might have gone back to Grishkino, and stayed at Taras's. Now we must sit here all night. Well, what was I thinking about? Yes, that God gives to the industrious, and not to the lazy, not to loafers and fools. It's time for a smoke, too."

He sat up, got his cigarette-case, and stretched himself flat on his stomach, to protect the light from the wind with the flaps of his coat; but the wind got in and put out one match after another. At last he managed to get a cigarette lit, and he began to smoke. The fact that he succeeded greatly delighted him. Though the wind smoked more of his cigarette than he did, nevertheless he got about three puffs, and felt better.

He again threw himself back in the sledge, wrapped himself up, and returned to his recollections and dreams; very unexpectedly he lost himself and fell asleep.

But suddenly something touched him and woke him up.

Whether it was Mukhortui pulling the straw from under him, or something within him that startled him, at all events he awoke, and his heart began to beat so quickly and violently that the sledge seemed to be shaking under him.

He opened his eyes. Everything around was the same as before; only it seemed a little lighter.

"The dawn," he said to himself; "it must be nearly morning."

But he instantly remembered that the light was only due to the rising of the moon.

He lifted himself, and looked first at the horse. Mukhortui was standing with his back to the wind, and shivering all over. The snow-covered sacking had fallen off on one side; the breeching had slipped down; the snowy head and the fluttering crest and mane, all were now clearly visible.

Vasili Andreyitch bent over the back of the sledge and looked behind. Nikita was still sitting in the old position which he had first taken. The sacking with which he had protected himself and his feet were covered with snow.

"I'm afraid the muzhik will be frozen; his clothes are so wretched. I might be held responsible. I declare they're such senseless people! They truly haven't the slightest forethought!" reflected Vasili Andreyitch; and he was tempted to take the sacking from the horse, to put over Nikita; but it was cold to get out and stir around, and besides, the horse might freeze to death.

"What made me bring him? It is all her stupidity!" thought Vasili Andreyitch, remembering his unattractive wife; and he turned again to his former place in the front of the sledge.

"My uncle once sat in snow all night, like this," he reflected, "and no harm came of it. And Sevastian also was dug out," he went on, remembering another case, "but he was dead, stiff like a frozen carcass. If we had only stopped at Grishkino, nothing would have happened."

Carefully covering himself, so that the warmth of the fur might not be wasted, but might protect his neck, knees, and the soles of his feet, he shut his eyes, trying to sleep again. But however much he tried, this time he could not lose himself; on the contrary, he felt alert and excited. Again he began to count his gains and the debts due to him; again he began to boast of his success, and to feel proud of himself and his position; but he was all the while disturbed by a lurking fear, and by the unpleasant regret that he had not stopped for the night at Grishkino.

"It would have been good to lie on the bench in a warm room!" He turned from side to side several times; he curled himself up trying to find a better position, more sheltered from the wind and snow, but all the time he felt uncomfortable; he rose again and changed his position, crossed his feet, shut his eyes, and lay silent; but either his crossed feet, in their high felt boots, began to ache, or the wind blew in somewhere; and thus lying for a short time, he again began the disagreeable reflection, how comfortably he would have rested in the warm house at Grishkino. Again he rose, changed his position, wrapped himself up, and again tucked himself in.

Once Vasili Andreyitch fancied he heard a distant cock-crow. He felt glad, and threw back his coat, and strained his ear to listen; but in spite of all his efforts he could hear nothing but the sound of the wind whistling against the shafts, and flapping the handkerchief, and the snow lashing the bark matting of the sledge.

Nikita had been motionless all the time, just as he had sat from the first, not stirring or even answering Vasili Andreyitch, though he spoke to him twice.

"He doesn't care in the least; he must be asleep," Vasili Andreyitch thought angrily, looking behind the sledge at Nikita, deeply covered with snow.

Twenty times Vasili Andreyitch thus rose and lay down. It seemed to him this night would never end.

"It must be near morning now," he thought once as he rose and glanced round him. "Let me look at my watch. I shall freeze if I unbutton my coat; but if I only know it is near morning, I shall feel better. We could begin to harness the horse."

At the bottom of his mind, Vasili Andreyitch knew that it could not be anywhere near morning; but he began to feel more and more afraid, and he chose both to assure himself and to deceive himself. He cautiously undid the hooks of his short coat, then putting his hand in at the bosom, he felt about until he got at the waistcoat. With great trouble, he drew out his silver watch enameled with flowers, and tried to examine it. Without a light, he could make out nothing.

Again he lay down flat on his elbows and his knees, as when he lighted the cigarette; got the matches, and proceeded to strike. This time he was more careful, and feeling for a match with the largest head, ignited it at the first stroke. When he brought the face of the watch into the light he could not believe his eyes. . . . It was not later than ten minutes past twelve. The whole night was still before him.

"Oh, what a long night!" thought Vasili Andreyitch, feeling the cold run down his back; and buttoning up again and wrapping his fur coat round him, he snuggled into the corner of the sledge with the intention of waiting patiently.

Suddenly, above the monotonous roar of the wind, he distinctly heard a new and a living sound. It grew gradually louder, and became quite clear; then began to die away with equal regularity. There could be no doubt it was a wolf. And this wolf was so near, that down the wind one could hear how he changed his cry by the movement of his jaws. Vasili Andreyitch turned back his collar and listened attentively. Mukhortui listened likewise, pricking up his ears, and when the wolf had ceased his chant he shifted his feet, and neighed warningly.

After this Vasili Andreyitch not only was unable to sleep, but even to keep calm. The more he tried to think of his accounts, of his business, reputation, importance, and property, more and more fear grew upon him; and above all his thoughts, one thought stood out predominantly and penetratingly:—the thought of his rashness in not stopping at Grishkino.

"The forest,—what do I care about the forest? There is plenty of business without that, thank God! Ah, if we had only stayed for the night!" said he to himself. "They say drunken men soon freeze to death," he thought, "and I have had some drink."

Then testing his own sensations, he felt that he began to shiver, either from cold or fear. He tried to wrap himself up and to lie down, as before; but he could not any longer do that. He could not stay in one position, wanted to rise, to do something so as to suppress his gathering fears, against which he felt helpless. Again he got his cigarettes and matches; but only three of the latter remained, and these were bad ones. All three rubbed away without lighting.

"The devil take you, curse you!" he objurgated, himself not knowing whom or what, and he threw away the cigarette. He was about to throw away the matchbox also, but stayed his hand, and thrust it into his pocket instead. He was so agitated that he could no longer remain in his place. He got out of the sledge, and, standing with his back to the wind, set his girdle again, tightly, and low down.

"What is the use of lying down? It is only waiting for death; much better mount the horse and get away!" the thought suddenly flashed into his mind. "The horse will not stand still with some one on his back. It's all the same to *him,* —thinking of Nikita,—if he does die. What sort of a life has he? He does not care much even about his life, but as for me,—thank God, I have something to live for!" . . .

Untying the horse from the sledge, he threw the reins over his neck, and tried to mount, but his coats and his boots were so heavy that he failed. Then he clambered on the sledge, and tried to mount from that; but the sledge tilted under his weight, and he failed again. At last, on a third attempt, he backed the horse to the sledge, and, cautiously balancing on the edge, got his body across the horse's back. Lying thus for a moment, he pushed himself once, twice, and finally threw one leg over and seated himself, supporting his feet on the loose breeching straps in place of stirrups. The shaking of the sledge roused Nikita, and he got up; Vasili Andreyitch thought he was speaking.

"Listen to you, fool? What, must I die in this way, for nothing?" exclaimed Vasili Andreyitch. Tucking under his knees the loose skirts of his coat, he turned the horse round, and rode away from the sledge in the direction where he expected to find the forest and the keeper's hut.

CHAPTER VII

Nikita had not stirred since he had covered himself with the matting and taken his seat behind the sledge. Like all men who live with nature, and are acquainted with poverty, he was patient, and could wait for hours, even days, without growing restless or irritated. When his master called him, he heard, but made no answer, because he did not want to stir. Although he still felt the warmth from the tea he had taken, and from the exercise of struggling through the snowdrifts, he knew the warmth would not last long, and that he could not warm himself again by moving about, for he was exhausted, and felt as a horse does when, in spite of the whip, it stops, and its master perceives that it must have food before it can work again. His foot, the one in the torn boot, was numb, and he could no longer feel his great toe. And, moreover, his whole body kept growing colder and colder.

The thought that he might and in all probability would die that night came upon him, but this thought did not seem especially unpleasant or especially awful. It did not seem to him especially unpleasant, because his life had not been a perpetual festival, but rather an incessant round of toil of which he was beginning to weary. And this thought did not seem to him especially awful, because, beyond the masters whom he served here, like Vasili Andreyitch, he felt himself dependent upon the Great Master; upon Him who had sent him into this life, and he knew that even after death he must remain in the power of that Master, and that that Master would not treat him badly.

"Is it a pity to leave what you are practised in, and used to? Well, what's to be done about it? You must get used to new things as well."

"Sins?" he thought, and recollected his drunkenness, the money wasted in drink, his ill-treatment of his wife, his profanity, neglect of church and of the fasts, and all things for which the priest reprimanded him at the confessional. "Of course, these are sins. But then, did I bring them on myself? Whatever I am, I suppose God made me so. Well, and about these sins? How can one help it?"

Thus ran his reflections, and after he had considered what might happen to him that night, he let it have the go-by, and gave himself up to whatever notions and memories came of their own accord into his mind. He remembered Marfa's visit, and the drunkenness among the peasants, and his own abstinence from drink; then he recalled how they had started on their present journey; Taras's house, and the talk about the break-up of the family; that reminded him of his own lad; then he thought of Mukhortui, with the sacking over him for warmth; and his master, rolling round in the sledge, and making it creak.

"I suppose he is vexed and angry because he started out," said Nikita to himself. "A man who lives such a life as his does not want to die; not like people of my kind."

And all these recollections and thoughts interwove and jumbled themselves in his brain, until he fell asleep.

When Vasili Andreyitch mounted the horse, he twisted aside the sledge, and the back of it, against which Nikita was leaning, slid away, and one of the runner-ends struck him in the side. Nikita awoke, and was compelled to change his position. Straightening his legs with difficulty, and throwing off the snow which covered them, he got up. Instantly an agonizing cold penetrated his whole frame. On making out what was happening, he wanted Vasili Andreyitch to leave him the sacking, which was no longer needed for the horse, so that he might put it round himself.

But Vasili Andreyitch did not wait, and disappeared in the mist of snow.

Thus left alone, Nikita considered what he should do. He felt that he had not strength enough to start off in search of some house; and it was no longer possible for him to sit down in his former place, for it was already covered with snow; and he knew he could not get warm in the sledge, having nothing to cover him. There seemed no warmth at all from his coat and sheepskin. It was a bitter moment. He felt as cold as if he had only his shirt on. "Our Father, who art in Heaven," he repeated; and the consciousness that he was not alone but that Some One heard him and would not desert him comforted him. He drew a deep sigh, and keeping the matting over his head, he crept into the sledge and lay down in the place where his master had lain.

But he could not possibly keep warm in the sledge. At first he shivered all over, then the shivering ceased, and little by little, he began to lose consciousness. Whether he was dying, or falling asleep, he knew not; but he was as ready for the one as for the other.

CHAPTER VIII

Meanwhile Vasili Andreyitch, using his feet and the straps of the harness, urged the horse in the direction where he, for some cause, expected to find the forest and the forester's hut. The snow blinded his eyes, and the wind, it seemed, was bent on staying him, but with head bent forward, and all the time pulling up his shuba between him and the cold pad, on which he could not settle himself, he kept urging on the horse. The dark bay, though with difficulty, obediently ambled on in the direction to which he was turned.

For five minutes he rode on; as it seemed to him, in a straight line; seeing nothing but the horse's head and the white waste, and hearing only the whistling of the wind about the horse's ears and collar of his own coat.

Suddenly a dark patch showed in front of him. His heart

began to beat with joy, and he rode on toward the object, already seeing in it the walls of village houses. But the dark patch was not stationary, it kept moving, and it was not a village but a patch of tall wormwood, growing on a strip of land and protruding through the snow, and shaking desperately under the blast of the wind which bent their heads all in one direction and whistled through them.

The sight of this wormwood tormented by the pitiless wind somehow made Vasili Andreyitch tremble, and he started to ride away hastily; not perceiving that in approaching the patch of wormwood, he had quite turned out of his first direction, and that now he was heading the opposite way, though he still supposed that he was riding toward where the forester's hut should be. But the horse seemed always to make toward the right, and so Vasili Andreyitch had to guide it toward the left.

Again a dark patch appeared before him; again he rejoiced, believing that now surely this was a village. But once more it was a patch of tall wormwood, once more the dry grass was shaking desperately, and, as before, frightening Vasili Andreyitch. But it could not be the same patch of grass, for near it was a horse-track, now disappearing in the snow. Vasili Andreyitch stopped, bent down, and looked carefully; a horse-track, not yet snow-covered; it could only be the hoof-prints of his own horse. He had evidently gone round in a small circle.

"And I shall perish in this way," he thought.

To overcome his terror, he urged on the horse with still greater energy, peering into the white mist of snow, wherein he saw nothing but flitting and fitful points of light which vanished the instant he looked at them. Once he thought he heard either the barking of dogs or the howling of wolves, but the sounds were so faint and indistinct, that he could not be sure whether he had heard them or imagined them; and he stopped and began to strain his ears and listen.

Suddenly a terrible, deafening cry beat upon his ears, and everything began to tremble and quake about him. Vasili Andreyitch seized the horse's neck, but that also shook, and the terrible cry grew still more frightful. For some seconds, Vasili Andreyitch could not collect himself, or understand what had happened. It was only this: Mukhortui, whether to encourage himself or to call for help, had neighed, loudly and resonantly.

"Ugh! Plague take you! You cursed brute, how you frightened me!" said Vasili Andreyitch to himself. But even when he understood the cause of his terror, he could not shake it off.

"I must consider and steady my nerves," he said to himself again, and saw at the same time he could not regain his self-control, but kept urging forward the horse without noting that he was now going with the wind, instead of against it. Especially when the horse walked slowly, his body, where it was exposed and where it touched the pad, was freezing and ached. His hands and legs shook and he was short of breath. He could see that he was likely to perish in the midst of this horrible snowy waste, and he could see no way of rescue. He forgot all about the forester's hut, and desired one thing only,—to get back to the sledge, that he might not perish alone, like that wormwood in the midst of the terrible waste of snow.

Suddenly the horse stumbled under him, caught in a snowdrift, and began to plunge, and fell on his side. Vasili Andreyitch jumped off as he did so, dragging with him the breeching on which his foot was supported, and turned the pad round by holding to it as he jumped.

As soon as Vasili Andreyitch was off his back, the horse struggled to his feet, plunged forward one leap and then another, and neighing again, with the sacking and breeching trailing after him, disappeared, leaving Vasili Andreyitch alone in the snowdrift.

He pressed on in pursuit of the horse, but the snow was so deep, and his coats were so heavy, that after he had gone not more than twenty paces, sinking over the knee at each step, he was out of breath, and stopped.

"The forest, the sheep, the farms, the shop, the taverns, the iron-roofed house and granary, my son!" thought he, "how can I leave them all? What does this really mean! It cannot be!"

These words flashed through his mind. Then somehow or other he recalled the wind-shaken wormwood which he had ridden past twice, and such a panic seized him that he lost all sense of the reality of what was happening. He asked himself, "Is not this all a dream?"—and tried to wake up. But there was nothing to wake up from! It was actual snow lashing his face and covering him and benumbing his right hand, from which he had dropped the glove; and it was a real desert in which he was now alone, like that wormwood, waiting for inevitable, speedy, and incomprehensible death.

"Queen in heaven, St. Nicholas, teacher of temperance!"

He recalled the Te Deums of the day; the shrine with the black image in a golden chasuble; the tapers which he sold for the shrine, and which, when they were at once returned to him hardly touched by the flame, he used to put back into the store-chest. And he began to implore that same Nicholas—the miracle-worker—to save him, vowing to the saint a Te Deum and tapers.

But in some way, here, he clearly and without a doubt realized that the image, chasuble, tapers, priests, masses, though they were all very important and necessary in their place, in the church, were of no service to him now; and that between those tapers and Te Deums, and his present disastrous plight, there could be no possible connection.

"I must not give up," he said to himself, "I must follow the horse's tracks, or they, too, will be snowed over." This idea struck him, and he made on. "He'll get away if I don't overtake him. But I mustn't hurry or else I shall be worse off and perish still more miserably."

But notwithstanding his resolution to walk quietly, he kept hurrying on, running, falling down every minute, rising and falling again. The hoof-prints were already almost indistinguishable where the snow was not deep. "I am lost!" thought Vasili Andreyitch, "if I lose this track and don't overtake the horse."

But at that instant, casting a glance in front, he saw something dark. It was Mukhortui, and not merely Mukhortui, but the sledge, and the shafts with the handkerchief.

Mukhortui, with the pad twisted round to one side, and the trailed breeching and sacking, was standing, not in his former place, but nearer to the shafts; and was shaking his head, which was drawn down by the bridle beneath his feet.

It turned out that Vasili Andreyitch had stuck in the same ravine into which he and Nikita had previously plunged, that the horse had led him back to the sledge, and that he had dismounted at not more than fifty paces from the place where the sledge lay.

CHAPTER IX

Vasili Andreyitch struggled back to the sledge, clutched hold of it, and stood so, motionless for a long time, trying to calm himself and to get back his breath. There was no sign of Nikita in his former place, but something covered with snow was lying in the sledge, and Vasili Andreyitch conjectured that it was Nikita. Vasili Andreyitch's terror had now altogether disappeared; if he felt any fear, it was of that state of terror which he had experienced when on the horse, and especially when he was alone in the snowdrift. By any and every means, he must keep away that terror; and in order to keep it away it was necessary for him to do something, to occupy himself with something.

Accordingly, the first thing he did was to turn his back to the wind and throw open his coat. As soon as he felt a little rested, he shook out the snow from his boots and from his left-hand glove,—the right-hand glove was lost beyond recovery and was undoubtedly already buried somewhere deep in the snow,—then he bound up his girdle again, tight and low-down, as he always did when he was going out of his shop to buy grain from the peasants' carts. He tightened his belt and prepared for action. The first thing which appeared to him necessary to do was to free the horse's leg. So Vasili Andreyitch did this; then, clearing the bridle, he tied Mukhortui to the iron cramp in front of the sledge, as before, and walking round the horse's quarters, he adjusted the pad, the breeching, and the sacking.

But as he did this, he perceived a movement in the sledge, and Nikita's head rose out of the snow that covered it. Obviously with great difficulty, the half-frozen peasant rose and sat up; and in a strange fashion, as if he were driving away flies, waved his hand before his face. He waved his hand and said something which Vasili Andreyitch interpreted as a call to himself.

Vasili Andreyitch left the sack unadjusted, and went to the sledge.

"What is the matter with you?" he asked. "What are you saying?"

"I am dy-y-ing, that's what's the matter," said Nikita, brokenly, struggling for speech. "Give what I have earned to the lad. Or to the wife; it's all the same."

"What, are you really frozen?" asked Vasili Andreyitch.

"I can feel I've got my death. Forgive . . . for Christ's sake . . ." said Nikita, in a sobbing voice, continuing to wave his hand before his face, as if driving away flies.

Vasili Andreyitch stood for half a minute silent and motionless; then suddenly, with the same resolution with which he used to strike hands over a good bargain, he took a step back, turned up the sleeves of his coat, and using both hands, began to rake the snow from off Nikita and the sledge. When he had brushed out, Vasili Andreyitch quickly took off his girdle, opened out his coat, and moving Nikita with a push, he lay down on him, covering him not only with the fur coat, but with the full length of his own body, which glowed with warmth.

Adjusting with his hands the skirts of his coat, so as to come between Nikita and the bark matting of the sledge, and tucking the tail of the coat between his knees, Vasili Andreyitch lay flat, with his head against the bark matting in the sledge-front; and now he no longer could hear either the stirring of the horse or the whistling of the wind; all he could hear was Nikita's breathing. At first, and for a long time, Nikita lay without a sign; then he gave a loud sigh, and moved.

"Ah, there you are! And yet you say 'die.' Lie still, get warm, and somehow we shall . . ." began Vasili Andreyitch.

But, to his own surprise, he could not speak: because his eyes were filled with tears, and his lower jaw began to quiver violently. He said no more—only gulped down something which rose in his throat.

"I was well scared, that is clear, and how weak I feel!" he thought of himself. But this weakness not only was not unpleasant to him, but rather gave him a peculiar and hitherto unknown delight.

"That's what we are!" he said to himself, experiencing a strange triumph and emotion. He lay quiet for some time, wiping his eyes with the fur of his coat and tucking under his knees the right skirt, which the wind kept turning up.

He felt a passionate desire to let some one else know of his happy condition.

"Mikita!" he said.

"It's comfortable, it's warm," came an answer from below.

"So it is, friend! I was nearly lost. And you would have been frozen, and I should have. . . ."

But here again his face began to quiver, and his eyes once more filled with tears, and he could say no more.

"Well, never mind," he thought, "I know well enough about myself, what I know."

And he kept quiet. Thus he lay for a long time.

Nikita warmed him from below, and the fur coat warmed

him from above; but his hands, with which he held the coat-skirts down on both sides of Nikita, and his feet, from which the wind kept lifting the coat, began to freeze. Especially cold was his right hand, unprotected by a glove. But he did not think either of his legs or of his hands. He thought only of how to warm the peasant who lay beneath him.

Several times he looked at the horse, and saw that his back was uncovered, and the sacking and breeching were hanging down nearly to the snow. He ought to get up and cover the horse; but he could not bring himself to leave Nikita for even a moment, and so disturb that happy situation in which he felt himself; he now no longer had any sense of terror.

"Never fear, we shan't lose him this time," he said to himself, about his way of warming Nikita, and with the same boastfulness as he used to speak of his buying and selling.

Thus Vasili Andreyitch continued lying an hour and then another and then a third, but he was unconscious of the passage of time.

At first his thoughts were filled with impressions of the snow-storm, the shafts of the sledge, the horse under the shaft-bow, all in confusion before his eyes; he remembered Nikita, lying under him; then mingling with these recollections rose others, of the festival, his wife, the commissary of police, the taper-box; then again of Nikita, this time lying under the taper-box. Then came apparitions of peasants selling and buying, and white walls, the iron-roofed houses, with Nikita lying underneath; then all was confused, one thing blending with another; and, like the colors in the rainbow, uniting in one white light, all the different impressions fused into one nothing; and he fell asleep.

For a long time he slept dreamlessly; but before daybreak visions visited him again. It seemed to him that he was once more standing beside the taper-box, and Tikhon's wife was asking him for a five-kopek candle for the festival-day; he wanted to take the taper and give it to her, but he could not move his hands, which hung down, thrust tightly into his pockets. He wanted to walk round the box, but his feet would not move; his goloshes, new and shiny, had grown to the stone floor, and he could neither move them, nor take out his feet.

All at once the box ceased to be a taper-box, and turned into a bed; and Vasili Andreyitch sees himself lying, face downward, on the taper-box, and yet it is his own bed in his own house. And thus he lies and is unable to get up; and yet he must get up, because Ivan Matveyitch, the commissary of police, will soon come for him, and he must go with Ivan Matveyitch either to bargain for the forest, or to set the breeching right on Mukhortui.

He asks his wife:—

"Well, Mikolavna, has he not come yet?"

"No," she says, "he has not."

He hears some one drive up to the front steps. It must be he. No, he has gone past.

"Mikolavna, Mikolavna! what, has he not come yet?"

"No."

And he lies on the bed and is still unable to rise, and is still waiting. And this waiting is painful, and yet pleasant.

All at once, his joy is fulfilled: the expected one has come; not Ivan Matveyitch, the police officer, but some one else, and yet the one for whom he has been waiting. He has come, and he calls to him; and he that called is he who had bidden him lie down on Nikita.

And Vasili Andreyitch is glad because that one has visited him.

"I am coming," he cries joyfully. And the cry awakens him!

He wakes; but wakes an entirely different person from what he had been when he fell asleep. He wants to rise, and cannot; to move his arm, and cannot,—his leg, and he cannot do that. He wants to turn his head, and cannot do even so much. He is surprised but not at all disturbed by this. He divines that this is death, and is not at all disturbed even by that. And he remembers that Nikita is lying under him, and that he has got warm, and is alive; and it seems to him that he is Nikita, and Nikita is he; that his life is not in himself, but in Nikita. He makes an effort to listen, and hears Nikita's breathing, even his slight snoring.

"Nikita is alive, and therefore I also am alive!" he says to himself, triumphantly.

He remembers his money, his shop, his house, his purchases and sales, the Mironofs' millions; and it is hard for him to understand why that man called Vasili Brekhunof had troubled himself with all those things with which he had troubled himself.

"Well, he did not know what it was all about," he thinks, concerning this Vasili Brekhunof. "I did not know; but now I do know. No mistake this time; now *I know*."

And again he hears the summons of that one who had before called him.

"I am coming, I am coming," he says with his whole joy-thrilled being. And he feels himself free, with nothing to encumber him more.

And nothing more, in this world, was seen, or heard, or felt by Vasili Andreyitch.

Round about the storm still eddied. The same whirlwinds of snow covered the dead Vasili Andreyitch's coat, and Mukhortui, all of a tremble, and the sledge, now hardly to be seen, with Nikita lying in the bottom of it, kept warm beneath his dead master.

CHAPTER X

Just before morning Nikita awoke. He was aroused by the cold again creeping along his back. He had dreamt that he was driving from the mill with a cartload of his master's flour, and that in crossing the brook, as he went past the bridge, the cart got stuck. And he sees himself go beneath the cart, and lift it, straightening up his back. But, wonderful!—the cart does not stir, it sticks to his back, so that he can neither lift it nor get out from under it. It was crushing his loins. And how cold it was! He must get away somehow.

"There! Stop!" he cries to whoever it is that presses his back with the load. "Take the sacks out!"

But the cart still presses him, always colder and colder; and suddenly a peculiar knocking awakes him completely, and he remembers everything. The cold cart,—that was his dead and frozen master, lying upon him. The knocking was from Mukhortui, who had struck twice on the sledge with his hoofs.

"Andreyitch, eh, Andreyitch!" calls Nikita, softly, straightening his back, and already having a suspicion of the truth.

But Andreyitch does not answer, and his body and legs are hard, and cold, and heavy, like iron weights.

"He must be dead. May his be the Kingdom of Heaven!" thinks Nikita.

He turns his head, digs with his hand through the snow about him, and opens his eyes. It is daylight. The wind still whistles through the shafts, and the snow is still falling; but with a difference, not lashing upon the bark matting, as before, but silently covering the sledge and horse, ever deeper and deeper; and the horse's breathing and stirring are no more to be heard.

"He must be frozen, too," thinks Nikita.

And, in fact, those hoof-strokes on the sledge were the last struggles of Mukhortui, by that time quite benumbed, to keep on his legs.

"God, Father, it seems Thou callest me as well," says Nikita, to himself. "Let Thy holy will be done. But it is hard. . . . Still you can't die twice, and you must die once. If it would only come quicker!" . . .

And he draws in his arm again, shutting his eyes; and he loses consciousness, with the conviction that this time he is really going to die altogether.

At dinner-time on the next day, the peasants with their shovels dug out Vasili Andreyitch and Nikita, only seventy yards from the road, and half a verst from the village. The snow had hidden the sledge, but the shafts and the handkerchief were still visible. Mukhortui, up to his belly in snow, with the breeching and sacking trailing from his back, stood all whitened, his dead head pressed in on the apple of his throat; his nostrils were fringed with icicles, his eyes filled with frost and frozen round as with tears. In that one night he had become so thin, that he was nothing but skin and bones.

Vasili Andreyitch was stiffened like a frozen carcass, and he lay with his legs spread apart, just as he was when they rolled him off Nikita. His prominent hawk-eyes were frozen, and his open mouth under his clipped mustache was filled with snow.

But Nikita, though chilled through, was alive. When he was roused, he imagined he was already dead, and that what they were doing with him was happening, not in this world, but in another. When he heard the shouts of the peasants who were digging him out and pulling the frozen Vasili Andreyitch from him he was surprised, at first, to think that in the other world, also, peasants should be shouting so, and that they had the same kind of a body. But when he understood that he was still here, in this world, he was sorry rather than glad; especially when he realized that the toes of both his feet were frozen.

Nikita lay in the hospital for two months. They cut off three toes from him, and the others recovered, so that he was able to work. For twenty years more he went on living, first as a farm-laborer, then as a watchman. He died at home, just as he wished, only this year,—laid under the holy images, with a lighted wax taper in his hands.

Before his death, he asked forgiveness from his old wife, and forgave her for the cooper; he took leave of his son and the grandchildren; and went away truly pleased that, in dying, he released his son and daughter-in-law from the added burden of his keep, and that he himself was, this time, really going out of a life grown wearisome to him, into that other one which with every passing year had grown clearer and more desirable to him.

Whether he is better off, or worse off, there, in the place where he awoke after that real death, whether he was disappointed or found things there just as he expected, is what we shall all of us soon learn.

The Lesson of the Master

BY HENRY JAMES
(1843-1916)

Perhaps no other American writer has been so completely an artist as was Henry James. James literally gave his life to his art, and he wrote a number of stories about the artist caught between the demands of art and the demands of life. The Lesson of the Master, first published in 1888, reveals not only James's devotion to his art, but also in its style and structure the superb craftsmanship that has made him one of the most influential writers in modern literature.

James was born in New York to the Swedenborgian philosopher, Henry James Sr., whose fame was to be eclipsed by that of his eldest son William, the renowned psychologist and spokesman for pragmatism, and by his second son, Henry Jr. The future writer, whose early reputation was based on his stories about Americans in Europe, spent many of his youthful years on that continent. After a year at Harvard Law School, James left the United States for a sojourn in Europe that lasted forty years. He settled in England, where he remained, with occasional trips to the Continent and to the United States, until he died. During his long career as a writer, James produced many novels, short novels, and stories, including such masterpieces as The Ambassadors, The Wings of the Dove, *and* The Golden Bowl.

The Lesson of the Master

CHAPTER I

He had been told the ladies were at church, but this was corrected by what he saw from the top of the steps—they descended from a great height in two arms, with a circular sweep of the most charming effect—at the threshold of the door which, from the long bright gallery, overlooked the immense lawn. Three gentlemen, on the grass, at a distance, sat under the great trees, while the fourth figure showed a crimson dress that told as a "bit of colour" amid the fresh rich green. The servant had so far accompanied Paul Overt as to introduce him to this view, after asking him if he wished first to go to his room. The young man declined that privilege, conscious of no disrepair from so short and easy a journey and always liking to take at once a general perceptive possession of a new scene. He stood there a little with his eyes on the group and on the admirable picture, the wide grounds of an old country-house near London—that only made it better—on a splendid Sunday in June. "But the lady, who's *she?*" he said to the servant before the man left him.

"I think she's Mrs. St. George, sir."

"Mrs. St. George the wife of the distinguished——" Then Paul Overt checked himself, doubting if a footman would know.

"Yes, sir—probably, sir," said his guide, who appeared to wish to intimate that a person staying at Summersoft would naturally be, if only by alliance, distinguished. His tone, however, made poor Overt himself feel for the moment scantly so.

"And the gentlemen?" Overt went on.

"Well, sir, one of them's General Fancourt."

"Ah yes, I know; thank you." General Fancourt was distinguished, there was no doubt of that, for something he had done, or perhaps even hadn't done—the young man couldn't remember which—some years before in India. The servant went away, leaving the glass doors open into the gallery, and Paul Overt remained at the head of the wide double staircase, saying to himself that the place was sweet and promised a pleasant visit, while he leaned on the balustrade of fine old ironwork which, like all the other details, was of the same period as the house. It all went together and spoke in one voice—a rich English voice of the early part of the eighteenth century. It might have been church-time on a summer's day in the reign of Queen Anne: the stillness was too perfect to be modern, the nearness counted so as distance, and there was something so fresh and sound in the originality of the large smooth house, the expanse of beautiful brickwork that showed for pink rather than red and that had been kept clear of messy creepers by the law under which a woman with a rare complexion disdains a veil. When Paul Overt became aware that the people under the trees had noticed him he turned back through the open doors into the great gallery which was the pride of the place. It marched across from end to end and seemed—with its bright colours, its high panelled windows, its faded flowered chintzes, its quickly-recognised portraits and pictures, the blue-and-white china of its cabinets and the attenuated festoons and rosettes of its ceiling—a cheerful upholstered avenue into the other century.

Our friend was slightly nervous; that went with his character as a student of fine prose, went with the artist's general disposition to vibrate; and there was a particular thrill in the idea that Henry St. George might be a member of the party. For the young aspirant he had remained a high literary figure, in spite of the lower range of production to which he had fallen after his three first great successes, the comparative absence of quality in his later work. There had been moments when Paul Overt almost shed tears for this; but now that he was near him—he had never met him—he was conscious only of the fine original source and of his own immense debt. After he had taken a turn or two up and down the gallery he came out again and descended the steps. He was but slenderly supplied with a certain social boldness —it was really a weakness in him—so that, conscious of a want of acquaintance with the four persons in the distance, he gave way to motions recommended by their not committing him to a positive approach. There was a fine English awkwardness in this—he felt that too as he sauntered vaguely and obliquely across the lawn, taking an independent line. Fortunately there was an equally fine English directness in the way one of the gentlemen presently rose and made as if to "stalk" him, though with an air of conciliation and reassurance. To this demonstration Paul Overt instantly responded, even if the gentleman were not his host. He was tall, straight and elderly and had, like the great house itself, a pink smiling face, and into the bargain a white moustache. Our young man met him halfway while he laughed and said: "Er—Lady Watermouth told us you were coming; she asked me just to look after you." Paul Overt thanked him, liking him on the spot, and turned round with him to walk towards the others. "They've all gone to church—all except us," the stranger continued as they went; "we're just sitting here—it's so jolly." Overt pronounced it jolly indeed: it was such a lovely place. He mentioned that he was having the charming impression for the first time.

"Ah, you've not been here before?" said his companion. "It's a nice little place—not much to *do*, you know." Overt wondered what he wanted to "do"—he felt that he himself was doing so much. By the time they came to where the others sat he had recognised his initiator for a military man— such was the turn of Overt's imagination—had found him thus still more sympathetic. He would naturally have a need for action, for deeds at variance with the pacific pastoral scene. He was evidently so good-natured, however, that he accepted the inglorious hour for what it was worth. Paul Overt shared it with him and his companions for the next twenty minutes; the latter looked at him and he looked at them without knowing much who they were, while the talk went on without much telling him even what it meant. It seemed indeed to mean nothing in particular; it wandered, with casual pointless pauses and short terrestrial flights, amid names of persons and places—names which, for our friend, had no great power of evocation. It was all sociable and slow, as was right and natural of a warm Sunday morning.

His first attention was given to the question, privately considered, of whether one of the two younger men would be Henry St. George. He knew many of his distinguished contemporaries by their photographs, but had never, as happened, seen a portrait of the great misguided novelist. One of the gentlemen was unimaginable—he was too young; and the other scarcely looked clever enough, with such mild un-discriminating eyes. If those eyes were St. George's the prob-lem presented by the ill-matched parts of his genius would be still more difficult of solution. Besides, the deportment of their proprietor was not, as regards the lady in the red dress, such as could be natural, toward the wife of his bosom, even to a writer accused by several critics of sacrificing too much to manner. Lastly, Paul Overt had a vague sense that if the gentleman with the expressionless eyes bore the name that had set his heart beating faster (he also had contra-dictory conventional whiskers—the young admirer of the celebrity had never in a mental vision seen *his* face in so vul-gar a frame) he would have given him a sign of recognition or friendliness, would have heard of him a little, would know something about "Ginistrella," would have an impression of how that fresh fiction had caught the eye of real criticism. Paul Overt had a dread of being grossly proud, but even mor-bid modesty might view the authorship of "Ginistrella" as constituting a degree of identity. His soldierly friend became clear enough: he was "Fancourt," but was also "the Gen-eral"; and he mentioned to the new visitor in the course of a few moments that he had but lately returned from twenty years' service abroad.

"And now you remain in England?" the young man asked.

"Oh yes; I've bought a small house in London."

"And I hope you like it," said Overt, looking at Mrs. St. George.

"Well, a little house in Manchester Square—there's a limit to the enthusiasm *that* inspires."

"Oh I meant being at home again—being back in Pic-cadilly."

"My daughter likes Piccadilly—that's the main thing. She's very fond of art and music and literature and all that kind of thing. She missed it in India and she finds it in Lon-don, or she hopes she'll find it. Mr. St. George has promised to help her—he has been awfully kind to her. She has gone to church—she's fond of that too—but they'll all be back in a quarter of an hour. You must let me introduce you to her —she'll be so glad to know you. I daresay she has read every blest word you've written."

"I shall be delighted—I haven't written so very many," Overt pleaded, feeling, and without resentment, that the General at least was vagueness itself about that. But he won-dered a little why, expressing this friendly disposition, it didn't occur to the doubtless eminent soldier to pronounce the word that would put him in relation with Mrs. St. George. If it was a question of introductions Miss Fancourt—apparently as yet unmarried—was far away, while the wife of his illustrious confrère was almost between them. This lady struck Paul Overt as altogether pretty, with a surprising juvenility and a high smartness of aspect, something that—he could scarcely have said why—served for mystification. St. George certainly had every right to a charming wife, but he himself would never have imagined the important little woman in the aggressively Parisian dress the partner for life, the *alter ego*, of a man of letters. That partner in general, he knew, that second self, was far from presenting herself in a single type: observation had taught him that she was not inveterately, not necessarily plain. But he had never before seen her look so much as if her prosperity had deeper foundations than an ink-spotted study-table littered with proof-sheets. Mrs. St. George might have been the wife of a gentleman who "kept" books rather than wrote them, who carried on great affairs in the City and made better bargains than those that poets mostly make with publishers. With this she hinted at a success more personal—a success peculiarly stamping the age in which society, the world of conversation, is a great drawing-room with the City for its ante-chamber. Overt numbered her years at first as some thirty, and then ended by believing that she might approach her fiftieth. But she somehow in this case juggled away the excess and the difference—you only saw them in a rare glimpse, like the rabbit in the conjuror's sleeve. She was extraordinarily white, and her every element and item was pretty; her eyes, her ears, her hair, her voice, her hands, her feet—to which her relaxed attitude in her wicker chair gave a great publicity—and the numerous ribbons and trinkets with which she was bedecked. She looked as if she had put on her best clothes to go to church and then had decided they were too good for that and had stayed at home. She told a story of some length about the shabby way Lady Jane had treated the Duchess, as well as an anecdote in relation to a purchase she had made in Paris—on her way back from Cannes; made for Lady Egbert, who had never refunded the money. Paul Overt suspected her of a tendency to figure great people as larger than life, until he noticed the manner in which she handled Lady Egbert, which was so sharply mutinous that it reassured him. He felt he should have understood her better if he might have met her eye; but she scarcely so much as glanced at him. "Ah here they come—all the good ones!" she said at last; and Paul Overt admired at his distance the return of the churchgoers—several persons, in couples and threes, advancing in a flicker of sun and shade at the end of a large green vista formed by the level grass and the over-arching boughs.

"If you mean to imply that *we're* bad, I protest," said one of the gentlemen—"after making one's self agreeable all the morning!"

"Ah if they've found you agreeable——!" Mrs. St. George gaily cried. "But if we're good the others are better."

"They must be angels then," said the amused General.

"Your husband was an angel, the way he went off at your bidding," the gentleman who had first spoken declared to Mrs. St. George.

"At my bidding?"

"Didn't you make him go to church?"

"I never made him do anything in my life but once—when I made him burn up a bad book. That's all!" At her "That's all!" our young friend broke into an irrepressible laugh; it lasted only a second, but it drew her eyes to him. His own met them, though not long enough to help him to understand her; unless it were a step towards this that he saw on the instant how the burnt book—the way she alluded to it!—would have been one of her husband's finest things.

"A bad book?" her interlocutor repeated.

"I didn't like it. He went to church because your daughter went," she continued to General Fancourt. "I think it my duty to call your attention to his extraordinary demonstrations to your daughter."

"Well, if you don't mind them I don't!" the General laughed.

"*Il s'attache à ses pas.* But I don't wonder—she's so charming."

"I hope she won't make him burn any books!" Paul Overt ventured to exclaim.

"If she'd make him write a few it would be more to the purpose," said Mrs. St. George. "He has been of a laziness of late——!"

Our young man stared—he was so struck with the lady's phraseology. Her "Write a few" seemed to him almost as good as her "That's all." Didn't she, as the wife of a rare artist, know what it was to produce *one* perfect work of art?

How in the world did she think they were turned off? His private conviction was that, admirably as Henry St. George wrote, he had written for the last ten years, and especially for the last five, only too much, and there was an instant during which he felt inwardly solicited to make this public. But before he had spoken a diversion was effected by the return of the absentees. They strolled up dispersedly—there were eight or ten of them—and the circle under the trees rearranged itself as they took their place in it. They made it much larger, so that Paul Overt could feel—he was always feeling that sort of thing, as he said to himself—that if the company had already been interesting to watch the interest would now become intense. He shook hands with his hostess, who welcomed him without many words, in the manner of a woman able to trust him to understand and conscious that so pleasant an occasion would in every way speak for itself. She offered him no particular facility for sitting by her, and when they had all subsided again he found himself still next General Fancourt, with an unknown lady on his other flank.

"That's my daughter—that one opposite," the General said to him without loss of time. Overt saw a tall girl, with magnificent red hair, in a dress of a pretty grey-green tint and of a limp silken texture, a garment that clearly shirked every modern effect. It had therefore somehow the stamp of the latest thing, so that our beholder quickly took her for nothing if not contemporaneous.

"She's very handsome—very handsome," he repeated while he considered her. There was something noble in her head, and she appeared fresh and strong.

Her good father surveyed her with complacency, remarking soon: "She looks too hot—that's her walk. But she'll be all right presently. Then I'll make her come over and speak to you."

"I should be sorry to give you that trouble. If you were to take me over *there*——!" the young man murmured.

"My dear sir, do you suppose I put myself out that way? I don't mean for you, but for Marian," the General added.

"*I* would put myself out for her soon enough," Overt replied; after which he went on: "Will you be so good as to tell me which of those gentlemen is Henry St. George?"

"The fellow talking to my girl. By Jove, he *is* making up to her—they're going off for another walk."

"Ah is that he—really?" Our friend felt a certain surprise, for the personage before him seemed to trouble a vision which had been vague only while not confronted with the reality. As soon as the reality dawned the mental image, retiring with a sigh, became substantial enough to suffer a slight wrong. Overt, who had spent a considerable part of his short life in foreign lands, made now, but not for the first time, the reflexion that whereas in those countries he had almost always recognised the artist and the man of letters by his personal "type," the mould of his face, the character of his head, the expression of his figure, and even the indications of his dress, so in England this identification was as little as possible a matter of course, thanks to the greater conformity, the habit of sinking the profession instead of advertising it, the general diffusion of the air of the gentleman —the gentleman committed to no particular set of ideas. More than once, on returning to his own country, he had said to himself about people met in society: "One sees them in this place and that, and one even talks with them; but to find out what they *do* one would really have to be a detective." In respect to several individuals whose work he was the opposite of "drawn to"—perhaps he was wrong—he found himself adding, "No wonder they conceal it—when it's so bad!" He noted that oftener than in France and in Germany his artist looked like a gentleman—that is, like an English one—while, certainly outside a few exceptions, his gentleman didn't look like an artist. St. George was not one of the exceptions; that circumstance he definitely apprehended before the great man had turned his back to walk off with Miss Fancourt. He certainly looked better behind than any foreign man of letters—showed for beautifully correct in his tall black hat and his superior frock coat. Somehow, all the same, these very garments—he wouldn't have minded them so much on a week-day—were disconcerting to Paul Overt, who forgot for the moment that the head of the profession was not a bit better dressed than himself. He had caught a glimpse of a regular face, a fresh colour, a brown moustache and a pair of eyes surely never visited by a fine frenzy, and he promised himself to study these denotements on the first occasion. His superficial sense was that their owner might have passed for a lucky stockbroker —a gentleman driving eastward every morning from a sanitary suburb in a smart dog-cart. That carried out the impression already derived from his wife. Paul's glance, after a moment, travelled back to this lady, and he saw how her own had followed her husband as he moved off with Miss Fancourt. Overt permitted himself to wonder a little if she were jealous when another woman took him away. Then he made out that Mrs. St. George wasn't glaring at the indifferent maiden. Her eyes rested but on her husband, and with unmistakable serenity. That was the way she wanted him to be —she liked his conventional uniform. Overt longed to hear more about the book she had induced him to destroy.

CHAPTER II

As they all came out from luncheon General Fancourt took hold of him with an "I say, I want you to know my girl!" as if the idea had just occurred to him and he hadn't spoken of it before. With the other hand he possessed himself all paternally of the young lady. "You know all about him. I've seen you with his books. She reads everything—everything!" he went on to Paul. The girl smiled at him and then laughed at her father. The General turned away and his daughter spoke—"Isn't papa delightful?"

"He is indeed, Miss Fancourt."

"As if I read you because I read 'everything'!"

"Oh I don't mean for saying that," said Paul Overt. "I liked him from the moment he began to be kind to me. Then he promised me this privilege."

"It isn't for you he means it—it's for me. If you flatter yourself that he thinks of anything in life but me you'll find you're mistaken. He introduces every one. He thinks me insatiable."

"You speak just like him," laughed our youth.

"Ah but sometimes I want to"—and the girl coloured. "I don't read everything—I read very little. But I *have* read you."

"Suppose we go into the gallery," said Paul Overt. She pleased him greatly, not so much because of this last remark —though that of course was not too disconcerting—as because, seated opposite to him at luncheon, she had given him for half an hour the impression of her beautiful face. Something else had come with it—a sense of generosity, of an enthusiasm which, unlike many enthusiasms, was not all manner. That was not spoiled for him by his seeing that the repast had placed her again in familiar contact with Henry St. George. Sitting next her this celebrity was also opposite our young man, who had been able to note that he multiplied the attentions lately brought by his wife to the General's notice. Paul Overt had gathered as well that this lady was not in the least discomposed by these fond excesses and that she gave every sign of an unclouded spirit. She had Lord Masham on one side of her and on the other the accomplished Mr. Mulliner, editor of the new high-class lively evening paper which was expected to meet a want felt in circles increasingly conscious that Conservatism must be made amusing, and unconvinced when assured by those of another political colour that it was already amusing enough. At the end of an hour spent in her company Paul Overt thought her still prettier than at the first radiation, and if her profane allusions to her husband's work had not still rung in his ears he should have liked her—so far as it could be a question of that in connexion with a woman to whom he had not yet spoken and to whom probably he should never speak if it were left to her. Pretty women were a clear need to this genius, and for the hour it was Miss Fancourt who supplied the want. If Overt had promised himself a closer view the occasion was now of the best, and it brought consequences felt by the young man as important. He saw more in St. George's face, which he liked the better for its not having told its whole story in the first three minutes. That story came out as one read, in short instalments—it was excusable that one's analogies should be somewhat professional—and the text was a style considerably involved, a language not easy to translate at sight. There were shades of meaning in it and a vague perspective of history which receded as you advanced. Two facts Paul had particularly heeded. The first of these was that he liked the measured mask much better at inscrutable rest than in social agitation; its almost convulsive smile above all displeased him (as much as any impression from that source could), whereas the quiet face had a charm that grew in proportion as stillness settled again. The change to the expression of gaiety excited, he made out, very much the private protest of a person sitting gratefully in the twilight when the lamp is brought in too soon. His second reflexion was that, though generally averse to the flagrant use of ingratiating arts by a man of age "making up" to a pretty girl, he was not in this case too painfully affected: which seemed to prove either that St. George had a light hand or the air of being younger than he was, or else that Miss Fancourt's own manner somehow made everything right.

Overt walked with her into the gallery, and they strolled to the end of it, looking at the pictures, the cabinets, the

charming vista, which harmonised with the prospect of the
summer afternoon, resembling it by a long brightness, with
great divans and old chairs that figured hours of rest. Such a
place as that had the added merit of giving those who came
into it plenty to talk about. Miss Fancourt sat down with her
new acquaintance on a flowered sofa, the cushions of which,
very numerous, were tight ancient cubes of many sizes, and
presently said: "I'm so glad to have a chance to thank
you."

"To thank me——?" He had to wonder.

"I liked your book so much. I think it splendid."

She sat there smiling at him, and he never asked himself
which book she meant; for after all he had written three or
four. That seemed a vulgar detail, and he wasn't even gratified by the idea of the pleasure she told him—her handsome
bright face told him—he had given her. The feeling she appealed to, or at any rate the feeling she excited, was something larger, something that had little to do with any quickened pulsation of his own vanity. It was responsive admiration
of the life she embodied, the young purity and richness of
which appeared to imply that real success was to resemble
that, to live, to bloom, to present the perfection of a fine type,
not to have hammered out headachy fancies with a bent back
at an ink-stained table. While her grey eyes rested on him—
there was a widish space between these, and the division of
her rich-coloured hair, so thick that it ventured to be smooth,
made a free arch above them—he was almost ashamed of
that exercise of the pen which it was her present inclination
to commend. He was conscious he should have liked better
to please her in some other way. The lines of her face were
those of a woman grown, but the child lingered on in her
complexion and in the sweetness of her mouth. Above all
she was natural—that was indubitable now; more natural
than he had supposed at first, perhaps on account of her
æsthetic toggery, which was conventionally unconventional,
suggesting what he might have called a tortuous spontaneity.
He had feared that sort of thing in other cases, and his fears
had been justified; for, though he was an artist to the essence,
the modern reactionary nymph, with the brambles of the
woodland caught in her folds and a look as if the satyrs had
toyed with her hair, made him shrink, not as a man of starch
and patent leather, but as a man potentially himself a poet
or even a faun. The girl was really more candid than her
costume, and the best proof of it was her supposing her liberal

character suited by any uniform. This was a fallacy, since if she was draped as a pessimist he was sure she liked the taste of life. He thanked her for her appreciation—aware at the same time that he didn't appear to thank her enough and that she might think him ungracious. He was afraid she would ask him to explain something he had written, and he always winced at that—perhaps too timidly—for to his own ear the explanation of a work of art sounded fatuous. But he liked her so much as to feel a confidence that in the long run he should be able to show her he wasn't rudely evasive. Moreover, she surely wasn't quick to take offence, wasn't irritable; she could be trusted to wait. So when he said to her, "Ah don't talk of anything I've done, don't talk of it *here;* there's another man in the house who's the actuality!"—when he uttered this short sincere protest it was with the sense that she would see in the words neither mock humility nor the impatience of a successful man bored with praise.

"You mean Mr. St. George—isn't he delightful?"

Paul Overt met her eyes, which had a cool morning-light that would have half-broken his heart if he hadn't been so young. "Alas I don't know him. I only admire him at a distance."

"Oh you *must* know him—he wants so to talk to you," returned Miss Fancourt, who evidently had the habit of saying the things that, by her quick calculation, would give people pleasure. Paul saw how she would always calculate on everything's being simple between others.

"I shouldn't have supposed he knew anything about me," he professed.

"He does then—everything. And if he didn't I should be able to tell him."

"To tell him everything?" our friend smiled.

"You talk just like the people in your book," she answered.

"Then they must all talk alike."

She thought a moment, not a bit disconcerted. "Well, it must be so difficult. Mr. St. George tells me it *is*—terribly. I've tried too—and I find it so. I've tried to write a novel."

"Mr. St. George oughtn't to discourage you," Paul went so far as to say.

"You do much more—when you wear that expression."

"Well, after all, why try to be an artist?" the young man pursued. "It's so poor—so poor!"

"I don't know what you mean," said Miss Fancourt, who looked grave.

"I mean as compared with being a person of action—as living your works."

"But what's art but an intense life—if it be real?" she asked. "I think it's the only one—everything else is so clumsy!" Her companion laughed, and she brought out with her charming serenity what next struck her. "It's so interesting to meet so many celebrated people."

"So I should think—but surely it isn't new to you."

"Why, I've never seen any one—any one: living always in Asia."

The way she talked of Asia somehow enchanted him. "But doesn't that continent swarm with great figures? Haven't you administered provinces in India and had captive rajahs and tributary princes chained to your car?"

It was as if she didn't care even *should* he amuse himself at her cost. "I was with my father, after I left school to go out there. It was delightful being with him—we're alone together in the world, he and I—but there was none of the society I like best. One never heard of a picture—never of a book, except bad ones."

"Never of a picture? Why, wasn't all life a picture?"

She looked over the delightful place where they sat. "Nothing to compare to this. I adore England!" she cried.

It fairly stirred in him the sacred chord. "Ah of course I don't deny that we must do something with her, poor old dear, yet!"

"She hasn't been touched, really," said the girl.

"Did Mr. St. George say that?"

There was a small and, as he felt, harmless spark of irony in his question; which, however, she answered very simply, not noticing the insinuation. "Yes, he says England hasn't been touched—not considering all there is," she went on eagerly. "He's so interesting about our country. To listen to him makes one want to do something."

"It would make *me* want to," said Paul Overt, feeling strongly, on the instant, the suggestion of what she said and that of the emotion with which she said it, and well aware of what an incentive, on St. George's lips, such a speech might be.

"Oh you—as if you hadn't! I should like so to hear you talk together," she added ardently.

"That's very genial of you; but he'd have it all his own way. I'm prostrate before him."

She had an air of earnestness. "Do you think, then, he's so perfect?"

"Far from it. Some of his later books seem to me of a queerness——!"

"Yes, yes—he knows that."

Paul Overt stared. "That they seem to me of a queerness——?"

"Well yes, or at any rate that they're not what they should be. He told me he didn't esteem them. He has told me such wonderful things—he's so interesting."

There was a certain shock for Paul Overt in the knowledge that the fine genius they were talking of had been reduced to so explicit a confession and had made it, in his misery, to the first comer; for though Miss Fancourt was charming what was she after all but an immature girl encountered at a country-house? Yet precisely this was part of the sentiment he himself had just expressed: he would make way completely for the poor peccable great man, not because he didn't read him clear, but altogether because he did. His consideration was half composed of tenderness for superficialities which he was sure their perpetrator judged privately, judged more ferociously than any one, and which represented some tragic intellectual secret. He would have his reasons for his psychology *à fleur de peau,* and these reasons could only be cruel ones, such as would make him dearer to those who already were fond of him. "You excite my envy. I have my reserves, I discriminate—but I love him," Paul said in a moment. "And seeing him for the first time this way is a great event for me."

"How momentous—how magnificent!" cried the girl. "How delicious to bring you together!"

"*Your* doing it—that makes it perfect," our friend returned.

"He's as eager as you," she went on. "But it's so odd you shouldn't have met."

"It's not really so odd as it strikes you. I've been out of England so much—made repeated absences all these last years."

She took this in with interest. "And yet you write of it as well as if you were always here."

"It's just the being away perhaps. At any rate the best bits, I suspect, are those that were done in dreary places abroad."

"And why were they dreary?"

"Because they were health-resorts—where my poor mother was dying."

"Your poor mother?"—she was all sweet wonder.

"We went from place to place to help her to get better. But she never did. To the deadly Riviera (I hate it!), to the high Alps, to Algiers, and far away—a hideous journey—to Colorado."

"And she isn't better?" Miss Fancourt went on.

"She died a year ago."

"Really?—like mine! Only that's years since. Some day you must tell me about your mother," she added.

He could at first, on this, only gaze at her. "What right things you say! If you say them to St. George I don't wonder he's in bondage."

It pulled her up for a moment. "I don't know what you mean. He doesn't make speeches and professions at all—he isn't ridiculous."

"I'm afraid you consider, then, that I am."

"No, I don't"—she spoke it rather shortly. And then she added: "He understands—understands everything."

The young man was on the point of saying jocosely: "And I don't—is that it?" But these words, in time, changed themselves to others slightly less trivial. "Do you suppose he understands his wife?"

Miss Fancourt made no direct answer, but after a moment's hesitation put it: "Isn't she charming?"

"Not in the least!"

"Here he comes. Now you must know him," she went on. A small group of visitors had gathered at the other end of the gallery and had been there overtaken by Henry St. George, who strolled in from a neighbouring room. He stood near them a moment, not falling into the talk but taking up an old miniature from a table and vaguely regarding it. At the end of a minute he became aware of Miss Fancourt and her companion in the distance; whereupon, laying down his miniature, he approached them with the same procrastinating air, his hands in his pockets and his eyes turned, right and left, to the pictures. The gallery was so long that this transit took some little time, especially as there was a moment when he stopped to admire the fine Gainsborough. "He says Mrs. St. George has been the making of him," the girl continued in a voice slightly lowered.

"Ah he's often obscure!" Paul laughed.

"Obscure?" she repeated as if she heard it for the first time.

Her eyes rested on her other friend, and it wasn't lost upon Paul that they appeared to send out great shafts of softness. "He's going to speak to us!" she fondly breathed. There was a sort of rapture in her voice, and our friend was startled. "Bless my soul, does she care for him like *that?*—is she in love with him?" he mentally inquired. "Didn't I tell you he was eager?" she had meanwhile asked of him.

"It's eagerness dissimulated," the young man returned as the subject of their observation lingered before his Gainsborough. "He edges toward us shyly. Does he mean that she saved him by burning that book?"

"That book? What book did she burn?" the girl quickly turned her face to him.

"Hasn't he told you, then?"

"Not a word."

"Then he doesn't tell you everything!" Paul had guessed that she pretty much supposed he did. The great man had now resumed his course and come nearer; in spite of which his more qualified admirer risked a profane observation. "St. George and the Dragon is what the anecdote suggests!"

His companion, however, didn't hear it; she smiled at the dragon's adversary. "He *is* eager—he is!" she insisted.

"Eager for you—yes."

But meanwhile she had called out: "I'm sure you want to know Mr. Overt. You'll be great friends, and it will always be delightful to me to remember I was here when you first met and that I had something to do with it."

There was a freshness of intention in the words that carried them off; nevertheless our young man was sorry for Henry St. George, as he was sorry at any time for any person publicly invited to be responsive and delightful. He would have been so touched to believe that a man he deeply admired should care a straw for him that he wouldn't play with such a presumption if it were possibly vain. In a single glance of the eye of the pardonable master he read—having the sort of divination that belonged to his talent—that his personage had ever a store of friendly patience, which was part of his rich outfit, but was versed in no printed page of a rising scribbler. There was even a relief, a simplification, in that: liking him so much already for what he had done, how could one have liked him any more for a perception which must at the best have been vague? Paul Overt got up, trying to show his compassion, but at the same instant he found himself encompassed by St. George's happy personal art—a

manner of which it was the essence to conjure away false
positions. It all took place in a moment. Paul was conscious
that he knew him now, conscious of his handshake and of
the very quality of his hand; of his face, seen nearer and consequently seen better, of a general fraternising assurance,
and in particular of the circumstance that St. George didn't
dislike him (as yet at least) for being imposed by a charming
but too gushing girl, attractive enough without such danglers.
No irritation at any rate was reflected in the voice with
which he questioned Miss Fancourt as to some project of a
walk—a general walk of the company round the park. He
had soon said something to Paul about a talk—"We must
have a tremendous lot of talk; there are so many things,
aren't there?"—but our friend could see this idea wouldn't in
the present case take very immediate effect. All the same he
was extremely happy, even after the matter of the walk had
been settled—the three presently passed back to the other
part of the gallery, where it was discussed with several members of the party; even when, after they had all gone out together, he found himself for half an hour conjoined with Mrs.
St. George. Her husband had taken the advance with Miss
Fancourt, and this pair were quite out of sight. It was the pret-
tiest of rambles for a summer afternoon—a grassy circuit,
of immense extent, skirting the limit of the park within. The
park was completely surrounded by its old mottled but perfect red wall, which, all the way on their left, constituted in
itself an object of interest. Mrs. St. George mentioned to him
the surprising number of acres thus enclosed, together with
numerous other facts relating to the property and the family,
and the family's other properties: she couldn't too strongly
urge on him the importance of seeing their other houses. She
ran over the names of these and rang the changes on them
with the facility of practice, making them appear an almost
endless list. She had received Paul Overt very amiably on his
breaking ground with her by the mention of his joy in having
just made her husband's acquaintance, and struck him as so
alert and so accommodating a little woman that he was
rather ashamed of his *mot* about her to Miss Fancourt;
though he reflected that a hundred other people, on a hundred occasions, would have been sure to make it. He got on
with Mrs. St. George, in short, better than he expected; but
this didn't prevent her suddenly becoming aware that she was
faint with fatigue and must take her way back to the house
by the shortest cut. She professed that she hadn't the strength

of a kitten and was a miserable wreck; a character he had been too preoccupied to discern in her while he wondered in what sense she could be held to have been the making of her husband. He had arrived at a glimmering of the answer when she announced that she must leave him, though this perception was of course provisional. While he was in the very act of placing himself at her disposal for the return the situation underwent a change; Lord Masham had suddenly turned up, coming back to them, overtaking them, emerging from the shrubbery—Overt could scarcely have said how he appeared—and Mrs. St. George had protested that she wanted to be left alone and not to break up the party. A moment later she was walking off with Lord Masham. Our friend fell back and joined Lady Watermouth, to whom he presently mentioned that Mrs. St. George had been obliged to renounce the attempt to go further.

"She oughtn't to have come out at all," her ladyship rather grumpily remarked.

"Is she so very much of an invalid?"

"Very bad indeed." And his hostess added with still greater austerity: "She oughtn't really to come to one!" He wondered what was implied by this, and presently gathered that it was not a reflexion on the lady's conduct or her moral nature: it only represented that her strength was not equal to her aspirations.

CHAPTER III

The smoking-room at Summersoft was on the scale of the rest of the place—high, light, commodious and decorated with such refined old carvings and mouldings that it seemed rather a bower for ladies who should sit at work at fading crewels than a parliament of gentlemen smoking strong cigars. The gentlemen mustered there in considerable force on the Sunday evening, collecting mainly at one end, in front of one of the cool fair fireplaces of white marble, the entablature of which was adorned with a delicate little Italian "subject." There was another in the wall that faced it, and, thanks to the mild summer night, a fire in neither; but a nucleus for aggregation was furnished on one side by a table in the chimney-corner laden with bottles, decanters and tall tumblers. Paul Overt was a faithless smoker; he would puff a cigarette for reasons with which tobacco had nothing to do. This was particularly the case on the occasion of which I speak; his motive was the vision of a little direct talk with Henry St. George. The "tremendous" communion of which the great man had held out hopes to him earlier in the day had not yet come off, and this saddened him considerably, for the party was to go its several ways immediately after breakfast on the morrow. He had, however, the disappointment of finding that apparently the author of "Shadowmere" was not disposed to prolong his vigil. He wasn't among the gentlemen assembled when Paul entered, nor was he one of those who turned up, in bright habiliments, during the next ten minutes. The young man waited a little, wondering if he had only gone to put on something extraordinary; this would account for his delay as well as contribute further to Overt's impression of his tendency to do the approved superficial thing. But he didn't arrive—he must have been putting on something more extraordinary than was probable. Our hero gave him up, feeling a little injured, a little wounded, at this loss of twenty coveted words. He wasn't angry, but he puffed his cigarette sighingly, with the sense of something rare possibly missed. He wandered away with his regret and moved slowly round the room, looking at the old prints on the walls. In this attitude he presently felt a hand on his shoulder and a friendly voice in his ear: "This is good. I hoped I should find you. I came down on purpose." St. George was there without a change of dress and with a fine face—his graver one—to which our young man all in a flutter responded. He explained that it was only for the Master—the idea of a little talk—that he had sat up, and that, not finding him, he had been on the point of going to bed.

"Well, you know, I don't smoke—my wife doesn't let me," said St. George, looking for a place to sit down. "It's very good for me—very good for me. Let us take that sofa."

"Do you mean smoking's good for you?"

"No, no—her not letting me. It's a great thing to have a wife who's so sure of all the things one can do without. One might never find them out one's self. She doesn't allow me to touch a cigarette." They took possession of a sofa at a distance from the group of smokers, and St. George went on: "Have you got one yourself?"

"Do you mean a cigarette?"

"Dear no—a wife!"

"No; and yet I'd give up my cigarette for one."

"You'd give up a good deal more than that," St. George returned. "However, you'd get a great deal in return. There's a something to be said for wives," he added, folding his arms and crossing his outstretched legs. He declined tobacco altogether and sat there without returning fire. His companion stopped smoking, touched by his courtesy; and after all they were out of the fumes, their sofa was in a faraway corner. It would have been a mistake, St. George went on, a great mistake for them to have separated without a little chat; "for I know all about you," he said. "I know you're very remarkable. You've written a very distinguished book."

"And how do you know it?" Paul asked.

"Why, my dear fellow, it's in the air, it's in the papers, it's everywhere." St. George spoke with the immediate familiarity of a confrère—a tone that seemed to his neighbour the very rustle of the laurel. "You're on all men's lips and, what's better, on all women's. And I've just been reading your book."

"Just? You hadn't read it this afternoon," said Overt.

"How do you know that?"

"I think you should know how I know it," the young man laughed.

"I suppose Miss Fancourt told you."

"No indeed—she led me rather to suppose you had."

"Yes—that's much more what she'd do. Doesn't she shed a rosy glow over life? But you didn't believe her?" asked St. George.

"No, not when you came to us there."

"Did I pretend? did I pretend badly?" But without waiting for an answer to this St. George went on: "You ought always to believe such a girl as that—always, always. Some women are meant to be taken with allowances and reserves; but you must take *her* just as she is."

"I like her very much," said Paul Overt.

Something in his tone appeared to excite on his companion's part a momentary sense of the absurd; perhaps it was the air of deliberation attending this judgement. St. George broke into a laugh to reply. "It's the best thing you can do with her. She's a rare young lady! In point of fact, however, I confess I hadn't read you this afternoon."

"Then you see how right I was in this particular case not to believe Miss Fancourt."

"How right? how can I agree to that when I lost credit by it?"

"Do you wish to pass exactly for what she represents you? Certainly you needn't be afraid," Paul said.

"Ah, my dear young man, don't talk about passing—for the likes of me! I'm passing away—nothing else than that. She has a better use for her young imagination (isn't it fine?) than in 'representing' in any way such a weary wasted used-up animal!" The Master spoke with a sudden sadness that produced a protest on Paul's part; but before the protest could be uttered he went on, reverting to the latter's striking novel: "I had no idea you were so good—one hears of so many things. But you're surprisingly good."

"I'm going to be surprisingly better," Overt made bold to reply.

"I see that, and it's what fetches me. I don't see so much else—as one looks about—that's going to be surprisingly better. They're going to be consistently worse—most of the things. It's so much easier to be worse—heaven knows I've found it so. I'm not in a great glow, you know, about what's breaking out all over the place. But you *must* be better, you really must keep it up. I haven't of course. It's very difficult —that's the devil of the whole thing, keeping it up. But I see you'll be able to. It will be a great disgrace if you don't."

"It's very interesting to hear you speak of yourself; but I don't know what you mean by your allusions to your having fallen off," Paul Overt observed with pardonable hypocrisy. He liked his companion so much now that the fact of any decline of talent or of care had ceased for the moment to be vivid to him.

"Don't say that—don't say that," St. George returned gravely, his head resting on the top of the sofa-back and his eyes on the ceiling. "You know perfectly what I mean. I haven't read twenty pages of your book without seeing that you can't help it."

"You make me very miserable," Paul ecstatically breathed.

"I'm glad of that, for it may serve as a kind of warning. Shocking enough it must be, especially to a young fresh mind, full of faith—the spectacle of a man meant for better things sunk at my age in such dishonour." St. George, in the same contemplative attitude, spoke softly but deliberately, and without perceptible emotion. His tone indeed suggested an impersonal lucidity that was practically cruel—cruel to himself—and made his young friend lay an argumentative hand on his arm. But he went on while his eyes seemed to follow the graces of the eighteenth-century ceiling: "Look at me well, take my lesson to heart—for it *is* a lesson. Let that good come of it at least that you shudder with your pitiful impression, and that this may help to keep you straight in the future. Don't become in your old age what I have in mine—the depressing, the deplorable illustration of the worship of false gods!"

"What do you mean by your old age?" the young man asked.

"It has made me old. But I like your youth."

Paul answered nothing—they sat for a minute in silence. They heard the others going on about the governmental majority. Then "What do you mean by false gods?" he inquired.

His companion had no difficulty whatever in saying, "The idols of the market; money and luxury and 'the world'; placing one's children and dressing one's wife; everything that drives one to the short and easy way. Ah the vile things they make one do!"

"But surely one's right to want to place one's children."

"One has no business to have any children," St. George placidly declared. "I mean of course if one wants to do anything good."

"But aren't they an inspiration—an incentive?"

"An incentive to damnation, artistically speaking."

"You touch on very deep things—things I should like to discuss with you," Paul said. "I should like you to tell me volumes about yourself. This is a great feast for *me!*"

"Of course it is, cruel youth. But to show you I'm still not incapable, degraded as I am, of an act of faith, I'll tie my vanity to the stake for you and burn it to ashes. You must come and see me—you must come and see us," the Master quickly substituted. "Mrs. St. George is charming; I don't know whether you've had any opportunity to talk with her. She'll be delighted to see you; she likes great celebrities, whether incipient or predominant. You must come and dine—my wife will write to you. Where are you to be found?"

"This is my little address"—and Overt drew out his pocket-book and extracted a visiting-card. On second thoughts, however, he kept it back, remarking that he wouldn't trouble his friend to take charge of it but would come and see him straightway in London and leave it at his door if he should fail to obtain entrance.

"Ah you'll probably fail; my wife's always out—or when she isn't out is knocked up from having *been* out. You must come and dine—though that won't do much good either, for my wife insists on big dinners." St. George turned it over further, but then went on: "You must come down and see us in the country, that's the best way; we've plenty of room and it isn't bad."

"You've a house in the country?" Paul asked enviously.

"Ah not like this! But we have a sort of place we go to— an hour from Euston. That's one of the reasons."

"One of the reasons?"

"Why my books are so bad."

"You must tell me all the others!" Paul longingly laughed.

His friend made no direct rejoinder to this, but spoke again abruptly. "Why have I never seen you before?"

The tone of the question was singularly flattering to our hero, who felt it to imply the great man's now perceiving he had for years missed something. "Partly, I suppose, because there has been no particular reason why you should see me. I haven't lived in the world—in your world. I've spent many years out of England, in different places abroad."

"Well, please don't do it any more. You must do England —there's such a lot of it."

"Do you mean I must write about it?"—and Paul struck the note of the listening candour of a child.

"Of course you must. And tremendously well, do you mind? That takes off a little of my esteem for this thing of yours—that it goes on abroad. Hang 'abroad'! Stay at home and do things here—do subjects we can measure."

"I'll do whatever you tell me," Overt said, deeply attentive. "But pardon me if I say I don't understand how you've been reading my book," he added. "I've had you before me all the afternoon, first in that long walk, then at tea on the lawn, till we went to dress for dinner, and all the evening at dinner and in this place."

St. George turned his face about with a smile. "I gave it but a quarter of an hour."

"A quarter of an hour's immense, but I don't understand where you put it in. In the drawing-room after dinner you weren't reading—you were talking to Miss Fancourt."

"It comes to the same thing, because we talked about 'Gin-istrella.' She described it to me—she lent me her copy."

"Lent it to you?"

"She travels with it."

"It's incredible," Paul blushed.

"It's glorious for you, but it also turned out very well for me. When the ladies went off to bed she kindly offered to send the book down to me. Her maid brought it to me in the hall, and I went to my room with it. I hadn't thought of coming here, I do that so little. But I don't sleep early, I always have to read an hour or two. I sat down to your novel on the spot, without undressing, without taking off anything but my coat. I think that's a sign my curiosity had been strongly roused about it. I read a quarter of an hour, as I tell you, and even in a quarter of an hour I was greatly struck."

"Ah the beginning isn't very good—it's the whole thing!" said Overt, who had listened to this recital with extreme interest. "And you laid down the book and came after me?" he asked.

"That's the way it moved me. I said to myself, 'I see it's off his own bat, and he's there, by the way, and the day's over, and I haven't said twenty words to him.' It occurred to me that you'd probably be in the smoking-room and that it wouldn't be too late to repair my omission. I wanted to do something civil to you, so I put on my coat and came down. I shall read your book again when I go up."

Our friend faced round in his place—he was touched as he had scarce ever been by the picture of such a demonstration in his favour. "You're really the kindest of men. *Cela s'est passé comme ça?*—and I've been sitting here with you all this time and never apprehended it and never thanked you!"

"Thank Miss Fancourt—it was she who wound me up. She has made me feel as if I had read your novel."

"She's an angel from heaven!" Paul declared.

"She is indeed. I've never seen any one like her. Her interest in literature's touching—something quite peculiar to herself; she takes it all so seriously. She feels the arts and she wants to feel them more. To those who practise them it's almost humiliating—her curiosity, her sympathy, her good faith. How can anything be as fine as she supposes it?"

"She's a rare organisation," the younger man sighed.

"The richest I've ever seen—an artistic intelligence really of the first order. And lodged in such a form!" St. George exclaimed.

"One would like to represent such a girl as that," Paul continued.

"Ah there it is—there's nothing like life!" said his companion. "When you're finished, squeezed dry and used up and you think the sack's empty, you're still appealed to, you still get touches and thrills, the idea springs up—out of the leap of the actual—and shows you there's always something to be done. But I shan't do it—she's not for me!"

"How do you mean, not for you?"

"Oh, it's all over—she's for you, if you like."

"Ah much less!" said Paul. "She's not for a dingy little man of letters; she's for the world, the bright rich world of bribes and rewards. And the world will take hold of her—it will carry her away."

"It will try—but it's just a case in which there may be a fight. It would be worth fighting, for a man who had it in him, with youth and talent on his side."

These words rang not a little in Paul Overt's consciousness—they held him briefly silent. "It's a wonder she has remained as she is; giving herself away so—with so much to give away."

"Remaining, you mean, so ingenuous—so natural? Oh she doesn't care a straw—she gives away because she overflows. She has her own feelings, her own standards; she doesn't keep remembering that she must be proud. And then she hasn't been here long enough to be spoiled; she has picked up a fashion or two, but only the amusing ones. She's a provincial—a provincial of genius," St. George went on; "her very blunders are charming, her mistakes are interesting. She has come back from Asia with all sorts of excited curiosities and unappeased appetites. She's first-rate herself and she expends herself on the second-rate. She's life herself and she takes a rare interest in imitations. She mixes all things up, but there are none in regard to which she hasn't perceptions. She sees things in a perspective—as if from the top of the Himalayas—and she enlarges everything she touches. Above all she exaggerates—to herself, I mean. She exaggerates you and me!"

There was nothing in that description to allay the agitation caused in our younger friend by such a sketch of a fine subject. It seemed to him to show the art of St. George's admired hand, and he lost himself in gazing at the vision—this hovered there before him—of a woman's figure which should be part of the glory of a novel. But at the end of a moment the thing had turned into smoke and out of the smoke—the last puff of a big cigar—proceeded the voice of General Fancourt, who had left the others and come and planted himself before the gentlemen on the sofa. "I suppose that when you fellows get talking you sit up half the night."

"Half the night?—*jamais de la vie!* I follow a hygiene"—and St. George rose to his feet.

"I see—you're hothouse plants," laughed the General. "That's the way you produce your flowers."

"I produce mine between ten and one every morning—I bloom with a regularity!" St. George went on.

"And with a splendour!" added the polite General, while Paul noted how little the author of "Shadowmere" minded, as he phrased it to himself, when addressed as a celebrated story-teller. The young man had an idea *he* should never get used to that; it would always make him uncomfortable—from the suspicion that people would think they had to—and he would want to prevent it. Evidently his great colleague had toughened and hardened—had made himself a surface. The group of men had finished their cigars and taken up their bedroom candlesticks; but before they all passed out Lord Watermouth invited the pair of guests who had been so absorbed together to "have" something. It happened that they both declined; upon which General Fancourt said: "Is that the hygiene? You don't water the flowers?"

"Oh I should drown them!" St. George replied; but, leaving the room still at his young friend's side, he added whimsically, for the latter's benefit, in a lower tone: "My wife doesn't let me."

"Well, I'm glad I'm not one of you fellows!" the General richly concluded.

The nearness of Summersoft to London had this consequence, chilling to a person who had had a vision of sociability in a railway-carriage, that most of the company, after breakfast, drove back to town, entering their own vehicles, which had come out to fetch them, while their servants returned by train with their luggage. Three or four young men, among whom was Paul Overt, also availed themselves of the common convenience; but they stood in the portico of the house and saw the others roll away. Miss Fancourt got into a victoria with her father after she had shaken hands with our hero and said, smiling in the frankest way in the world, "I *must* see you more. Mrs. St. George is so nice; she has promised to ask us both to dinner together." This lady and her husband took their places in a perfectly-appointed brougham—she required a closed carriage—and as our young man waved his hat to them in response to their nods and flourishes he reflected that, taken together, they were an honourable image of success of the material rewards and the social credit of literature. Such things were not the full measure, but he nevertheless felt a little proud for literature.

CHAPTER IV

Before a week had elapsed he met Miss Fancourt in Bond Street, at a private view of the works of a young artist in "black-and-white" who had been so good as to invite him to the stuffy scene. The drawings were admirable, but the crowd in the one little room was so dense that he felt himself up to his neck in a sack of wool. A fringe of people at the outer edge endeavoured by curving forward their backs and presenting, below them, a still more convex surface of resistance to the pressure of the mass, to preserve an interval between their noses and the glazed mounts of the pictures; while the central body, in the comparative gloom projected by a wide horizontal screen hung under the skylight and allowing only a margin for the day, remained upright dense and vague, lost in the contemplation of its own ingredients. This contemplation sat especially in the sad eyes of certain female heads, surmounted with hats of strange convolution and plumage, which rose on long necks above the others. One of the heads, Paul perceived, was much the most beautiful of the collection, and his next discovery was that it belonged to Miss Fancourt. Its beauty was enhanced by the glad smile she sent him across surrounding obstructions, a smile that drew him to her as fast as he could make his way. He had seen for himself at Summersoft that the last thing her nature contained was an affectation of indifference; yet even with this circumspection he took a fresh satisfaction in her not having pretended to wait his arrival with composure. She smiled as radiantly as if she wished to make him hurry, and as soon as he came within earshot she broke out in her voice of joy: "He's here—he's here; he's coming back in a moment!"

"Ah your father?" Paul returned as she offered him her hand.

"Oh dear no, this isn't in my poor father's line. I mean Mr. St. George. He has just left me to speak to some one— he's coming back. It's he who brought me—wasn't it charming?"

"Ah that gives him a pull over me—I couldn't have 'brought' you, could I?"

"If you had been so kind as to propose it—why not you as well as he?" the girl returned with a face that, expressing no cheap coquetry, simply affirmed a happy fact.

"Why he's a *père de famille*. They've privileges," Paul explained. And then quickly: "Will you go to see places with *me*?" he asked.

"Anything you like," she smiled. "I know what you mean, that girls have to have a lot of people——!" Then she broke off: "I don't know; I'm free. I've always been like that—I can go about with any one. I'm so glad to meet you," she added with a sweet distinctness that made those near her turn round.

"Let me at least repay that speech by taking you out of this squash," her friend said. "Surely people aren't happy here!"

"No, they're awfully *mornes*, aren't they? But I'm very happy indeed and I promised Mr. St. George to remain on this spot till he comes back. He's going to take me away. They send him invitations for things of this sort—more than he wants. It was so kind of him to think of me."

"They also send me invitations of this kind—more than *I* want. And if thinking of *you* will do it——!" Paul went on.

"Oh, I delight in them—everything that's life, everything that's London!"

"They don't have private views in Asia, I suppose," he laughed. "But what a pity that for this year, even in this gorged city, they're pretty well over."

"Well, next year will do, for I hope you believe we're going to be friends always. Here he comes!" Miss Fancourt continued before Paul had time to respond.

He made out St. George in the gaps in the crowd, and this perhaps led to his hurrying a little to say: "I hope that doesn't mean I'm to wait till next year to see you."

"No, no—aren't we to meet at dinner on the twenty-fifth?" she panted with an eagerness as happy as his own.

"That's almost next year. Is there no means of seeing you before?"

She stared with all her brightness. "Do you mean you'd *come*?"

"Like a shot, if you'll be so good as to ask me!"

"On Sunday then—this next Sunday?"

"What have I done that you should doubt it?" the young man asked with delight.

Miss Fancourt turned instantly to St. George, who had now joined them, and announced triumphantly:

"He's coming on Sunday—this next Sunday!"

"Ah my day—my day too!" said the famous novelist, laughing, to their companion.

"Yes, but not yours only. You shall meet in Manchester Square; you shall talk—you shall be wonderful!"

"We don't meet often enough," St. George allowed, shaking hands with his disciple. "Too many things—ah too many things! But we must make it up in the country in September. You won't forget you've promised me that?"

"Why, he's coming on the twenty-fifth—you'll see him then," said the girl.

"On the twenty-fifth?" St. George asked vaguely.

"We dine with you; I hope you haven't forgotten. He's dining out that day," she added gaily to Paul.

"Oh bless me, yes—that's charming! And you're coming? My wife didn't tell me," St. George said to him. "Too many things—too many things!" he repeated.

"Too many people—too many people!" Paul exclaimed, giving ground before the penetration of an elbow.

"You oughtn't to say that. They all read you."

"Me? I should like to see them! Only two or three at most," the young man returned.

"Did you ever hear anything like that? He knows, haughtily, how good he is!" St. George declared, laughing, to Miss Fancourt. "They read *me*, but that doesn't make me like them any better. Come away from them, come away!" And he led the way out of the exhibition.

"He's going to take me to the Park," Miss Fancourt observed to Overt with elation as they passed along the corridor that led to the street.

"Ah does he go there?" Paul asked, taking the fact for a somewhat unexpected illustration of St. George's *mœurs*.

"It's a beautiful day—there'll be a great crowd. We're going to look at the people, to look at types," the girl went on. "We shall sit under the trees; we shall walk by the Row."

"I go once a year—on business," said St. George, who had overheard Paul's question.

"Or with a country cousin, didn't you tell me? I'm the country cousin!" she continued over her shoulder to Paul as their friend drew her toward a hansom to which he had signalled. The young man watched them get in; he returned, as he stood there, the friendly wave of the hand with which, ensconced in the vehicle beside her, St. George took leave of him. He even lingered to see the vehicle start away and lose itself in the confusion of Bond Street. He followed it with his eyes; it put to him embarrassing things. "She's not for *me!*" the great novelist had said emphatically at Summersoft; but his manner of conducting himself toward her appeared not quite in harmony with such a conviction. How could he have behaved differently if she *had* been for him? An indefinite envy rose in Paul Overt's heart as he took his way on foot alone; a feeling addressed alike, strangely enough, to each of the occupants of the hansom. How much he should like to rattle about London with such a girl! How much he should like to go and look at "types" with St. George!

The next Sunday at four o'clock he called in Manchester Square, where his secret wish was gratified by his finding Miss Fancourt alone. She was in a large bright friendly occupied room, which was painted red all over, draped with the quaint cheap florid stuffs that are represented as coming from southern and eastern countries, where they are fabled to serve as the counterpanes of the peasantry, and bedecked with pottery of vivid hues, ranged on casual shelves, and with many water-colour drawings from the hand (as the visitor learned) of the young lady herself, commemorating with a brave breadth the sunsets, the mountains, the temples and palaces of India. He sat an hour—more than an hour, two hours—and all the while no one came in. His hostess was so good as to remark, with her liberal humanity, that it was delightful they weren't interrupted: it was so rare in London, especially at that season, that people got a good talk. But luckily now, of a fine Sunday, half the world went out of town, and that made it better for those who didn't go, when these others were in sympathy. It was the defect of London—one or two or three, the very short list of those she recognised in the teeming world-city she adored—that there were too few good chances for talk: you never had time to carry anything far.

"Too many things, too many things!" Paul said, quoting St. George's exclamation of a few days before.

"Ah yes, for him there are too many—his life's too complicated."

"Have you seen it *near*? That's what I should like to do; it might explain some mysteries," her visitor went on. She asked him what mysteries he meant, and he said: "Oh peculiarities of his work, inequalities, superficialities. For one who looks at it from the artistic point of view it contains a bottomless ambiguity."

She became at this, on the spot, all intensity. "Ah do describe that more—it's so interesting. There are no such suggestive questions. I'm so fond of them. He thinks he's a failure—fancy!" she beautifully wailed.

"That depends on what his ideal may have been. With his gifts it ought to have been high. But till one knows what he really proposed to himself—! Do *you* know by chance?" the young man broke off.

"Oh he doesn't talk to me about himself. I can't make him. It's too provoking."

Paul was on the point of asking what, then, he did talk about, but discretion checked it and he said instead: "Do you think he's unhappy at home?"

She seemed to wonder. "At home?"

"I mean in his relations with his wife. He had a mystifying little way of alluding to her."

"Not to me," said Marian Fancourt with her clear eyes. "That wouldn't be right, would it?" she asked gravely.

"Not particularly; so I'm glad he doesn't mention her to you. To praise her might bore you, and he has no business to do anything else. Yet he knows you better than me."

"Ah but he respects *you!*" the girl cried as with envy.

Her visitor stared a moment, then broke into a laugh. "Doesn't he respect you?"

"Of course, but not in the same way. He respects what you've done—he told me so the other day."

Paul drank it in, but retained his faculties. "When you went to look at types?"

"Yes—we found so many: he has such an observation of them! He talked a great deal about your book. He says it's really important."

"Important! Ah the grand creature!"—and the author of the work in question groaned for joy.

"He was wonderfully amusing, he was inexpressibly droll, while we walked about. He sees everything; he has so many compassions and images, and they're always exactly right. *C'est d'un trouvé*, as they say!"

"Yes, with his gifts, such things as he ought to have done!" Paul sighed.

"And don't you think he *has* done them?"

Ah it was just the point. "A part of them, and of course

even that part's immense. But he might have been one of the greatest. However, let us not make this an hour of qualifications. Even as they stand," our friend earnestly concluded, "his writings are a mine of gold."

To this proposition she ardently responded, and for half an hour the pair talked over the Master's principal productions. She knew them well—she knew them even better than her visitor, who was struck with her critical intelligence and with something large and bold in the movement in her mind. She said things that startled him and that evidently had come to her directly; they weren't picked-up phrases—she placed them too well. St. George had been right about her being first-rate, about her not being afraid to gush, not remembering that she must be proud. Suddenly something came back to her, and she said: "I recollect that he did speak of Mrs. St. George to me once. He said, apropos of something or other, that she didn't care for perfection."

"That's a great crime in an artist's wife," Paul returned.

"Yes, poor thing!" and the girl sighed with a suggestion of many reflexions, some of them mitigating. But she presently added: "Ah perfection, perfection—how one ought to go in for it! I wish *I* could."

"Every one can in his way," her companion opined.

"In *his* way, yes—but not in hers. Women are so hampered —so condemned! Yet it's a kind of dishonour if you don't, when you want to *do* something, isn't it?" Miss Fancourt pursued, dropping one train in her quickness to take up another, an accident that was common with her. So these two young persons sat discussing high themes in their electric drawing-room, in their London "season"—discussing, with extreme seriousness, the high theme of perfection. It must be said in extenuation of this eccentricity that they were interested in the business. Their tone had truth and their emotion beauty; they weren't posturing for each other or for someone else.

The subject was so wide that they found themselves reducing it; the perfection to which for the moment they agreed to confine their speculations was that of the valid, the exemplary work of art. Our young woman's imagination, it appeared, had wandered far in that direction, and her guest had the rare delight of feeling in their conversation a full interchange. This episode will have lived for years in his memory and even in his wonder; it had the quality that fortune distils in a single drop at a time—the quality that lubri-

cates many ensuing frictions. He still, whenever he likes, has
a vision of the room, the bright red sociable talkative room
with the curtains that, by a stroke of successful audacity, had
the note of vivid blue. He remembers where certain things
stood, the particular book open on the table and the almost
intense odour of the flowers placed, at the left, somewhere
behind him. These facts were the fringe, as it were, of a fine
special agitation which had its birth in those two hours and
of which perhaps the main sign was in its leading him inwardly and repeatedly to breathe, "I had no idea there was
any one like this—I had no idea there was any one like
this!" Her freedom amazed him and charmed him—it seemed
so to simplify the practical question. She was on the footing
of an independent personage—a motherless girl who had
passed out of her teens and had a position and responsibilities, who wasn't held down to the limitations of a
little miss. She came and went with no dragged duenna, she
received people alone, and, though she was totally without
hardness, the question of protection or patronage had no
relevancy in regard to her. She gave such an impression of
the clear and the noble combined with the easy and the natural that in spite of her eminent modern situation she suggested no sort of sisterhood with the "fast" girl. Modern she
was indeed, and made Paul Overt, who loved old colour,
the golden glaze of time, think with some alarm of the mud-
dled palette of the future. He couldn't get used to her interest in the arts he cared for; it seemed too good to be real
—it was so unlikely an adventure to tumble into such a well
of sympathy. One might stray into the desert easily—that
was on the cards and that was the law of life; but it was
too rare an accident to stumble on a crystal well. Yet if her
aspirations seemed at one moment too extravagant to be real
they struck him at the next as too intelligent to be false. They
were both high and lame, and, whims for whims, he preferred them to any he had met in a like relation. It was probable enough she would leave them behind—exchange them
for politics or "smartness" or mere prolific maternity, as was
the custom of scribbling daubing educated flattered girls in
an age of luxury and a society of leisure. He noted that the
water-colours on the walls of the room she sat in had mainly
the quality of being naïves, and reflected that naïveté in art
is like a zero in a number: its importance depends on the
figure it is united with. Meanwhile, however, he had fallen in
love with her. Before he went away, at any rate, he said to

her: "I thought St. George was coming to see you to-day, but he doesn't turn up."

For a moment he supposed she was going to cry "*Comment donc?* Did you come here only to meet him?" But the next he became aware of how little such a speech would have fallen in with any note of flirtation he had as yet perceived in her. She only replied: "Ah yes, but I don't think he'll come. He recommended me not to expect him." Then she gaily but all gently added: "He said it wasn't fair to you. But I think I could manage two."

"So could I," Paul Overt returned, stretching the point a little to meet her. In reality his appreciation of the occasion was so completely an appreciation of the woman before him that another figure in the scene, even so esteemed a one as St. George, might for the hour have appealed to him vainly. He left the house wondering what the great man had meant by its not being fair to him; and, still more than that, whether he had actually stayed away from the force of that idea. As he took his course through the Sunday solitude of Manchester Square, swinging his stick and with a good deal of emotion fermenting in his soul, it appeared to him he was living in a world strangely magnanimous. Miss Fancourt had told him it was possible she should be away, and that her father should be, on the following Sunday, but that she had the hope of a visit from him in the other event. She promised to let him know should their absence fail, and then he might act accordingly. After he had passed into one of the streets that open from the Square he stopped, without definite intentions, looking sceptically for a cab. In a moment he saw a hansom roll through the place from the other side and come a part of the way toward him. He was on the point of hailing the driver when he noticed a "fare" within; then he waited, seeing the man prepare to deposit his passenger by pulling up at one of the houses. The house was apparently the one he himself had just quitted; at least he drew that inference as he recognised Henry St. George in the person who stepped out of the hansom. Paul turned off as quickly as if he had been caught in the act of spying. He gave up his cab—he preferred to walk; he would go nowhere else. He was glad St. George hadn't renounced his visit altogether—that would have been too absurd. Yes, the world was magnanimous, and even he himself felt so as, on looking at his watch, he noted but six o'clock, so that he could mentally congratulate his successor on having an hour still to sit in

Miss Fancourt's drawing-room. He himself might use that hour for another visit, but by the time he reached the Marble Arch the idea of such a course had become incongruous to him. He passed beneath that architectural effort and walked into the Park till he had got upon the spreading grass. Here he continued to walk; he took his way across the elastic turf and came out by the Serpentine. He watched with a friendly eye the diversions of the London people, he bent a glance almost encouraging on the young ladies paddling their sweethearts about the lake and the guardsmen tickling tenderly with their bearskins the artificial flowers in the Sunday hats of their partners. He prolonged his meditative walk; he went ino Kensington Gardens, he sat upon the penny chairs, he looked at the little sailboats launched upon the round pond and was glad he had no engagement to dine. He repaired for this purpose, very late, to his club, where he found himself unable to order a repast and told the waiter to bring whatever there was. He didn't even observe what he was served with, and he spent the evening in the library of the establishment, pretending to read an article in an American magazine. He failed to discover what it was about; it appeared in a dim way to be about Marian Fancourt.

Quite later in the week she wrote to him that she was not to go into the country—it had only just been settled. Her father, she added, would never settle anything, but put it all on her. She felt her responsibility—she had to—and since she was forced this was the way she had decided. She mentioned no reasons, which gave our friend all the clearer field for bold conjecture about them. In Manchester Square on this second Sunday he esteemed his fortune less good, for she had three or four other visitors. But there were three or four compensations; perhaps the greatest of which was that, learning how her father had after all, at the last hour, gone out of town alone, the bold conjecture I just now spoke of found itself becoming a shade more bold. And then her presence was her presence, and the personal red room was there and was full of it, whatever phantoms passed and vanished, emitting incomprehensible sounds. Lastly, he had the resource of staying till every one had come and gone and of believing this grateful to her, though she gave no particular sign. When they were alone together she came to his point. "But St. George did come—last Sunday. I saw him as I looked back."

"Yes, but it was the last time."

"The last time?"

"He said he would never come again."

Paul Overt stared. "Does he mean he wishes to cease to see you?"

"I don't know what he means," the girl bravely smiled. "He won't at any rate see me here."

"And pray why not?"

"I haven't the least idea," said Marian Fancourt, whose visitor found her more perversely sublime than ever yet as she professed this clear helplessness.

CHAPTER V

"Oh I say, I want you to stop a little," Henry St. George said to him at eleven o'clock the night he dined with the head of the profession. The company—none of it indeed *of* the profession—had been numerous and was taking its leave; our young man, after bidding good night to his hostess, had put out his hand in farewell to the master of the house. Besides drawing from the latter the protest I have cited this movement provoked a further priceless word about their chance now to have a talk, their going into his room, his having still everything to say. Paul Overt was all delight at this kindness; nevertheless he mentioned in weak jocose qualification the bare fact that he had promised to go to another place which was at a considerable distance.

"Well, then, you'll break your promise, that's all. You quite awful humbug!" St. George added in a tone that confirmed our young man's ease.

"Certainly I'll break it—but it was a real promise."

"Do you mean to Miss Fancourt? You're following her?" his friend asked.

He answered by a question. "Oh, is *she* going?"

"Base imposter!" his ironic host went on. "I've treated you handsomely on the article of that young lady: I won't make another concession. Wait three minutes—I'll be with you." He gave himself to his departing guests, accompanied the long-trained ladies to the door. It was a hot night, the windows were open, the sound of the quick carriages and of the linkmen's call came into the house. The affair had rather glittered; a sense of festal things was in the heavy air: not only the influence of that particular entertainment, but the suggestion of the wide hurry of pleasure which in London on summer nights fills so many of the happier quarters of the complicated town. Gradually Mrs. St. George's drawing-room emptied itself; Paul was left alone with his hostess, to whom he explained the motive of his waiting. "Ah yes, some intellectual, some *professional,* talk," she leered; "at this season doesn't one miss it? Poor dear Henry, I'm so glad!" The young man looked out of the window a moment, at the called hansoms that lurched up, at the smooth broughams that rolled away. When he turned round Mrs. St. George had disappeared; her husband's voice rose to him from below— he was laughing and talking, in the portico, with some lady who awaited her carriage. Paul had solitary possession, for some minutes, of the warm deserted rooms where the covered tinted lamplight was soft, the seats had been pushed about and the odour of flowers lingered. They were large, they were pretty, they contained objects of value; everything in the picture told of a "good house." At the end of five minutes a servant came in with a request from the Master that he would join him downstairs; upon which, descending, he followed his conductor through a long passage to an apartment thrown out, in the rear of the habitation, for the special requirements, as he guessed, of a busy man of letters.

St. George was in his shirt-sleeves in the middle of a large high room—a room without windows, but with a wide skylight at the top, that of a place of exhibition. It was furnished as a library, and the serried bookshelves rose to the ceiling, a surface of incomparable tone produced by dimly-gilt "backs" interrupted here and there by the suspension of old prints and drawings. At the end furthest from the door of admission was a tall desk, of great extent, at which the person using it could write only in the erect posture of a clerk in a counting-house; and stretched from the entrance to this structure was a wide plain band of crimson cloth, as straight as a garden-path and almost as long, where, in his mind's eye, Paul at once beheld the Master pace to and fro during vexed hours—hours, that is, of admirable composition. The servant gave him a coat, an old jacket with a hang of experience, from a cupboard in the wall, retiring afterwards with the garment he had taken off. Paul Overt welcomed the coat; it was a coat for talk, it promised confidences—having visibly received so many—and had tragic literary elbows. "Ah we're practical—we're practical!" St. George said as he saw his visitor look the place over. "Isn't it a good big cage for going round and round? My wife invented it and she locks me up here every morning."

Our young man breathed—by way of tribute—with a certain oppression. "You don't miss a window—a place to look out?"

"I did at first awfully; but her calculation was just. It saves time, it has saved me many months in these ten years. Here I stand, under the eye of day—in London of course, very often, it's rather a bleared old eye—walled in to my trade. I can't get away—so the room's a fine lesson in concentration. I've learnt the lesson, I think; look at that big bundle of proof and acknowledge it." He pointed to a fat roll of papers on one of the tables, which had not been undone.

"Are you bringing out another——?" Paul asked in a tone the fond deficiencies of which he didn't recognise till his companion burst out laughing, and indeed scarce even then.

"You humbug, you humbug!"—St. George appeared to enjoy caressing him, as it were, with that opprobrium. "Don't I know what you think of them?" he asked, standing there with his hands in his pockets and with a new kind of smile. It was as if he were going to let his young votary see him all now.

"Upon my word in that case you know more than I do!" the latter ventured to respond, revealing a part of the torment of being able neither clearly to esteem nor distinctly to renounce him.

"My dear fellow," said the more and more interesting Master, "don't imagine I talk about my books specifically; they're not a decent subject—*il ne manquerait plus que ça!* I'm not so bad as you may apprehend. About myself, yes, a little, if you like; though it wasn't for that I brought you down here. I want to ask you something—very much indeed; I value this chance. Therefore sit down. We're practical, but there *is* a sofa, you see—for she does humour my poor bones so far. Like all really great administrators and disciplinarians she knows when wisely to relax." Paul sank into the corner of a deep leathern couch, but his friend remained standing and explanatory. "If you don't mind, in this room, this is my habit. From the door to the desk and from the desk to the door. That shakes up my imagination gently; and don't you see what a good thing it is that there's no window for her to fly out of? The eternal standing as I write (I stop at that bureau and put it down, when anything comes, and so we go on) was rather wearisome at first, but we adopted it with an eye to the long run: you're in better order—if your legs don't break down!—and you can keep it up for more years. Oh we're practical—we're practical!" St. George repeated, going to the table and taking up all mechanically the bundle of proofs. But, pulling off the wrapper, he had a change of attention that appealed afresh to our hero. He lost himself a moment, examining the sheets of his new book, while the younger man's eyes wandered over the room again.

"Lord, what good things I should do if I had such a charming place as this to do them in!" Paul reflected. The outer world, the world of accident and ugliness, was so successfully excluded, and within the rich protecting square, beneath the patronising sky, the dream-figures, the summoned company, could hold their particular revel. It was a fond prevision of Overt's rather than an observation on actual data, for which occasions had been too few, that the Master thus more closely viewed would have the quality, the charming gift, of flashing out, all surprisingly, in personal intercourse and at moments of suspended or perhaps even of diminished expectation. A happy relation with him would be a thing proceeding by jumps, not by traceable stages.

"Do you read them—really?" he asked, laying down the proofs on Paul's inquiring of him how soon the work would be published. And when the young man answered, "Oh yes, always," he was moved to mirth again by something he caught in his manner of saying that. "You go to see your grandmother on her birthday—and very proper it is, especially as she won't last for ever. She has lost every faculty and every sense; she neither sees, nor hears, nor speaks; but all customary pieties and kindly habits are respectable. Only you're strong if you *do* read 'em! *I* couldn't, my dear fellow. You *are* strong, I know; and that's just a part of what I wanted to say to you. You're very strong indeed. I've been going into your other things—they've interested me immensely. Some one ought to have told me about them before—some one I could believe. But whom can one believe? You're wonderfully on the right road—it's awfully decent work. Now do you mean to keep it up?—that's what I want to ask you."

"Do I mean to do others?" Paul asked, looking up from his sofa at his erect inquisitor and feeling partly like a happy little boy when the schoolmaster is gay, and partly like some pilgrim of old who might have consulted a world-famous oracle. St. George's own performance had been infirm, but as an adviser he would be infallible.

"Others—others? Ah the number won't matter; one other would do, if it were really a further step—a throb of the same effort. What I mean is have you it in your heart to go in for some sort of decent perfection?"

"Ah decency, ah perfection——!" the young man sincerely sighed. "I talked of them the other Sunday with Miss Fancourt."

It produced on the Master's part a laugh of odd acrimony. "Yes, they'll 'talk' of them as much as you like! But they'll do little to help one to them. There's no obligation of course; only you strike me as capable," he went on. "You must have thought it all over. I can't believe you're without a plan. That's the sensation you give me, and it's so rare that it really stirs one up—it makes you remarkable. If you haven't a plan, if you *don't* mean to keep it up, surely you're within your rights; it's nobody's business, no one can force you, and not more than two or three people will notice you don't go straight. The others—*all* the rest, every blest soul in England, will think you do—will think you *are* keeping it up: upon my honour they will! I shall be one of the two or three who know better. Now the question is whether you can do it for two or three. Is that the stuff you're made of?"

It locked his guest a minute as in closed throbbing arms. "I could do it for one, if you were the one."

"Don't say that; I don't deserve it; it scorches me," he protested with eyes suddenly grave and glowing. "The 'one' is of course one's self, one's conscience, one's idea, the singleness of one's aim. I think of that pure spirit as a man thinks of a woman he has in some detested hour of his youth loved and forsaken. She haunts him with reproachful eyes, she lives for ever before him. As an artist, you know, I've married for money." Paul stared and even blushed a little, confounded by this avowal; whereupon his host, observing the expression of his face, dropped a quick laugh and pursued: "You don't follow my figure. I'm not speaking of my dear wife, who had a small fortune—which, however, was not my bribe. I fell in love with her, as many other people have done. I refer to the mercenary muse whom I led to the altar of literature. Don't, my boy, put your nose into *that* yoke. The awful jade will lead you a life!"

Our hero watched him, wondering and deeply touched. "Haven't you been happy?"

"Happy? It's a kind of hell."

"There are things I should like to ask you," Paul said after a pause.

"Ask me anything in all the world. I'd turn myself inside out to save you."

"To 'save' me?" he quavered.

"To make you stick to it—to make you see it through. As I said to you the other night at Summersoft, let my example be vivid to you."

"Why, your books are not so bad as that," said Paul, fairly laughing and feeling that if ever a fellow had breathed the air of art——!

"So bad as what?"

"Your talent's so great that it's in everything you do, in what's less good as well as in what's best. You've some forty volumes to show for it—forty volumes of wonderful life, of rare observation, of magnificent ability."

"I'm very clever, of course I know that"—but it was a thing, in fine, this author made nothing of. "Lord, what rot they'd all be if I hadn't been! I'm a successful charlatan," he went on—"I've been able to pass off my system. But do you know what it is? It's *carton-pierre*."

"*Carton-pierre?*" Paul was struck, and gaped.

"Lincrusta-Walton!"

"Ah don't say such things—you make me bleed!" the younger man protested. "I see you in a beautiful fortunate home, living in comfort and honour."

"Do you call it honour?"—his host took him up with an intonation that often comes back to him. "That's what I want *you* to go in for. I mean the real thing. This is brummagem."

"Brummagem?" Paul ejaculated while his eyes wandered, by a movement natural at the moment, over the luxurious room.

"Ah they make it so well to-day—it's wonderfully deceptive!"

Our friend thrilled with the interest and perhaps even more with the pity of it. Yet he wasn't afraid to seem to patronise when he could still so far envy. "Is it deceptive that I find you living with every appearance of domestic felicity—blest with a devoted, accomplished wife, with children whose acquaintance I haven't yet had the pleasure of making, but who *must* be delightful young people, from what I know of their parents?"

St. George smiled as for the candour of his question. "It's all excellent, my dear fellow—heaven forbid I should deny it. I've made a great deal of money; my wife has known how to take care of it, to use it without wasting it, to put a good bit of it by, to make it fructify. I've got a loaf on the shelf; I've got everything in fact but the great thing."

"The great thing?" Paul kept echoing.

"The sense of having done the best—the sense which is the real life of the artist and the absence of which is his death, of having drawn from his intellectual instrument the finest music that nature had hidden in it, of having played it as it should be played. He either does that or he doesn't—and if he doesn't he isn't worth speaking of. Therefore, precisely, those who really know *don't* speak of him. He may still hear a great chatter, but what he hears most is the incorruptible silence of Fame. I've squared her, you may say, for my little hour—but what's my little hour? Don't imagine for a moment," the Master pursued, "that I'm such a cad as to have brought you down here to abuse or to complain of my wife to you. She's a woman of distinguished qualities, to whom my obligations are immense; so that, if you please, we'll say nothing about her. My boys—my children are all boys—are straight and strong, thank God, and have no poverty of growth about them, no penury of needs. I receive periodically the most satisfactory attestation from Harrow, from Oxford, from Sandhurst—oh we've done the best for them!—of their eminence as living thriving consuming organisms."

"It must be delightful to feel that the son of one's loins is at Sandhurst," Paul remarked enthusiastically.

"It is—it's charming. Oh I'm a patriot!"

The young man then could but have the greater tribute of questions to pay. "Then what did you mean—the other night at Summersoft—by saying that children are a curse?"

"My dear youth, on what basis are we talking?" and St. George dropped upon the sofa at a short distance from him. Sitting a little sideways he leaned back against the opposite arm with his hands raised and interlocked behind his head. "On the supposition that a certain perfection's possible and even desirable—isn't it so? Well, all I say is that one's children interfere with perfection. One's wife interferes. Marriage interferes."

"You think, then, the artist shouldn't marry?"

"He does so at his peril—he does so at his cost."

"Not even when his wife's in sympathy with his work?"

"She never is—she can't be! Women haven't a conception of such things."

"Surely they on occasion work themselves," Paul objected.

"Yes, very badly indeed. Oh of course, often, they think they understand, they think they sympathise. Then it is they're most dangerous. Their idea is that you shall do a great lot and get a great lot of money. Their great nobleness and virtue, their exemplary conscientiousness as British females, is in keeping you up to that. My wife makes all my bargains with my publishers for me, and has done so for twenty years. She does it consummately well—that's why I'm really pretty well off. Aren't you the father of their innocent babes, and will you withhold from them their natural sustenance? You asked me the other night if they're not an immense incentive. Of course they are—there's no doubt of that!"

Paul turned it over; it took, from eyes he had never felt open so wide, so much looking at. "For myself I've an idea I need incentives."

"Oh well, then, *n'en parlons plus!*" his companion handsomely smiled.

"*You* are an incentive, I maintain," the young man went on. "You don't affect me in the way you'd apparently like to. Your great success is what I see—the pomp of Ennismore Gardens!"

"Success?"—St. George's eyes had a cold fine light. "Do you call it success to be spoken of as you'd speak of me if you were sitting here with another artist—a young man intelligent and sincere like yourself? Do you call it success to make you blush—as you *would* blush!—if some foreign critic (some fellow, of course I mean, who should know what he was talking about and should have shown you he did, as foreign critics like to show it) were to say to you: 'He's the one, in this country, whom they consider the most perfect, isn't he?' Is it success to be the occasion of a young Englishman's having to stammer as you would have to stammer at such a moment for old England? No, no; success is to have made people wriggle to another tune. Do try it!"

Paul continued all gravely to glow. "Try what?"

"Try to do some really good work."

"Oh I want to, heaven knows!"

"Well, you can't do it without sacrifices—don't believe that for a moment," the Master said. "I've made none. I've had everything. In other words, I've missed everything."

"You've had the full rich masculine human general life, with all the responsibilities and duties and burdens and sorrows and joys—all the domestic and social initiations and complications. They must be immensely suggestive, immensely amusing," Paul anxiously submitted.

"Amusing?"

"For a strong man—yes."

"They've given me subjects without number, if that's what you mean; but they've taken away at the same time the power to use them. I've touched a thousand things, but which one of them have I turned into gold? The artist has to do only with that—he knows nothing of any baser metal. I've led the life of the world, with my wife and my progeny; the clumsy conventional expensive materialised vulgarised brutalised life of London. We've got everything handsome, even a carriage—we're perfect Philistines and prosperous hospitable eminent people. But, my dear fellow, don't try to stultify yourself and pretend you don't know what we *haven't* got. It's bigger than all the rest. Between artists—come!" the Master wound up. "You know as well as you sit there that you'd put a pistol-ball into your brain if you had written my books!"

It struck his listener that the tremendous talk promised by him at Summersoft had indeed come off, and with a promptitude, a fulness, with which the latter's young imagination had scarcely reckoned. His impression fairly shook him and he throbbed with the excitement of such deep soundings and such strange confidences. He throbbed indeed with the conflict of his feelings—bewilderment and recognition and alarm, enjoyment and protest and assent, all commingled with tenderness (and a kind of shame in the participation) for the sores and bruises exhibited by so fine a creature, and with a sense of the tragic secret nursed under his trappings. The idea of *his*, Paul Overt's, becoming the occasion of such an act of humility made him flush and pant, at the same time that his consciousness was in certain directions too much alive not to swallow—and not intensely to taste—every offered spoonful of the revelation. It had been his odd fortune to blow upon the deep waters, to make them surge and break in waves of strange eloquence. But how couldn't he give out a passionate contradiction of his host's last extravagance, how couldn't he enumerate to him the parts of his work he loved, the splendid things he had found in it, beyond the compass of any other writer of the day? St. George listened a while, courteously; then he said, laying his hand on his visitor's: "That's all very well; and if your idea's to do nothing better there's no reason you shouldn't have as many good things as I—as many human and material appendages, as many sons or daughters, a wife with as many gowns, a house with as many servants, a stable with as many horses, a heart with as many aches." The Master got up when he had spoken thus—he stood a moment—near the sofa, looking down on his agitated pupil. "Are you possessed of any property?" it occurred to him to ask.

"None to speak of."

"Oh well then there's no reason why you shouldn't make a goodish income—if you set about it the right way. Study *me* for that—study me well. You may really have horses."

Paul sat there some minutes without speaking. He looked straight before him—he turned over many things. His friend had wandered away, taking up a parcel of letters from the table where the roll of proofs had lain. "What was the book Mrs. St. George made you burn—the one she didn't like?" our young man brought out.

"The book she made me burn—how did you know that?" The Master looked up from his letters quite without the facial convulsion the pupil had feared.

"I heard her speak of it at Summersoft."

"Ah yes—she's proud of it. I don't know—it was rather good."

"What was it about?"

"Let me see." And he seemed to make an effort to remember. "Oh yes—it was about myself." Paul gave an irrepressible groan for the disappearance of such a production, and the elder man went on: "Oh but *you* should write it—*you* should do me." And he pulled up—from the restless motion that had come upon him; his fine smile a generous glare. "There's a subject, my boy: no end of stuff in it!"

Again Paul was silent, but it was all tormenting. "Are there no women who really understand—who can take part in a sacrifice?"

"How can they take part? They themselves are the sacrifice. They're the idol and the altar and the flame."

"Isn't there even *one* who sees further?" Paul continued.

For a moment St. George made no answer; after which, having torn up his letters, he came back to the point all ironic. "Of course I know the one you mean. But not even Miss Fancourt."

"I thought you admired her so much."

"It's impossible to admire her more. Are you in love with her?" St. George asked.

"Yes," Paul Overt presently said.

"Well, then, give it up."

Paul stared. "Give up my 'love'?"

"Bless me, no. Your idea." And then as our hero but still gazed: "The one you talked with her about. The idea of a decent perfection."

"She'd help it—she'd help it!" the young man cried.

"For about a year—the first year, yes. After that she'd be as a millstone round its neck."

Paul frankly wondered. "Why, she has a passion for the real thing, for good work—for everything you and I care for most."

" 'You and I' is charming, my dear fellow!" his friend laughed. "She has it indeed, but she'd have a still greater passion for her children—and very proper too. She'd insist on everything's being made comfortable, advantageous, propitious for them. That isn't the artist's business."

"The artist—the artist! Isn't he a man all the same?"

St. George had a grand grimace. "I mostly think not. You know as well as I what he has to do: the concentration, the finish, the independence he must strive for from the moment he begins to wish his work really decent. Ah my young friend, his relation to women, and especially to the one he's most intimately concerned with, is at the mercy of the damning fact that whereas he can in the nature of things have but one standard, they have about fifty. That's what makes them so superior," St. George amusingly added. "Fancy an artist with a change of standards as you'd have a change of shirts or of dinner-plates. To *do* it—to do it and make it divine—is the only thing he has to think about. 'Is it done or not?' is his only question. Not 'Is it done as well as a proper solicitude for my dear little family will allow?' He has nothing to do with the relative—he has only to do with the absolute; and a dear little family may represent a dozen relatives."

"Then you don't allow him the common passions and affections of men?" Paul asked.

"Hasn't he a passion, an affection, which includes all the

rest? Besides, let him have all the passions he likes—if he only keeps his independence. He must be able to be poor."

Paul slowly got up. "Why, then, did you advise me to make up to her?"

St. George laid a hand on his shoulder. "Because she'd make a splendid wife! And I hadn't read you then."

The young man had a strained smile. "I wish you had left me alone!"

"I didn't know that that wasn't good enough for you," his host returned.

"What a false position, what a condemnation of the artist, that he's a mere disfranchised monk and can produce his effect only by giving up personal happiness. What an arraignment of art!" Paul went on with a trembling voice.

"Ah you don't imagine by chance that I'm defending art? 'Arraignment'—I should think so! Happy the societies in which it hasn't made its appearance, for from the moment it comes they have a consuming ache, they have an incurable corruption, in their breast. Most assuredly is the artist in a false position! But I thought we were taking him for granted. Pardon me," St. George continued: " 'Ginistrella' made me!"

Paul stood looking at the floor—one o'clock struck, in the stillness, from a neighbouring church-tower. "Do you think she'd ever look at me?" he put to his friend at last.

"Miss Fancourt—as a suitor? Why shouldn't I think it? That's why I've tried to favour you—I've had a little chance or two of bettering your opportunity."

"Forgive my asking you, but do you mean by keeping away yourself?" Paul said with a blush.

"I'm an old idiot—my place isn't there," St. George stated gravely.

"I'm nothing yet, I've no fortune; and there must be so many others," his companion pursued.

The Master took this considerably in, but made little of it. "You're a gentleman and a man of genius. I think you might do something."

"But if I must give that up—the genius?"

"Lots of people, you know, think I've kept mine," St. George wonderfully grinned.

"You've a genius for mystification!" Paul declared, but grasping his hand gratefully in attenuation of this judgment.

"Poor dear boy, I do worry you! But try, try, all the same. I think your chances are good and you'll win a great prize."

Paul held fast the other's hand a minute; he looked into the strange deep face. "No, I *am* an artist—I can't help it!"

"Ah show it then!" St. George pleadingly broke out. "Let me see before I die the thing I most want, the thing I yearn for: a life in which the passion—ours—is really intense. If you can be rare don't fail of it! Think what it is—how it counts—how it lives!"

They had moved to the door and he had closed both his hands over his companion's. Here they paused again and our hero breathed deep. "I want to live!"

"In what sense?"

"In the greatest."

"Well, then, stick to it—see it through."

"With your sympathy—your help?"

"Count on that—you'll be a great figure to me. Count on my highest appreciation, my devotion. You'll give me satisfaction—if that has any weight with you!" After which, as Paul appeared still to waver, his host added: "Do you remember what you said to me at Summersoft?"

"Something infatuated, no doubt!"

" 'I'll do anything in the world you tell me.' You said that."

"And you hold me to it?"

"Ah what am I?" the Master expressively sighed.

"Lord, what things I shall have to do!" Paul almost moaned as he departed.

CHAPTER VI

"It goes on too much abroad—hang abroad!" These or something like them had been the Master's remarkable words in relation to the action of "Ginistrella"; and yet, though they had made a sharp impression on the author of that work, like almost all spoken words from the same source, he a week after the conversation I have noted left England for a long absence and full of brave intentions. It is not a perversion of the truth to pronounce that encounter the direct cause of his departure. If the oral utterance of the eminent writer had the privilege of moving him deeply it was especially on his turning it over at leisure, hours and days later, that it appeared to yield him its full meaning and exhibit its extreme importance. He spent the summer in Switzerland

and, having in September begun a new task, determined not to cross the Alps till he should have made a good start. To this end he returned to a quiet corner he knew well, on the edge of the Lake of Geneva and within sight of the towers of Chillon: a region and a view for which he had an affection that sprang from old associations and was capable of mysterious revivals and refreshments. Here he lingered late, till the snow was on the nearer hills, almost down to the limit to which he could climb when his stint, on the shortening afternoons, was performed. The autumn was fine, the lake was blue, and his book took form and direction. These felicities, for the time, embroidered his life, which he suffered to cover him with its mantle. At the end of six weeks he felt he had learnt St. George's lesson by heart, had tested and proved its doctrine. Nevertheless he did a very inconsistent thing: before crossing the Alps he wrote to Marian Fancourt. He was aware of the perversity of this act, and it was only as a luxury, an amusement, the reward of a strenuous autumn, that he justified it. She had asked of him no such favour when, shortly before he left London, three days after their dinner in Ennismore Gardens, he went to take leave of her. It was true she had had no ground—he hadn't named his intention of absence. He had kept his counsel for want of due assurance: it was that particular visit that was, the next thing, to settle the matter. He had paid the visit to see how much he really cared for her, and quick departure, without so much as an explicit farewell, was the sequel to this inquiry, the answer to which had created within him a deep yearning. When he wrote her from Clarens he noted that he owed her an explanation (more than three months after!) for not having told her what he was doing.

She replied now briefly but promptly, and gave him a striking piece of news: that of the death, a week before, of Mrs. St. George. This exemplary woman had succumbed, in the country, to a violent attack of inflammation of the lungs —he would remember that for a long time she had been delicate. Miss Fancourt added that she believed her husband was overwhelmed by the blow; he would miss her too terribly—she had been everything in life to him. Paul Overt, on this, immediately wrote to St. George. He would from the day of their parting have been glad to remain in communication with him, but had hitherto lacked the right excuse for troubling so busy a man. Their long nocturnal talk came back to him in every detail, but this was no bar to an expres-

sion of proper sympathy with the head of the profession,
for hadn't that very talk made it clear that the late accomplished lady was the influence that ruled his life? What catastrophe could be more cruel than the extinction of such an
influence? This was to be exactly the tone taken by St.
George in answering his young friend upwards of a month
later. He made no allusion of course to their important discussion. He spoke of his wife as frankly and generously as if
he had quite forgotten that occasion, and the feeling of deep
bereavement was visible in his words. "She took everything
off my hands—off my mind. She carried on our life with the
greatest art, the rarest devotion, and I was free, as few men
can have been, to drive my pen, to shut myself up with my
trade. This was a rare service—the highest she could have
rendered me. Would I could have acknowledged it more
fitly!"

A certain bewilderment, for our hero, disengaged itself
from these remarks: they struck him as a contradiction, a
retractation, strange on the part of a man who hadn't the
excuse of witlessness. He had certainly not expected his cor-
respondent to rejoice in the death of his wife, and it was
perfectly in order that the rupture of a tie of more than
twenty years should have left him sore. But if she had been
so clear a blessing what in the name of consistency had the
dear man meant by turning *him* upside down that night—by
dosing him to that degree, at the most sensitive hour of his
life, with the doctrine of renunciation? If Mrs. St. George
was an irreparable loss, then her husband's inspired advice
had been a bad joke and renunciation was a mistake. Overt
was on the point of rushing back to London to show that, for
his part, he was perfectly willing to consider it so, and he
went so far as to take his manuscript of the first chapters of
his new book out of his table-drawer and insert it into a
pocket of his portmanteau. This led to his catching a glimpse
of certain pages he hadn't looked at for months, and that
accident, in turn, to his being struck with the high promise
they revealed—a rare result of such retrospections, which it
was his habit to avoid as much as possible: they usually
brought home to him that the glow of composition might be
purely subjective and misleading emotion. On this occasion
a certain belief in himself disengaged itself whimsically from
the serried erasures of his first draft, making him think it
best after all to pursue his present trial to the end. If he could
write so well under the rigour of privation it might be a mis-

take to change the conditions before that spell had spent itself. He would go back to London of course, but he would go back only when he should have finished his book. This was the vow he privately made, restoring his manuscript to the table-drawer. It may be added that it took him a long time to finish his book, for the subject was as difficult as it was fine, and he was literally embarrassed by the fulness of his notes. Something within him warned him he must make it supremely good—otherwise he should lack, as regards his private behaviour, a handsome excuse. He had a horror of this deficiency and found himself as firm as need be on the question of the lamp and the file. He crossed the Alps at last and spent the winter, the spring, the ensuing summer, in Italy, where still, at the end of a twelvemonth, his task was unachieved. "Stick to it—see it through"; this general injunction of St. George's was good also for the particular case. He applied it to the utmost, with the result that when in its slow order the summer had come round again he felt he had given all that was in him. This time he put his papers into his portmanteau, with the address of his publisher attached, and took his way northward.

He had been absent from London for two years; two years which, seeming to count as more, had made such a difference in his own life—through the production of a novel far stronger, he believed, than "Ginistrella"—that he turned out into Piccadilly, the morning after his arrival, with a vague expectation of changes, of finding great things had happened. But there were few transformations in Piccadilly—only three or four big red houses where there had been low black ones—and the brightness of the end of June peeped through the rusty railings of the Green Park and glittered in the varnish of the rolling carriages as he had seen it in other, more cursory Junes. It was a greeting he appreciated; it seemed friendly and pointed, added to the exhilaration of his finished book, of his having his own country and the huge oppressive amusing city that suggested everything, that contained everything, under his hand again. "Stay at home and do things here—do subjects we can measure," St. George had said; and now it struck him he should ask nothing better than to stay at home for ever. Late in the afternoon he took his way to Manchester Square, looking out for a number he hadn't forgotten. Miss Fancourt, however, was not at home, so that he turned rather dejectedly from the door. His movement brought him face to face with a gentleman just approaching it and recognised on another glance as Miss Fancourt's father. Paul saluted this personage, and the General returned the greeting with his customary good manner—a manner so good, however, that you could never tell whether it meant he placed you. The disappointed caller felt the impulse to address him; then, hesitating, became both aware of having no particular remark to make, and convinced that though the old soldier remembered him he remembered him wrong. He therefore went his way without computing the irresistible effect his own evident recognition would have on the General, who never neglected a chance to gossip. Our young man's face was expressive, and observation seldom let it pass. He hadn't taken ten steps before he heard himself called after with a friendly semi-articulate "Er—I beg your pardon!" He turned round and the General, smiling at him from the porch, said: "Won't you come in? I won't leave you the advantage of me!" Paul declined to come in, and then felt regret, for Miss Fancourt, so late in the afternoon, might return at any moment. But her father gave him no second chance; he appeared mainly to wish not to have struck him as ungracious. A further look at the visitor had recalled something, enough at least to enable him to say: "You've come back, you've come back?" Paul was on the point of replying that he had come back the night before, but he suppressed, the next instant, this strong light on the immediacy of his visit and, giving merely a general assent, alluded to the young lady he deplored not having found. He had come late in the hope she would be in. "I'll tell her—I'll tell her," said the old man; and then he added quickly, gallantly: "You'll be giving us something new? It's a long time, isn't it?" Now he remembered him right.

"Rather long. I'm very slow," Paul explained. "I met you at Summersoft a long time ago."

"Oh yes—with Henry St. George. I remember very well. Before his poor wife——" General Fancourt paused a moment, smiling a little less. "I daresay you know."

"About Mrs. St. George's death? Certainly—I heard at the time."

"Oh no, I mean—I mean he's to be married."

"Ah I've not heard that!" But just as Paul was about to add "To whom?" the General crossed his intention.

"When did you come back? I know you've been away— by my daughter. She was very sorry. You ought to give her something new."

"I came back last night," said our young man, to whom something had occurred which made his speech for the moment a little thick.

"Ah most kind of you to come so soon. Couldn't you turn up at dinner?"

"At dinner?" Paul just mechanically repeated, not liking to ask whom St. George was going to marry, but thinking only of that.

"There are several people, I believe. Certainly St. George. Or afterwards if you like better. I believe my daughter expects——" He appeared to notice something in the visitor's raised face (on his steps he stood higher) which led him to interrupt himself, and the interruption gave him a momentary sense of awkwardness, from which he sought a quick

Paul gaped again. "To be married?"

"To Mr. St. George—it has just been settled. Odd marriage, isn't it?" Our listener uttered no opinion on this point: he only continued to stare. "But I daresay it will do—she's so awfully literary!" said the General. "Perhaps, then, you haven't heard she's to be married."

Paul had turned very red. "Oh it's a surprise—very interesting, very charming! I'm afraid I can't dine—so many thanks!"

"Well, you must come to the wedding!" cried the General. "Oh I remember that day at Summersoft. He's a great man, you know."

"Charming—charming!" Paul stammered for retreat. He shook hands with the General and got off. His face was red and he had the sense of its growing more and more crimson. All the evening at home—he went straight to his rooms and remained there dinnerless—his cheek burned at intervals as if it had been smitten. He didn't understand what had happened to him, what trick had been played him, what treachery practised. "None, none," he said to himself. "I've nothing to do with it. I'm out of it—it's none of my business." But that bewildered murmur was followed again and again by the incongruous ejaculation: "Was it a plan—was it a plan?" Sometimes he cried to himself, breathless, "Have I been duped, sold, swindled?" If at all, he was an absurd; an abject victim. It was as if he hadn't lost her till now. He had renounced her, yes; but that was another affair—that was a closed but not a locked door. Now he seemed to see the door quite slammed in his face. Did he expect her to wait—was she to give him his time like that: two years at a stretch?

He didn't know what he had expected—he only knew what he hadn't. It wasn't this—it wasn't this. Mystification, bitterness and wrath rose and boiled in him when he thought of the deference, the devotion, the credulity with which he had listened to St. George. The evening wore on and the light was long; but even when it had darkened he remained without a lamp. He had flung himself on the sofa, where he lay through the hours with his eyes either closed or gazing at the gloom, in the attitude of a man teaching himself to bear something, to bear having been made a fool of. He had made it too easy—that idea passed over him like a hot wave. Suddenly, as he heard eleven o'clock strike, he jumped up, remembering what General Fancourt had said about his coming after dinner. He'd go—he'd see her at least; perhaps he should see what it meant. He felt as if some of the elements of a hard sum had been given him and the others were wanting: he couldn't do his sum till he had got all his figures.

He dressed and drove quickly, so that by half-past eleven he was at Manchester Square. There were a good many carriages at the door—a party was going on; a circumstance which at the last gave him a slight relief, for now he would rather see her in a crowd. People passed him on the staircase; they were going away, going "on" with the hunted herdlike movement of London society at night. But sundry groups remained in the drawing-room, and it was some minutes, as she didn't hear him announced, before he discovered and spoke to her. In this short interval he had seen St. George talking to a lady before the fireplace; but he at once looked away, feeling unready for an encounter, and therefore couldn't be sure the author of "Shadowmere" noticed him. At all events he didn't come over; though Miss Fancourt did as soon as she saw him—she almost rushed at him, smiling rustling radiant beautiful. He had forgotten what her head, what her face offered to the sight; she was in white, there were gold figures on her dress and her hair was a casque of gold. He saw in a single moment that she was happy, happy with an aggressive splendour. But she wouldn't speak to him of that, she would speak only of himself.

"I'm so delighted; my father told me. How kind of you to come!" She struck him as so fresh and brave, while his eyes moved over her, that he said to himself irresistibly: "Why to *him*, why not to youth, to strength, to ambition, to a future? Why, in her rich young force, to failure, to abdication, to superannuation?" In his thought at that sharp moment he blasphemed even against all that had been left of his faith in the peccable master. "I'm so sorry I missed you," she went on. "My father told me. How charming of you to have come so soon!"

"Does that surprise you?" Paul Overt asked.

"The first day? No, from you—nothing that's nice." She was interrupted by a lady who bade her good-night, and he seemed to read that it cost her nothing to speak to him in that tone; it was her old liberal lavish way, with a certain added amplitude that time had brought; and if this manner began to operate on the spot, at such a juncture in her history, perhaps in the other days too it had meant just as little or as much—a mere mechanical charity, with the difference now that she was satisfied, ready to give but in want of nothing. Oh she was satisfied—and why shouldn't she be? Why shouldn't she have been surprised at his coming the first day —for all the good she had ever got from him? As the lady continued to hold her attention Paul turned from her with a strange irritation in his complicated artistic soul and a sort of disinterested disappointment. She was so happy that it was almost stupid—a disproof of the extraordinary intelligence he had formerly found in her. Didn't she know how bad St. George could be, hadn't she recognised the awful thinness——? If she didn't she was nothing, and if she did why such an insolence of serenity? This question expired as our young man's eyes settled at last on the genius who had advised him in a great crisis. St. George was still before the chimney-piece, but now he was alone—fixed, waiting, as if he meant to stop after every one—and he met the clouded gaze of the young friend so troubled as to the degree of his right (the right his resentment would have enjoyed) to regard himself as a victim. Somehow the ravage of the question was checked by the Master's radiance. It was as fine in its way as Marian Fancourt's, it denoted the happy human being; but also it represented to Paul Overt that the author of "Shadowmere" had now definitely ceased to count—ceased to count as a writer. As he smiled a welcome across the place he was almost *banal*, was almost smug. Paul fancied that for a moment he hesitated to make a movement, as if, for all the world, he *had* his bad conscience; then they had already met in the middle of the room and had shaken hands—expressively, cordially on St. George's part. With which they had passed back together to where the elder man had been standing, while St. George said: "I hope you're never go-

ing away again. I've been dining here; the General told me."
He was handsome, he was young, he looked as if he had still
a great fund of life. He bent the friendliest, most unconfess-
ing eyes on his disciple of a couple of years before; asked
him about everything, his health, his plans, his late occupations, the new book. "When will it be out—soon, soon, I
hope? Splendid, eh? That's right; you're a comfort, you're a
luxury! I've read you all over again these last six months."
Paul waited to see if he'd tell him what the General had told
him in the afternoon and what Miss Fancourt, verbally at
least, of course hadn't. But as it didn't come out he at last
put the question, "Is it true, the great news I hear—that
you're to be married?"

"Ah you *have* heard it, then?"

"Didn't the General tell you?" Paul asked.

The Master's face was wonderful. "Tell me what?"

"That he mentioned it to me this afternoon?"

"My dear fellow, I don't remember. We've been in the
midst of people. I'm sorry, in the case, that I lose the pleasure, myself, of announcing to you a fact that touches me so
nearly. It *is* a fact, strange as it may appear. It has only just
become one. Isn't it ridiculous?" St. George made this speech
without confusion, but on the other hand, so far as our friend
could judge, without latent impudence. It struck his interlocutor that, to talk so comfortably and coolly, he must
simply have forgotten what had passed between them. His
next words, however, showed he hadn't, and they produced,
as an appeal to Paul's own memory, an effect which would
have been ludicrous if it hadn't been cruel. "Do you recall
the talk we had at my house that night, into which Miss Fancourt's name entered? I've often thought of it since."

"Yes; no wonder you said what you did"—Paul was careful to meet his eyes.

"In the light of the present occasion? Ah but there was no
light then. How could I have foreseen this hour?"

"Didn't you think it probable?"

"Upon my honour, no," said Henry St. George. "Certainly
I owe you that assurance. Think how my situation has
changed."

"I see—I see," our young man murmured.

His companion went on as if, now that the subject had
been broached, he was, as a person of imagination and tact,
quite ready to give every satisfaction—being both by his genius and his method so able to enter into everything another

might feel. "But it's not only that; for honestly, at my age, I never dreamed—a widower with big boys and with so little else! It has turned out differently from anything one could have dreamed, and I'm fortunate beyond all measure. She has been so free, and yet she consents. Better than any one else perhaps—for I remember how you liked her before you went away, and how she liked you—you can intelligently congratulate me."

"She has been so free!" Those words made a great impression on Paul Overt, and he almost writhed under that irony in them as to which it so little mattered whether it was designed or casual. Of course she had been free, and appreciably perhaps by his own act; for wasn't the Master's allusion to her having liked him a part of the irony too? "I thought that by your theory you disapproved of a writer's marrying."

"Surely—surely. But you don't call me a writer?"

"You ought to be ashamed," said Paul.

"Ashamed of marrying again?"

"I won't say that—but ashamed of your reasons."

The elder man beautifully smiled. "You must let me judge of them, my good friend."

"Yes; why not? For you judged wonderfully of mine."

The tone of these words appeared suddenly, for St. George, to suggest the unsuspected. He stated as if divining a bitterness. "Don't you think I've been straight?"

"You might have told me at the time perhaps."

"My dear fellow, when I say I couldn't pierce futurity——!"

"I mean afterwards."

The Master wondered. "After my wife's death?"

"When this idea came to you."

"Ah never, never! I wanted to save you, rare and precious as you are."

Poor Overt looked hard at him. "Are you marrying Miss Fancourt to save me?"

"Not absolutely, but it adds to the pleasure. I shall be the making of you," St. George smiled. "I was greatly struck, after our talk, with the brave devoted way you quitted the country, and still more perhaps with your force of character in remaining abroad. You're very strong—you're wonderfully strong."

Paul tried to sound his shining eyes; the strange thing was that he seemed sincere—not a mocking fiend. He turned away, and as he did so heard the Master say something about his giving them all the proof, being the joy of his old age. He faced him again, taking another look. "Do you mean to say you've stopped writing?"

"My dear fellow, of course I have. It's too late. Didn't I tell you?"

"I can't believe it!"

"Of course you can't—with your own talent! No, no; for the rest of my life I shall only read *you*."

"Does she know that—Miss Fancourt?"

"She will—she will." Did he mean this, our young man wondered, as a covert intimation that the assistance he should derive from that young lady's fortune, moderate as it was, would make the difference of putting it in his power to cease to work ungratefully an exhausted vein? Somehow, standing there in the ripeness of his successful manhood, he didn't suggest that any of his veins were exhausted. "Don't you remember the moral I offered myself to you that night as pointing?" St. George continued. "Consider at any rate the warning I am at present."

This was too much—he *was* the mocking fiend. Paul turned from him with a mere nod for good-night and the sense in a sore heart that he might come back to him and his easy grace, his fine way of arranging things, some time in the far future, but couldn't fraternise with him now. It was necessary to his soreness to believe for the hour in the intensity of his grievance—all the more cruel for its not being a legal one. It was doubtless in the attitude of hugging this wrong that he descended the stairs without taking leave of Miss Fancourt, who hadn't been in view at the moment he quitted the room. He was glad to get out into the honest dusky unsophisticating night, to move fast, to take his way home on foot. He walked a long time, going astray, paying no attention. He was thinking of too many other things. His steps recovered their direction, however, and at the end of an hour he found himself before his door in the small inexpensive empty street. He lingered, questioning himself still before going in, with nothing around and above him but moonless blackness, a bad lamp or two and a few far-away dim stars. To these last faint features he raised his eyes; he had been saying to himself that he should have been "sold" indeed, diabolically sold, if now, on his new foundation, at the end of a year, St. George were to put forth something of his prime quality—something of the type of "Shadowmere" and finer than his finest. Greatly as he admired his talent Paul literally hoped such an incident wouldn't occur; it seemed to him just then that he shouldn't be able to bear it. His late adviser's words were still in his ears—"You're very strong, wonderfully strong." Was he really? Certainly he would have to be, and it might a little serve for revenge. *Is* he? the reader may ask in turn, if his interest has followed the perplexed young man so far. The best answer to that perhaps is that he's doing his best, but that it's too soon to say. When the new book came out in the autumn Mr. and Mrs. St. George found it really magnificent. The former still has published nothing, but Paul doesn't even yet feel safe. I may say for him, however, that if this event were to occur he would really be the very first to appreciate it: which is perhaps a proof that the Master was essentially right and that Nature had dedicated him to intellectual, not to personal passion.

The Metamorphosis

BY FRANZ KAFKA
(1883-1924)

Franz Kafka wrote slowly and with meticulous care, striving for and achieving a remarkable, clear, precise prose. He had just entered his forties when he died. His novels— The Trial, The Castle, Amerika—*were not yet in print. He left the manuscripts to Max Brod, his biographer, telling Brod to destroy them. Fortunately Brod decided otherwise and the novels were published. Kafka's reputation since his death has grown steadily, and he is ranked by many critics among the greatest of the modern writers. He combined in his fiction realistic detail with symbolic, dreamlike situations and scenes that reveal the anxieties and the isolation of modern man. Though he wrote in German, Kafka was born in Prague, Czechoslovakia, to a well-to-do family. He studied law, then worked in the office of the workmen's compensation division of the Austrian government. The profound effect of Kafka's family life on his personality, especially his alienation from his father, is reflected in many of his stories, including* The Metamorphosis, *first published in 1916.*

The Metamorphosis

When Gregor Samsa awoke one morning from a troubled dream, he found himself changed into some kind of monstrous vermin.

He lay on his back, which was as hard as armor plate. By raising his head a little, he could see the arch of his large brown belly, divided into bowed corrugations. The bedcover was sliding off the top of the curve; Gregor's legs, pitiably thin compared with their former size, fluttered uselessly before his eyes.

"What has happened?" he pondered. It was no dream. His room, a man's room—though rather small—lay still within its four familiar walls. Above the table, upon which was scattered a collection of cloth samples—Samsa was a commercial traveler—hung a picture that he had recently cut from a newspaper and had put in a gilded frame. The picture showed a lady sitting very straight, wearing a small fur hat and a fur boa; into a heavy muff her arm was thrust up to the elbow.

Gregor looked toward the window; he could hear rain falling on the panes; the foggy weather saddened him. "Supposing I go to sleep again for awhile and forget all this stupidity?" he thought; but it was absolutely out of the question. He was used to sleeping on his right side and in his present plight he could not get into that position. No matter how violently he tried to throw himself on his side, he always turned over on his back. He tried a hundred times, keeping his eyes closed so that he should not see his trembling legs; he did not give up until he felt a slight but deep pain in his side, a pain he had never known before.

"God!" he thought, "What a job I've chosen. Traveling day in, day out. A much more vexing occupation than working in the office! Apart from business itself, the bother of traveling: the anxieties of changing trains, the irregular, inferior meals, the ever changing faces never seen again, people with whom one had no chance to be friendly. To hell with it all!" He felt a little itch above his stomach and wriggled nearer to the bedpost, pulling himself slowly on his back so that he might more easily raise his head; he saw, right where he was itching, a few little white points, whose purpose he could not guess; he tried to scratch the place with one of his feet but he drew it back quickly: the contact made him shudder.

He returned to his former position. He said to himself: "Nothing is more degrading than always to have to rise so early. A man must have his sleep. Other travelers can live like harem women. When I return to the hotel in the morning to enter my orders, I find those gentlemen still at breakfast. I'd like to see what my boss would say if I tried it; I would be sacked immediately. Who knows if that wouldn't be a good thing, after all! If it weren't for my parents, I would have given notice long ago; I would have gone to the boss and I wouldn't have minced matters. He would have fallen from his desk. That's a funny thing; to sit on a desk so as to speak to one's employees from such a height, especially when one is hard of hearing and people must come close! Still, all hope is not lost; once I have got together the money my parents owe him—that will be in about five or six years—I shall certainly do it. Then I'll take the big step! Meanwhile, I must get up; my train goes at five."

He looked at the alarm clock which was ticking on the chest. "My God!" he thought; it was half-past six; quarter to seven was not far off. Hadn't the alarm rung? From the bed he could see that the little hand was set at four, sure enough; the alarm had sounded. But had he been able to sleep calmly through that furniture-shattering din? Calmly, no; his sleep had not been calm; but he had slept only the sounder for that. What should he do now?

The next train went at seven; to catch it he must hurry madly, and his collection of samples was not packed; besides, he himself did not feel at all rested nor inclined to move. And even if he did catch the train, his employer's anger was inevitable, since the firm's errand boy would have been waiting at the five o'clock train and would have notified the firm of his lapse. He was just a toady to his boss, a stupid and servile boy. Supposing Gregor pretended to be ill? But that would be foolish, and suspicious, too; during the four years he had been with the firm he had never had the slightest illness. The manager would come with the Health Insurance doctor; he would reproach his parents for their son's idleness and would cut short any objections by giving the doctor's arguments that no people are sick, only idle. And would he be so far wrong, in such a case? Gregor felt in very good fettle, apart from his unnecessary need for more sleep after such a long night; he even had an unusually keen appetite.

Just as he was rapidly turning these thoughts over in his mind without being able to decide to leave the bed—while the alarm clock struck a quarter to seven—he heard a cautious knock on his door, close by the head of his bed.

"Gregor," someone called—it was his mother—"It is a quarter to seven. Didn't you want to catch the train?"

What a soft voice! Gregor trembled as he heard his own voice reply. It was unmistakably his former voice, but with it could be heard, as if from below, a painful whining, which only allowed the words their real shape for a moment, immediately to confuse their sound so that one wondered if one had really heard right. Gregor would have liked to answer fully and to give an explanation but, in these circumstances, he contented himself by saying, "Yes, yes, thank you, mother. I am just getting up." No doubt the door prevented her from judging the change in Gregor's voice, for the explanation reassured his mother, who went away, shuffling in her slippers. But because of this little dialogue the other members of the family had become aware that, contrary to custom, Gregor was still in the house, and his father started to knock on one of the side doors, softly, but with his fists.

"Gregor, Gregor," he cried, "what is the matter?" And, after a moment, in a warning tone, "Gregor! Gregor!"

At the other side door, the young man's sister softly called, "Gregor, aren't you well? Do you need anything?"

"I am getting ready," said Gregor, answering both sides and forcing himself to pronounce carefully and to separate each word with a long pause, to keep a natural voice.

His father went back to breakfast, but the sister still whispered, "Gregor, open the door, I beg you." But Gregor had no intention of answering this request; on the contrary, he complimented himself on having developed the habit of always locking his door, as if in a hotel.

He would get up quietly, without being bothered by anyone; he would dress, and, above all, he would have breakfast; then would come the time to reflect, for he felt it was not in bed that a reasonable solution could be found. He recalled how often an unusual position adopted in bed had resulted in slight pains which proved imaginary as soon as he arose, and Gregor was curious to see his present hallucination gradually dissolve. As for the change in his voice, his private opinion was that it was the prelude to some serious quinsy, the occupational malady of travelers.

He had no difficulty in turning back the coverlet; he needed only to blow himself up a little, and it fell of its own accord. But beyond that he was impeded by his tremendous girth. To get up, he needed arms and hands; but he had only numerous little legs, in perpetual vibration, over which he had no control. Before he could bend one leg, he first had to stretch it out; and when at last he had performed the desired movement, all the other legs worked uncontrollably, in intensely painful agitation. "I must not stay uselessly in bed," said Gregor to himself.

To get his body out of bed, he first tried moving the hind part. But unfortunately this hind part, which he had not yet seen, and of which he could form no very precise idea, went so slowly it proved to be very difficult to move; he summoned all his strength to throw himself forward but, ill-calculating his course, he hurled himself violently against one of the bedposts, and the searing pain he felt showed that the lower part of his body was without doubt the most sensitive.

He then tried to start with the fore part of his body and cautiously turned his head toward the side of the bed. In this he succeeded quite easily, and the rest of his body, despite its weight and size, followed the direction of his head. But when his head left the bed and was hanging in mid-air, he was afraid to continue any further; if he were to fall in this position; it would be a miracle if he did not crack his head; and this was no moment to lose his senses—better to stay in bed.

But when, panting with his efforts, he again found himself stretched out just as before, when he saw his little legs struggling more wildly than ever, despairing of finding any means of bringing peace and order into this chaotic procedure, he once again realized that he absolutely could not stay in bed and that it was perfectly reasonable to sacrifice everything to the slightest chance of getting out. At the same time he did not forget that cool and wise reflection would be far better than desperate resolutions. Ordinarily, at such moments he turned his eyes to the window to gain encouragement and hope. But the fog prevented him from seeing the other side of the street; the window gave him neither confidence nor strength. "Seven o'clock already," he said as he listened once more to the sound of the alarm clock. "Seven o'clock already, and the fog has got no thinner!" He lay back again for a moment, breathing weakly, as though, in the complete silence, he could calmly await the return to his normal self.

Then he said, "Before a quarter past it is absolutely essential for me to be up. But someone will be sent from the office to ask for me before then, for the place opens at seven." And he began to rock on his back in order to get his whole body out of bed in one movement. In this manner he would be able to protect his head by raising it sharply as he fell. His back seemed to be hard; nothing would be risked by falling on it to the floor; his only fear was that the noise of his fall, which would surely resound through the whole house, might arouse terror, or, at the very least, uneasiness. However, that would have to be risked.

When Gregor had half his body out of bed—the new method seemed more like a game than a task, for he had only to swing himself on his back—he began to think how easily he could have got up if only he had had a little assistance. Two strong people—he thought of his father and the servant girl—would have been quite enough; they would have needed only to pass their arms under his round back, raise it from the bed, quickly lean forward with their burden, and then wait carefully till he had completed the operation of settling himself on the ground, where he hoped his feet would at last find a way of working together. But even if the doors had not been closed, would it have been wise for him to call for help? At this idea, despite his misery, he could not repress a smile.

Now he had progressed so far that, by sharply accentuating his swinging movement, he felt he was nearly losing his balance; he would have to take a serious decision, for in five minutes it would be a quarter to eight—but suddenly there was a knock at the front door.

"Someone from the office," he said to himself, and he felt his blood run cold, while his little legs quickened their saraband. For a moment all was quiet.

"They're not going to the door," thought Gregor, in an access of absurd hope. But of course the maid, with a firm tread, went to the door and opened it. Gregor needed to hear only the caller's first words of greeting to know immediately who it was—the manager himself. Why was Gregor, particularly, condemned to work for a firm where the worst was suspected at the slightest inadvertence of the employees? Were the employees, without exception, all scoundrels? Was there among their number not one devoted, faithful servant, who, if it did so happen that by chance he missed a few hours work one morning, might have found himself so numbed with remorse that he just could not leave his bed? Would it not have been enough to send some apprentice to put things right—if it was necessary to make inquiries at all—instead of the manager himself having to come, in order to let the whole innocent family know that the clearing-up of so suspicious an affair could only be entrusted to a person of his importance? These thoughts so irritated Gregor that he swung himself out of bed with all his might. This made a loud thud, but not the terrible crash that he had feared. The carpet somewhat softened the blow, and Gregor's back was more elastic than he had thought; thus his act was not accompanied by any din. Only his head had been slightly hurt. Gregor had not raised it enough, and it had been knocked by his fall. In pain and anger he turned over a little to rub it on the carpet.

"Something fell in there just then," cried the manager, in the room on the left. Gregor tried to imagine his employer's face if such a mishap had occurred to him; for such a thing was possible, he had to admit. But, as if in brutal reply, the manager began pacing up and down in the next room, making his patent-leather boots creak.

And in the other room on the right, Gregor's sister whispered to warn her brother, "Gregor, the manager is here."

"I know," said Gregor to himself, but he dared not raise his voice enough for his sister to hear.

"Gregor," said his father in the room on the left, "the manager has come to find out why you didn't catch the early train. We don't know what to say. He wants to speak to you personally. So please open the door. I'm sure he will be kind enough to excuse the untidiness of your room."

"Good morning, good morning, Mr. Samsa," interrupted the manager, cordial and brisk.

"He is not well," said his mother to the manager, while his father went on shouting through the door. "Believe me, he is not well, sir. How else could Gregor have missed the train?

The boy thinks of nothing but his work! It makes me upset to see how he never goes out after supper; do you know he's just spent a whole week here and been at home every evening! He sits down with us at the table and stays there, quietly reading the paper or studying his timetables. His greatest indulgence is to do a little fretwork. Just lately he made a small picture frame. It was finished in two or three evenings, and you'd be surprised how pretty it is; it is hanging up in his room. As soon as Gregor opens his door, you will be able to see it. I am so glad you came, sir, because without you we would never have got Gregor to open his door, he is so obstinate; and surely he must be ill, even though he denied it this morning."

"I am coming," said Gregor slowly and carefully, but he continued to lie still, so as not to miss a word of the conversation.

"I can offer no other suggestion," declared the manager. "Let us only hope it is nothing serious. However, we businessmen must often—fortunately or not, as you will—do our jobs and ignore our little indispositions."

"Well, can the manager come in now?" asked his father impatiently, knocking on the door again.

"No," said Gregor. In the room on the left there was a painful silence; in that on the right the sister began to sob.

Why did she not go to the others? Possibly she had just got out of bed and was not yet dressed. And why did she weep? Because he did not get up to let the manager in, because he risked losing his position, and because the boss would once more worry his parents about their old debts? These were misplaced troubles! Gregor was still there and had not the slightest intention of letting his family down. At this very moment he was stretched out on the carpet, and nobody seeing him in this state could seriously have demanded that he should let the manager enter his room. But it was not on account of this slight impoliteness—for which in normal times he could easily have made his excuses later—that Gregor would be dismissed. And he thought it would be more reasonable, just now, to leave him alone rather than to upset him with tears and speeches. But it was just this uncertainty which was making the others uneasy and which excused their behavior.

"Herr Samsa," now cried the manager, raising his voice, "What is the matter? You barricade yourself in your room, you don't answer yes or no, you needlessly upset your parents, and you neglect your professional duties in an unheard-of manner. I am speaking in the name of your employer and of your parents, and I beg you seriously to give us a satisfactory explanation immediately. I am astonished, astonished! I took you for a quiet, reasonable young man, and here you suddenly give yourself airs, behaving in an absolutely fantastic manner! The head of the firm, speaking to me this morning in your absence, suggested an explanation which I rejected; he mentioned the samples which were entrusted to you a while ago. I gave him my word of honor that this had nothing to do with the affair, but now that I have been witness to your obstinacy, I can assure you, Herr Samsa, that it deprives me of any wish to defend you. Your job is by no means safe! I had intended to tell you this in private but, since you oblige me to waste my time here for nothing, I see no reason for keeping quiet before your parents. I'd have you know that lately your work has been far from satisfactory; we realize, of course, that the time of the year is not propitious for big business, but you must understand, Herr Samsa, that a period with no business at all should not and can not be tolerated!"

Gregor was beside himself; in his anxiety he forgot everything else. "But, sir," he cried, "I will open the door immediately. I will open it. I felt a little ill; a slight giddiness prevented me from getting up. I am still in bed. But I feel better already. I am just getting up. Only a moment's patience. I am not quite so well as I thought. But I am all right, really. How can it be that illness should take one so quickly? Only yesterday I felt quite well, my parents can tell you; and then last evening I had a slight symptom. They must have noticed it. Why didn't I let them know at the office! But then, one always thinks one will be able to get rid of an illness without staying at home. Please, sir, spare my parents. The complaints you made just now are really without foundation. No one has even suggested them before. Perhaps you have not seen the last orders I sent in. I will leave on the eight-o'clock train; these few moments of rest have done me a great deal of good. Please don't stay, sir, I shall be at the office immediately; and please inform the director of what has happened and put in a good word for me."

And while Gregor hastily cried these words, scarcely realizing what he said, he had, with an ease due to his previous exertions, approached the chest of drawers, against which

he now tried to raise himself. He wanted to open the door;
he wanted to be seen and to speak with the manager. He was
curious to know what impression he would make on these
people who were so imperiously demanding his presence. If
he frightened them, that would be reassuring, for he would
stop being cross-questioned and be left in peace. If they
took everything quietly then he, too, need not be alarmed.
And if he hurried he might still catch the eight o'clock train.
The chest was polished, and Gregor slipped on it several times but, by a supreme effort, he managed to get upright. He paid no attention to the pains in his stomach,
though they were hurting him. He let himself drop forward
to the top of a nearby chair and clung there with his little
legs. Then, finding himself master of his body, he stayed very
quiet in order to listen to what the manager had to say.

"Did you understand a word of what he said?" the
manager asked the parents. "Is he trying to make fools of
us?"

"Good heavens," cried the mother, already in tears. "Perhaps he is seriously ill, and here we are torturing him! Grete!
Grete!" she called.

"Mother!" cried the daughter from the other side. They
were separated by Gregor's room.

"Fetch a doctor immediately. Gregor is ill. A doctor,
quickly! Did you hear him speak?"

"It was an animal's voice," said the manager; after the
cries of the women, his voice seemed curiously gentle.

"Anna, Anna!" shouted the father through the hall into
the kitchen, clapping his hands. "Get a locksmith, quick!"
And already the two young girls—how could his sister have
dressed so soon?—ran along the corridor with rustling skirts
and opened the front door. No one heard the door close; no
doubt it had been left open, as is the custom in houses to
which a great misfortune has come.

However, Gregor had become calmer. Doubtless they had
not understood his words, though they had seemed clear
enough to him, clearer, indeed, than the first time; perhaps
his ears were becoming more accustomed to the sounds. But
at least they were obliged to realize that his case was not normal, and they were ready, now, to help him. The assurance
and resourcefulness with which the first steps had been taken
comforted him considerably. He felt himself integrated into
human society once again, and, without differentiating between them, he hoped for great and surprising things from

the locksmith and the doctor. To clear his throat for the decisive conversation which he would have to hold soon, he coughed a little, but as quietly as possible, for he feared that even his cough might not sound human. Meanwhile, in the next room, it had become quiet. Perhaps his parents were sitting at table in a secret conference with the manager; perhaps everyone was leaning against the door, listening.

Gregor made his way slowly toward it with the chair; then he abandoned the chair and flung himself at the door, holding himself erect against the woodwork—for the bottoms of his feet secreted a sticky substance—and he rested a moment from his efforts. After this, he tried to turn the key in the lock with his mouth. Unfortunately, it seemed he had no proper teeth. How could he take hold of the key? In compensation, instead of teeth he possessed a pair of very strong mandibles and succeeded in seizing the key in the lock, regardless of the pain this caused him; a brownish liquid flowed out of his mouth, spread over the lock, and dropped to the floor.

"Listen!" said the manager in the next room. "He is just turning the key."

This was valuable encouragement for Gregor; he would have liked his father, his mother, everybody, to start calling to him, "Courage, Gregor, go on, push hard!" And, with the idea that everyone was following his efforts with passionate attention, he clutched the key with all the power of his jaws until he was nearly unconscious. Following the progress of the turning key, he twisted himself around the lock, hanging on by his mouth, and, clinging to the key, pressed it down again, whenever it slipped, with all the weight of his body. The clear click of the lock as it snapped back awoke Gregor from his momentary coma.

"I have dispensed with the locksmith," he thought, and sighed and leaned his head against the handle to open one panel of the double doors completely.

This method, the only possible one, prevented the others from seeing him for some time, even with the door open. Still erect, he had to grope his way round the door with great caution in order not to spoil his entry by falling flat on his back; so he was concentrating toward this end, with all his attention absorbed by the maneuver, when he heard the manager utter a sonorous, "Oh!" such as the roaring of the wind produces, and saw him—he was just by the door—press his hand over his open mouth and slowly stagger back as if some invisible and intensely powerful force were driving him from the spot. His mother—who, despite the presence of the manager, was standing by with her hair in curlers, still disordered by sleep—began to look at the father, clasping her hands; then she made two steps toward Gregor and fell backward into the family circle in the midst of a confusion of skirts which spread around her, while her face, falling on her breast, was concealed from sight. The father clenched his fists with a menacing air, as if to beat Gregor back into his room; then he looked around the dining room in perplexity, covered his eyes with his hand, and wept with great sobs which shook his powerful chest.

Gregor did not enter the room; he stood against the closed half of the double doors, allowing only a part of his body to be seen, while, above, he turned his head to one side to see what would happen. Meanwhile, it had grown much lighter; on either side of the street a part of the long, dark building opposite could clearly be seen—it was a hospital, with regular windows startlingly pitting its façade; it was still raining, but in great separate drops which fell to the ground, one by one. The breakfast crockery was spread all over the table, for breakfast was the most important meal of the day for Gregor's father; he would prolong it for hours while he read various newspapers. On the wall hung a photograph of Gregor in lieutenant's uniform, taken while he was in military service; he was smiling; his hand lay on the hilt of his sword. By his expression, he seemed happy to be alive; by his gesture, he appeared to command respect for his rank. The living-room door was ajar, and, as the front door was also open, the balcony and the first steps of the stairway could just be seen.

"Now," said Gregor, and he realized that he was the only one to have kept calm, "now I will get dressed, collect my samples, and go. Will you, will you let me go? Surely you can now see, sir, that I am not obstinate, that I do mean to work; commercial traveling is tiresome, I admit, but without it I cannot live. Where are you going, sir? To the office? Yes? Will you give them a faithful account of what has happened? After all, anyone might find for a moment that they were incapable of resuming their work, but that's just a good opportunity to review the work they have been doing, and to bear in mind that, once the obstacle is removed, they will be able to return with twice the heart. I owe so much to the director, as you know very well. I have my parents and my sister to consider. I am in an awkward position, but I shall return to work. Only, please do not make things more difficult for me; they are hard enough as it is. Take my part at the office. I know only too well they don't like travelers. They think we earn our money too easily, that we lead too grand a life. I realize that the present situation doesn't encourage the removal of this prejudice; but you, sir, the manager, can judge the circumstances better than the rest of the staff, better than the director himself—though this is between ourselves—for in his executive capacity he is often easily misled by an employee's prejudice. You know quite well that the traveler, who is hardly ever in the office the whole year round, is often the victim of scandal, of a chance, undeserved complaint against which he is powerless to defend himself, for he does not even know that he is being accused; he only learns of it as he returns, exhausted, at the end of his trip, when the sad consequences of an affair, whose circumstances he can no longer recall, painfully confront him. Please, sir, don't leave me without a word to show that you think all this at least a little reasonable."

But, at Gregor's first words, the manager had turned away and only glanced back, with snarling lips, over his trembling shoulder. During Gregor's speech, he had not stood still for a moment; instead, he had retreated furtively, step by step, toward the door—always keeping Gregor in sight—as if some secret law forbade him to leave the room. He had already reached the hall and, as he took the very last step out of the living room, one would have thought the floor was burning his shoes, so sharply did he spring. Then he stretched his hand toward the balustrade, as if some unearthly deliverance awaited him at the foot of the stairs.

Gregor realized that, if he were to keep his job, on no account must the manager be allowed to leave in this condition. Unfortunately, his parents did not realize the position very clearly; they had for so long held the idea that Gregor was settled in the firm for life and were so taken up with their present troubles that they had little thought for such a contingency. But Gregor had more foresight. The manager must be stopped, calmed, convinced, and finally won over. The future of Gregor and of his family depended on it! If only his sister were there! She had understood, she had actually begun to weep while Gregor still lay quietly on his back. And the manager, who liked women, would have listened to her; he would have let himself be guided by her; she would have closed the door and would have proved to him, in the hall, how unreasonable his terror was. But she was not there; Gregor himself must manage this affair. And without even considering whether he would ever be able to return to work, nor whether his speech had been understood, he let go of the doorpost to glide through the opening and overtake the manager (who was clutching the balustrade with both hands in a ridiculous manner), vainly sought for a foothold, and, uttering a cry, he fell, with his frail little legs crumpled beneath him.

Suddenly, for the first time that whole morning, he experienced a feeling of physical well-being; his feet were on firm ground; he noticed with joy that his legs obeyed him wonderfully and were even eager to carry him wherever he might wish. But while, under the nervous influence of his need for haste, he hesitated on the spot, not far from his mother, he saw her suddenly jump, fainting though she seemed to be, and throw her arms about with outspread fingers, crying, "Help, for God's sake, help!" She turned her head, the better to see Gregor; then, in flagrant contradiction, she began to retreat madly, having forgotten that behind her stood the table, still laden with breakfast things. She staggered against it and sat down suddenly, like one distraught, regardless of the fact that, at her elbow, the overturned coffeepot was making a pool of coffee on the carpet.

"Mother, mother," whispered Gregor, looking up at her. The manager had quite gone out of his mind. Seeing the coffee spilling, Gregor could not prevent himself from snapping his jaws several times in the air, as if he were eating. Thereupon his mother again began to shriek and quickly jumped up from the table and fell into the arms of the father, who had rushed up behind her. But Gregor had no time to bother about them. The manager was already on the stairs; with his chin on the balustrade, he was looking back for the last time.

Gregor summoned all his courage to try to bring him back; the manager must have suspected something of the sort, for he leaped several steps at a single bound and disappeared with a cry of "Huh!" which resounded in the hollow of the stair well. This flight had the unfortunate effect of causing Gregor's father—who till now had remained master of himself—to lose his head completely; instead of running after the manager, or at least not interfering with Gregor in his pursuit, he seized in his right hand the manager's walking stick, which had been left behind on a chair with his overcoat and hat, took up in his left a newspaper from the table, and began stamping his feet and brandishing the newspaper and the cane to drive Gregor back into his room. Gregor's prayers were unavailing, were not even understood; he had turned to his father a supplicating head, but, meek though he showed himself, his father merely stamped all the louder. In the dining room, despite the cold, the mother had opened the window wide and was leaning out as far as possible, pressing her face in her hands. A great rush of air swept the space between the room and the stairway; the curtains billowed, the papers rustled, and a few sheets flew over the carpet. But the father pursued Gregor pitilessly, whistling and whooping like a savage, and Gregor, who was not used to walking backward, progressed but slowly.

Had he been able to turn around, he could have reached his room quickly, but he feared to make his father impatient by the slowness of his turning and feared also that at any moment he might receive a mortal blow on his head or on his back from this menacing stick. Soon Gregor had no choice; for he realized with terror that when he was going backward he was not master of his direction and, still fearfully watching the attitude of his father out of the corner of his eye, he began his turning movement as quickly as possible, which was really only very slowly. Perhaps his father realized his good intention for, instead of hindering this move, he guided him from a little distance away, helping Gregor with the tip of the stick. If only he had left off that insupportable whistling! Gregor was completely losing his head. He had nearly completed his turn when, bewildered by the din, he mistook his direction and began to go back to his former position. When at last, to his great joy, he found himself facing the half-opened double doors, he discovered that his body was too big to pass through without hurt. Naturally, it never occurred to his father, in his present state, to open the other half of the double doors in order to allow Gregor to pass. He was dominated by the one fixed idea that Gregor should be made to return to his room as quickly as possible. He would never have entertained the long-winded performance which Gregor would have needed to rear up and pass inside. Gregor heard him storming behind him, no doubt to urge him through as though there were no obstacle in his path; the hubbub no longer sounded like the voice of one single father.

Now was no time to play, and Gregor—come what may—hurled himself into the doorway. There he lay, jammed in a slanting position, his body raised up on one side and his flank crushed by the door jamb, whose white paint was now covered with horrible brown stains. He was caught fast and could not free himself unaided; on one side his little legs fluttered in the air, on the other they were painfully pressed under his body; then his father gave him a tremendous blow from behind with the stick. Despite the pain, this was almost a relief; he was lifted bodily into the middle of the room and fell, bleeding thickly. The door was slammed by a thrust of the stick, and then, at last, all was still.

II

It was dusk when Gregor awoke from his heavy, deathlike sleep. Even had he not been disturbed, he would doubtless soon have awakened, for he felt he had had his fill of rest and sleep; however, he seemed to have been awakened by the cautious, furtive noise of a key turning in the lock of the hall door. The reflection of the electric tramway lay dimly here and there about the ceiling and on the upper parts of the furniture, but below, where Gregor was, it was dark. Slowly he dragged himself toward the door to ascertain what had happened and fumbled around clumsily with his feelers, whose use he was at last learning to appreciate. His left side seemed to him to be one long, irritating scar, and he limped about on his double set of legs. One of his legs had been seriously injured during the morning's events—it was a miracle that only one should be hurt—and it dragged lifelessly behind.

When he reached the door, he realized what had attracted him: the smell of food. For there was a bowl of sweetened milk in which floated little pieces of bread. He could have laughed with delight, his appetite had grown so since morning; he thrust his head up to the eyes in the milk. But he drew it back quickly; his painful left side gave him some difficulty, for he could only eat by convulsing his whole body and snorting; also, he could not bear the smell of milk, which once had been his favorite drink and which his sister had no doubt prepared for this special reason. He turned from the bowl in disgust and dragged himself to the middle of the room.

The gas was lit in the dining room; he could see it through the cracks of the door. Now was the time when, ordinarily, his father would read aloud to his family from the evening paper, but this time Gregor heard nothing. Perhaps this traditional reading, which his sister always retailed to him in her conversation and in her letters, had not lapsed entirely from the customs of the household. But everywhere was still, and yet surely someone was in the room.

"What a quiet life my family has led," thought Gregor, staring before him in the darkness, and he felt very proud, for it was to him that his parents and his sister owed so placid a life in so nice a flat. What would happen now, if this peace, this satisfaction, this well-being should end in terror and disaster? In order to dissipate such gloomy thoughts, Gregor began to take a little exercise and crawled back and forth over the floor.

Once during the evening he saw the door on the left open slightly, and once it was the door on the right; someone had wished to enter but had found the task too risky. Gregor resolved to stop by the dining-room door and to entice the hesitant visitor as best he might or at least to see who it was; but the door never opened again, and Gregor waited in vain. That morning, when the door had been locked, everyone had tried to invade his room; but now that they had succeeded in opening it no one came to see him; they had even locked his doors on the outside.

Not till late was the light extinguished, and Gregor could guess that his parents and his sister had been waiting till then, for he heard them all go off on tiptoe. Now no one would come to him till the morning, and so he would have the necessary time to reflect on the ordering of his new life; but his great room, in which he was obliged to remain flat on his stomach on the floor, frightened him in a way that he could not understand—for he had lived in it for the past five years—and, with a half-involuntary action of which he was a little ashamed, he hastily slid under the couch; he soon found that here his back was a little crushed and he could not raise his head; he only regretted that his body was too large to go entirely under the couch.

He spent the whole night there, sometimes in a half-sleep from which the pangs of hunger would wake him with a start, sometimes ruminating on his misfortune and his vague hopes, always concluding that his duty was to remain docile and to try to make things bearable for his family, whatever unpleasantness the situation might impose upon them.

Early in the morning he had a chance to test the strength

of his new resolutions; it was still almost dark; his sister, already half dressed, opened the hall door and looked in curiously. She did not see Gregor at once but when she perceived him under the sofa—"Heavens, he must be somewhere; he can't have flown away!"—she was overcome by an unmanageable terror and rushed off, slamming the door. Then, repenting her gesture, she opened it again and entered on tiptoe, as if it were the room of a stranger or one seriously ill. Gregor stretched his head out from the side of the sofa and watched her. Would she notice that he had left the milk, and not from lack of appetite? Would she bring him something which suited his taste better? If she did not do so of her own accord, he would rather have died of hunger than draw her attention to these things, despite his overwhelming desire to rush out of his hiding place, to throw himself at his sister's feet, and to beg for something to eat. But suddenly the sister saw the full bowl in astonishment. A little milk had been spilled around it; using a piece of paper, she took up the bowl without touching it and carried it off to the kitchen. Gregor waited anxiously to see what she would bring him in its place and racked his brains to guess. But he had never realized to what lengths his sister's kindness would go. In order to discover her brother's likes, she brought a whole choice of eatables spread on an old newspaper. There were half-rotted stumps of vegetables, the bones of yesterday's dinner covered with a thick white sauce, a few currants and raisins, some almonds, some cheese that Gregor, a few days before, had declared uneatable, a stale loaf, a piece of salted bread and butter, and another without salt. Besides this she brought back the bowl which had become so important to Gregor. This time it was filled with water, and, guessing that her brother would not like to eat before her, she very kindly retired, closing and locking the door to show him that he might eat in peace. Now that his meal was ready, Gregor felt all his legs trembling. His wounds seemed cured, for he felt not the slightest hindrance, and he was astonished to remember that when he had been human and had cut his finger slightly only a few months ago, it had pained him for several days after.

"Have I become less sensitive?" he wondered; but already he had begun sucking at the cheese, which had suddenly and imperiously attracted him above all the other food. Gluttonously he swallowed in turn the cheese, the vegetables, and the sauce, his eyes moist with satisfaction; as to the fresh things, he wanted none of them; their smell repelled him, and, in order to eat, he separated them from the others.

When he had finished and was idly making up his mind to return to his place, his sister slowly began to turn the key in the lock to give him the signal for retreat. He was very frightened, though he was half asleep, and hurried to reach the sofa. It needed great determination to remain beneath it during the time, however short, that his sister was in the room; his heavy meal had so swollen his body that he could scarcely breathe in his retreat. Between two fits of suffocation he saw, with his eyes filled with tears, that his sister, intending no harm, was sweeping up the remains of his meal with the very things that he had not touched, as if he needed them no more; she put the refuse into a bucket, which she covered with a wooden lid and hastily carried away. Hardly had she turned the handle before Gregor struggled out from his hiding place to expand his body to its proper size.

So he was fed each day; in the morning, before his parents and the maid were awake, and in the afternoon, when lunch was over and while his parents were taking their nap and the maid had been provided with some task or other by his sister. Certainly they did not wish Gregor to die of hunger but perhaps they preferred to know nothing about his meals except by hearsay—they could not have borne to see him—perhaps, also, in order to diminish their disgust, his sister was taking pains to spare them the slightest trouble. He must realize that they, too, had their share of misfortune.

Gregor never learned what excuses they had made to rid themselves of the doctor and the locksmith, for, as no one attempted to understand him, no one, not even his sister, imagined that he could understand them. He had to be content, when she came into his room, to listen to her invoking the saints between her sighs. It was only much later, when Grete had become somewhat accustomed to the new situation—to which she never really became reconciled—that Gregor would occasionally overhear an expression which showed some kindness or allowed him to guess at such a meaning. When he had eaten all the food off the newspaper she would say, "He liked what I brought today"; at other times, when he had no appetite—and lately this had become more frequent—she would say, almost sadly, "Now he has left it all."

But even if he could learn no news directly, Gregor overheard a good deal of what was said in the dining room; as soon as he heard anyone speak, he would hurry to the most propitious door and press his whole body close against it. At first, especially, there was little conversation which did not bear more or less directly on his predicament. For two whole days, the mealtimes were given over to deliberating on the new attitude which must be maintained toward Gregor; even between meals they spoke mostly on the same theme, for now at least two members of the household always remained at home, each one fearing to remain alone and, particularly, to leave Gregor unwatched.

It was not very clear how much the maid knew of what had happened, but, on the very first day, she had fallen on her knees and begged his mother to let her go; and a quarter of an hour later she had left the house in tearful gratitude, as if her release were the greatest evidence of the kindness she had met with in the house; and of her own accord she took a long and boring oath never to reveal the secret to anyone. Now his sister and his mother had to look after the cooking; this entailed little trouble, for the appetite of the Samsa family had gone. Occasionally Gregor would hear one member of the family vainly exhorting another to eat. The reply was always the same: "Thank you, I have had enough," or some such phrase. Perhaps, also, they did not drink. Often his sister would ask her father if he would like some beer; she would cheerfully offer to fetch it, or, faced with her father's silence, she would say, to remove any scruples on his part, that the landlady could go for it, but her father would always reply with a loud, "No!" and nothing more would be said.

In the course of the very first day, the father had clearly explained their precise financial situation to his wife and daughter. From time to time he would get up from the table and hunt for some paper or account book in his Wertheim safe, which he had saved from the crash when his business had failed five years before. He could be heard opening the complicated locks of the safe and closing it again after he had taken out what he sought. Ever since he became a prisoner, nothing had given Gregor such pleasure as these financial explanations. He had always imagined that his father had been unable to save a penny from the ruins of his business; in any case, his father had never said anything to undeceive him, and Gregor had never questioned him upon the matter; he had done all he could to help his family to forget as quickly as possible the disaster which had plunged them into such despair.

He had set to work with splendid ardor; in less than no time, from being a junior clerk he had been promoted to the position of traveler, with all the benefits of such a post; and his successes were suddenly transformed into hard cash which could be spread on the table before the surprised and delighted eyes of his family. Those were happy times—they had never since recovered such a sense of delight, though Gregor now earned enough to feed the whole Samsa family. Everyone had grown accustomed to it, his family as much as himself; they took the money gratefully, he gave it willingly, but the act was accompanied by no remarkable effusiveness. Only his sister had remained particularly affectionate toward Gregor, and it was his secret plan to have her enter the conservatory next year regardless of the considerable cost of such an enterprise, which he would try to meet in some way; for, unlike him, Grete was very fond of music and wished to take up the study of the violin. This matter of the conservatory recurred often in the brief conversations between Gregor and his sister, whenever Gregor had a few days to spend with his family; they hardly ever spoke of it except as a dream impossible to realize; his parents did not much like the innocent allusions to the subject, but Gregor thought very seriously of it and had promised himself that he would solemnly announce his plan next Christmas eve.

It was ideas of this kind, ideas completely unsuited to his present situation, which now passed constantly through Gregor's mind while he held himself pressed erect against the door, listening. He would get so tired that he could no longer hear anything; then he would let himself go and allow his head to fall against the door; but he would draw it back immediately, for the slightest noise was noticed in the dining room and would be followed by an interval of silence.

"What can he be doing now?" his father would say after a moment's pause, turning, no doubt, toward the door; the interrupted conversation would only gradually be resumed.

His father was often obliged to repeat his explanations in order to recall forgotten details or to make them understood by his wife, who did not always grasp them the first time. Gregor thus learned, by what the father said, that, despite all their misfortunes, his parents had been able to save a certain amount from their former property—little enough, it is true, but it had been augmented, to some extent, by interest. Also, they had not spent all the money that Gregor, keeping only a few shillings for himself, had handed over to his family each week, enabling them to gather together a little capital. Behind his door, Gregor nodded his head in approval; he was so happy at this unexpected foresight and thrift. Doubtless, with these savings his father could have more rapidly paid off the debt he had contracted to Gregor's employer, which would have brought nearer the date of Gregor's release; but under the circumstances it was much better that his father had acted as he had.

Unfortunately this money was not quite sufficient to enable the family to live on its interest; it would last a year, perhaps two, but no more. It was a sum which must not be touched, which must be kept for a case of urgent necessity. As for money on which to live, that would have to be earned. Now, despite his good health, the father was nevertheless an old man who had ceased to work five years before and who could not be expected to entertain any foolish hopes of getting employment; during these five years of retirement—his first holiday in a life entirely devoted to work and unsuccess —he had become very fat and moved with great difficulty. And the old mother would not be able to earn much, suffering as she did from asthma, for even now it was an effort for her to get about the house; she passed a good deal of her time each day lying on the sofa, panting and wheezing under the open window. And was the breadwinner to be the sister, who was still but a child, seventeen years old, so suited to the life she had led till then, nicely dressed, getting plenty of sleep, helping in the house, taking part in a few harmless little entertainments, and playing her violin? Whenever the conversation fell on this topic, Gregor left the door and lay on the leather sofa, whose coolness was so soothing to his body, burning as it was with anxiety and shame.

Often he lay all night, sleepless, and hearing no sound for hours on end save the creak of the leather as he turned. Or, uncomplainingly, he would push his armchair toward the window, crawl up on it, and, propped on the seat, he would lean against the window, not so much to enjoy the view as to recall the sense of release he once used to feel whenever he looked across the pavements; for now he was daily becoming more shortsighted, he could not even make out the hospital opposite, which he had cursed when he was human because he could see it all too clearly; and had he not known so well that he was living in Charlottenstrasse, a quiet but entirely urban street, he might have thought his window gave out on a desert, where the gray of the sky and the gray of the earth merged indistinguishably together. His attentive sister had only to see the armchair by the window twice to understand; from then on, each time she tidied the room she would push the armchair to the window, and would always leave its lower half open.

If only Gregor had been able to speak to his sister, to thank her for all she was doing for him, he could have borne her services easier; but as it was, they pained and embarrassed him. Grete naturally tried to hide any appearance of blame or trouble regarding the situation, and as time went on she played her part even better, but she could not prevent her brother from realizing his predicament more and more clearly. Each time she entered his room, it was terrible for Gregor. Hardly had she entered, when, despite the pains she always took to spare the others the sight of its interior, she would not even take time to shut the door but would run to the window, open it hastily with a single push, as if to escape imminent suffocation, and would stand there for a minute, however cold it might be, breathing deeply. Twice a day she terrified Gregor with this rush and clatter; he shrank trembling under the couch the whole time; he knew his sister would have spared him this had she been able to stand being in the room with him with the window shut.

One day—it must have been a month after Gregor's change, and his sister had no grounds for astonishment at his appearance—she came a little earlier than usual and found him looking out of the window, motionless and in such a position as to inspire terror. If she had not liked to enter, that would not have surprised Gregor, for his position prevented her from opening the window. But not only would she not enter; she sprang back, slammed the door, and locked it; a stranger might have thought that Gregor was lying in wait for his sister, to attack her. Naturally he hid himself under the couch immediately, but he had to wait till midday for Grete's return, and, when she did come, she appeared unusually troubled. He realized that his appearance was still disgusting to the poor girl, that it would always be so, and that she must fiercely resist her own impulse to flee the moment she caught sight of the tiniest part of Gregor's body protruding from under the sofa. To spare her this sight, he took a sheet on his back, dragged it to the sofa—a task which occupied some hours—and spread it in such a way that his sister could see nothing under the sofa, even if she stooped.

Had she found this precaution unnecessary, she would have taken the sheet away, for she guessed that Gregor did not so completely shut himself away for pleasure; but she left the sheet where it lay, and Gregor, prudently parting the curtain with his head to see what impression this new arrangement had made upon his sister, thought he detected a look of gratitude in her face.

During the first fortnight his parents had not been able to bring themselves to enter his room, and he often heard them praising the zeal of his sister, whom they had regarded, so far, as a useless young girl and of whom they had often complained. But now, both his father and mother would wait quite frequently outside Gregor's door while his sister was tidying the room, and scarcely had she come out again before they would make her tell them in detail exactly how she had found the room, what Gregor had eaten, and, in detail, what he was doing at that moment; they would ask her, too, if there were the slightest signs of improvement. His mother seemed impatient to see Gregor, but the father and sister restrained her with argument to which she listened very attentively and with which she wholly agreed. Later, however, they had to use force, and when his mother began to cry, "Let me go to Gregor! My poor boy! Don't you understand that I must see him!" Gregor thought that perhaps it would be as well if his mother did come in, not every day, of course, but perhaps once a week; she would understand things better than his sister, who was but a child, for all her courage, and had perhaps taken on such a difficult task out of childish lightheartedness.

Gregor's wish to see his mother was soon realized. Gregor avoided showing himself at the window during the day, out of consideration to his parents; but his restricted walks around the floor did not fully compensate him for this self-denial, nor could he bear to lie still for long, even during the night; he took no more pleasure in eating, and it soon became his habit to distract himself by walking—around the room, back and forth along the walls, and across the ceiling, on which he would hang; it was quite a different matter from walking across the floor. His breathing became freer, a light, swinging motion went through his body, and he felt so elated that now and then, to his own surprise, he would let himself go and fall to the floor. But by now, knowing better how to manage his body, he succeeded in rendering these falls harmless. His sister soon noticed his new pastime, for he left sticky marks here and there in his track, and Grete took it into her head to help him in his walks by removing all the furniture likely to be a hindrance, particularly the chest and the desk. Unfortunately, she was not strong enough to manage this on her own and dared not ask the help of her father; as for the maid, she certainly would have refused, for if this sixteen-year-old child had worked bravely since the former cook had left, it was on condition that she could stay continually barricaded in the kitchen, whose doors she would only open on special demand. So there was nothing else for it; Grete would have to enlist the mother's help one day when the father was away.

The mother gladly consented, but her exclamations of joy were hushed before Gregor's door. The sister first made sure that everything was in order in the room; then she allowed the mother to enter. In his great haste, Gregor had pulled the sheet down further than usual, and the many folds in which it fell gave the scene the air of a still life. This time he refrained from peeping under the sheet to spy on his mother but he was delighted to have her near.

"You may come in; he is not in sight," said his sister; and, taking her mother by the hand, she led her into the room. Then Gregor heard the two frail women struggling to remove the heavy old chest; the sister undertook the hardest part of the task, despite the warnings of her mother, who feared she might do herself some harm. It took a long time. They had been struggling with the chest for four hours when the mother declared that it might be best to leave it where it was, that it was too heavy for them, that they would not finish moving it before the father returned, and that, with the chest in the middle of the room, Gregor would be considerably impeded in his movements, and, finally, who knew whether he might not be displeased by the removal of his furniture?

The mother thought he would be; the sight of the bare walls struck cold at her heart; might Gregor not feel the same, having long grown so accustomed to the furniture, and would he not feel forsaken in his empty room? "Isn't it a fact," said the mother in a low voice—she had spoken in whispers ever since she entered the room, so that Gregor, whose hiding place she had not yet discovered, might not overhear, not so much what she was saying—for she was persuaded that he could not understand—but the very sound of her voice. "Isn't it a fact that when we remove the furniture, we seem to imply that we are giving up all hope of seeing him cured and are wickedly leaving him to his fate? I think it would be better to keep the room just as it was before, so that Gregor will find nothing changed when he comes back to us and will be able the more easily to forget what has happened meanwhile."

Hearing his mother's words, Gregor realized how these two monotonous months, in the course of which nobody had addressed a word to him, must have affected his mind; he could not otherwise explain his desire for an empty room. Did he really wish to allow this warm, comfortable room with its genial furniture to be transformed into a cavern in which, in rapid and complete forgetfulness of his human past, he might exercise his right to crawl all over the walls? It seemed he was already so near to forgetting; and it had required nothing less than his mother's voice, which he had not heard for so long, to rouse him. Nothing should be removed, everything must stay as it is, he could not bear to forego the good influence of his furniture, and, if it prevented him from indulging his crazy impulses, then so much the better.

Unfortunately, his sister was not of this opinion; she had become accustomed to assume authority over her parents where Gregor was concerned—this was not without cause—and now the mother's remarks were enough to make her decide to remove not only the desk and the chest—which till now had been their only aim—but all the other furniture as well, except the indispensable sofa. This was not the result of mere childish bravado, nor the outcome of that new feeling of self-confidence which she had just acquired so unexpectedly and painfully. No, she really believed that Gregor had need of plenty of room for exercise and that, as far as she could see, he never used the furniture. Perhaps, also, the romantic character of girls of her age was partly responsible for her decision, a sentiment which strove to satisfy itself on every possible occasion and which now drove her to dramatize her brother's situation to such an extent so that she could devote herself to Gregor even more passionately than hitherto; for in a room over whose bare walls Gregor reigned alone, no one but Grete dare enter and stay.

She did not allow herself to be turned from her resolve by her mother, made irresolute by the oppressive atmosphere of the room, and who did not hesitate now to remove the chest as best she could. Gregor could bear to see the chest removed, at a pinch, but the desk must stay. And hardly had the women left the room, panting as they pushed the chest, than Gregor put out his head to examine the possibilities of making a prudent and tactful appearance. But unfortunately it was his mother who returned first, while Grete, in the side room, her arms around the chest, was rocking it from side to side without being able to settle it in position. The mother was not used to the sight of Gregor; it might give her a serious shock. Terrified, he hastened to retreat to the other end of the sofa, but he could not prevent the sheet from fluttering slightly, which immediately attracted his mother's attention. She stopped short, stood stockstill for a moment, then hurried back to Grete.

Gregor assured himself that nothing extraordinary was happening—they were merely removing a few pieces of furniture—but the coming and going of the women, their little cries, the scraping of the furniture over the floor, seemed to combine in such an excruciating din that, however much he withdrew his head, contracted his legs, and pressed himself to the ground, he had to admit that he could not bear this torture much longer. They were emptying his room, taking away from him all that he loved; they had already removed the chest in which he kept his saw and his fretwork outfit; now they were shifting his desk, which had stood so solid and fast to the floor all the time it was in use, that desk on which he had written his lessons while he was at the commercial school, at the secondary school, even at the preparatory school. However, he could no longer keep pace with their intentions, for so absent minded had he become he had almost forgotten their existence, now that fatigue had quietened them and the clatter of their weary feet could no longer be heard.

So he came out—the women were only leaning against the desk in the next room, recovering their breath—and he found himself so bewildered that he changed his direction four times; he really could not decide what he should first salvage—when suddenly he caught sight of the picture of the woman in furs which assumed tremendous importance on the bare wall; he hastily climbed up and pressed himself against the glass, which stuck to his burning belly and refreshed him delightfully. This picture, at least, which Gregor entirely covered, should not be snatched away from him by anyone. He turned his head toward the dining-room door to observe the women as they returned.

They had had but a short rest and were already coming back; Grete's arm was round her mother's waist, supporting her.

"Well, what shall we take now?" said Grete, and she looked around. Her eyes met those of Gregor on the wall. If she succeeded in keeping her presence of mind, it was only for her mother's sake, toward whom she leaned her head to prevent her from seeing anything and said, a little too quickly and with a trembling voice, "Come, wouldn't it be better to go back to the living room for a minute?" The girl's intention was clear to Gregor: she wished to put her mother in a safe place and then to drive him from the wall. Well, let her try! He lay over his picture, and he would not let it go. He would rather leap into his sister's face.

But Grete had merely disquieted her mother; now she turned, saw the gigantic brown stain spread over the wallpaper and, before she realized that it was Gregor she was seeing, she cried, "O God! O God!" in a screaming, raucous voice, fell on the sofa with outspread arms in a gesture of complete renunciation, and gave no further sign of life. "You, Gregor!" cried the sister, raising her fist and piercing Gregor with a look. It was the first word she had addressed to him directly ever since his metamorphosis. Then she ran to get some smelling salts from the dining room to rouse her mother from her swoon. Gregor decided to help—there was still time to save the picture—alas, he found he had stuck fast to the glass and had to make a violent effort to detach himself; then he hurried into the dining room as if able to give his sister some good advice, but he was obliged to content himself with remaining passively behind her while she rummaged among the bottles, and he frightened her so terribly when she turned around that a bottle fell and broke on the floor, a splinter wounded Gregor in the face, and a corrosive medicine flowed round his feet; then Grete hastily grabbed up all the bottles she could carry and rushed in to her mother, slamming the door behind her with her foot. Now Gregor was shut out from his mother, who perhaps was nearly dead through his fault; he dared not open the door lest he drive away his sister, who must stay by his mother; so there was nothing to do but wait, and, gnawed by remorse and distress, he began to wander over the walls, the furniture, and the ceilings so rapidly that everything began to spin around him, till in despair he fell heavily on to the middle of the huge table.

A moment passed; Gregor lay stretched there; around all was still; perhaps that was a good sign. But suddenly he heard a knock. The maid was naturally barricaded in her kitchen; Grete herself must go to the door. His father had returned. "What has happened?" were his first words; no doubt Grete's expression had explained everything.

The girl replied in a stifled voice—probably she leaned her face against her father's breast—"Mother fainted, but she is better now. Gregor has got out."

"I was waiting for that," said the father. "I told you all along, but you women will never listen."

Gregor realized by these words that his father had mis-understood Grete's brief explanation and imagined that his son had broken loose in some reprehensible way. There was no time to explain. Gregor had to find some way of pacifying his father, so he quickly crawled to the door of his room and pressed himself against it for his father to see, as he came in, how he had every intention of returning to his own room immediately and that it was not at all necessary to drive him back with violence; one had only to open the door and he would quickly withdraw.

But his father was in no mood to notice these fine points. As he entered; he cried, "Ah!" in a tone at once of joy and anger; Gregor turned his head away from the door and lifted it toward his father. He was astonished. He had never imagined his father as he stood before him now; it is true that for some time now he had neglected to keep himself acquainted with the events of the house, preferring to devote himself to his new mode of existence, and he had therefore been unaware of a certain change of character in his family. And yet—and yet, was that really his father? Was it really the same man who once had lain wearily in bed when Gregor had been leaving on his journeys, who met him, on his re-turn, in his nightshirt, seated in an armchair out of which he could not even lift himself, throwing his arms high to show how pleased he was? Was this that same old man who, on the rare walks which the family would take together, two or three Sundays a year and on special holidays, would hob-ble between Gregor and his mother, while they walked slower and slower for him, as he, covered with an old coat, carefully set his stick before him and prudently worked his way forward; and yet, despite their slowness, he would be obliged to stop, whenever he wished to say anything, and call his escort back to him? How upstanding he had become since then!

Now he was wearing a blue uniform with gold buttons, without a single crease, just as you see the employees of banking houses wearing; above the big, stiff collar his double chin spread its powerful folds; under his bristly eyebrows the watchful expression of his black eyes glittered young and purposefully; his white hair, ordinarily untidy, had been carefully brushed till it shone. He threw on to the sofa his cap, ornamented with the gilded monogram of some bank, making it describe the arc of a circle across the room, and, with his hands in his trouser pockets, the long flaps of his coat turned back, he walked toward Gregor with a menacing air. He himself did not know what he was going to do; however, he raised his feet very high, and Gregor, astonished at the enormous size of the soles of his boots, took care to remain still, for he knew that, from the first day of his metamorphosis, his father had held the view that the greatest severity was the only attitude to take up toward Gregor. Then he began to beat a retreat before his father's approach, halting when the other stopped and beginning again at his father's slightest move. In this way they walked several times round the room without any decisive result; it did not even take on the appearance of a pursuit, so slow was their pace.

Gregor was provisionally keeping to the floor; he feared that if his father saw him climbing about the walls or rushing across the ceiling, he might take this maneuver for some refinement of bad behavior. However, he had to admit that he could not go on much longer in this way; in the little time his father needed to take a step, Gregor had to make a whole series of gymnastic movements and, as he had never had good lungs, he now began to pant and wheeze; he tried to recover his breath quickly in order to gather all his strength for a supreme effort, scarcely daring to open his eyes, so stupefied that he could think of no other way to safety than by pursuing his present course; he had already forgotten that the walls were at his disposal, and the carefully carved furniture, all covered with festoons of plush and lace as it was. Suddenly something flew sharply by him, fell to the ground, and rolled away. It was an apple, carelessly thrown; a second one flew by. Paralyzed with terror, Gregor stayed still. It was useless to continue his course, now that his father had decided to bombard him. He had emptied the bowls of fruit

on the sideboard, filled his pockets, and now threw apple
after apple, without waiting to take aim.

These little red apples rolled about the floor as if electrified,
knocking against each other. One lightly-thrown apple
struck Gregor's back and fell off without doing any harm,
but the next one literally pierced his flesh. He tried to drag
himself a little further away, as if a change of position could
relieve the shattering agony he suddenly felt, but he seemed
to be nailed fast to the spot and stretched his body helplessly,
not knowing what to do. With his last, hopeless glance, he
saw his door opened suddenly, and, in front of his sister, who
was shouting at the top of her voice, his mother came running in, in her petticoat, for his sister had partly undressed
her that she might breathe easier in her swoon. And his
mother, who ran to the father, losing her skirts one by one,
stumbled forward, thrust herself against her husband, embraced him, pressed him to her, and, with her hands clasped
at the back of his neck—already Gregor could see no more
—begged him to spare Gregor's life.

III

The apple that no one dared extract from Gregor's back remained embedded in his flesh as a palpable memory, and the
grave wound which he had now borne for a month seemed
to have reminded his father that Gregor, despite his sad and
terrible change, remained none the less a member of the
family and must not be treated as an enemy; on the contrary, duty demanded that disgust be overcome and Gregor
be given all possible help.

His wound had made him lose, irremediably, no doubt,
much of his agility; now, merely to cross his room required a
long, long time, as if he were an aged invalid; his walks across
the walls could no longer be considered. But this aggravation
of his state was largely compensated for, in his opinion, by
the fact that now, every evening, the dining-room door was
left open; for two hours he would wait for this. Lying in
the darkness of his room, invisible to the diners, he could observe the whole family gathered round the table in the lamplight, and he could, by common consent, listen to all they
had to say—it was much better than before.

It must be admitted that they no longer held those lively
conversations of which, in former times, he had always
thought with such sadness as he crept into his damp bed in

some little hotel room. Most of the time, now, they discussed nothing in particular after dinner. The father would soon settle himself to doze in his armchair; the mother and daughter would bid each other be silent; the mother, leaning forward in the light, would sew at some fine needlework for a lingerie shop, and the sister, who had obtained a job as a shop assistant, would study shorthand or French in the hope of improving her position. Now and then the father would wake up and, as if he did not know that he had been asleep, would say to his wife, "How late you are sewing to-night!" and would fall off to sleep again, while the mother and sister would exchange a tired smile.

By some capricious obstinacy, the father always refused to take off his uniform, even at home; his dressing gown hung unused in the wardrobe, and he slept in his armchair in full livery, as if to keep himself always ready to carry out some order; even in his own home he seemed to await his superior's voice. Moreover, the uniform had not been new when it was issued to him, and now each day it became more shabby, despite the care which the two women devoted to it; and Gregor often spent the evening staring dully at this coat, so spotted and stained, whose polished buttons always shone so brightly, and in which the old man slept, uncomfortably but peacefully.

As soon as the clock struck ten, the mother, in a low voice, tried to rouse her husband and to encourage him to go to bed, as it was impossible to get proper sleep in such a position, and he must sleep normally before returning to work at six the next morning. But, with the obstinacy which had characterized him ever since he had obtained his position at the bank, he would stay at the table although he regularly dropped off to sleep, and thus it would become more and more difficult to induce him to change his armchair for the bed. The mother and sister might insist with their little warnings; he stayed there just the same, slowly nodding his head, his eyes shut tight, and would not get up. The mother might shake him by the wrist, might whisper endearments in his ear; the daughter might abandon her work to assist her mother, but all in vain. The old man would merely sink deeper in his chair. At last the two women would have to take him under the arms to make him open his eyes; then he would look at each in turn and say, "What a life! Is this the hard-earned rest of my old days?" and, leaning on the two women, he would rise painfully, as if he were a tremendous weight, and would allow himself to be led to the door by his wife and daughter; then he would wave them off and continue alone, while the mother and sister, the one quickly throwing down her pen, the other her needle, would run after him to help.

Who in the overworked and overtired family had time to attend to Gregor, except for his most pressing needs? The household budget was ever more and more reduced; at last the maid was dismissed. In her place, a gigantic charwoman, with bony features and white hair, which stood up all around her head, came, morning and evening, to do the harder work. The rest was done by the mother, over and above her interminable mending and darning. It even happened that they were obliged to sell various family trinkets which formerly had been worn proudly by the mother and sister at ceremonies and festivals, as Gregor discovered one evening when he heard them discussing the price they hoped to get. But their most persistent complaints were about this flat, which was so much larger than they needed and which had now become too expensive for the family purse; they could not leave, they said, for they could not imagine how Gregor could be moved. Alas, Gregor understood that it was not really he who was the chief obstacle to this removal, for he might easily have been transported in a large wooden box pierced with a few air holes. No, what particularly prevented the family from changing their residence was their own despair, the idea that they had been stricken by such a misfortune as had never before occurred in the family or within the circle of their acquaintances.

Of all the deprivations which the world imposes on poor people, not one had been spared them; the father took his day-time meals with the lesser employees of the bank, the mother was killing herself mending the linen of strangers, the sister ran here and there behind her counter at the customers' bidding; but the family had energy for nothing further. It seemed to poor Gregor that his wound reopened whenever his mother and sister, returning from putting the father to bed, would leave their work in disorder and bring their chairs nearer to each other, till they were sitting almost cheek to cheek; then the mother would say, pointing to Gregor's room, "Close the door, Grete," and he would once more be left in darkness, while, outside, the two women mingled their tears or, worse, sat at the table staring with dry eyes.

These days and nights brought Gregor no sleep. From time to time he thought of taking the family affairs in hand, as he once used, the very next time the door was opened; at the end of a long perspective of time he dimly saw in his mind his employer and the manager, the clerks and apprentices, the porter with his narrow ideas, two or three acquaintances from other offices, a provincial barmaid—a fleeting but dear memory—and a cashier in a hat shop, whom he had pursued earnestly but too slowly; they passed through his mind in confusion, mingled with unknown and forgotten faces; but none of them could bring help to him or his family; nothing was to be gained from them. He was pleased to be able to dismiss them from his mind but now he no longer cared what happened to his family; on the contrary, he only felt enraged because they neglected to tidy his room and, though nothing imaginable could excite his appetite, he began making involved plans for a raid on the larder, with a view to taking such food as he had a right to, even if he was not hungry. Nowadays his sister no longer tried to guess what might please him; she made a hasty appearance twice a day, in the morning and in the afternoon, before going to her shop, and pushed a few scraps of food into the room with her foot; in the evening, without even bothering to see whether he had touched his meal or whether he had left it entirely—and this was usually the case—she would sweep up the remains with a whisk of the broom.

As for tidying up the room, which Grete now did in the evenings, it could not have been done in a more hasty manner. Great patches of dirt streaked the wall, little heaps of dust and ordure lay here and there about the floor. At first Gregor would place himself in the filthiest places whenever his sister appeared, so that this might seem a reproach to her. But he could have stayed there for weeks, and still Grete would not have altered her conduct; she saw the dirt as well as he but she had finally decided to take no further trouble. This did not prevent her from taking even more jealous care than ever to insure that no other member of the family should presume on her right to the tidying of the room.

Once the mother undertook to give Gregor's room a great cleaning which required several buckets of water, and this deluge deeply upset poor Gregor, crouched under his sofa in bitter immobility—but the mother's punishment soon came. Hardly had the sister, coming home in the evening, noticed the difference in Gregor's room, than, feeling deeply offended, she ran crying and screaming into the dining room, despite the appeal of her mother, who raised her hands in supplication; the father, who was quietly seated at table, leaped up, astonished but powerless to pacify her. Then he, too, became agitated; shouting, he began to attack the mother, on the one hand, for not leaving the care and cleaning of Gregor's room to the girl and, on the other hand, he forbade his daughter ever again to dare to clean it; the mother tried to draw the old man, quivering with anger as he was, into the bedroom; the daughter, shaken with sobs, was banging on the table with her little fists, while Gregor loudly hissed with rage to think that no one had the decency or consideration to close the door and thus spare him the sight of all this trouble and uproar.

But even if the sister, tired out by her work in the shop, could not bother to look after Gregor as carefully as hitherto, she could still have arranged that he should not be neglected without necessarily calling on the aid of her mother, for there was always the charwoman. This old woman, whose bony frame had helped her out of worse trouble during her long life, could not really be said to feel any disgust with Gregor. Though she was not inquisitive, she had opened his door one day and had stood with her hands folded over her stomach, astonished at the sight of Gregor, who began to trot here and there in his alarm, though she had no thought of chasing him. From that day, morning and evening, the old woman never lost an opportunity of opening the door a little to peer into the room.

At first she would call Gregor to make him come out crying in a familiar tone, "Come on, you old cockroach!" or, "Hey, look at the old cockroach!" To such invitations Gregor would not respond; instead he remained motionless beneath his sofa as if the door had not been opened. If they had only ordered the charwoman to clean his room out each day instead of allowing her to go on teasing and upsetting him! Early one morning, when heavy rain—perhaps a sign of approaching spring—beat on the roofs, Gregor was so annoyed by the old woman as she began to bait him again that he suddenly turned on her, in a somewhat cumbersome and uncertain manner, it must be admitted, but with every intention of attacking her. She was not at all frightened of him; there was a chair by the door; she took it up and brandished it, opening wide her mouth with the obvious intention

of not closing it until she had brought the chair down with a
crash on Gregor's back. "Ah, is that all?" she asked, seeing
him return to his former position, and she quietly put the
chair back in its place.

Nowadays Gregor hardly ate at all. When, by some
chance, he passed by his scraps, he would amuse himself by
taking a piece of food in his mouth and keeping it there for
hours, usually spitting it out in the end. At first he had
thought that his loss of appetite was due to the misery into
which the state of his room had plunged him; no doubt this
was a mistake, for he had soon become reconciled to the
squalor of his surroundings. His family had got into the
habit of piling into his room whatever could not be accom-
modated elsewhere, and this meant a great deal, now that
one of the rooms had been let to three lodgers. They were
very earnest and serious men; all three had thick beards—as
Gregor saw one day when he was peering through a crack
in the door—and they were fanatically tidy; they insisted on
order, not only in their own room, but also, now that they
were living here, throughout the whole household, and especially in the kitchen.

They had brought with them all that they needed, and this
rendered superfluous a great many things about the house
which could neither be sold nor thrown away, and which
were now all stacked in Gregor's room, as were the ash
bucket and the rubbish bin. Everything that seemed for the
moment useless would be dumped in Gregor's room by the
charwoman, who was always in a breathless hurry to get
through her work; he would just have time to see a hand
brandishing some unwanted utensil, and then the door would
slam again. Perhaps the old woman intended to return and
find the objects she so carelessly relegated here when she
needed them and had time to search; or perhaps she meant
to throw them all away some day, but in actual fact they
stayed in the room, on the very spot where they had first
fallen, so that Gregor was obliged to pick his way among
the rubbish to make a place for himself—a game for which
his taste began to grow, in spite of the appalling misery and
fatigue which followed these peregrinations, leaving him
paralyzed for hours. As the lodgers sometimes dined at home
in the living room, the door of this room would be shut on
certain evenings; however, Gregor no longer attached any
importance to this; for some while, now, he had ceased to
profit by those evenings when the family would open the

door and he would remain shrinking in the darkest corner of his room, where the family could not see him.

One day the woman forgot to close the dining-room door, and it was still ajar when the lodgers came in and lit the gas. They sat down at the table in the places that had previously been occupied by the father, the mother, and Gregor; each unfolded his napkin and took up his knife and fork. Soon the mother appeared in the doorway with a plate of meat; the sister followed her, carrying a dish of potatoes. When their meal had been set before them, the lodgers leaned over to examine it, and the one who was seated in the middle and who appeared to have some authority over the others, cut a piece of meat as it lay on the dish to ascertain whether it was tender or whether he should send it back to the kitchen. He seemed satisfied, however, and the two women, who had been anxiously watching, gave each other a smile of relief.

The family itself lived in the kitchen. However, the father, before going into the kitchen, always came into the dining room and bowed once with his cap in his hand, then made his way around the table. The boarders rose together and murmured something in their beards. Once they were alone, they began to eat in silence. It seemed curious to Gregor that he could hear the gnashing of their teeth above all the clatter of cutlery; it was as if they wanted to prove to him that one must have real teeth in order to eat properly, and that the best mandibles in the world were but an unsatisfactory substitute. "I am hungry," thought Gregor sadly, "but not for these things. How these lodgers can eat! And in the meantime I might die, for all they care."

He could not remember hearing his sister play since the arrival of the lodgers; but this evening the sound of the violin came from the kitchen. The lodgers had just finished their meal; the middle one had brought a newspaper and had given a page to each of the others; now they all three read, leaning back in their chairs and smoking. The sound of the violin attracted their attention, and they rose and walked on tiptoe toward the hall door, where they halted and remained very close together.

Apparently they had been heard in the kitchen, for the father cried, "Does the violin upset you gentlemen? We'll stop it immediately."

"On the contrary," said the man in the middle. "Would Fräulein Samsa not like to come in and play to us here in the dining room, where it is much nicer and more comfortable?"

"Oh, thank you," said the father, as if he were the violinist.

The gentlemen walked back across the room and waited. Soon the father came in with the music stand, the mother with the sheets of music, and the sister with the violin. The sister calmly prepared to play; her parents, who had never before let their rooms, were exaggeratedly polite to the boarders and were afraid to seem presumptuous by sitting in their own chairs; the father leaned against the door, his right hand thrust between two buttons of his livery coat; but one of the gentlemen offered the mother a chair, in which she finally sat, not daring to move from her corner throughout the performance.

The girl now began to play, while her father and mother, from either side, watched the movement of her hands. Attracted by the music, Gregor had crawled forward a little and had thrust his head into the room. He was no longer astonished that nowadays he had entirely lost that consideration for others, that anxiety to cause no trouble that once had been his pride. Yet never had he more reason to remain hidden, for now, because of the dirt that lay about his room, flying up at the slightest movement, he was always covered with dust and fluff, with ends of cotton and hairs, and with morsels of stale food, which stuck to his back or to his feet and which he trailed after him wherever he went; his apathy had grown too great for him to bother any more about cleaning himself several times a day by lying on his back and rubbing himself on the carpet, as once he used to do. And this filthy state did not prevent him from crawling over the spotless floor without a moment's shame.

So far, no one had noticed him. The family was too absorbed by the music of the violin, and the lodgers, who had first stood with their hands in their pockets, very close to the music stand—which disturbed the sister a great deal as she was obliged to see their image dancing amid the notes—had at last retired toward the window, where they stood speaking together half aloud, with lowered heads, under the anxious gaze of the father, who was watching attentively. It had become only too evident that they had been deceived in their hopes of hearing some beautiful violin piece, or at least some amusing little tune; it seemed that what the girl was playing bored them and that now they only tolerated her out of politeness. By the way in which they puffed the smoke of their cigars, by the energy with which they blew it toward the ceiling through the mouth or the nose, one could guess how fidgety they were becoming. And the sister was playing so nicely. Her face leaning to one side, her glance followed the score carefully and sadly. Gregor crawled forward a little more and put his head as near as possible to the floor to meet her gaze. Could it be that he was only an animal, when music moved him so? It seemed to him to open a way toward that unknown nourishment he so longed for. He resolved to creep up to his sister and to pull at her dress, to make her understand that she must come with him, for no one here would appreciate her music as much as he. He would never let her out of his room—at least, while he lived—for once, his horrible shape would serve him some useful purpose; he would be at all doors at once, repulsing intruders with his raucous breath; but his sister would not be forced to stay there; she must live with him of her own accord; she would sit by him on the sofa, hearing what he had to say; then he would tell her in confidence that he had firmly intended to send her to the Conservatory and had planned to let everyone know last Christmas—was Christmas really past?—without listening to any objections, had his misfortune not overtaken him too soon. His sister, moved by this explanation, would surely burst into tears, and Gregor, climbing up on her shoulder, would kiss her neck; this would be all the easier, for she had worn neither collar nor ribbon ever since she had been working in the shop.

"Herr Samsa," cried the middle lodger, and he pointed at Gregor, who slowly came into the room. The violin was suddenly silenced, the middle lodger turned to his friends, grinning and shaking his head, then once more he stared at Gregor. The father seemed to consider it more urgent to reassure the lodgers than to drive his son from the room, though the lodgers did not seem to be at all upset by the spectacle; in fact, Gregor seemed to amuse them more highly than did the violin. The father hurried forward and, with outstretched arms, tried to drive them into their room, hiding Gregor from them with his body. Now they began to be really upset, but it is not known whether this was on account of the father's action or because they had been living with such a monstrous neighbor as Gregor without being made aware of it. They demanded explanations, waving their arms in the air; and, fidgeting nervously with their beards, they retreated toward their own door. Meanwhile the sister had re-

covered from the distress that the sudden interruption of her
music had caused her; after remaining a moment completely
at a loss, with the violin and the bow hanging from her helpless hands, following the score with her eyes as if she were
still playing, she suddenly came back to life, laid the violin
in her mother's lap—the mother sat suffocating in her
chair, her lungs working violently—and rushed into the next
room, toward which the lodgers were rapidly retreating before Herr Samsa's onslaught. One could see how quickly,
under Grete's practised hand, pillows and covers were set in
order on the beds. The lodgers had not yet reached the room
when their beds were already prepared, and Grete had
slipped out. The father seemed so possessed by his strange
fury that he had quite forgotten the respect due to lodgers.

He drove them to the door of the room, where the middle
lodger suddenly came to a stop, stamping thunderously on
the floor. "I wish to inform you," said this man, raising his
hand and looking around for the two women, "that in view
of the disgusting circumstances which govern this family and
this house"—and here he spat quickly on the carpet—"I
hereby immediately give up my room. Naturally, you will not
get a penny for the time I have been living here; on the
contrary, I am considering whether I should not claim compensation from you, damages which should easily be awarded
in any court of law; it is a matter about which I shall inquire,
believe me." He was silent and stared into space, as if awaiting something. Accordingly, his two friends also spoke up:
"We, too, give our notice." Thereupon the gentleman in
the middle seized the door handle, and they went inside. The
door closed with a crash.

The father stumbled toward his chair, put his trembling
hands upon the arms, and let himself drop into it; he looked
exactly as if he were settling himself for his customary evening nap, but the way his head drooped heavily from side to
side showed that he was thinking of something other than
sleep. All this time Gregor had stayed still on the spot where
he had surprised the lodgers. He felt completely paralyzed
with bewilderment at the checking of his plans—perhaps,
also, with weakness due to his prolonged fasting. He feared
that the whole household would fall upon him immediately;
he foresaw the precise moment when this catastrophe
would happen, and now he waited. Even the violin did not
frighten him as it fell with a clatter from the trembling
fingers of his mother, who until now had held it in her lap.

"My dear parents," said his sister, who beat with her hand on the table by way of introduction. "Things cannot go on like this. Even if you do not realize it, I can see it quite clearly. I will not mention my brother's name when I speak of this monster here; I merely want to say: we must find some means of getting rid of it. We have done all that is humanly possible to care for it, to put up with it; I believe that nobody could reproach us in the least."

"She's a thousand times right," said the father. But the mother who had not yet recovered her breath, coughed helplessly behind her hand, her eyes haggard.

The sister hurried toward her mother and held her forehead. Grete's words seemed to have made up the father's mind; he sat up in his armchair and fidgeted with his cap among the dishes on the table, from which the lodgers' meal had not yet been cleared; from time to time he stared at Gregor.

"We must find a way of getting rid of it," repeated the sister, now speaking only to her father, for her mother, shaken by her coughing, could hear nothing. "It will bring you both to the grave. I can see it coming. When people have to work all day, as we must, we cannot bear this eternal torture each time we come home at night. I can stand it no longer." And she wept so bitterly that her tears fell on her mother's face, who wiped them off with a mechanical movement of her hand.

"But what can we do, child?" said the father in a pitiful voice. It was surprising to see how well he understood his daughter.

The sister merely shrugged her shoulders as a sign of the perplexity which, during her tears, had replaced her former assurance.

"If he could only understand us," said the father in a half-questioning tone, but the sister, through her tears, made a violent gesture with her hand as a sign that this was not to be thought of.

"If only he could understand us," repeated the father—and he shut his eyes as he spoke, as if to show that he agreed with the sister that such a thing was quite impossible. "If only he could understand us, perhaps there would be some way of coming to an agreement. But as it is . . ."

"It must go!" cried the sister. "That's the only way out. You must get the idea out of your head that this is Gregor. We have believed that for too long, and that is the cause of all our unhappiness. How could it be Gregor? If it were really he, he would long ago have realized that he could not live with human beings and would have gone off on his own accord. I haven't a brother any longer, but we can go on living and can honor his memory. In his place we have this monster that pursues us and drives away our lodgers; perhaps it wants the whole flat to itself, to drive us out into the streets. Look, father, look!" she suddenly screamed, "it's beginning again!" And in an access of terror, which Gregor could not understand, she let go her mother so suddenly that she bounced in the seat of the armchair; it seemed as if the sister would rather sacrifice her mother than stay near Gregor; she hastily took refuge behind her father, who was very upset by her behavior and now stood up, spreading his arms to protect her.

But Gregor had no thought of frightening anyone, least of all his sister. He had merely started to turn around in order to go back to his room; but it must be realized that this looked very alarming, for his weakness obliged him to assist his difficult turning movement with his head, which he raised and lowered many times, clutching at the carpet with his mandibles. At last he ceased and stared at the family. It seemed they realized his good intentions. They were watching him in mute sadness. The mother lay in her armchair, her outstretched legs pressed tightly together, her eyes nearly closed with fatigue; the father and sister were sitting side by side, and the girl's arm was round her father's neck.

"Now, perhaps, they will let me turn," thought Gregor, and he once more set about his task. He could not repress a sigh of weariness; he was obliged to rest from time to time. However, no one hurried him; they left him entirely alone. When he had completed his turn, he immediately beat a retreat, crawling straight ahead. He was astonished at the distance which separated him from his room; he did not realize that this was due merely to his weak state, and that a little before he could have covered the distance without noticing it. His family did not disturb him by a single cry, a single exclamation; but this he did not even notice, so necessary was it to concentrate all his will on getting back to his room. It was only when he had at long last reached his door that he thought of turning his head, not completely, because his neck had become very stiff, but sufficiently to reassure himself that nothing had changed behind him; only his sister was now standing up. His last look was toward his mother, who, by this time, was fast asleep.

Hardly was he in his room before the door was slammed, locked, and double bolted. So sudden was the crash that Gregor's legs gave way. It was his sister who had rushed to the door. She had stood up so as to be ready immediately and at the right moment had run forward so lightly that he had not heard her come; as she turned the key in the lock, she cried to her parents, "At last!"

"What now?" asked Gregor, looking around himself in the darkness. He soon discovered that he could not move. This did not surprise him in the least; it seemed to him much more remarkable that such frail legs had hitherto been able to bear his weight. Now he experienced a feeling of relative comfort. True, his whole body ached, but it seemed that these aches became less and less until finally they disappeared. Even the rotted apple embedded in his back hardly hurt him now; no more did the inflammation of the surrounding parts, covered with fine dust, cause him any further discomfort. He thought of his family in tender solicitude. He realized that he must go, and his opinion on this point was even more firm, if possible, than that of his sister. He lay in this state of peaceful and empty meditation till the clock struck the third morning hour. He saw the landscape grow lighter through the window; then, against his will, his head fell forward and his last feeble breath streamed from his nostrils.

When the charwoman arrived early in the morning—and though she had often been forbidden to do so, she always slammed the door so loudly in her vigor and haste that once she was in the house it was impossible to get any sleep—she did not at first notice anything unusual as she paid her customary morning visit to Gregor. She imagined that he was deliberately lying motionless in order to play the role of an "injured party," as she herself would say—she deemed him capable of such refinements; as she had a long broom in her hand, she tried to tickle him from the doorway. Meeting with little success, she grew angry; she gave him one or two hard pushes, and it was only when his body moved unresistingly before her thrusts that she became curious. She quickly realized what had happened, opened her eyes wide, and whistled in astonishment, but she did not stay in the room; she ran to the bedroom, opened the door, and loudly shouted into the darkness, "Come and look! He's stone dead! He's lying there, absolutely dead as a doornail!"

Herr and Frau Samsa sat up in their bed and tried to calm each other; the old woman had frightened them so much and they did not realize the sense of her message immediately. But now they hastily scrambled out of bed, Herr Samsa on one side, his wife on the other; Herr Samsa put the coverlet over his shoulders, Frau Samsa ran out, clad only in her nightdress; and it was thus that they rushed into Gregor's room. Meanwhile, the dining-room door was opened—Grete had been sleeping there since the arrival of the lodgers—she was fully dressed, as if she had not slept all night, and the pallor of her face seemed to bear witness to her sleeplessness.

"Dead?" said Frau Samsa, staring at the charwoman with a questioning look, though she could see as much for herself without further examination.

"I should say so," said the charwoman, and she pushed Gregor to one side with her broom, to support her statement. Frau Samsa made a movement as if to hold back the broom, but she did not complete her gesture.

"Well," said Herr Samsa, "we can thank God for that!" He crossed himself and signed the three women to do likewise.

Grete, whose eyes had never left the corpse, said, "Look how thin he was! It was such a long time since he had eaten anything. His meals used to come out of the room just as they were taken in." And, indeed, Gregor's body was quite flat and dry; this could be seen more easily now that he was no longer supported on his legs and there was nothing to deceive one's sight.

"Come with us a moment, Grete!" said Frau Samsa with a sad smile, and Grete followed her parents into their bedroom, not without turning often to gaze at the corpse. The charwoman closed the door and opened the French windows. Despite the early hour, the fresh morning air had a certain warmth. It was already the end of March.

The three lodgers came out of their room and gazed around in astonishment for their breakfast; they had been forgotten. "Where is our breakfast?" the middle lodger petulantly demanded of the old woman. But she merely laid her finger to her mouth and signed them, with a mute and urgent gesture, to follow her into Gregor's room. So they entered and stood around Gregor's corpse, with their hands in the pockets of their rather shabby coats, in the middle of the room already bright with sunlight.

Then the bedroom door opened and Herr Samsa appeared in his uniform with his wife on one arm, his daughter on the other. All seemed to have been weeping, and from time to time Grete pressed her face against her father's arm.

"Leave my house immediately!" said Herr Samsa, and he pointed to the door, while the women still clung to his arms.

Somewhat disconcerted, the middle lodger said with a timid smile, "Whatever do you mean?"

The two others clasped their hands behind their backs and kept on rubbing their palms together, as if they were expecting some great dispute which could only end in triumph for them.

"I mean exactly what I say!" answered Herr Samsa and, in line with the two women, he marched straight at the lodger. The latter, however, stood quietly in his place, his eyes fixed on the floor, as if reconsidering what he should do.

"Well, then, we will go," he said at last, raising his eyes to Herr Samsa as if searching, in a sudden access of humility, for some slight approval of his resolution.

Herr Samsa merely nodded several times, opening his eyes very wide. Thereupon the lodger walked away with big strides and soon reached the anteroom; his two friends, who for some while had ceased wringing their hands, now bounded after him, as if afraid Herr Samsa might reach the door before them and separate them from their leader. Once they had gained the hall, they took down their hats from the pegs, grabbed their sticks from the umbrella stand, bowed silently, and left the flat.

With a suspicion which, it appears, was quite unjustified, Herr Samsa ran out onto the landing after them with the women and leaned over the balustrade to watch the three men as they slowly, but steadily, descended the interminable stairway, disappearing once as they reached a certain point on each floor, and then, after a few seconds, coming into view again. As they went farther down the staircase, so the Samsa family's interest diminished, and when they had been met and passed by a butcher's boy who came proudly up the stairs with his basket on his head, Herr Samsa and the women quickly left the landing and went indoors again with an air of relief.

They decided to spend the whole day resting; perhaps they

might take a walk in the country; they had earned a respite and needed it urgently. And so they sat down to the table to write three letters of excuse: Herr Samsa to the manager of the Bank, Frau Samsa to her employer, and Grete to the head of her department at the shop. The charwoman came in while they were writing and announced that her work was done and that she was going. The three writers at first merely nodded their heads, without raising their eyes, but, as the old woman did not leave, they eventually laid down their pens and looked crossly at her.

"Well?" asked Herr Samsa. The charwoman was standing in the doorway, smiling as if she had some very good news to tell them but which she would not impart till she had been begged to. The little ostrich feather which stood upright on her hat and which had always annoyed Herr Samsa so much ever since the old woman had entered their service, now waved lightly in all directions.

"Well, what is it?" asked Frau Samsa, toward whom the old woman had always shown so much more respect than to the others.

"Well . . ." she replied, and she laughed so much she could hardly speak for some while. "Well, you needn't worry about getting rid of that thing in there, I have fixed it already."

Frau Samsa and Grete leaned over the table as if to resume their letter-writing; Herr Samsa, noticing that the woman was about to launch forth into a detailed explanation, cut her short with a peremptory gesture of his outstretched hand. Then, prevented from speaking, she suddenly remembered that she was in a great hurry and, crying, "Goodbye, everyone," in a peevish tone, she half turned and was gone in a flash, savagely slamming the door behind her.

"This evening we must sack her," declared Herr Samsa; but neither his wife nor his daughter answered; the old woman had not been able to disturb their newly won tranquillity. They arose, went to the window, and stood there, with their arms around each other; Herr Samsa, turning toward them in his armchair, stared at them for a moment in silence. Then he cried, "Come, come, it's all past history now; you can start paying a little attention to me." The women immediately hurried to him, kissed him, and sat down to finish their letters.

Then they left the apartment together, something they had been unable to do for many months past, and they boarded a tram that would take them into the country. There were no other passengers in the compartment, which was warm and bright in the sun. Casually leaning back in their seats, they discussed their future. On careful reflection, they decided that things were not nearly so bad as they might have been, for—and this was a point they had not hitherto realized—they had all three found really interesting occupations which looked even more promising in the future. They decided to effect what really should be the greatest improvement as soon as possible: to move from their flat. They would take a smaller, cheaper flat, one more practical, and in a better neighborhood than the present one, which Gregor had chosen. Hearing their daughter speak in more and more lively tones, Herr and Frau Samsa noticed almost together that, during this affair, Grete had blossomed into a fine strapping girl, despite the make-up which made her cheeks look pale. They became calmer; almost unconsciously they exchanged glances; it occurred to both of them that it would soon be time for her to find a husband. And it seemed to them that their daughter's gestures were a confirmation of these new dreams of theirs, an encouragement for their good intentions, when, at the end of the journey, the girl rose before them and stretched her young body.

Daughters of the Vicar

BY D. H. LAWRENCE
(1885-1930)

The 1960 court decision permitting the publication in the United States of Lady Chatterley's Lover *pleased the many ardent Lawrence readers who had long considered his powerful studies of the sexual forces at work in the human being as lasting works of art. Lawrence was born in Nottingham, England, the son of a coal miner. His novel* Sons and Lovers *(1913) reflects the environmental and psychological influences of these early years. Restless and intense, Lawrence traveled widely, spending much time in Italy. He visited Mexico and settled for a short time in New Mexico, the locale of* The Plumed Serpent *(1926).*

Daughters of the Vicar *represents the early Lawrence: straightforward naturalism, without mysticism or philosophy, rooted in his native scene; yet its theme, social range, and elaborate pattern prefigure his later development as characterized by* Lady Chatterley's Lover. *We recognize the well-bred family drained of all life, the girls who search for their individuality, the pressures to marry for status and economic security. Against this background, the typical Lawrencian struggle is waged between the emotionally emasculated and the shy, intense youth who lives in response to his nature.* Daughters of the Vicar *was included in a collection entitled* The Prussian Officer, *published in 1914.*

Daughters of the Vicar

Mr. Lindley was first vicar of Aldecross. The cottages of this tiny hamlet had nestled in peace since their beginning, and the country folk had crossed the lanes and farm-land, two or three miles, to the parish church at Greymeed, on the bright Sunday mornings.

But when the pits were sunk, blank rows of dwellings started up beside the high roads, and a new population, skimmed from the floating scum of workmen, was filled in, the cottages and the country people almost obliterated.

To suit the convenience of these new collier-inhabitants, a church must be built at Aldecross. There was not too much money. And so the little building crouched like a humped stone-and-mortar mouse, with two little turrets at the west corners for ears, in the fields near the cottages and the apple trees, as far as possible from the dwellings down the high road. It had an uncertain, timid look about it. And so they planted big-leaved ivy, to hide its shrinking newness. So that now the little church stands buried in its greenery, stranded and sleeping among the fields, while the brick houses elbow nearer and nearer, threatening to crush it down. It is already obsolete.

The Reverend Ernest Lindley, aged twenty-seven, and newly married, came from his curacy in Suffolk to take charge of his church. He was just an ordinary young man, who had been to Cambridge and taken orders. His wife was a self-assured young woman, daughter of a Cambridgeshire rector. Her father had spent the whole of his thousand a year, so that Mrs. Lindley had nothing of her own. Thus the young married people came to Aldecross to live on a stipend of about a hundred and twenty pounds, and to keep up a superior position.

They were not very well received by the new, raw, disaf-

fected population of colliers. Being accustomed to farm la-
bourers, Mr. Lindley had considered himself as belonging in-
disputably to the upper or ordering classes. He had to be
humble to the county families, but still, he was of their
kind, whilst the common people were something different.
He had no doubts of himself.

He found, however, that the collier population refused to
accept this arrangement. They had no use for him in their
lives, and they told him so, callously. The women merely
said: "they were throng," or else: "Oh, it's no good you coming here, we're Chapel." The men were quite good-humoured
so long as he did not touch them too nigh, they were cheerfully contemptuous of him, with a preconceived contempt
he was powerless against.

At last, passing from indignation to silent resentment,
even if he dared have acknowledged it, to conscious hatred
of the majority of his flock, and unconscious hatred of himself, he confined his activities to a narrow round of cottages,
and he had to submit. He had no particular character, having always depended on his position in society to give him
position among men. Now he was so poor, he had no social
standing even among the common vulgar tradespeople of
the district, and he had not the nature nor the wish to make
his society agreeable to them, nor the strength to impose
himself where he would have liked to be recognised. He
dragged on, pale and miserable and neutral.

At first his wife raged with mortification. She took on airs
and used a high hand. But her income was too small, the
wrestling with tradesmen's bills was too pitiful, she only met
with general, callous ridicule when she tried to be impressive.

Wounded to the quick of her pride, she found herself isolated in an indifferent, callous population. She raged indoors
and out. But soon she learned that she must pay too heavily
for her outdoor rages, and then she only raged within the
walls of the rectory. There her feeling was so strong that she
frightened herself. She saw herself hating her husband, and
she knew that, unless she were careful, she would smash her
form of life and bring catastrophe upon him and upon herself. So in very fear she went quiet. She hid, bitter and beaten
by fear, behind the only shelter she had in the world, her
gloomy, poor parsonage.

Children were born one every year; almost mechanically,
she continued to perform her maternal duty, which was
forced upon her. Gradually, broken by the suppressing of

her violent anger and misery and disgust, she became an invalid and took to her couch.

The children grew up healthy, but unwarmed and rather rigid. Their father and mother educated them at home, made them very proud and very genteel, put them definitely and cruelly in the upper classes, apart from the vulgar around them. So they lived quite isolated. They were good-looking, and had that curiously clean, semi-transparent look of the genteel, isolated and poor.

Gradually Mr. and Mrs. Lindley lost all hold on life, and spent their hours, weeks and years merely haggling to make ends meet, and bitterly repressing and pruning their children into gentility, urging them to ambition, weighting them with duty. On Sunday morning the whole family, except the mother, went down the lane to church, the long-legged girls in skimpy frocks, the boys in black coats and long, grey, unfitting trousers. They passed by their father's parishioners with mute clear faces, childish mouths closed in pride that was like a doom to them, and childish eyes already unseeing. Miss Mary, the eldest, was the leader. She was a long, slim thing with a fine profile and a proud, pure look of submission to a high fate. Miss Louisa, the second, was short and plump and obstinate-looking. She had more enemies than ideals. She looked after the lesser children, Miss Mary after the elder. The collier children watched the pale, distinguished procession of the vicar's family pass mutely by, and they were impressed by the air of gentility and distance, they made mock of the trousers of the small sons, they felt inferior in themselves, and hate stirred their hearts.

In her time, Miss Mary received as governess a few little daughters of tradesmen; Miss Louisa managed the house and went among her father's church-goers, giving lessons on the piano to the colliers' daughters at thirteen shillings for twenty-six lessons.

II

One winter morning, when his daughter Mary was about twenty years old, Mr. Lindley, a thin, unobtrusive figure in his black overcoat and his wideawake, went down into Aldecross with a packet of white papers under his arm. He was delivering the parish almanacs.

A rather pale, neutral man of middle age, he waited while the train thumped over the level-crossing, going up to the pit which rattled busily just along the line. A wooden-legged man hobbled to open the gate, Mr. Lindley passed on. Just at his left hand, below the road and the railway, was the red roof of a cottage, showing through the bare twigs of apple trees. Mr. Lindley passed round the low wall, and descended the worn steps that led from the highway down to the cottage which crouched darkly and quietly away below the rumble of passing trains and the clank of coal-carts, in a quiet little underworld of its own. Snowdrops with tight-shut buds were hanging very still under the bare currant bushes.

The clergyman was just going to knock when he heard a clinking noise, and turning saw through the open door of a black shed just behind him an elderly woman in a black lace cap stooping among reddish big cans, pouring a very bright liquid into a tundish. There was a smell of paraffin. The woman put down her can, took the tundish and laid it on a shelf, then rose with a tin bottle. Her eyes met those of the clergyman.

"Oh, is it you, Mr. Lin'ley!" she said, in a complaining tone. "Go in."

The minister entered the house. In the hot kitchen sat a big, elderly man with a great grey beard, taking snuff. He grunted in a deep, muttering voice, telling the minister to sit down, and then took no more notice of him, but stared vacantly into the fire. Mr. Lindley waited.

The woman came in, the ribbons of her black lace cap, or bonnet, hanging on her shawl. She was of medium stature, everything about her was tidy. She went up a step out of the kitchen, carrying the paraffin-tin. Feet were heard entering the room up the step. It was a little haberdashery shop, with parcels on the shelves of the walls, a big, old-fashioned sewing-machine with tailor's work lying round it, in the open space. The woman went behind the counter, gave the child who had entered the paraffin-bottle, and took from her a jug.

"My mother says shall yer put it down," said the child, and she was gone. The woman wrote in a book, then came into the kitchen with her jug. The husband, a very large man, rose and brought more coal to the already hot fire. He moved slowly and sluggishly. Already he was going dead; being a tailor, his large form had become an encumbrance to him. In his youth he had been a great dancer and boxer. Now he was taciturn, and inert. The minister had nothing to say, so he sought for his phrases. But John Durant took no notice, existing silent and dull.

Mrs. Durant spread the cloth. Her husband poured himself beer into a mug, and began to smoke and drink.

"Shall you have some?" he growled through his beard at the clergyman, looking slowly from the man to the jug, capable of this one idea.

"No, thank you," replied Mr. Lindley, though he would have liked some beer. He must set the example in a drinking parish.

"We need a drop to keep us going," said Mrs. Durant.

She had rather a complaining manner. The clergyman sat on uncomfortably while she laid the table for the half-past ten lunch. Her husband drew up to eat. She remained in her little round arm-chair by the fire.

She was a woman who would have liked to be easy in her life, but to whose lot had fallen a rough and turbulent family, and a slothful husband who did not care what became of himself or anybody. So, her rather good-looking square face was peevish, she had that air of having been compelled all her life to serve unwillingly, and to control where she did not want to control. There was about her, too, that masterful aplomb of a woman who has brought up and ruled her sons: but even them she had ruled unwillingly. She had enjoyed managing her little haberdashery shop, riding in the carrier's cart to Nottingham, going through the big warehouses to buy her goods. But the fret of managing her sons she did not like. Only she loved her youngest boy, because he was her last, and she saw herself free.

This was one of the houses the clergyman visited occasionally. Mrs. Durant, as part of her regulation, had brought up all her sons in the Church. Not that she had any religion. Only, it was what she was used to. Mr. Durant was without religion. He read the fervently evangelical *Life of John Wesley* with a curious pleasure, getting from it a satisfaction as from the warmth of the fire, or a glass of brandy. But he cared no more about John Wesley, in fact, than about John Milton, of whom he had never heard.

Mrs. Durant took her chair to the table.

"I don't feel like eating," she sighed.

"Why—aren't you well?" asked the clergyman, patronising.

"It isn't that," she sighed. She sat with shut, straight mouth. "I don't know what's going to become of us."

But the clergyman had ground himself down so long that he could not easily sympathise.

"Have you any trouble?" he asked.

"Ay, have I any trouble!" cried the elderly woman. "I shall end my days in the workhouse."

The minister waited unmoved. What could she know of poverty in her little house of plenty!

"I hope not," he said.

"And the one lad as I wanted to keep by me——" she lamented.

The minister listened without sympathy, quite neutral.

"And the lad as would have been a support to my old age! What is going to become of us?" she said.

The clergyman, justly, did not believe in the cry of poverty, but wondered what had become of the son.

"Has anything happened to Alfred?" he asked.

"We've got word he's gone for a Queen's sailor," she said sharply.

"He has joined the Navy!" exclaimed Mr. Lindley. "I think he could scarcely have done better—to serve his Queen and country on the sea . . ."

"He is wanted to serve *me*," she cried. "And I wanted my lad at home."

Alfred was her baby, her last, whom she had allowed herself the luxury of spoiling.

"You will miss him," said Mr. Lindley, "that is certain. But this is no regrettable step for him to have taken—on the contrary."

"That's easy for you to say, Mr. Lindley," she replied tartly. "Do you think I want my lad climbing ropes at another man's bidding, like a monkey——"

"There is no *dishonour*, surely, in serving in the Navy?"

"Dishonour this· dishonour that," cried the angry old woman. "He goes and makes a slave of himself, and he'll rue it."

Her angry, scornful impatience nettled the clergyman, and silenced him for some moments.

"I do not see," he retorted at last, white at the gills and inadequate, "that the Queen's service is any more to be called slavery than working in a mine."

"At home he was at home, and his own master. *I* know he'll find a difference."

"It may be the making of him," said the clergyman. "It will take him away from bad companionship and drink."

Some of the Durants' sons were notorious drinkers, and Alfred was not quite steady.

"And why indeed shouldn't he have his glass?" cried the mother. "He picks no man's pocket to pay for it!"

The clergyman stiffened at what he thought was an allusion to his own profession, and his unpaid bills.

"With all due consideration, I am glad to hear he has joined the Navy," he said.

"Me with my old age coming on, and his father working very little! I'd thank you to be glad about something else besides that, Mr. Lindley."

The woman began to cry. Her husband, quite impassive, finished his lunch of meat-pie, and drank some beer. Then he turned to the fire, as if there were no one in the room but himself.

"I shall respect all men who serve God and their country on the sea, Mrs. Durant," said the clergyman stubbornly.

"That is very well, when they're not your sons who are doing the dirty work. It makes a difference," she replied tartly.

"I should be proud if one of my sons were to enter the Navy."

"Ay—well—we're not all of us made alike——"

The minister rose. He put down a large folded paper.

"I've brought the almanac," he said.

Mrs. Durant unfolded it.

"I do like a bit of colour in things," she said, petulantly.

The clergyman did not reply.

"There's that envelope for the organist's fund——" said the old woman, and rising, she took the thing from the mantelpiece, went into the shop, and returned sealing it up.

"Which is all I can afford," she said.

Mr. Lindley took his departure, in his pocket the envelope containing Mrs. Durant's offering for Miss Louisa's services. He went from door to door delivering the almanacs, in dull routine. Jaded with the monotony of the business, and with the repeated effort of greeting half-known people, he felt barren and rather irritable. At last he returned home.

In the dining-room was a small fire. Mrs. Lindley, growing very stout, lay on her couch. The vicar carved the cold mutton: Miss Louisa, short and plump and rather flushed, came in from the kitchen; Miss Mary, dark, with a beautiful white brow and grey eyes, served the vegetables; the children chattered a little, but not exuberantly. The very air seemed starved.

"I went to the Durants," said the vicar, as he served out small portions of mutton; "it appears Alfred has run away to join the Navy."

"Do him good," came the rough voice of the invalid.

Miss Louisa, attending to the youngest child, looked up in protest.

"Why has he done that?" asked Mary's low, musical voice.

"He wanted some excitement, I suppose," said the vicar. "Shall we say grace?"

The children were arranged, all bent their heads, grace was pronounced, at the last word every face was being raised to go on with the interesting subject.

"He's just done the right thing, for once," came the rather deep voice of the mother; "save him from becoming a drunken sot, like the rest of them."

"They're not *all* drunken, mama," said Miss Louisa, stubbornly.

"It's no fault of their upbringing if they're not. Walter Durant is a standing disgrace."

"As I told Mrs. Durant," said the vicar, eating hungrily, "it is the best thing he could have done. It will take him away from temptation during the most dangerous years of his life —how old is he—nineteen?"

"Twenty," said Miss Louisa.

"Twenty!" repeated the vicar. "It will give him wholesome discipline and set before him some sort of standard of duty and honour—nothing could have been better for him. But——"

"We shall miss him from the choir," said Miss Louisa, as if taking opposite sides to her parents.

"That is as it may be," said the vicar. "I prefer to know he is safe in the Navy than running the risk of getting into bad ways here."

"Was he getting into bad ways?" asked the stubborn Miss Louisa.

"You know, Louisa, he wasn't quite what he used to be," said Miss Mary gently and steadily. Miss Louisa shut her rather heavy jaw sulkily. She wanted to deny it, but she knew it was true.

For her he had been a laughing, warm lad, with something kindly and something rich about him. He had made her feel warm. It seemed the days would be colder since he had gone.

"Quite the best thing he could do," said the mother with emphasis.

"I think so," said the vicar. "But his mother was almost abusive because I suggested it."

He spoke in an injured tone.

"What does she care for her children's welfare?" said the invalid. "Their wages is all her concern."

"I suppose she wanted him at home with her," said Miss Louisa.

"Yes, she did—at the expense of his learning to be a drunkard like the rest of them," retorted her mother.

"George Durant doesn't drink," defended her daughter.

"Because he got burned so badly when he was nineteen—in the pit—and that frightened him. The Navy is a better remedy than that, at least."

"Certainly," said the vicar. "Certainly."

And to this Miss Louisa agreed. Yet she could not but feel angry that he had gone away for so many years. She herself was only nineteen.

III

It happened when Miss Mary was twenty-three years old that Mr. Lindley was very ill. The family was exceedingly poor at the time, such a lot of money was needed, so little was forthcoming. Neither Miss Mary nor Miss Louisa had suitors. What chance had they? They met no eligible young men in Aldecross. And what they earned was a mere drop in a void. The girls' hearts were chilled and hardened with fear of this perpetual, cold penury, this narrow struggle, this horrible nothingness of their lives.

A clergyman had to be found for the church work. It so happened the son of an old friend of Mr. Lindley's was waiting three months before taking up his duties. He would come and officiate, for nothing. The young clergyman was keenly expected. He was not more than twenty-seven, a Master of Arts of Oxford, had written his thesis on Roman Law. He came of an old Cambridgeshire family, had some private means, was going to take a church in Northamptonshire with a good stipend, and was not married. Mrs. Lindley incurred new debts, and scarcely regretted her husband's illness.

But when Mr. Massy came there was a shock of disappointment in the house. They had expected a young man with a pipe and a deep voice, but with better manners than Sidney, the eldest of the Lindleys. There arrived instead a small, chétif man, scarcely larger than a boy of twelve, spectacled, timid in the extreme, without a word to utter at first; yet with a certain inhuman self-sureness.

"What a little abortion!" was Mrs. Lindley's exclamation to herself on first seeing him, in his buttoned-up clerical coat. And for the first time for many days she was profoundly thankful to God that all her children were decent specimens.

He had not normal powers of perception. They soon saw that he lacked the full range of human feelings, but had rather a strong philosophical mind, from which he lived. His body was almost unthinkable, in intellect he was something definite. The conversation at once took a balanced, abstract tone when he participated. There was no spontaneous exclamation, no violent assertion or expression of personal conviction, but all cold, reasonable assertion. This was very hard on Mrs. Lindley. The little man would look at her, after one of her pronouncements, and then give, in his thin voice, his own calculated version, so that she felt as if she were tumbling into thin air through a hole in the flimsy floor on which their conversation stood. It was she who felt a fool. Soon she was reduced to a hardy silence.

Still, at the back of her mind, she remembered that he was an unattached gentleman, who would shortly have an income altogether of six or seven hundred a year. What did the man matter, if there were pecuniary ease! The man was a trifle thrown in. After twenty-two years her sentimentality was ground away, and only the millstone of poverty mattered to her. So she supported the little man as a representative of a decent income.

His most irritating habit was that of a sneering little giggle, all on his own, which came when he perceived or related some illogical absurdity on the part of another person. It was the only form of humour he had. Stupidity in thinking seemed to him exquisitely funny. But any novel was unintelligibly meaningless and dull, and to an Irish sort of humour he listened curiously, examining it like mathematics, or else simply not hearing. In normal human relationship he was not there. Quite unable to take part in simple everyday talk, he padded silently round the house, or sat in the dining-room looking nervously from side to side, always apart in a cold, rarefied little world of his own. Sometimes he made an ironic remark, that did not seem humanly relevant, or he gave his little laugh, like a sneer. He had to defend himself and his own insufficiency. And he answered questions grudgingly, with a yes or no, because he did not see their import and was nervous. It seemed to Miss Louisa he scarcely distinguished one person from another, but that he liked to be near to her, or to Miss Mary, for some sort of contact which stimulated him unknown.

Apart from all this, he was the most admirable workman. He was unremittingly shy, but perfect in his sense of duty: as far as he could conceive Christianity, he was a perfect Christian. Nothing that he realised he could do for anyone did he leave undone, although he was so incapable of coming into contact with another being that he could not proffer help. Now he attended assiduously to the sick man, investigated all the affairs of the parish or the church which Mr. Lindley had in control, straightened out accounts, made lists of the sick and needy, padded round with help and to see what he could do. He heard of Mrs. Lindley's anxiety about her sons, and began to investigate means of sending them to Cambridge. His kindness almost frightened Miss Mary. She honoured it so, and yet she shrank from it. For, in it all Mr. Massy seemed to have no sense of any person, any human being whom he was helping: he only realised a kind of mathematical working out, solving of given situations, a calculated well-doing. And it was as if he had accepted the Christian tenets as axioms. His religion consisted in what his scrupulous, abstract mind approved of.

Seeing his acts, Miss Mary must respect and honour him. In consequence she must serve him. To this she had to force herself, shuddering and yet desirous, but he did not perceive it. She accompanied him on his visiting in the parish, and whilst she was cold with admiration for him, often she was touched with pity for the little padding figure with bent shoulders, buttoned up to the chin in his overcoat. She was a handsome, calm girl, tall, with a beautiful repose. Her clothes were poor, and she wore a black silk scarf, having no furs. But she was a lady. As the people saw her walking down Aldecross beside Mr. Massy they said:

"My word, Miss Mary's got a catch. Did you ever see such a sickly little shrimp!"

She knew they were talking so, and it made her heart grow hot against them, and she drew herself as it were protectively towards the little man beside her. At any rate, she could see and give honour to his genuine goodness.

He could not walk fast, or far.

"You have not been well?" she asked, in her dignified way.

"I have an internal trouble."

He was not aware of her slight shudder. There was silence, whilst she bowed to recover her composure, to resume her gentle manner towards him.

He was fond of Miss Mary. She had made it a rule of hospitality that he should always be escorted by herself or by her sister on his visits in the parish, which were not many. But some mornings she was engaged. Then Miss Louisa took her place. It was no good Miss Louisa's trying to adopt to Mr. Massy an attitude of queenly service. She was unable to regard him save with aversion. When she saw him from behind, thin and bent-shouldered, looking like a sickly lad of thirteen, she disliked him exceedingly, and felt a desire to put him out of existence. And yet a deeper justice in Mary made Louisa humble before her sister.

They were going to see Mr. Durant, who was paralysed and not expected to live. Miss Louisa was crudely ashamed at being admitted to the cottage in company with the little clergyman.

Mrs. Durant was, however, much quieter in the face of her real trouble.

"How is Mr. Durant?" asked Louisa.

"He is no different—and we don't expect him to be," was the reply. The little clergyman stood looking on.

They went upstairs. The three stood for some time looking at the bed, at the grey head of the old man on the pillow, the grey beard over the sheet. Miss Louisa was shocked and afraid.

"It is so dreadful," she said, with a shudder.

"It is how I always thought it would be," replied Mrs. Durant.

Then Miss Louisa was afraid of her. The two women were uneasy, waiting for Mr. Massy to say something. He stood, small and bent, too nervous to speak.

"Has he any understanding?" he asked at length.

"Maybe," said Mrs. Durant. "Can you hear, John?" she asked loudly. The dull blue eye of the inert man looked at her feebly.

"Yes, he understands," said Mrs. Durant to Mr. Massy. Except for the dull look in his eyes, the sick man lay as if dead. The three stood in silence. Miss Louisa was obstinate but heavy-hearted under the load of unlivingness. It was Mr. Massy who kept her there in discipline. His non-human will dominated them all.

Then they heard a sound below, a man's footsteps, and a man's voice called subduedly:

"Are you upstairs, mother?"

Mrs. Durant started and moved to the door. But already a quick, firm step was running up the stairs.

"I'm a bit early, mother," a troubled voice said, and on the landing they saw the form of the sailor. His mother came and clung to him. She was suddenly aware that she needed something to hold on to. He put his arms round her, and bent over her, kissing her.

"He's not gone, mother?" he asked anxiously, struggling to control his voice.

Miss Louisa looked away from the mother and son who stood together in the gloom on the landing. She could not bear it that she and Mr. Massy should be there. The latter stood nervously, as if ill at ease before the emotion that was running. He was a witness nervous, unwilling, but dispassionate. To Miss Louisa's hot heart it seemed all, all wrong that they should be there.

Mrs. Durant entered the bedroom, her face wet.

"There's Miss Louisa and the vicar," she said, out of voice and quavering.

Her son, red-faced and slender, drew himself up to salute. But Miss Louisa held out her hand. Then she saw his hazel eyes recognise her for a moment, and his small white teeth showed in a glimpse of the greeting she used to love. She was covered with confusion. He went round to the bed; his boots clicked on the plaster floor, he bowed with dignity.

"How are you, dad?" he said, laying his hand on the sheet, faltering. But the old man stared fixedly and unseeing. The son stood perfectly still for a few minutes, then slowly recoiled. Miss Louisa saw the fine outline of his breast, under the sailor's blue blouse, as his chest began to heave.

"He doesn't know me," he said, turning to his mother. He gradually went white.

"No, my boy!" cried the mother, pitiful, lifting her face. And suddenly she put her face against his shoulder, he was stooping down to her, holding her against him, and she cried aloud for a moment or two. Miss Louisa saw his sides heaving, and heard the sharp hiss of his breath. She turned away, tears streaming down her face. The father lay inert upon the white bed, Mr. Massy looked queer and obliterated, so little now that the sailor with his sun-burned skin was in the room. He stood waiting. Miss Louisa wanted to die, she wanted to have done. She dared not turn round again to look.

"Shall I offer a prayer?" came the frail voice of the clergy-man, and all kneeled down.

Miss Louisa was frightened of the inert man upon the bed. Then she felt a flash of fear of Mr. Massy, hearing his thin, detached voice. And then, calmed, she looked up. On the far side of the bed were the head of the mother and son, the one in the black lace cap, with the small white nape of the neck beneath, the other, with brown, sun-scorched hair too close and wiry to allow of a parting, and neck tanned firm, bowed as if unwillingly. The great grey beard of the old man did not move, the prayer continued. Mr. Massy prayed with a pure lucidity that they all might conform to the higher Will. He was like something that dominated the bowed heads, something dispassionate that governed them inexorably. Miss Louisa was afraid of him. And she was bound, during the course of the prayer, to have a little reverence for him. It was like a foretaste of inexorable, cold death, a taste of pure justice.

That evening she talked to Mary of the visit. Her heart, her veins were possessed by the thought of Alfred Durant as he held his mother in his arms; then the break in his voice, as she remembered it again and again, was like a flame through her; and she wanted to see his face more distinctly in her mind, ruddy with the sun, and his golden-brown eyes, kind and careless, strained now with a natural fear, the fine nose tanned hard by the sun, the mouth that could not help smiling at her. And it went through her with pride, to think of his figure, a fine jet of life.

"He is a handsome lad," said she to Miss Mary, as if he had not been a year older than herself. Underneath was the deeper dread, almost hatred, of the inhuman being of Mr. Massy. She felt she must protect herself and Alfred from him.

"When I felt Mr. Massy there," she said, "I almost hated him. What right had he to be there!"

"Surely he has all right," said Miss Mary after a pause. "He is *really* a Christian."

"He seems to me nearly an imbecile," said Miss Louisa.

Miss Mary, quiet and beautiful, was silent for a moment:

"Oh, no," she said. "Not *imbecile*——"

"Well then—he reminds me of a six months' child—or a five months' child—as if he didn't have time to get developed enough before he was born."

"Yes," said Miss Mary, slowly. "There is something lacking. But there is something wonderful in him: and he is really *good*——"

"Yes," said Miss Louisa, "it doesn't seem right that he should be. What right has *that* to be called goodness!"

"But it *is* goodness," persisted Mary. Then she added, with a laugh: "And come, you wouldn't deny that as well."

There was a doggedness in her voice. She went about very quietly. In her soul, she knew what was going to happen. She knew that Mr. Massy was stronger than she, and that she must submit to what he was. Her physical self was prouder, stronger than he, her physical self disliked and despised him. But she was in the grip of his moral, mental being. And she felt the days allotted out to her. And her family watched.

IV

A few days after, old Mr. Durant died. Miss Louisa saw Alfred once more, but he was stiff before her now, treating her not like a person, but as if she were some sort of will in command and he a separate, distinct will waiting in front of her. She had never felt such utter steel-plate separation from anyone. It puzzled her and frightened her. What had become of him? And she hated the military discipline—she was antagonistic to it. Now he was not himself. *He was the will which obeys set over against* the will which commands. She hesitated over accepting this. He had put himself out of her range. He had ranked himself inferior, subordinate to her. And that was how he could get away from her, that was how he would avoid all connection with her: by fronting her impersonally from the opposite camp, by taking up the abstract position of an inferior.

She went brooding steadily and sullenly over this, brooding and brooding. Her fierce, obstinate heart could not give way. It clung to its own rights. Sometimes she dismissed him. Why should he, her inferior, trouble her?

Then she relapsed to him, and almost hated him. It was his way of getting out of it. She felt the cowardice of it, his calmly placing her in a superior class, and placing himself inaccessibly apart, in an inferior, as if she, the sentient woman who was fond of him, did not count. But she was not going to submit. Dogged in her heart she held on to him.

V

In six months' time Miss Mary had married Mr. Massy. There had been no love-making, nobody had made any remark. But everybody was tense and callous with expectation. When one day Mr. Massy asked for Mary's hand, Mr. Lindley started and trembled from the thin, abstract voice of the little man. Mr. Massy was very nervous, but so curiously absolute.

"I shall be very glad," said the vicar, "but of course the decision lies with Mary herself." And his still feeble hand shook as he moved a Bible on his desk.

The small man, keeping fixedly to his idea, padded out of the room to find Miss Mary. He sat a long time by her, while she made some conversation, before he had readiness to speak. She was afraid of what was coming, and sat stiff in apprehension. She felt as if her body would rise and fling him aside. But her spirit quivered and waited. Almost in expectation she waited, almost wanting him. And then she knew he would speak.

"I have already asked Mr. Lindley," said the clergyman, while suddenly she looked with aversion at his little knees, "if he would consent to my proposal." He was aware of his own disadvantage, but his will was set.

She went cold as she sat, and impervious, almost as if she had become stone. He waited a moment nervously. He would not persuade her. He himself never even heard persuasion, but pursued his own course. He looked at her, sure of himself, unsure of her, and said:

"Will you become my wife, Mary?"

Still her heart was hard and cold. She sat proudly.

"I should like to speak to mama first," she said.

"Very well," replied Mr. Massy. And in a moment he padded away.

Mary went to her mother. She was cold and reserved.

"Mr. Massy has asked me to marry him, mama," she said. Mrs. Lindley went on staring at her book. She was cramped in her feeling.

"Well, and what did you say?"

They were both keeping calm and cold.

"I said I would speak to you before answering him."

This was equivalent to a question. Mrs. Lindley did not want to reply to it. She shifted her heavy form irritably on the couch. Miss Mary sat calm and straight, with closed mouth.

"Your father thinks it would not be a bad match," said the mother, as if casually.

Nothing more was said. Everybody remained cold and shut-off. Miss Mary did not speak to Miss Louisa, the Reverend Ernest Lindley kept out of sight.

At evening Miss Mary accepted Mr. Massy.

"Yes, I will marry you," she said, with even a little movement of tenderness towards him. He was embarrassed, but satisfied. She could see him making some movement towards her, could feel the male in him, something cold and triumphant, asserting itself. She sat rigid, and waited.

When Miss Louisa knew, she was silent with bitter anger against everybody, even against Mary. She felt her faith wounded. Did the real things to her not matter after all? She wanted to get away. She thought of Mr. Massy. He had some curious power, some unanswerable right. He was a will that they could not controvert. Suddenly a flush started in her. If he had come to her she would have flipped him out of the room. He was never going to touch *her*. And she was glad. She was glad that her blood would rise and exterminate the little man, if he came too near to her, no matter how her judgment was paralysed by him, no matter how he moved in abstract goodness. She thought she was perverse to be glad, but glad she was. "I would just flip him out of the room," she said, and she derived great satisfaction from the open statement. Nevertheless, perhaps she ought still to feel that Mary, on her plane, was a higher being than herself. But then Mary was Mary, and she was Louisa, and that also was inalterable.

Mary, in marrying him, tried to become a pure reason such as he was, without feeling or impulse. She shut herself up, she shut herself rigid against the agonies of shame and the terror of violation which came at first. She *would* not feel, and she *would* not feel. She was a pure will acquiescing to him. She elected a certain kind of fate. She would be good and purely just, she would live in a higher freedom than she had ever known, she would be free of mundane care, she was a pure will towards right. She had sold herself, but she had a new freedom. She had got rid of her body. She had sold a lower thing, her body, for a higher thing, her freedom from material things. She considered that she paid for all she got from her husband. So, in kind of independence, she moved proud and free. She had paid with her body: that was henceforward out of consideration. She was glad to be rid of it. She had bought her position in the world—that henceforth was taken for granted. There remained only the direction of her activity towards charity and high-minded living.

She could scarcely bear other people to be present with her and her husband. Her private life was her shame. But then, she could keep it hidden. She lived almost isolated in the rectory of the tiny village miles from the railway. She

suffered as if it were an insult to her own flesh, seeing the
repulsion which some people felt for her husband, or the
special manner they had of treating him, as if he were a
"case." But most people were uneasy before him, which
restored her pride.

If she had let herself, she would have hated him, hated his
padding round the house, his thin voice devoid of human
understanding, his bent little shoulders and rather incomplete face that reminded her of an abortion. But rigorously
she kept her position. She took care of him and was just to
him. There was also a deep, craven fear of him, something
slave-like.

There was not much fault to be found with his behaviour.
He was scrupulously just and kind according to his lights. But
the male in him was cold and self-complete, and utterly dom-
ineering. Weak, insufficient little thing as he was, she had
not expected this of him. It was something in the bargain she
had not understood. It made her hold her head, to keep still.
She knew, vaguely, that she was murdering herself. After
all, her body was not quite so easy to get rid of. And this
manner of disposing of it—ah, sometimes she felt she must
rise and bring about death, lift her hand for utter denial of
everything, by a general destruction.

He was almost unaware of the conditions about him. He
did not fuss in the domestic way, she did as she liked in the
house, indeed, she was a great deal free of him. He would
sit obliterated for hours. He was kind, and almost anxiously
considerate. But when he considered he was right, his will
was just blindly male, like a cold machine. And on most
points he was logically right, or he had with him the right of
the creed they both accepted. It was so. There was nothing
for her to go against.

Then she found herself with child, and felt for the first
time horror, afraid before God and man. This also she had
to go through—it was the right. When the child arrived, it
was a bonny, healthy lad. Her heart hurt in her body, as she
took the baby between her hands. The flesh that was trampled and silent in her must speak again in the boy. After all,
she had to live—it was not so simple after all. Nothing was
finished completely. She looked and looked at the baby, and
almost hated it, and suffered an anguish of love for it. She
hated it because it made her live again in the flesh, when she
could not live in the flesh, she could not. She wanted to tram-
ple her flesh down, down, extinct, to live in the mind. And

now there was this child. It was too cruel, too racking. For she must love the child. Her purpose was broken in two again. She had to become amorphous, purposeless, without real being. As a mother, she was a fragmentary, ignoble thing.

Mr. Massy, blind to everything else in the way of human feeling, became obsessed by the idea of his child. When it arrived, suddenly it filled the whole world of feeling for him. It was his obsession, his terror was for its safety and well-being. It was something new, as if he himself had been born a naked infant, conscious of his own exposure, and full of apprehension. He who had never been aware of anyone else, all his life, now was aware of nothing but the child. Not that he ever played with it, or kissed it, or tended it. He did nothing for it. But it dominated him, it filled, and at the same time emptied his mind. The world was all baby for him.

This his wife must also bear, his question: "What is the reason that he cries?"—his reminder, at the first sound: "Mary, that is the child,"—his restlessness if the feeding-time were five minutes past. She had bargained for this—now she must stand by her bargain.

VI

Miss Louisa, at home in the dingy vicarage, had suffered a great deal over her sister's wedding. Having once begun to cry out against it, during the engagement, she had been silenced by Mary's quiet: "I don't agree with you about him, Louisa, I *want* to marry him." Then Miss Louisa had been angry deep in her heart, and therefore silent. This dangerous state started the change in her. Her own revulsion made her recoil from the hitherto undoubted Mary.

"I'd beg the streets barefoot first," said Miss Louisa, thinking of Mr. Massy.

But evidently Mary could perform a different heroism. So she, Louisa the practical, suddenly felt that Mary, her ideal, was questionable after all. How could she be pure—one cannot be dirty in act and spiritual in being. Louisa distrusted Mary's high spirituality. It was no longer genuine for her. And if Mary were spiritual and misguided, why did not her father protect her? Because of the money. He disliked the whole affair, but he backed away, because of the money. And the mother frankly did not care: her daughters could do as they liked. Her mother's pronouncement:

"Whatever happens to *him*, Mary is safe for life,"—so evidently and shallowly a calculation, incensed Louisa.

"I'd rather be safe in the workhouse," she cried.

"Your father will see to that," replied her mother brutally. This speech, in its directness, so injured Miss Louisa that she hated her mother deep, deep in her heart, and almost hated herself. It was a long time resolving itself out, this hate. But it worked and worked, and at last the young woman said:

"They are wrong—they are all wrong. They have ground out their souls for what isn't worth anything, and there isn't a grain of love in them anywhere. And I *will* have love. They want us to deny it. They've never found it, so they want to say it doesn't exist. But I *will* have it. I *will* love—it is my birthright. I will love the man I marry—that is all I care about."

So Miss Louisa stood isolated from everybody. She and Mary had parted over Mr. Massy. In Louisa's eyes, Mary was degraded, married to Mr. Massy. She could not bear to think of her lofty, spiritual sister degraded in the body like this. Mary was wrong, wrong, wrong: she was not superior, she was flawed, incomplete. The two sisters stood apart. They still loved each other, they would love each other as long as they lived. But they had parted ways. A new solitariness came over the obstinate Louisa, and her heavy jaw set stubbornly. She was going on her own way. But which way? She was quite alone, with a blank world before her. How could she be said to have any way? Yet she had her fixed will to love, to have the man she loved.

VII

When her boy was three years old, Mary had another baby, a girl. The three years had gone by monotonously. They might have been an eternity, they might have been brief as a sleep. She did not know. Only, there was always a weight on top of her, something that pressed down her life. The only thing that had happened was that Mr. Massy had had an operation. He was always exceedingly fragile. His wife had soon learned to attend to him mechanically, as part of her duty.

But this third year, after the baby girl had been born, Mary felt oppressed and depressed. Christmas drew near: the gloomy, unleavened Christmas of the rectory, where all the days were of the same dark fabric. And Mary was afraid. It was as if the darkness were coming upon her.

"Edward, I should like to go home for Christmas," she said, and a certain terror filled her as she spoke.

"But you can't leave baby," said her husband, blinking.

"We can all go."

He thought, and stared in his collective fashion.

"Why do you wish to go?" he asked.

"Because I need a change. A change would do me good, and it would be good for the milk."

He heard the will in his wife's voice, and was at a loss. Her language was unintelligible to him. But somehow he felt that Mary was set upon it. And while she was breeding, either about to have a child, or nursing, he regarded her as a special sort of being.

"Wouldn't it hurt baby to take her by the train?" he said.

"No," replied the mother, "why should it?"

They went. When they were in the train it began to snow. From the window of his first-class carriage the little clergyman watched the big flakes sweep by, like a blind drawn across the country. He was obsessed by thought of the baby, and afraid of the draughts of the carriage.

"Sit right in the corner," he said to his wife, "and hold baby close back."

She moved at his bidding, and stared out of the window. His eternal presence was like an iron weight on her brain. But she was going partially to escape for a few days.

"Sit on the other side, Jack," said the father. "It is less draughty. Come to this window."

He watched the boy in anxiety. But his children were the only beings in the world who took not the slightest notice of him.

"Look, mother, look!" cried the boy. "They fly right in my face"—he meant the snowflakes.

"Come into this corner," repeated his father, out of another world.

"He's jumped on this one's back, mother, an' they're riding to the bottom!" cried the boy, jumping with glee.

"Tell him to come on this side," the little man bade his wife.

"Jack, kneel on this cushion," said the mother, putting her white hand on the place.

The boy slid over in silence to the place she indicated, waited still for a moment, then almost deliberately, stridently cried:

"Look at all those in the corner, mother, making a heap," and he pointed to the cluster of snowflakes with finger pressed dramatically on the pane, and he turned to his mother a bit ostentatiously.

"All in a heap!" she said.

He had seen her face, and had her response, and he was somewhat assured. Vaguely uneasy, he was reassured if he could win her attention.

They arrived at the vicarage at half-past two, not having had lunch.

"How are you, Edward?" said Mr. Lindley, trying on his side to be fatherly. But he was always in a false position with his son-in-law, frustrated before him, therefore, as much as possible, he shut his eyes and ears to him. The vicar was looking thin and pale and ill-nourished. He had gone quite grey. He was, however, still haughty; but, since the growing-up of his children, it was a brittle haughtiness, that might break at any moment and leave the vicar only an impoverished, pitiable figure. Mrs. Lindley took all the notice of her daughter, and of the children. She ignored her son-in-law. Miss Louisa was clucking and laughing and rejoicing over the baby. Mr. Massy stood aside, a bent, persistent little figure.

"Oh a pretty!—a little pretty! oh a cold little pretty come in a railway train!" Miss Louisa was cooing to the infant, crouching on the hearth-rug, opening the white woollen wraps and exposing the child to the fireglow.

"Mary," said the little clergyman, "I think it would be better to give baby a warm bath; she may take cold."

"I think it is not necessary," said the mother, coming and closing her hand judiciously over the rosy feet and hands of the mite. "She is not chilly."

"Not a bit," cried Miss Louisa. "She's not caught cold."

"I'll go and bring her flannels," said Mr. Massy, with one idea.

"I can bath her in the kitchen then," said Mary, in an altered, cold tone.

"You can't, the girl is scrubbing there," said Miss Louisa. "Besides, she doesn't want a bath at this time of day."

"She'd better have one," said Mary, quietly, out of submission. Miss Louisa's gorge rose, and she was silent. When the little man padded down with the flannels on his arm, Mrs. Lindley asked:

"Hadn't *you* better take a hot bath, Edward?"

But the sarcasm was lost on the little clergyman. He was absorbed in the preparations round the baby.

The room was dull and threadbare, and the snow outside seemed fairy-like by comparison, so white on the lawn and tufted on the bushes. Indoors the heavy pictures hung obscurely on the walls, everything was dingy with gloom.

Except in the fireglow, where they had laid the bath on the hearth. Mrs. Massy, her black hair always smoothly coiled and queenly, kneeled by the bath, wearing a rubber apron, and holding the kicking child. Her husband stood holding the towels and the flannels to warm. Louisa, too cross to share in the joy of the baby's bath, was laying the table. The boy was hanging on the door-knob, wrestling with it to get out. His father looked round.

"Come away from the door, Jack," he said ineffectually. Jack tugged harder at the knob as if he did not hear. Mr. Massy blinked at him.

"He must come away from the door, Mary," he said. "There will be a draught if it is opened."

"Jack, come away from the door, dear," said the mother, dexterously turning the shiny wet baby on to her towelled knee, then glancing round: "Go and tell Auntie Louisa about the train."

Louisa, also afraid to open the door, was watching the scene on the hearth. Mr. Massy stood holding the baby's flannel, as if assisting at some ceremonial. If everybody had not been subduedly angry, it would have been ridiculous.

"I want to see out of the window," Jack said. His father turned hastily.

"Do you mind lifting him on to a chair, Louisa," said Mary hastily. The father was too delicate.

When the baby was flannelled, Mr. Massy went upstairs and returned with four pillows, which he set in the fender to warm. Then he stood watching the mother feed her child, obsessed by the idea of his infant.

Louisa went on with her preparations for the meal. She could not have told why she was so sullenly angry. Mrs. Lindley, as usual, lay silently watching.

Mary carried her child upstairs, followed by her husband with the pillows. After a while he came down again.

"What is Mary doing? Why doesn't she come down to eat?" asked Mrs. Lindley.

"She is staying with baby. The room is rather cold. I will ask the girl to put in a fire." He was going absorbedly to the door.

"But Mary has had nothing to eat. It is *she* who will catch cold," said the mother, exasperated.

Mr. Massy seemed as if he did not hear. Yet he looked at his mother-in-law, and answered:

"I will take her something."

He went out. Mrs. Lindley shifted on her couch with anger. Miss Louisa glowered. But no one said anything, because of the money that came to the vicarage from Mr. Massy.

Louisa went upstairs. Her sister was sitting by the bed, reading a scrap of paper.

"Won't you come down and eat?" the younger asked.

"In a moment or two," Mary replied, in a quiet, reserved voice, that forbade anyone to approach her.

It was this that made Miss Louisa most furious. She went downstairs, and announced to her mother:

"I am going out. I may not be home to tea."

VIII

No one remarked on her exit. She put on her fur hat, that the village people knew so well, and the old Norfolk jacket. Louisa was short and plump and plain. She had her mother's heavy jaw, her father's proud brow, and her own grey, brooding eyes that were very beautiful when she smiled. It was true, as the people said, that she looked sulky. Her chief attraction was her glistening, heavy, deep-blonde hair, which shone and gleamed with a richness that was not entirely foreign to her.

"Where am I going?" she said to herself, when she got outside in the snow. She did not hesitate, however, but by mechanical walking found herself descending the hill towards Old Aldecross. In the valley that was black with trees, the colliery breathed in stertorous pants, sending out high conical columns of steam that remained upright, whiter than the snow on the hills, yet shadowy, in the dead air. Louisa would not acknowledge to herself whither she was making her way, till she came to the railway crossing. Then the bunches of snow in the twigs of the apple tree that leaned towards the fence told her she must go and see Mrs. Durant. The tree was in Mrs. Durant's garden.

Alfred was now at home again, living with his mother in the cottage below the road. From the highway hedge, by the railway crossing, the snowy garden sheered down steeply, like the side of a hole, then dropped straight in a wall. In this depth the house was snug, its chimney just level with the road. Miss Louisa descended the stone stairs, and stood below in the little back-yard, in the dimness and the semi-secrecy.

A big tree leaned overhead, above the paraffin-hut. Louisa felt secure from all the world down there. She knocked at the open door, then looked round. The tongue of garden narrowing in from the quarry bed was white with snow: she thought of the thick fringes of snowdrops it would show beneath the currant bushes in a month's time. The ragged fringe of pinks hanging over the garden brim behind her was whitened now with snowflakes, that in summer held white blossom to Louisa's face. It was pleasant, she thought, to gather flowers that stooped to one's face from above.

She knocked again. Peeping in, she saw the scarlet glow of the kitchen, red firelight falling on the brick floor and on the bright chintz cushions. It was alive and bright as a peep-show. She crossed the scullery, where still an almanac hung. There was no one about. "Mrs. Durant," called Louisa softly, "Mrs. Durant."

She went up the brick step into the front room, that still had its little shop counter and its bundles of goods, and she called from the stair-foot. Then she knew Mrs. Durant was out.

She went into the yard, to follow the old woman's footsteps up the garden path.

She emerged from the bushes and raspberry canes. There was the whole quarry bed, a wide garden white and dimmed, brindled with dark bushes, lying half submerged. On the left, overhead, the little colliery train rumbled by. Right away at the back was a mass of trees.

Louisa followed the open path, looking from right to left, and then she gave a cry of concern. The old woman was sitting rocking slightly among the ragged snowy cabbages. Louisa ran to her, found her whimpering with little, involuntary cries.

"Whatever have you done?" cried Louisa, kneeling in the snow.

"I've—I've— I was pulling a brussel-sprout stalk—and—oh-h!—something tore inside me. I've had a pain," the old woman wept from shock and suffering, gasping between her whimpers,—"I've had a pain there—a long time—and now—oh—oh!" She panted, pressed her hand on her side, leaned as if she would faint, looking yellow against the snow. Louisa supported her.

"Do you think you could walk now?" she asked.

"Yes," gasped the old woman.

Louisa helped her to her feet.

"Get the cabbage—I want it for Alfred's dinner," panted Mrs. Durant. Louisa picked up the stalk of brussel-sprouts, and with difficulty got the old woman indoors. She gave her brandy, laid her on the couch, saying:

"I'm going to send for a doctor—wait just a minute."

The young woman ran up the steps to the public-house a few yards away. The landlady was astonished to see Miss Louisa.

"Will you send for a doctor at once to Mrs. Durant," she said, with some of her father in her commanding tone.

"Is something the matter?" fluttered the landlady in concern.

Louisa, glancing out up the road, saw the grocer's cart driving to Eastwood. She ran and stopped the man, and told him.

Mrs. Durant lay on the sofa, her face turned away, when the young woman came back.

"Let me put you to bed," Louisa said. Mrs. Durant did not resist.

Louisa knew the ways of the working people. In the bottom drawer of the dresser she found dusters and flannels. With the old pit-flannel she snatched out the oven shelves, wrapped them up, and put them in the bed. From the son's bed she took a blanket, and, running down, set it before the fire. Having undressed the little old woman, Louisa carried her upstairs.

"You'll drop me, you'll drop me!" cried Mrs. Durant.

Louisa did not answer, but bore her burden quickly. She could not light a fire, because there was no fire-place in the bedroom. And the floor was plaster. So she fetched the lamp, and stood it lighted in one corner.

"It will air the room," she said.

"Yes," moaned the old woman.

Louisa ran with more hot flannels, replacing those from the oven shelves. Then she made a bran-bag and laid it on the woman's side. There was a big lump on the side of the abdomen.

"I've felt it coming a long time," moaned the old lady, when the pain was easier, "but I've not said anything; I didn't want to upset our Alfred."

Louisa did not see why "our Alfred" should be spared.

"What time is it?" came the plaintive voice.

"A quarter to four."

"Oh!" wailed the old lady, "he'll be here in half an hour, and no dinner ready for him."

"Let me do it?" said Louisa, gently.

"There's that cabbage—and you'll find the meat in the pantry—and there's an apple-pie you can hot up. But *don't you* do it——!"

"Who will, then?" asked Louisa.

"I don't know," moaned the sick woman, unable to consider.

Louisa did it. The doctor came and gave serious examination. He looked very grave.

"What is it, doctor?" asked the old lady, looking up at him with old, pathetic eyes in which already hope was dead.

"I think you've torn the skin in which a tumour hangs," he replied.

"Ay!" she murmured, and she turned away.

"You see, she may die any minute—and it *may* be swaled away," said the old doctor to Louisa.

The young woman went upstairs again.

"He says the lump may be swaled away, and you may get quite well again," she said.

"Ay!" murmured the old lady. It did not deceive her. Presently she asked:

"Is there a good fire?"

"I think so," answered Louisa.

"He'll want a good fire," the mother said. Louisa attended to it.

Since the death of Durant, the widow had come to church occasionally, and Louisa had been friendly to her. In the girl's heart the purpose was fixed. No man had affected her as Alfred Durant had done, and to that she kept. In her heart, she adhered to him. A natural sympathy existed between her and his rather hard, materialistic mother.

Alfred was the most lovable of the old woman's sons. He had grown up like the rest, however, headstrong and blind to everything but his own will. Like the other boys, he had insisted on going into the pit as soon as he left school, because that was the only way speedily to become a man, level with all the other men. This was a great chagrin to his mother, who would have liked to have this last of her sons a gentleman.

But still he remained constant to her. His feeling for her was deep and unexpressed. He noticed when she was tired, or when she had a new night-cap. And he bought little things for her occasionally. She was not wise enough to see how much he lived by her.

At the bottom he did not satisfy her, he did not seem manly enough. He liked to read books occasionally, and better still he liked to play the piccolo. It amused her to see his head nod over the instrument as he made an effort to get the right note. It made her fond of him, with tenderness, almost pity, but not with respect. She wanted a man to be fixed, going his own way without knowledge of women. Whereas she knew Alfred depended on her. He sang in the choir because he liked singing. In the summer he worked in the garden, attended to the fowls and pigs. He kept pigeons. He played on Saturday in the cricket or football team. But to her he did not seem the man, the independent man her other boys had been. He was her baby—and whilst she loved him for it, she was a little bit contemptuous of him.

There grew up a little hostility between them. Then he began to drink, as the others had done; but not in their blind, oblivious way. He was a little self-conscious over it. She saw this, and she pitied it in him. She loved him most, but she was not satisfied with him because he was not free of her. He could not quite go his own way.

Then at twenty he ran away and served his time in the Navy. This had made a man of him. He had hated it bitterly, the service, the subordination. For years he fought with himself under the military discipline, for his own self-respect, struggling through blind anger and shame and a cramping sense of inferiority. Out of humiliation and self-hatred he rose into a sort of inner freedom. And his love for his mother, whom he idealised, remained the fact of hope and of belief.

He came home again, nearly thirty years old, but naïve and inexperienced as a boy, only with a silence about him that was new: a sort of dumb humility before life, a fear of living. He was almost quite chaste. A strong sensitiveness had kept him from women. Sexual talk was all very well among men, but somehow it had no application to living women. There were two things for him, the *idea* of women, with which he sometimes debauched himself, and real women, before whom he felt a deep uneasiness, and a need to draw away. He shrank and defended himself from the approach of any woman. And then he felt ashamed. In his innermost soul he felt he was not a man, he was less than the normal man. In Genoa he went with an under-officer to a drinking-house where the cheaper sort of girl came in to look for lovers. He sat there with his glass, the girls looked at him, but they never came to him. He knew that if they did come he could only pay for food and drink for them, because he felt a pity for them, and was anxious lest they lacked good necessities. He could not have gone with one of them; he knew it, and was ashamed, looking with curious envy at the swaggering, easy-passionate Italian whose body went to a woman by instinctive impersonal attraction. They were men, he was not a man. He sat feeling short, feeling like a leper. And he went away imagining sexual scenes between himself and a woman, walking wrapt in this indulgence. But when the ready woman presented herself, the very fact that she was a palpable woman made it impossible for him to touch her. And this incapacity was like a core of rottenness in him.

So several times he went, drunk, with his companions, to the licensed prostitute-houses abroad. But the sordid insignificance of the experience appalled him. It had not been anything really: it meant nothing. He felt as if he were, not physically, but spiritually impotent: not actually impotent, but intrinsically so.

He came home with this secret, never changing burden of his unknown, unbestowed self torturing him. His Navy training left him in perfect physical condition. He was sensible of, and proud of his body. He bathed and used dumb-bells, and kept himself fit. He played cricket and football. He read books and began to hold fixed ideas which he got from the Fabians. He played his piccolo, and was considered an expert. But at the bottom of his soul was always this canker of shame and incompleteness: he was miserable beneath all his healthy cheerfulness, he was uneasy and felt despicable among all his confidence and superiority of ideas. He would have changed with any mere brute, just to be free of himself, to be free of this shame of self-consciousness. He saw some collier lurching straight forward without misgiving, pursuing his own satisfactions, and he envied him. Anything, he would have given for this spontaneity and this blind stupidity which went to its own satisfaction direct.

IX

He was not unhappy in the pit. He was admired by the men, and well enough liked. It was only he himself who felt the difference between himself and the others. He seemed to hide his own stigma. But he was never sure that the others did not really despise him for a ninny, as being less a man than they were. Only he pretended to be more manly, and was surprised by the ease with which they were deceived. And, being naturally cheerful, he was happy at work. He was sure of himself there. Naked to the waist, hot and grimy with labour, they squatted on their heels for a few minutes and talked, seeing each other dimly by the light of the safety lamps, while the black coal rose jutting round them, and the props of wood stood like little pillars in the low, black, very dark temple. Then the pony came and the gang-lad with a message from Number 7, or with a bottle of water from the horse-trough or some news of the world above. The day passed pleasantly enough. There was an ease, a go-as-you-please about the day underground, a delightful camaraderie of men shut off alone from the rest of the world, in a danger-ous place, and a variety of labour, holing, loading, timbering, and a glamour of mystery and adventure in the atmosphere, that made the pit not unattractive to him when he had again got over his anguish of desire for the open air and the sea.

This day there was much to do and Durant was not in humour to talk. He went on working in silence through the afternoon.

"Loose-all" came, and they tramped to the bottom. The white-washed underground office shone brightly. Men were putting out their lamps. They sat in dozens round the bottom of the shaft, down which black, heavy drops of water fell continuously into the sump. The electric lights shone away down the main underground road.

"Is it raining?" asked Durant.

"Snowing," said an old man, and the younger was pleased. He liked to go up when it was snowing.

"It'll just come right for Christmas?" said the old man.

"Ay," replied Durant.

"A green Christmas, a fat churchyard," said the other sententiously.

Durant laughed, showing his small, rather pointed teeth.

The cage came down, a dozen men lined on. Durant no-ticed tufts of snow on the perforated, arched roof of the chain, and he was pleased. He wondered how it liked its ex-cursion underground. But already it was getting soppy with black water.

He liked things about him. There was a little smile on his face. But underlying it was the curious consciousness he felt in himself.

The upper world came almost with a flash, because of the

glimmer of snow. Hurrying along the bank, giving up his lamp at the office, he smiled to feel the open about him again, all glimmering round him with snow. The hills on either hand were pale blue in the dusk, and the hedges looked savage and dark. The snow was trampled between the railway lines. But far ahead, beyond the black figures of miners moving home, it became smooth again, spreading right up to the dark wall of the coppice.

To the west there was a pinkness, and a big star hovered half revealed. Below, the lights of the pit came out crisp and yellow among the darkness of the buildings, and the lights of Old Aldecross twinkled in rows down the bluish twilight.

Durant walked glad with life among the miners, who were all talking animatedly because of the snow. He liked their company, he liked the white dusky world. It gave him a little thrill to stop at the garden gate and see the light of home down below, shining on the silent blue snow.

X

By the big gate of the railway, in the fence, was a little gate, that he kept locked. As he unfastened it, he watched the kitchen light that shone on to the bushes and the snow outside. It was a candle burning till night set in, he thought to himself. He slid down the steep path to the level below. He liked making the first marks in the smooth snow. Then he came through the bushes to the house. The two women heard his heavy boots ring outside on the scraper, and his voice as he opened the door.

"How much worth of oil do you reckon to save by that candle, mother?" He liked a good light from the lamp.

He had just put down his bottle and snap-bag and was hanging his coat behind the scullery door, when Miss Louisa came upon him. He was startled, but he smiled.

His eyes began to laugh—then his face went suddenly straight, and he was afraid.

"Your mother's had an accident," she said.

"How?" he exclaimed.

"In the garden," she answered. He hesitated with his coat in his hands. Then he hung it up and turned to the kitchen.

"Is she in bed?" he asked.

"Yes," said Miss Louisa, who found it hard to deceive him.

He was silent. He went into the kitchen, sat down heavily in his father's old chair, and began to pull off his boots. His head was small, rather finely shapen. His brown hair, close and crisp, would look jolly whatever happened. He wore heavy, moleskin trousers that gave off the stale, exhausted scent of the pit. Having put on his slippers, he carried his boots into the scullery.

"What is it?" he asked, afraid.

"Something internal," she replied.

He went upstairs. His mother kept herself calm for his coming! Louisa felt his tread shake the plaster floor of the bedroom above.

"What have you done?" he asked.

"It's nothing, my lad," said the old woman, rather hard. "It's nothing. You needn't fret, my boy, it's nothing more the matter with me than I had yesterday, or last week. The doctor said I'd done nothing serious."

"What were you doing?" asked her son.

"I was pulling up a cabbage, and I suppose I pulled too hard; for, oh—there was such a pain——"

Her son looked at her quickly. She hardened herself.

"But who doesn't have a sudden pain sometimes, my boy? We all do."

"And what's it done?"

"I don't know," she said, "but I don't suppose it's anything."

The big lamp in the corner was screened with a dark green screen, so that he could scarcely see her face. He was strung tight with apprehension and many emotions. Then his brow knitted.

"What did you go pulling your inside out at cabbages for," he asked, "and the ground frozen? You'd go on dragging and dragging, if you killed yourself."

"Somebody's got to get them," she said.

"You needn't do yourself harm."

But they had reached futility.

Miss Louisa could hear plainly downstairs. Her heart sank. It seemed so hopeless between them.

"Are you sure it's nothing much, mother?" he asked, appealing, after a little silence.

"Ay, it's nothing," said the old woman, rather bitter.

"I don't want you to—to—to be badly—you know."

"Go an' get your dinner," she said. She knew she was going to die: moreover, the pain was torture just then. "They're only cosseting me up a bit because I'm an old woman.

Miss Louisa's *very* good—and she'll have got your dinner ready, so you'd better go and eat it."

He felt stupid and ashamed. His mother put him off. He had to turn away. The pain burned in his bowels. He went downstairs. The mother was glad he was gone, so that she could moan with pain.

He had resumed the old habit of eating before he washed himself. Miss Louisa served his dinner. It was strange and exciting to her. She was strung up tense, trying to understand him and his mother. She watched him as he sat. He was turned away from his food, looking in the fire. Her soul watched him, trying to see what he was. His black face and arms were uncouth, he was foreign. His face was masked black with coal-dust. She could not see him, she could not know him. The brown eyebrows, the steady eyes, the coarse, small moustache above the closed mouth—these were the only familiar indications. What was he, as he sat there in his pit-dirt? She could not see him, and it hurt her.

She ran upstairs, presently coming down with flannels and the bran-bag, to heat them, because the pain was on again. He was half-way through his dinner. He put down the fork, suddenly nauseated.

"They will soothe the wrench," she said. He watched, useless and left out.

"Is she bad?" he asked.

"I think she is," she answered.

It was useless for him to stir or comment. Louisa was busy. She went upstairs. The poor old woman was in a white, cold sweat of pain. Louisa's face was sullen with suffering as she went about to relieve her. Then she sat and waited. The pain passed gradually, the old woman sank into a state of coma. Louisa still sat silently by the bed. She heard the sound of water downstairs. Then came the voice of the old mother, faint, but unrelaxing:

"Alfred's washing himself—he'll want his back washing——"

Louisa listened anxiously, wondering what the sick woman wanted.

"He can't bear if his back isn't washed——" the old woman persisted, in a cruel attention to his needs. Louisa rose and wiped the sweat from the yellowish brow.

"I will go down," she said soothingly.

"If you would," murmured the sick woman.

Louisa waited a moment. Mrs. Durant closed her eyes,

having discharged her duty. The young woman went down-stairs. Herself, or the man, what did they matter? Only the suffering woman must be considered.

Alfred was kneeling on the hearth-rug, stripped to the waist, washing himself in a large panchion of earthenware. He did so every evening, when he had eaten his dinner; his brothers had done so before him. But Miss Louisa was strange in the house.

He was mechanically rubbing the white lather on his head, with a repeated, unconscious movement, his hand every now and then passing over his neck. Louisa watched. She had to brace herself to this also. He bent his head into the water, washed it free of soap, and pressed the water out of his eyes.

"Your mother said you would want your back wash-ing," she said.

Curious how it hurt her to take part in their fixed routine of life! Louisa felt the almost repulsive intimacy being forced upon her. It was all so common, so like herding. She lost her own distinctness.

He ducked his face round, looking up at her in what was a very comical way. She had to harden herself.

"How funny he looks with his face upside down," she thought. After all, there was a difference between her and the common people. The water in which his arms were plunged was quite black, the soap-froth was darkish. She could scarcely conceive him as human. Mechanically, under the influence of habit, he groped in the black water, fished out soap and flannel, and handed them backward to Louisa. Then he remained rigid and submissive, his two arms thrust straight in the panchion, supporting the weight of his shoul-ders. His skin was beautifully white and unblemished, of an opaque, solid whiteness. Gradually Louisa saw it: this also was what he was. It fascinated her. Her feelings of separate-ness passed away: she ceased to draw back from contact with him and his mother. There was this living centre. Her heart ran hot. She had reached some goal in this beautiful, clear, male body. She loved him in a white, impersonal heat. But the sun-burnt, reddish neck and ears: they were more personal, more curious. A tenderness rose in her, she loved even his queer ears. A person—an intimate being he was to her. She put down the towel and went upstairs again, troubled in her heart. She had only seen one human being in her life—and that was Mary. All the rest were strangers.

Now her soul was going to open, she was going to see another. She felt strange and pregnant.

"He'll be more comfortable," murmured the sick woman
abstractedly, as Louisa entered the room. The latter did not
answer. Her own heart was heavy with its own responsibility.
Mrs. Durant lay silent awhile, then she murmured plaintively:

"You mustn't mind, Miss Louisa."

"Why should I?" replied Louisa, deeply moved.

"It's what we're used to," said the old woman.

And Louisa felt herself excluded again from their life. She
sat in pain, with the tears of disappointment distilling in
her heart. Was that all?

Alfred came upstairs. He was clean, and in his shirt-sleeves.
He looked a workman now. Louisa felt that she and he were
foreigners, moving in different lives. It dulled her again. Oh,
if she could only find some fixed relations, something sure
and abiding.

"How do you feel?" he said to his mother.

"It's a bit better," she replied wearily, impersonally.
This strange putting herself aside, this abstracting herself
and answering him only what she thought good for him to
hear, made the relations between mother and son poignant
and cramping to Miss Louisa. It made the man so ineffectual,
so nothing. Louisa groped as if she had lost him. The mother
was real and positive—he was not very actual. It puzzled and
chilled the young woman.

"I'd better fetch Mrs. Harrison?" he said, waiting for his
mother to decide.

"I suppose we shall have to have somebody," she replied.

Miss Louisa stood by, afraid to interfere in their business.
They did not include her in their lives, they felt she had
nothing to do with them, except as a help from outside. She
was quite external to them. She felt hurt and powerless
against this unconscious difference. But something patient
and unyielding in her made her say:

"I will stay and do the nursing: you can't be left."

The other two were shy, and at a loss for an answer.

"We'll manage to get somebody," said the old woman
wearily. She did not care very much what happened, now.

"I will stay until to-morrow, in any case," said Louisa.
"Then we can see."

"I'm sure you've no right to trouble yourself," moaned the
old woman. But she must leave herself in my hands.

Miss Louisa felt glad that she was admitted, even in an

official capacity. She wanted to share their lives. At home they would need her, now Mary had come. But they must manage without her.

"I must write a note to the vicarage," she said.

Alfred Durant looked at her inquiringly, for her service. He had always that intelligent readiness to serve, since he had been in the Navy. But there was a simple independence in his willingness, which she loved. She felt nevertheless it was hard to get at him. He was so deferential, quick to take the slightest suggestion of an order from her, implicitly, that she could not get at the man in him.

He looked at her very keenly. She noticed his eyes were golden brown, with a very small pupil, the kind of eyes that can see a long way off. He stood alert, at military attention. His face was still rather weather-reddened.

"Do you want pen and paper?" he asked, with deferential suggestion to a superior, which was more difficult for her than reserve.

"Yes please," she said.

He turned and went downstairs. He seemed to her so self-contained, so utterly sure in his movement. How was she to approach him? For he would take not one step towards her. He would only put himself entirely and impersonally at her service, glad to serve her, but keeping himself quite removed from her. She could see he felt real joy in doing anything for her, but any recognition would confuse him and hurt him. Strange it was to her, to have a man going about the house in his shirt-sleeves, his waistcoat unbuttoned, his throat bare, waiting on her. He moved well, as if he had plenty of life to spare. She was attracted by his completeness. And yet, when all was ready, and there was nothing more for him to do, she quivered, meeting his questioning look.

As she sat writing, he placed another candle near her. The rather dense light fell in two places on the overfoldings of her hair till it glistened heavy and bright, like a dense golden plumage folded up. Then the nape of her neck was very white, with fine down and pointed wisps of gold. He watched it as if it were a vision, losing himself. She was all that was beyond him, of revelation and exquisiteness. All that was ideal and beyond him, she was that—and he was lost to himself in looking at her. She had no connection with him. He did not approach her. She was there like a wonderful distance. But it was a treat, having her in the house. Even

with this anguish for his mother tightening about him, he was
sensible of the wonder of living this evening. The candles
glistened on her hair, and seemed to fascinate him. He felt a
little awe of her, and a sense of uplifting, that he and she and
his mother should be together for a time, in the strange, unknown atmosphere. And, when he got out of the house, he
was afraid. He saw the stars above ringing with fine brightness, the snow beneath just visible, and a new night was gathering round him. He was afraid almost with obliteration.
What was this new night ringing about him, and what was
he? He could not recognise himself nor any of his surroundings. He was afraid to think of his mother. And yet his
chest was conscious of her, and of what was happening to
her. He could not escape from her, she carried him with her
into an unformed, unknown chaos.

XI

He went up the road in an agony, not knowing what it was
all about, but feeling as if a red-hot iron were gripped round
his chest. Without thinking, he shook two or three tears on
to the snow. Yet in his mind he did not believe his mother
would die. He was in the grip of some greater consciousness.
As he sat in the hall of the vicarage, waiting whilst Mary put
things for Louisa into a bag, he wondered why he had been
so upset. He felt abashed and humbled by the big house, he
felt again as if he were one of the rank and file. When Miss
Mary spoke to him, he almost saluted.

"An honest man," thought Mary. And the patronage was
applied as salve to her own sickness. She had station, so she
could patronise: it was almost all that was left to her. But
she could not have lived without having a certain position.
She could never have trusted herself outside a definite place,
nor respected herself except as a woman of superior class.

As Alfred came to the latch-gate, he felt the grief at
his heart again, and saw the new heavens. He stood a moment
looking northward to the Plough climbing up the night, and
at the far glimmer of snow in distant fields. Then his grief
came on like physical pain. He held tight to the gate, biting
his mouth, whispering "Mother!" It was a fierce, cutting,
physical pain of grief, that came on in bouts, as his mother's
pain came on in bouts, and was so acute he could scarcely
keep erect. He did not know where it came from, the pain,

nor why. It had nothing to do with his thoughts. Almost it had nothing to do with him. Only it gripped him and he must submit. The whole tide of his soul, gathering in its unknown towards this expansion into death, carried him with it helplessly, all the fritter of his thought and consciousness caught up as nothing, the heave passing on towards its breaking, taking him farther than he had ever been. When the young man had regained himself, he went indoors, and there he was almost gay. It seemed to excite him. He felt in high spirits: he made whimsical fun of things. He sat on one side of his mother's bed, Louisa on the other, and a certain gaiety seized them all. But the night and the dread was coming on.

Alfred kissed his mother and went to bed. When he was half undressed the knowledge of his mother came upon him, and the suffering seized him in its grip like two hands, in agony. He lay on the bed screwed up tight. It lasted so long, and exhausted him so much, that he fell asleep, without having the energy to get up and finish undressing. He awoke after midnight to find himself stone cold. He undressed and got into bed, and was soon asleep again.

At a quarter to six he woke, and instantly remembered. Having pulled on his trousers and lighted a candle, he went into his mother's room. He put his hand before the candle flame so that no light fell on the bed.

"Mother!" he whispered.

"Yes," was the reply.

There was a hesitation.

"Should I go to work?"

He waited, his heart was beating heavily.

"I think I'd go, my lad."

His heart went down in a kind of despair.

"You want me to?"

He let his hand down from the candle flame. The light fell on the bed. There he saw Louisa lying looking up at him. Her eyes were upon him. She quickly shut her eyes and half buried her face in the pillow, her back turned to him. He saw the rough hair like bright vapour about her round head, and the two plaits flung coiled among the bedclothes. It gave him a shock. He stood almost himself, determined. Louisa cowered down. He looked, and met his mother's eyes. Then he gave way again, and ceased to be sure, ceased to be himself.

"Yes, go to work, my boy," said the mother.

"All right," replied he, kissing her. His heart was down at despair, and bitter. He went away.

"Alfred!" cried his mother faintly.

He came back with beating heart.

"What, mother?"

"You'll always do what's right, Alfred?" the mother asked, beside herself in terror now he was leaving her. He was too terrified and bewildered to know what she meant.

"Yes," he said.

She turned her cheek to him. He kissed her, then went away in bitter despair. He went to work.

XII

By midday his mother was dead. The word met him at the pit-mouth. As he had known, inwardly, it was not a shock to him, and yet he trembled. He went home quite calmly, feeling only heavy in his breathing.

Miss Louisa was still at the house. She had seen to everything possible. Very succinctly, she informed him of what he needed to know. But there was one point of anxiety for her.

"You *did* half expect it—it's not come as a blow to you?" she asked, looking up at him. Her eyes were dark and calm and searching. She too felt lost. He was so dark and inchoate.

"I suppose—yes," he said stupidly. He looked aside, unable to endure her eyes on him.

"I could not bear to think you might not have guessed," she said.

He did not answer.

He felt it a great strain to have her near him at this time. He wanted to be alone. As soon as the relatives began to arrive, Louisa departed and came no more. While everything was arranging, and a crowd was in the house, whilst he had business to settle, he went well enough, with only those uncontrollable paroxysms of grief. For the rest, he was superficial. By himself, he endured the fierce, almost insane bursts of grief which passed again and left him calm, almost clear, just wondering. He had not known before that everything could break down, that he himself could break down, and all be a great chaos, very vast and wonderful. It seemed as if life in him had burst its bounds, and he was lost in a great, bewildering flood, immense and unpeopled. He himself was broken and spilled out amid it all. He could only breathe panting in silence. Then the anguish came on again.

When all the people had gone from the Quarry Cottage, leaving the young man alone with an elderly housekeeper, then the long trial began. The snow had thawed and frozen, a fresh fall had whitened the grey, this then began to thaw. The world was a place of loose grey slosh. Alfred had nothing to do in the evenings. He was a man whose life had been filled up with small activities. Without knowing it, he had been centralised, polarised in his mother. It was she who had kept him. Even now, when the old housekeeper had left him, he might still have gone on in his old way. But the force and balance of his life was lacking. He sat pretending to read, all the time holding his fists clenched, and holding himself in, enduring he did not know what. He walked the black and sodden miles of field-paths, till he was tired out: but all this was only running away from whence he must return. At work he was all right. If it had been summer he might have escaped by working in the garden till bedtime. But now, there was no escape, no relief, no help. He, perhaps, was made for action rather than for understanding; for doing than for being. He was shocked out of his activities, like a swimmer who forgets to swim.

For a week, he had the force to endure this suffocation and struggle, then he began to get exhausted, and knew it must come out. The instinct of self-preservation became strongest. But there was the question: Where was he to go? The public-house really meant nothing to him, it was no good going there. He began to think of emigration. In another country he would be all right. He wrote to the emigration offices.

On the Sunday after the funeral, when all the Durant people had attended church, Alfred had seen Miss Louisa, impassive and reserved, sitting with Miss Mary, who was proud and very distant, and with the other Lindleys, who were people removed. Alfred saw them as people remote. He did not think about it. They had nothing to do with his life. After service Louisa had come to him and shaken hands.

"My sister would like you to come to supper one evening, if you would be so good."

He looked at Miss Mary, who bowed. Out of kindness, Mary had proposed this to Louisa, disapproving of her even as she did so. But she did not examine herself closely.

"Yes," said Durant awkwardly, "I'll come if you want me." But he vaguely felt that it was misplaced.

"You'll come to-morrow evening, then, about half-past six."

He went. Miss Louisa was very kind to him. There could be no music, because of the babies. He sat with his fists clenched on his thighs, very quiet and unmoved, lapsing, among all those people, into a kind of muse or daze. There was nothing between him and them. They knew it as well as he. But he remained very steady in himself, and the evening passed slowly. Mrs. Lindley called him "young man."

"Will you sit here, young man?"

He sat there. One name was as good as another. What had they to do with him?

Mr. Lindley kept a special tone for him, kind, indulgent, but patronising. Durant took it all without criticism or offence, just submitting. But he did not want to eat—that troubled him, to have to eat in their presence. He knew he was out of place. But it was his duty to stay yet awhile. He answered precisely, in monosyllables.

When he left he winced with confusion. He was glad it was finished. He got away as quickly as possible. And he wanted still more intensely to go right away, to Canada.

Miss Louisa suffered in her soul, indignant with all of them, with him too, but quite unable to say why she was indignant.

XIII

Two evenings after, Louisa tapped at the door of the Quarry Cottage, at half-past six. He had finished dinner, the woman had washed up and gone away, but still he sat in his pit-dirt. He was going later to the New Inn. He had begun to go there because he must go somewhere. The mere contact with other men was necessary to him, the noise, the warmth, the forgetful flight of the hours. But still he did not move. He sat alone in the empty house till it began to grow on him like something unnatural.

He was in his pit-dirt when he opened the door.

"I have been wanting to call—I thought I would," she said, and she went to the sofa. He wondered why she wouldn't use his mother's round arm-chair. Yet something stirred in him, like anger, when the housekeeper placed herself in it.

"I ought to have been washed by now," he said, glancing at the clock, which was adorned with butterflies and cherries, and the name of "T. Brooks, Mansfield." He laid his black hands along his mottled dirty arms. Louisa looked at him. There was the reserve, and the simple neutrality towards her, which she dreaded in him. It made it impossible for her to approach him.

"I am afraid," she said, "that I wasn't kind in asking you to supper."

"I'm not used to it," he said, smiling with his mouth, showing the interspaced white teeth. His eyes, however, were steady and unseeing.

"It's not *that*," she said hastily. Her repose was exquisite and her dark grey eyes rich with understanding. He felt afraid of her as she sat there, as he began to grow conscious of her.

"How do you get on alone?" she asked.

He glanced away to the fire.

"Oh——" he answered, shifting uneasily, not finishing his answer.

Her face settled heavily.

"How close it is in this room. You have such immense fires. I will take off my coat," she said.

He watched her take off her hat and coat. She wore a cream cashmir blouse embroidered with gold silks. It seemed to him a very fine garment, fitting her throat and wrists close. It gave him a feeling of pleasure and cleanness and relief from himself.

"What were you thinking about, that you didn't get washed?" she asked, half intimately. He laughed, turning aside his head. The whites of his eyes showed very distinct in his black face.

"Oh," he said, "I couldn't tell you."

There was a pause.

"Are you going to keep this house on?" she asked.

He stirred in his chair, under the question.

"I hardly know," he said. "I'm very likely going to Canada."

Her spirit became very quiet and attentive.

"What for?" she asked.

Again he shifted restlessly on his seat.

"Well,"—he said slowly—"to try the life."

"But which life?"

"There's various things—farming or lumbering or mining. I don't mind much what it is."

"And is that what you want?"

He did not think in these times, so he could not answer.

"I don't know," he said, "till I've tried."

She saw him drawing away from her for ever.

"Aren't you sorry to leave this house and garden?" she asked.

"I don't know," he answered reluctantly. "I suppose our Fred would come in—that's what he's wanting."

"You don't want to settle down?" she asked.

He was leaning forward on the arms of his chair. He turned to her. Her face was pale and set. It looked heavy and impassive, her hair shone richer as she grew white. She was to him something steady and immovable and eternal presented to him. His heart was hot in an anguish of suspense. Sharp twitches of fear and pain were in his limbs. He turned his whole body away from her. The silence was unendurable. He could not bear her to sit there any more. It made his heart get hot and stifled in his breast.

"Were you going out to-night?" she asked.

"Only to the New Inn," he said.

Again there was silence.

She reached for her hat. Nothing else was suggested to her. She *had* to go. He sat waiting for her to be gone, for relief. And she knew that if she went out of that house as she was, she went out a failure. Yet she continued to pin on her hat; in a moment she would have to go. Something was carrying her.

Then suddenly a sharp pang, like lightning, seared her from head to foot, and she was beyond herself.

"Do you want me to go?" she asked, controlled, yet speaking out of a fiery anguish, as if the words were spoken from her without her intervention.

He went white under his dirt.

"Why?" he asked, turning to her in fear, compelled.

"Do you want me to go?" she repeated.

"Why?" he asked again.

"Because I wanted to stay with you," she said, suffocated, with her lungs full of fire.

His face worked, he hung forward a little, suspended, staring straight into her eyes, in torment, in an agony of chaos, unable to collect himself. And as if turned to stone, she looked back into his eyes. The souls were exposed bare for a few moments. It was agony. They could not bear it. He dropped his head, whilst his body jerked with little sharp twitchings.

She turned away for her coat. Her soul had gone dead in her. Her hands trembled, but she could not feel any more. She drew on her coat. There was a cruel suspense in the room. The moment had come for her to go. He lifted his head. His eyes were like agate, expressionless, save for the black points of torture. They held her, she had no will, no life any more. She felt broken.

"Don't you want me?" she said helplessly.

A spasm of torture crossed his eyes, which held her fixed. "I—I——" he began, but he could not speak. Something drew him from his chair to her. She stood motionless, spellbound, like a creature given up as prey. He put his hand tentatively, uncertainly, on her arm. The expression of his face was strange and inhuman. She stood utterly motionless. Then clumsily he put his arms round her, and took her, cruelly, blindly, straining her till she nearly lost consciousness, till he himself had almost fallen.

Then, gradually, as he held her gripped, and his brain reeled round, and he felt himself falling, falling from himself, and whilst she, yielded up, swooned to a kind of death of herself, a moment of utter darkness came over him, and they began to wake up again as if from a long sleep. He was himself.

After a while his arms slackened, she loosened herself a little, and put her arms round him, as he held her. So they held each other close, and hid each against the other for assurance, helpless in speech. And it was ever her hands that trembled more closely upon him, drawing him nearer into her, with love.

And at last she drew back her face and looked up at him, her eyes wet, and shining with light. His heart, which saw, was silent with fear. He was with her. She saw his face all sombre and inscrutable, and he seemed eternal to her. And all the echo of pain came back into the rarity of bliss, and all her tears came up.

"I love you," she said, her lips drawn to sobbing. He put down his head against her, unable to hear her, unable to bear the sudden coming of the peace and passion that almost broke his heart. They stood together in silence whilst the thing moved away a little.

At last she wanted to see him. She looked up. His eyes were strange and glowing, with a tiny black pupil. Strange, they were, and powerful over her. And his mouth came to hers, and slowly her eyelids closed, as his mouth sought hers closer and closer, and took possession of her.

They were silent for a long time, too much mixed up with passion and grief and death to do anything but hold each other in pain and kiss with long, hurting kisses wherein fear was transfused into desire. At last she disengaged herself. He felt as if his heart were hurt, but glad, and he scarcely dared look at her.

"I'm glad," she said also.

He held her hands in passionate gratitude and desire. He had not yet the presence of mind to say anything. He was dazed with relief.

"I ought to go," she said.

He looked at her. He could not grasp the thought of her going, he knew he could never be separated from her any more. Yet he dared not assert himself. He held her hands tight.

"Your face is black," she said.

He laughed.

"Yours is a bit smudged," he said.

They were afraid of each other, afraid to talk. He could only keep her near to him. After a while she wanted to wash her face. He brought her some warm water, standing by and watching her. There was something he wanted to say, that he dared not. He watched her wiping her face, and making tidy her hair.

"They'll see your blouse is dirty," he said.

She looked at her sleeves and laughed for joy.

He was sharp with pride.

"What shall you do?" he asked.

"How?" she said.

He was awkward at a reply.

"About me," he said.

"What do you want me to do?" she laughed.

He put his hand out slowly to her. What did it matter!

"But make yourself clean," she said.

XIV

As they went up the hill, the night seemed dense with the unknown. They kept close together, feeling as if the darkness were alive and full of knowledge, all around them. In silence they walked up the hill. At first the street lamps went their way. Several people passed them. He was more shy than she, and would have let her go had she loosened in the least. But she held firm.

Then they came into the true darkness, between the fields. They did not want to speak, feeling closer together in silence.

So they arrived at the vicarage gate. They stood under the naked horse-chestnut tree.

"I wish you didn't have to go," he said.

She laughed a quick little laugh.

"Come to-morrow," she said, in a low tone, "and ask father."

She felt his hand close on hers.

She gave the same sorrowful little laugh of sympathy. Then she kissed him, sending him home.

At home, the old grief came on in another paroxysm, obliterating Louisa, obliterating even his mother for whom the stress was raging like a burst of fever in a wound. But something was sound in his heart.

XV

The next evening he dressed to go to the vicarage, feeling it was to be done, not imagining what it would be like. He would not take this seriously. He was sure of Louisa, and this marriage was like fate to him. It filled him also with a blessed feeling of fatality. He was not responsible, neither had her people anything really to do with it.

They ushered him into the little study, which was fireless. By and by the vicar came in. His voice was cold and hostile as he said:

"What can I do for you, young man?"

He knew already, without asking.

Durant looked up at him, again like a sailor before a superior. He had the subordinate manner. Yet his spirit was clear.

"I wanted, Mr. Lindley——" he began respectfully, then all the colour suddenly left his face. It seemed now a violation to say what he had to say. What was he doing there? But he stood on, because it had to be done. He held firmly to his own independence and self-respect. He must not be indecisive. He must put himself aside: the matter was bigger than just his personal self. He must not feel. This was his highest duty.

"You wanted——" said the vicar.

Durant's mouth was dry, but he answered with steadiness:

"Miss Louisa—Louisa—promised to marry me——"

"You asked Miss Louisa if she would marry you—yes——" corrected the vicar. Durant reflected he had not asked her this:

"If she would marry me, sir. I hope you—don't mind."

He smiled. He was a good-looking man, and the vicar could not help seeing it.

"And my daughter was willing to marry you?" said Mr. Lindley.

"Yes," said Durant seriously. It was pain to him, nevertheless. He felt the natural hostility between himself and the elder man.

"Will you come this way?" said the vicar. He led into the dining-room, where were Mary, Louisa, and Mrs. Lindley. Mr. Massy sat in a corner with a lamp.

"This young man has come on your account, Louisa?" said Mr. Lindley.

"Yes," said Louisa, her eyes on Durant, who stood erect, in discipline. He dared not look at her, but he was aware of her.

"You don't want to marry a collier, you little fool," cried Mrs. Lindley harshly. She lay obese and helpless upon the couch, swathed in a loose dove-grey gown.

"Oh, hush, Mother," cried Mary, with quiet intensity and pride.

"What means have you to support a wife?" demanded the vicar's wife roughly.

"I!" Durant replied, starting. "I think I can earn enough."

"Well, and how much?" came the rough voice.

"Seven and six a day," replied the young man.

"And will it get to be any more?"

"I hope so."

"And are you going to live in that poky little house?"

"I think so," said Durant, "if it's all right."

He took small offence, only was upset, because they would not think him good enough. He knew that, in their sense, he was not.

"Then she's a fool, I tell you, if she marries you," cried the mother roughly, casting her decision.

"After all, mama, it is Louisa's affair," said Mary distinctly, "and we must remember——"

"As she makes her bed, she must lie—but she'll repent it," interrupted Mrs. Lindley.

"And after all," said Mr. Lindley, "Louisa cannot quite hold herself free to act entirely without consideration for her family."

"What do you want, Papa?" asked Louisa sharply.

"I mean that if you marry this man, it will make my posi-

tion very difficult for me, particularly if you stay in this parish. If you were moving quite away, it would be simpler.
But living here in a collier's cottage, under my nose, as it
were—it would be almost unseemly. I have my position to
maintain, and a position which may not be taken lightly."

"Come over here, young man," cried the mother, in her
rough voice, "and let us look at you."

Durant, flushing, went over and stood—not quite at attention, so that he did not know what to do with his hands.
Miss Louisa was angry to see him standing there, obedient
and acquiescent. He ought to show himself a man.

"Can't you take her away and live out of sight?" said the
mother. "You'd both of you be better off."

"Yes, we can go away," he said.

"Do you want to?" asked Miss Mary clearly.

He faced round. Mary looked very stately and impressive.
He flushed.

"I do if it's going to be a trouble to anybody," he said.

"For yourself, you would rather stay?" said Mary.

"It's my home," he said, "and that's the house I was born
in."

"Then"—Mary turned clearly to her parents, "I really don't
see how you can make the conditions, papa. He has his own
rights, and if Louisa wants to marry him——"

"Louisa, Louisa!" cried the father impatiently. "I cannot
understand why Louisa should not behave in the normal way.
I cannot see why she should only think of herself, and leave
her family out of count. The thing is enough in itself, and
she ought to try to ameliorate it as much as possible. And
if——"

"But I love the man, papa," said Louisa.

"And I hope you love your parents, and I hope you want
to spare them as much of the—the loss of prestige as possible."

"We *can* go away to live," said Louisa, her face breaking
to tears. At last she was really hurt.

"Oh yes, easily," Durant replied hastily, pale, distressed.

There was dead silence in the room.

"I think it would really be better," murmured the vicar,
mollified.

"Very likely it would," said the rough-voiced invalid.

"Though I think we ought to apologise for asking such a
thing," said Mary haughtily.

"No," said Durant. "It will be best all round." He was glad there was no more bother.

"And shall we put up the banns here or go to the registrar?" he asked clearly, like a challenge.

"We will go to the registrar," replied Louisa decidedly.

Again there was a dead silence in the room.

"Well, if you will have your own way, you must go your own way," said the mother emphatically.

All the time Mr. Massy had sat obscure and unnoticed in a corner of the room. At this juncture he got up, saying:

"There is baby, Mary."

Mary rose and went out of the room, stately; her little husband padded after her. Durant watched the fragile, small man go, wondering.

"And where," asked the vicar, almost genial, "do you think you will go when you are married?"

Durant started.

"I was thinking of emigrating," he said.

"To Canada? Or where?"

"I think to Canada."

"Yes, that would be very good."

Again there was a pause.

"We shan't see much of you then, as a son-in-law," said the mother, roughly but amicably.

"Not much," he said.

Then he took his leave. Louisa went with him to the gate. She stood before him in distress.

"You won't mind them, will you?" she said humbly.

"I don't mind them, if they don't mind me!" he said. Then he stooped and kissed her.

"Let us be married soon," she murmured, in tears.

"All right," he said. "I'll go to-morrow to Barford."